Seize

Seize the Beat

The Evolution of American Music

Brian Q. Torff

McFarland & Company, Inc., Publishers
Jefferson, North Carolina

All photographs were taken by the author.

Library of Congress Cataloguing-in-Publication Data

Names: Torff, Brian, author.
Title: Seize the beat : the evolution of American music / Brian Q. Torff.
Description: Jefferson, North Carolina : McFarland & Company, Inc., Publishers, 2023. | Includes bibliographical references and index.
Identifiers: LCCN 2022055553 | ISBN 9781476690773 (paperback : acid free paper) ∞
ISBN 9781476648576 (ebook)
Subjects: LCSH: Popular music—United States—History and criticism. | Popular music—Social aspects—United States—History.
Classification: LCC ML3477 .T67 2023 | DDC 781.640973—dc23/eng/20221123
LC record available at https://lccn.loc.gov/2022055553

British Library cataloguing data are available

ISBN (print) 978-1-4766-9077-3
ISBN (ebook) 978-1-4766-4857-6

Front cover image © Zarya Maxim Alexandrovich/Shutterstock

Printed in the United States of America

McFarland & Company, Inc., Publishers
Box 611, Jefferson, North Carolina 28640
www.mcfarlandpub.com

To Sarah,
for her love and the tap on my shoulder

Table of Contents

Preface

American music is the sound of surprise. Someone puts a rabbit and a chicken together and out comes an elephant. Yet in this spirit of experimentation, a mistake is made when we fail to value or even remember our innovations. Music is more than collective sound; it reveals volumes about who we are as a people and as a nation.

Our nation's material wealth is at odds with a prevailing cultural illiteracy. Clearly, somebody dropped the ball. You can't truly know yourself without understanding the messages that surround you. Whether as a performing musician or as a music professor in front of a classroom of students (they can be a tough crowd), cultural understanding can go well beyond—it's got a great beat; I can dance to it. Exploring our past enables us to move into the future.

Bus stop around the corner from the Stax Museum, Memphis, Tennessee.

1

We realize that no artist of any merit ever learned their craft out of a textbook. This book is a collection of freewheeling essays without boundaries, exploring the stories that lie between the beats in our vast musical heritage. I leave hip-hop and country to those who have lived it, but I'm happy to hear someone rap over a country tune, a freedom born of "don't fence me in."

I have taken the liberty of freely mixing genres in order to make connections for students as well as a general readership.

Music is always trying to tell us something.

When we seize the beat, that is when great sailing begins.

Prologue:
Music for a Pandemic

Let's face it.

If the year 2020 were a fish, we'd throw it back.

As of this writing, the year is not even over. If one hundred years from now they invent a way-back machine, I would recommend they skip right over it. It has been historic on many levels—massive death and illness, hurricanes, tornadoes, power outages, a deranged president, no leadership, and nothing to do at night. Silence is golden but not with the ambulances passing by.

How will we make music? What should art look and sound like now that the audience is in hiding? It all hit the fan around my sixty-sixth birthday—March 16, 2020. I have been a professional musician, composer, bandleader, and university professor for over forty years. I am an academic backdoor man. I sneaked in the back when no one was watching. I was now faced with a challenging task, trying to guide my weary students through the semester, despite everything looking bleak. Baseball without crowds, bizarre outdoor events, and masked people with looks of suspicion. Billy the Kid comes to the masses.

My students missed out on huge parts of their lives. Internships and senior recitals were canceled, and no one walked in their caps and gowns. Time to learn the hard life lesson of disappointment. No celebration, just silence. I went onto campus in June and it was a ghost town, just me and the asbestos removal guys. It reminded me of the Baron von Blixen quote, "Life is life and fun is fun, but it's all so quiet when the goldfish die."

I decided a few things as life grounded to a halt. I would write this book as I reflect on music which has even greater meaning now that it has been largely taken away. Instead of churning it out while taking it for granted, it was time for a new perspective. It slowly emerged. I started composing music like a child with finger paints, making it up as

3

I went along. I wanted it to sound like an open field, based on a photo I took in rural Mississippi in 2017.

I began harmonica lessons.

I dreamed of music made by bass, a cajon drum, digital loops music coming from a paint brush, sounding like nothing else. And I started working on my singing. Like many people, I hate the sound of my own voice, but the art is in getting past that to the point where you are no longer nauseous. I can now sing without Dramamine, so that is progress.

I performed once in late July. It was surreal. The audience wore masks and the musicians were great distances from one another. It felt like singing in a windstorm. We were all happy to be out of the house and alive. We must live and figure out not only how to do that but also how to express the storm outside and in. Concerts online? I'm not sure; it feels like a substitute at best.

Maybe I'll just put all the musical equipment and a drummer in a car, pull up to the nearest electrical outlet, and start playing. In Africa, they don't need to announce and promote live music; they just do it.

As the fall semester draws near, I am haunted by the image of careening through a riptide in a barrel toward Niagara Falls. We just don't know how we will land, intact or in pieces. Like Proud Mary, we keep rolling on the river.

Keep writing, keep playing, keep fishing, and, when necessary, throw back the little ones.

I am a working, veteran professional musician transformed into a classroom griot. It is my job to get people thinking by dispensing knowledge, raising questions, listening, and illuminating—followed by marking papers and filing grades. It is a big responsibility to pass down stories that are largely ignored by the outside world. No Grammys are awarded for teachers, but they are essential. I feel strongly that university students paying enormous tuition should not have to wait until they reach college to discover their cultural identity.

This book is a collection of personal essays consisting of my discoveries and insights (if I have had any) from the past decades of a dual life, teacher and performer. Avoiding unnecessary academic formality, this work takes an open view of contemporary music. It delves into the societal impact of art on American culture—when we had American culture, that is. We can talk about that later.

American popular music is our story in sound. *Seize the Beat* is not genre specific largely because no one music style has the final word. They all tell a different story.

It is said that when a griot dies, a library burns up. All that knowledge that was disseminated by the oral tradition is now silent. But not really, for what was passed on through dance, story, song, and drum-beat now lives in the hearts and minds of those who were there to learn it. I am not a library, but I have some experiences and stories to tell. This book is an attempt to convey aspects of what I truly believe is important regarding American culture. It is an exploration into discovery based on my experience, a sense of having been there.

We play music in school, if we are lucky, but few teachers tell us what the music means. I distrust most academic jargon and try to avoid theoretical smoke screens—using big words when small words will do. It is a case of too much living from the neck up and not enough big beat from the body.

I do not have all the answers and have failed more times than I can count in this crazy music profession. Success is hard earned and careers rarely become easier, but I would not trade a life in music for anything, nor would I stop teaching it. I was hooked from an early age and I can tell you that once it gets into your veins, you are in a lot of trouble. If you can see it through, past all the disappointments and uncertainty, you come to realize that music is a great gift to the performer, listener, and dancer. We are on the same team.

We don't have to play an instrument, paint, or draw to benefit from the arts. It has much to teach us. Like jazz, life is an improvised song, full of twists, turns, and surprises. The blues teaches us about hard times and how to overcome them. People who develop a similar resilience stand a much better chance of having a happy, well-lived life. Music reveals the mistakes of the past and moves our culture forward. Discovering an individual musician's greatness reveals extraordinary human characteristics and sometimes tragic flaws, all at the same time. They are not gone; they inspire, resonate, and sing on.

Take Them by Surprise

Labor Day has passed and it is the first morning of another school year at Fairfield University. A group of twenty-five students file into my basement music studio/classroom containing a grand piano, music posters, and African masks that peer out onto desks built like tanks, having outlived many generations of students.

The eighteen- to twenty-one-year-olds take their seats; they know not what awaits them. Students are strange and variable animals. They either roll in with enthusiastic, animated conversation or sit warily in icy silence. Many stare into smartphones that offer a guaranteed com-panion in uncertain situations. As soon as they are seated, I request for all to stand up and join me in the middle of the room. "We are about to perform an African ring shout," I declare in my booming Midwest voice. Arranged in a semicircle, some students smile sheepishly, a few look terrified, and the rest wonder why they must take this music course with a lunatic liberal arts professor. "He is probably some burned-out hippie from the '60s, so we'll humor him. Besides, I am going to be an accountant, so what do I need this for, huh? My father would be furious if he knew I was wasting my time and his money with this tree-hugging nutcase." I get it; this is a tough time for the liberal arts. Higher education becomes more corporate all the time, and a trade school mentality flies in the face of employers who seek graduates who are actually trained in some aspect of the arts. They are looking for creative graduates who think in new ways, can improvise and shift with changing trends, and collectively interact with others as if they are a band. Employers know that the arts require a self-discipline that they want to see in the workplace.

Following my lead, the class begins to move their feet in a unified tempo, though I never gave them one. Body clocks are in sync, hands clap, and a chant of "aché" begins to form, albeit softly, far too meek to raise the spirits. "More," I command. The energy begins to heat the room. Now we are getting somewhere, without the assistance of numerous Budweisers.

Being a teacher has been my other life, away from concert halls, loading docks and back stages, airports and van rides. It is the performance coming to the classroom. We are discovering music through the infinitely layered stories it can reveal. I explain the African ring shout concept coming to America through slavery. It was a rock landing in a silent pool of water. The dozens and dozens of concentric circles from its splash represent the sounds, styles, and voices that have evolved since the first slave ship came to this country in 1619. I add my African djembe into the mix, and the students begin to smile. The journey has begun; maybe this won't be so bad after all.

I was a teacher for many years before I realized that I was taking on the griot role. He (usually male, alas) is a storyteller, historian, and educator with the purpose of passing on tribal heritage to the next generation. It must be done in call-and-response style; texting won't do. Aché is the inner spirit and life force that is our engine, setting everything in motion. If I can get the class to understand this concept, they can apply it to their own lives.

Music is a basic form of communication. We do this through our voices, sung or spoken. Musical instruments have an immense power— they can express the inexpressible. We are moved by dynamic music; it transports us to another dimension, resulting in an unforgettable experience that defies translation. Did you ever go to a great concert or musical event, then upon being asked about it, stumble over an explanation? You had to be there.

More than being present as a listener, you must be engaged like a musician on the stage. The band plays more than instruments that make sound; they play on and off the audience. The subtle, or sometimes not so subtle, audience cues are read by a live band. They inspire the music, oftentimes turning the music in new directions. I have seen this thousands of times, but the instruments don't play themselves. It is the musician's inner spirit that runs through the sax, guitar, or trumpet and delivers the authentic voice of the player, revealing how that person feels at a given moment.

An impassive, indifferent audience can pull down a performance. If the audience is sharp and attentive, everyone may be in for a great night, but if they are distracted by cell phones, it may be a very long one. I came up before the digital era and social media. It certainly was a different game back then. In the 1960s and early '70s there were only three or four television channels and live music performances on TV were rare. We relied on radio to deliver the music that made us dance. The FM band delivered an interesting and eclectic mix of underground rock, folk, blues, and psychedelia. We bought albums with covers that told a story, if we could figure it out. Vinyl enforced a holistic type of listening; random play would scratch and ruin a record, so you were forced to listen to one side of music without interruption. When the band came to town and took the stage, the excitement was palpable. What would we hear? What would this look like? Where would this take us? Sans cell phones, we were, for the most part, riveted to the performance. This created a special relationship between artist and audience. I am not saying all of this is superior to today, but it certainly was a different experience than what would be delivered by digital music decades later. The law of unintended consequences moves into the future.

Rewind Is Never an Option

It is important to realize a basic fact about American popular music's evolution. We hit play and sometimes fast forward, but rewind is never an option. It is a forward-looking art that embraces change to suit a new generation. As much as we may love the music of our youthful golden years, we will never go back to those days, no matter how much we may long for them. This has been proven time and time again. When

I was a rock band–playing teenager in the era of the Beatles and Stones, I often would hear parents and grandparents exclaim, "The big bands are coming back. Just you wait." It never happened. The thrilling time of the 1930s swing bands à la Benny Goodman, Count Basie, and Glenn Miller became a haunted ballroom. Bobby-sock girls swooned to Frank Sinatra in the mid–'40s, but Ol' Blue Eyes soon gave way to Elvis Presley a decade later. Teenagers (a new marketing concept at the time) of the '50s related to the grinding, boogie-woogie rocking sound of a new musical sex symbol. The old icons wouldn't do.

The seeds of the future are sown in the past. By the early '60s, Elvis and pop music had grown stagnant and homogenized. Change was in the air, requiring a new sound and image. The Beatles, arriving in the United States a few months after John F. Kennedy's assassination, were a tidal wave that knocked Elvis and the '50s out for good. English accents and long hair had replaced greasers with sideburns. One era makes another obsolete, or at the very least, a distant, nostalgic memory. It doesn't take very long for a musical style to be perceived as old fashioned. Every generation demands the new and must have its own music, clothes, slang, and form of rebellion. We are perpetually a country in transition.

Post–World War II America has had an intolerance for aging. Popular music demands a young sound and image that is socially relevant. MTV certainly proved that if you no longer had the look, you couldn't play the game. Rock, pop, and hip-hop stars age out of the art form as their social connection to youth is fleeting. On some level, kids need to see themselves in the music. Does this relate to me, my problems, my desires, my neighborhood, and my friends? Perennial forms such as blues, jazz, and folk music reach a smaller but far more loyal audience who age with the music. The respect for older artists such as Aretha Franklin, B.B. King, Duke Ellington, and Miles Davis grew in their later years. They were masters who still had something to say.

We can never go back. This has been proven by dismal costume party attempts to re-create Woodstock. The famous Fillmore East is now a bank, the legendary Hit Factory recording studio in New York City are high-priced condos, and the well-known Chicago jazz club the London House became at first a Burger King. So goes American culture.

It is true that classic American musical forms become that way because new generations keep rediscovering their brilliance. The release of Miles Davis's *Kind of Blue* in 1959 brought minimal sales; fifty years later it had sold more than five million copies and is rightfully considered an indispensable jazz recording. So too with the rerelease of forty-one tracks of the phantom Delta blues singer-guitarist Robert

Johnson, who went from mythic obscurity to being the most heralded of all the country blues artists. Beware of ghosts who bring the past forward.

Bob Dylan knew that.

Yet we must acknowledge that though classic American music will be revered and remembered, it will never again be "popular" or part of the contemporary mainstream. This is not a bad thing. When fewer people know about something, it does not diminish its value. Every generation has its own slang. Music is an ever-changing language that adapts to the times. Without change, the art world would stagnate.

There is a world of difference between an artist who has a "hit" and one who creates an authentically new musical form. Artists are known for their hit songs, as witnessed by excited audiences who yell out these song title requests at concerts ad nauseam, often before they have played their opening number. Hit songs produce income, sell tickets, place artists on streaming lists, increase radio airplay, sell merchandise, and create a demand for television appearances. It brings a visibility that can take a local band playing on a Saturday night in front of a few dozen people for beer money to stadiums of screaming fans with all the perks attached. Once they were a few feet away; now you see them on big screens.

Here is the catch-22: Hit songs are extremely difficult to come by because no one, no matter what they claim, knows what makes a hit. It is an elusive and unpredictable phenomenon. When the hits stop coming, careers move into a reverse trajectory and you are an oldies band before you know it. Audiences are fickle beings with an ever-shortening attention span. They move on to the next new thing, leaving you in the hotel lobby with a list of cancellations.

Music is a tough and, at times, ugly business.

The alternate career type is not the roller-coaster success story but a place in the record books. These are the artists who have relatively long and steady careers based on far more than popularity, on respect and lasting influence. Creating more than hits, they invented a new form. Louis Armstrong turned jazz into an improvised art form based on the soloist. Muddy Waters electrified the blues and provided a gateway to rock and roll and the Rolling Stones. Little Richard created the icon of what an outrageous rock star should look and sound like. They were different, did not fit the norm, and, most importantly, they took plenty of risk. Bob Dylan built on the Walt Whitman American past and was crazy enough to merge beat poetry and folk music, while Kool Herc taught us the breaks. The list goes on and on of artists who changed our musical landscape while deeply affecting our lives. They created a form, a blueprint that future generations could use as a springboard to create their own sound, a new launching pad. That, my friends, is greatness.

Music that takes on greater meaning endures. It resonates not only when it is contemporary but for generations to come. When Aretha Franklin died, her life work was heralded far beyond being a commercially successful celebrity. Her music meant volumes to people who found inspiration in songs such as "Respect," "Think," "Chain of Fools," and "Do Right Woman, Do Right Man." Her authentic urban expression spoke to the struggles of the common people. Aretha moved beyond entertainment into an artistic level rarely seen. Music has the power to enlighten, inspire, and track social progress, or the lack thereof.

There lies a strange paradox in music between performers who create original music and the incessant American demand for covers of popular songs. Yes, we appreciate the work of great artists, but initially there is an almost insurmountable wall in attempting to get this music heard. People love the familiar songs that are comforting and well known. This is why bands have always had to meet the needs of audiences who want to hear familiar hits as opposed to debuting exciting new music. Go into any bar, club, or concert hall and you will find an audience waiting for what they know.

An artist performing on American stages can generally anticipate an audience that will be disappointed if they do not hear their favorite songs. Bands that once enjoyed the musical freedom that obscurity gives them now find themselves beholden to an audience that wants the same ten songs, over and over again. They are caught in the web of either being hit parade machines or risk-taking artists who challenge their audience. I have never had this problem and I'm probably luckier than I realize. I just don't get the best table in the restaurant.

This is an American phenomenon. European and Asian audiences want artists to present fresh material that shows both creativity and risk. Their expectations are based on this principle: give us your best shot. The standard for European culture is imbued from an early age and its value is obvious when walking through the streets of Paris. When Duke Ellington toured Europe, many audiences and critics were disappointed to hear medleys of his numerous hits. In America, they expect it; Ellington had piles of new material that he knew could only be sparsely sprinkled in a program of audience favorites. He had to lead them gently.

Why is this? The standard for creative art in foreign countries with far older cultures than America was set centuries ago. An artist must strive for a creative, authentic, and distinctive voice that makes Picasso, Van Gogh, Stravinsky, and Bartok stand out from the pack. Museums walls are filled with originality in some shape or form, not secondhand copies. Art is the search for individual expression and self-realization.

Risk-takers are the people we end up studying. They picked their influences wisely and had the vision to advance into unknown regions that only they could discover. It sounds simple, yet it takes great courage. Artists must be persistent while battling the demons of self-doubt. This is a hard road—the stones in our passway.

So why this book? I find that Americans love music but have little or no appreciation of its cultural significance. We cherish our favorite artists and their songs but have little understanding of music's meaning in the social context in which it was created. I believe the fault is partially due to our misguided public school curriculums. Unlike European education, which sends a message that art is essential to life and the development of a human being, America takes the careless attitude of "let the marketplace take care of it when it comes to the arts." Our K–12 curriculums have mostly cut down or eliminated the arts, seeing it as a nonessential. Really?

Try telling that to Louis Armstrong, who found himself playing a bugle in a New Orleans Home for Colored Waifs. It took him off the streets, and Armstrong became one of the most important and famous individuals of the twentieth century. Yes, the arts do matter. When music is valued, it is a gateway to understanding our nation's cultural evolution. It teaches us volumes about who we are. This is badly needed right now in a divided nation.

America has done a poor job telling our story because in order to do that you must confront and fully acknowledge the diverse groups of people who created it. Music is one of the most effective ways of discovering who we are, who we were, and where we might be headed. The arts engage critical thinking. It is all about the decisions an artist makes when putting the work together, followed by the critical thinking that engages audiences as they perceive the finished product.

It is also important to realize that artists fail regularly. That can teach us a lot. A writer, musician, or painter begins a work knowing full well that they are entering into the unknown. If they are lucky, they may have an idea or inspiration, but molding that into an evolved, developed, and coherent entity is extremely challenging—you don't always hit your target. Many people have the common misconception that the arts are solely about passion. Fuhgeddaboudit. Passion is a good word gone bad through overuse. (The emperor of overused words is "like," which, when used in every other sentence, encourages mass murder.) Yes, an artist must have a passion for their work. It is not a nine-to-five job; it is a fundamental part of their identity, but folks, passion will not be nearly enough. It is the creative act of pulling that inspiration out of thin air and transforming it into something that will resonate, first with the creator, and second with the audience. The '50s and '60s were filled with misguided people who thought that drugs, passion, and spontaneity would result in great art. They underestimated the craft involved. A study of an artist is usually a look into the work ethic of an extremely disciplined person. No, you just don't "pick up a sax and blow," as stated by a famous beat poet; just ask Charlie Parker, Jimi Hendrix, Mary Lou Williams, and John Coltrane for starters.

Music Is the Art of Discovery

No one can tell you what is good or what you should like. Music is the art of discovery. Taking a music class is helpful, but it does not compare with the experience of self-discovery that might occur long after the class is a faint memory. It is the person who stumbles upon Coltrane, Miles, Rakim, J Dilla, Big Mama Thornton, Bill Evans, or Joni Mitchell, feeling that they have added something essential to their lives. They experience this sense of discovery.

Music teaches us the art of listening. A great band stands on this principle. You might have an ensemble of virtuosos and it can sound terribly disjointed, largely because no one is listening to anyone but themselves. It is not just the playing but also the quality of the listening and creative call-and-response interaction that comprise a performance. The same is true of conversation, whether with friends or in the workplace. The quality of listening will affect the outcome, always. We live in a call-and-response world. We always have.

Beginning a new piece of music, a book, or any work of art is the hardest part. We dance around it for as long as possible and then, giving ourselves a firm kick in the pants, we just do it. I have had the incredibly good fortune to perform, compose, and teach music for many decades.

I strongly believe that America is a great land of musical and cultural innovation whose story is effectively told through the art lens.

In *Seize the Beat,* I hope to convey what I have discovered in music over many years. It is a long road: from club to concert hall, bar room to classroom, as a performer, composer, and educator. A career in music is a tough business and one must know the odds going in, realizing that this is marathon, not a sprint. Music, like boxing, requires a good cut man in your corner. These essays will not be glamorized. I seek connections between music and society by asking among other questions,

"What does this mean?" The essay is a wonderful form for exploring what you know and have seen. It takes some nerve to be a personal essayist; my work is cut out for me. Of course, this book is not all inclusive. I leave hip-hop, country music, and other styles to the people who have lived it.

I don't believe in force-feeding knowledge, yet it is incredibly important to learn about our past. It has much to teach us about beauty and life in a better world, but another thing that is essential is this: music must be a product of its time. My students know and love hip-hop in various forms. The artists, words, dress, language, and culture allow them to relate to life in the present. It is true that music is more visual than it once was; now we listen first with our eyes. A simple video on YouTube can be more powerful than an elaborately produced recording. Some might say this started with the MTV era, but people have always been visually oriented. We did not have the technology back in the day. Perhaps we were waiting for its arrival.

History matters; we just haven't taught it very well. The William Faulkner quote, "The past is never dead; it's not even past," certainly applies to music. We build on past forms if we are smart enough to know what those forms say and how to build new ideas based on them. Have a hit record and you are lucky; count your blessings. Create a musical form and your legacy will last forever. It is an infinite gift that keeps on teaching. American music brings the past forward. We would do well to remember that.

I believe music has the capacity to transform a life; it did mine. I also think that art's main purpose is to raise humanity above the daily hatred, anger, ignorance, bigotry, greed, and violence to envision not a utopian existence but a world of better possibilities. We judge a civilization by the art they create, not the material possessions they acquire. It is the yardstick by which we measure the books, songs, poems, plays, paintings, and films that tell a

The author's Shure 55SH microphone, AKG K240 headphones, and Hohner Special 20 harmonica.

story of what life meant back then and how people felt. We turn to the arts in this critically low point in America and the world.

I hope this book deepens your understanding of what music is, what it does, and how it can affect us. It is a cultural weather vane picking up shifts in the wind. It might surprise you in some way—as surprised as my students are at the end of their first African ring shout. Something just happened, but you don't know what it is, do you, dear students?

The rock hit the water; the ripples form and grow infinitely.

The lights go on.

I can see it in their faces.

1

How We Listen

When I became a professional musician, I quickly learned that my job was to react to what pianist George Shearing played and to the phrases that Frank Sinatra and Cleo Laine sang. I would play a new idea and pianist Erroll Garner would look up, startled, laugh, and play his response. In music, we live in the moment. Music, like life, is dependent on people who are interested in both sides of the conversation. Husbands take note.

There once was a Chicago band in the early '70s called the Flock. At one point on their first album, in a quiet breakdown before a long jam section, you hear a faint voice in the background ask, "Where will this take us?" That is music's great question. We never know—that is the beauty of it all. Improvised music, leaning heavily on extemporaneous expression, can enter new sound spectrums if the stars align. In live performance, the band requires an audience willing to go along for the ride—to see where it takes us. In order to do this, they will need to listen—carefully. More than passive observers, an audience participates in the creative process, though few realize it.

I have seen my student's facial expressions change dramatically when I play some blues harmonica, demonstrate something (usually badly) on the piano, slide guitar, or African djembe drum. Music moves the air and they feel it like waves crashing the shoreline.

Focused listening has become increasingly rare in a modern age. We are more distracted than ever. Never in human history have there been so many screens, gadgets, and gizmos, and we are just getting started, folks. Virtually every type of music is a click away and easier to access than ever. Many people no longer own music; they rent it through streaming. We'll discuss that later. The upside is, you have the world's music at your fingertips. Who wouldn't want that convenience? Hip-hop, African drumming, vintage rock, Eastern European folk songs, and Cajun fiddle music are but a few choices among the infinite playlist.

You are waiting for the downside; I can feel it.

A Sea of Digital BBs and Buddys

Our technology increases while our attention span gets shorter. Go to a concert and you often witness an audience that is only partially there, not there. At any moment, they will pull out their smartphones, text, twitter, shoot a selfie (look at me!), take video of the stage, upload it to Facebook, and check their email. My wife and I went to a B.B. King/Buddy Guy concert and I saw more screen images from handheld devices than I did of the two blues masters. It was a sea of digital BBs and Buddys lighting up the crowd. Were those phone-hugging people really experiencing a live event or documenting their coolness for their "friends" on social media? It is a case of being present and absent at the same time—a great deal is missed.

Music is made on multiple dimensions. I don't just play the bass; I must look to catch every little expression from the other musicians. Visual cues can pull the music in any direction, and the audience can be in on it, if they are paying attention. The gift of music is its spontaneity—it gives us the moment, and sharing that with an audience is one of my greatest joys. The atmosphere surrounding an audience is an essential part of the experience. All those rock concerts I saw in Chicago's Auditorium Theatre were great, but I am just as nostalgic for the hall itself. It felt like community and being there was a life-changing experience.

I was paying attention.

From a performer's standpoint I can tell you that a disconnected audience is quite disconcerting. It is as hard to make a musical connection with an audience engaged on smartphones as it is having an intimate dinner conversation with people unable to tear themselves away from the social media prompts, beckoning them like a disturbed lighthouse.

Let me give you an example of how an audience can affect a performance. Just down the street from Chicago's Wrigley Field, home of the Chicago Cubs and mecca to fanatics like me, stands the Cubby Bear Lounge. I recall seeing Maceo Parker, the veteran saxophonist who logged many miles with James Brown, at the Cubby Bear Lounge. His band played a tight, funky set until they made the mistake of playing a slow, dreamy ballad, when suddenly—a catastrophe, almost the entire audience walked out—time for a smoke, a text, in search of something more instantly gratifying. In the era of technology, audiences easily slip out of the performer's net. The crestfallen faces of the musicians said it all. My students readily admit their digital addictions (I do not allow cell phones in class, à la Attila the Hun), but what can we do? The horse and buggy have left the stable and I can't find a crank to a Model T Ford.

You don't have to be an expert to listen and enjoy music—that is the beauty of it. No talent is required to be a great listener. You need an open mind and imagination that is willing to be inhabited by sound. I have always felt that people are far too impressed by musical talent. Are musicians, music critics, or obsessed fans the only people who listen intently? They can go overboard as well. Those who don't play instruments are mystified by those who do—as if a secret spy code has been broken. One morning I was in a coffee shop in West Los Angeles and heard a guy, probably in his sixties, talking loudly into his cell phone. "And then he played a solo that was just sick, and they changed keys which was awesome, and he used some stomp pedals and it was just insane." Oye—yet you have to love the guy's enthusiasm for artistry. What great musicians do is not magic, but it can have a magical impact. I go to the Metropolitan Museum of Art and become absorbed by visual brilliance with the knowledge that it is beyond my capability. I can write my name on a good day.

Perhaps we should review the audience and leave the performance alone for a while. A great listening crowd dramatically uplifts the musical quality; it inspires the band and makes them reach deeper into their gifts. Let's look at two examples in jazz and rock. Duke Ellington, a master jazz composer, arranger, songwriter, bandleader, stylish dresser, and all-around ladies' man, hit a career low point in the 1950s. Rock had stolen the thunder from jazz, taking everything but the hubcaps. Elvis was king and the Duke was relegated to the shadows.

Then lighting struck off the docks at Newport, Rhode Island. Ellington and his magnificent big band played the 1956 Newport Jazz Festival, featuring a thrilling performance of "Diminuendo and Crescendo in Blue." The musical fire ignited the audience, driving it into a frenzy, spurred on by tenor saxophonist Paul Gonsalves. But the best part was an attractive, dancing blonde woman possessed by the music and dancing her heart out. Bands notice these things. *Someone should have sent her flowers.* Duke Ellington was born again, his career back on track with his face on the cover of *Time* magazine. It was the audience experience, the call and response that occurred that night, that made it seem magical. If you were there, you were lucky.

In the mid–'60s, the British rock band Cream (Eric Clapton, Jack Bruce, and Ginger Baker) came to America. They appeared at Bill Graham's Fillmore West in San Francisco, a city loved by musicians for their open and enthusiastic audiences. Cream, a trio of virtuosos, had to up their game because the audience demanded inventive, spontaneous improvisations. The San Francisco fans actually helped define Cream's style. An audience can tell a performer a lot about themselves. Through their reactions to a performance, they are telegraphing honest, deeply felt feelings when the music hits a nerve. This often comes as a surprise to musicians who live with this daily sound. Their fans can relay why the music truly moves them and this is priceless.

An indifferent crowd (and there are many of them) can kill a night. They can bring down a performance resulting in heavy drinking after the show. Back at the hotel, the band wonders where they went wrong; perhaps a day job might have been a better choice. I have found the best way to get people to listen in a New York jazz club is to tack on an enormous cover charge—that is, soak 'em. Cover charge = prestige = listening. People don't talk through Broadway shows with a ticket price close to a second mortgage for the same reason. Money should not command attention. I have been taken aback many times by audiences who talked through a legendary artist's performance.

Musicians Listen in Split-Screen Mode

You can't have a great performance from the stage without listening. A rock band, orchestra, jazz ensemble, or string quartet count interaction as an essential ingredient in an inspired performance. It is the sound that you don't hear from the stage that counts. I believe musicians exist in split-screen mode. They hear themselves on one side, while focusing on all the other musical sounds on the other, blending and shaping their sound in combination with the collective tone. The mark of a mature and selfless musician is one who can instantly adapt to the moment by sharing and interacting with the rest of the group. So what happens when a band doesn't truly listen to one another? When musicians fail to control their egos (this can happen frequently), they overplay, subjecting all to a punishment of far too many notes. They usually get louder, not unlike a person who raises their voice in a foreign country when people don't understand their language. Maybe speaking English louder will get these Italian people to understand....

Music as communication is a team effort. Duke Ellington was known to occasionally admonish his band at rehearsals with the words "Listen, listen," when they weren't paying close enough attention to the overall sound. Music is a conversation among the musicians and then with the audience; if everyone is on board, you're in for a special night. When I was young, I went to concerts like a sponge, absorbing the sights and sounds in front of me. I honestly had no idea what was going on; I could only put together some pieces of the story. That is OK; art reveals itself over the long run.

Music Is Conversation Set to Pitch

Remember suffering through middle school concerts? Sure you do. Children are too busy trying to play their instruments to worry about what the other kids are doing, but listening, as a skilled conductor knows, must come sooner or later. An accomplished musician knows the entire musical score, not just their part. They hear it in its entirety. Music is basically a conversation set to pitch. Our best friends in life are not just talkers; they are empathetic listeners, and we need them. It is their reaction to dialogue that makes conversation truly rewarding. If only we could get members of Congress to realize this.

So what happens when technology dominates the music? Live music is where real humans play music together, but today this is not always the case. When the sequencers, loops, auto tune, pre-recorded tracks, and sequenced light shows take over, that is something different altogether. I have attended concerts that began impressively, filled with strong ensemble playing and virtuoso solos, only to devolve halfway through into a live screen saver. How did this happen? Stay tuned for '70s mega-stadium events and MTV. A concert is one thing, but a show is another. Both can be great, but the lines often blur.

A concert generally focuses on the music and the people who create it in front of you. There is hopefully some degree of showmanship, but don't ask that of Bob Dylan. In jazz, Miles Davis let the music speak for itself, but when huge arena concerts took over, it was time for a show biz presentation necessary to engage an intimate audience of 50,000 people. The group Kiss sure went through a lot of makeup in those days. Later in this book you'll hear what Keith Richards says about concerts in baseball stadiums. He never played for the Yankees.

How best can we go about listening as a creative act? First, try focusing without unnecessary distraction, be open, engaged, and willing to expend a little effort. This won't hurt a bit. We love what is familiar and comforting. New music requires an open-minded audience, one that is willing to go into new and uncharted directions. We change the channel on the unfamiliar—nothing learned, nothing discovered. Try not to compare what you are hearing to what you already know and like; be a blank slate. I personally love the sound of surprise, something when you least expect it. You may be in new territory, and giving it a chance means multiple plays. Musicians use repetition when they practice; it is the only way to reach a new level. It also drives the neighbors crazy. In rapture, I practice something over and over again, trying to master the challenges. Meanwhile, my wife is in the next room plotting to poison me. Try listening to a song three or four times in succession and you will hear more each time.

The Three Listening Levels (Borrowed from Aaron Copland)

Aaron Copland, who epitomized America in sound with pieces such as *Rodeo, Billy the Kid,* and *Appalachian Spring,* is one of my favorite classical composers. Only in America could a Brooklyn Jew like Copland capture a panoramic sound painting of the majestic Wild West. (He had never ridden a horse through Flatbush.) I loved the plain, straightforward way in which he explained music. Copland broke listening down into three basic levels. I have modernized them a bit, but they still ring true with my students who have rarely, if ever, given the listening process any thought. You can't blame them; we are inundated with music and it is easy to take sound for granted.

Level 1: Listening on the Surface

You can hardly turn it off. The first level is the surface plane which takes in the bombardment of noise humans face every day. We are so inundated by screens and sounds that no wonder we have less room to focus. Music isn't easy to escape; it fills most public spaces—waiting rooms, bars, restaurants, elevators, airports, and even gas pumps with speakers in them (Who's idea was that?). It's enough to make you want to live alone in the mountains. Television screens attack us from all sides with opinions that never stop. Silence is not golden to the talking heads (not the band, mind you).

Background sound provides companionship when we are alone or stuck in traffic. Most music that lives on the first level is pop music—no surprise there. It is geared toward an audience that wants simple, straightforward, danceable, and singable melodies. The truth is, popular music of the past one hundred years hasn't changed much in that regard. Did you just ask why? Humans love a melody they can sing or at least hum, and above all, like our beating hearts, we are drawn to rhythm. We have a physical reaction to music; it is the aché, our inner life force. Pop music from Elvis to the Beatles to Taylor Swift is mostly for the six- to sixteen-year-old set. We enjoy the music of our youth. Don't blame Madonna.

No judgment is being made here. There is good pop and dreadful stuff, always was, always will be. In the '50s, pop singers like Patti Page were singing, "How Much Is That Doggie in the Window," complete with dogs barking. Only in America. (Yes, I know. That is an incomplete sentence and I can envision the words "See me" written in red pen by my sixth-grade English teacher.) Pop music is the business of making hits, not providing social uplift, but you can sometimes sneak a message in when no one is looking.

Pop and early rock and roll has been a young person's game for a long time, certainly since the '50s. It provides community and a way to connect with friends. "Are you a Beatle or a Stones?" was the burning question of the mid–'60s. We were deep thinkers. The word *fan* never came into it; your eleven-year-old identity was tied up in this critical choice. If you were a "Beatles," you were a nice boy or girl; if you were a "Stones," you were the most sinister sixth-grader to have ever walked the earth.

In pop music, the story remains the same. You are what you listen to, and in our youth, that is very important as we try on new identities, hoping no one is watching. When recalling my youth, my recurring mantra seems to be, "What was I thinking? Did I really wear those clothes? What was with that hair? I looked like my springer spaniel. Maybe there was something wrong with the mirror in my bedroom. Yeah, let's go with that." Music tells us a great deal about who we are and what we are going through at that moment.

Level 2: Gimme a Picture I Can Dance To...

The second listening level is the visual/expressive plane. As we mature, our imagination interacts with music. Sound becomes vivid, reminding us of a person, place, time, and memory. These connections are incredibly strong, lasting a lifetime. It is well known that some Alzheimer's patients are unable to speak, yet they can sing song lyrics of their youth from memory. It is a stunning thing to see. Hear a song of your past and you are transported to a time you can see, hear, and even smell. It is the incalculable power of music and how it interacts with the brain. No, I'm not about to get all neuroscientist on you. There is no quicker way to get my eyes to glaze over than a person analyzing music through the cerebral cortex. It takes all the fun out of it for me, and professional musicians would rather not dissect their art.

Big business knows how to work the visual. Film and television would be static mediums without their soundtracks. We rarely go to a movie and notice the music, but without it, virtually none of the film's emotional values would be believable. It would be a bunch of actors talking to each other. Who wants to see that? Answer: other actors. We hear the spoken word; we feel music.

Television commercials count on music to sell the product's image and connect to a targeted demographic. If you are selling BMWs, you might hear either classical music or cool jazz in the background, appealing to an older, sophisticated, and affluent audience. Selling hamburgers, you need hip-hop, or at the very least, classic rock. The music and the product are selling an identity, a lifestyle that you are supposed to desire.

When music videos came along, the visual sold the song in a new way that radio could not. Once upon a time, during the prehistoric early 1980s, there was something called MTV. It was a cable station that showed music videos, which were short films that acted out the song, sort of the way Elvis did in *Blue Hawaii*. Never mind.

That music video format was tailor-made for the expressive plane. Highly creative works such as Peter Gabriel's "Sledgehammer" or Herbie Hancock's "Rocket," mixed with inane videos whose visual content surpassed the music. Milli Vanilli and Vanilla Ice come to mind. The song became secondary to the visual image. We began to listen more and more with our eyes—another example of the law of unintended consequences. If you were an older performer from a previous era, you were most likely out of luck and looking for a Geico ad you could sponsor. At least MTV resulted in performers with very spiffy outfits.

This was a watershed moment in American culture. For better or worse, the tables were turned, and stagnant '80s radio, drowning in corporate demographic spreadsheets, lost its impact and influence. The major record labels, always slow to catch on, soon bought into making their own music videos in an attempt to save a music industry in free fall mode. These long-lasting effects are felt today. The TV show *American Bandstand,* from the long-ago '60s, was now MTV in the '80s, and video would pretty much kill, or at least permanently maim, the radio star.

My Cassette Is Stuck Again

Image conquered again, and it was a game changer. The music became digital, CDs replaced vinyl at over twice the price, and I still couldn't extract my Buffalo Springfield cassette from my Volkswagen Rabbit. Life is hard.

Technology shapes an audience. People who recall the '50s have noted how different their communities felt upon the introduction of television. Before people had TVs, you'd finish supper, do the dishes, then go out and play with other kids in the neighborhood, while parents sat outside on warm summer nights and socialized. Along came TV, people discovered their new favorite shows, and gradually there was less playing and socializing and more watching in silent American dens and living rooms. Besides, who could tear themselves away from *Leave It to Beaver*?

Bring on the new world.

Level 3: The Deep Dive

Despite being visual people, we can go even deeper into the third listening level—the musical plane. Imagine a room without distractions (try a monastery); it's just you and the music. Focus all your attention on what you hear—the singer, lyrics, individual musical instruments, and so on. This level is like peeling away the layers of an onion. The more you listen, the more the music comes to you in newly revealed depth and nuance. You begin hearing things you may have never previously encountered. I always tell my students, it is OK to not know; figuring things out happens over time with much patient repetition and then discovery.

Music was a big mystery to me when I was young. I heard the singer and the words to pop, rock, soul, blues, jazz, and Motown, but what was all that other sound that filled the aural background? I knew there were musical instruments buzzing about, but what were they doing in the big picture? Going to concerts had a big impact on me. I could see and connect sounds and visual images, plus those rock concerts had an interesting aroma.

Music may start out as a confusing white noise, but with repeated hearings, we familiarize the sounds and begin to put them in some kind of order. Once it becomes familiar, you are on the way to knowing and maybe even loving the piece, not always, but it is possible. You can't get there if you don't try. Where will this take us? We never know. My father used to say to my brother and me at the dinner table, "You don't have to love it; just eat it." Ah, parents.

We only had vinyl in those days and they scratched very easily. All those ticks and pops discouraged dropping the needle and placing it somewhere else in the song. Today, through modern digital convenience, you can guide the song anywhere you like. Result: yesterday we heard albums; today, singles.

The third listening plane reveals the character of the vocals, the sound and blend of the instruments, and the ever-present beat, tone, and story in the music. An artist's background history indicates the important influences that go into creating their sound. Examples would be the impact of the early rocker Buddy Holly on the Beatles, who took the Holly instrumentation and songwriting approach as a springboard for their own ideas. Jazz trumpeter Louis Armstrong's instrumental and vocal phrasing were essential to a young Billie Holiday. You can even hear that trumpet tone in her voice. Blues singer and guitarist Muddy Waters was the gateway for the Rolling Stones and Eric Clapton, among others. As bumbling British teenagers, hearing the driving, sexual tone of Muddy's "Mannish Boy" gave them a musical home, a place to hang their hat. Folk singer Woody Guthrie's topical songs were the recipe Bob Dylan needed to craft his lyrics into a contemporary worldview. What bop trumpet innovator Dizzy Gillespie said about Louis Armstrong could be expressed by all of those mentioned here—"No him, no me." It took Armstrong's genius to open the doors to jazz improvisation and provide a gateway for future generations in search of their own voice, or in the case of 1920s blues diva Bessie Smith, who influenced blues-rock vocalist Janis Joplin. It was a case of "No her, no me." Janis, with her unique style, took the essence of Bessie and put it on a rock and roll stage. The past was born again in a new era.

The mistake is to think that you can absorb it all on the first listening. Unless it is very straightforward, and admittedly, most pop music is, there is too much to digest on a first go-round. Repetition is our best friend, whether practicing an instrument or evolving into a deeper listener. Every time you hit rewind, you will hear more, make new associations, and find undiscovered sounds. Trust me on this. I still hear new things in recordings that have been important to me over a lifetime. The music keeps giving.

A life of touring has taught me a lot about American music. People make music based on what they hear in the streets, feel on the dance floor, and what's cooking in the kitchen. Every town has its own sonic story, a diverse group of musicians with the same American dream but each with its own distinctive feel and beat, a rhythm of life.

Being in San Francisco, I could feel the eccentric freedom that released Janis Joplin and the Grateful Dead. Driving down Sunset Boulevard in Hollywood, with its glamour and decadence, made me feel the Doors' dark music in the city of night.

Visiting the locations of Sun Studios, Stax Records, and the grave of Elvis Presley in Memphis created an atmosphere in the air as thick as barbecue sauce, a cultural ground zero for American music. You could taste it.

Driving down old Highway 61 in Mississippi and stopping at Clarksdale, Rosedale, Merrigold, Helena, Arkansas, and the old Stovall Plantation in Coahoma County, was like visiting the most important European cathedrals. This was the land where the Delta blues was born, and for me, the music still hung in the air.

The dilapidated southern juke joint I saw in Rosedale, Mississippi— ceiling falling in on an ancient pool table—was a symbol of America's musical crossroads. The endless miles of cotton fields were a reminder not to make the mistake of romanticizing the place; desperate poverty has kept gentrification away and the vestiges of Jim Crow rambles on.

In my hometown of Chicago, on the south and west side, Muddy Water's electric blues sprung from the Black migration while Record Row defined a soul sound.

Detroit's Motown Records, in a small house on West Grand Boulevard, was a crossover sound for young America as Detroit ghetto kids became stars in Las Vegas.

I still need to visit Muscle Shoals, Alabama, where Black and white musicians working together during the height of '60s racism made historic recordings.

There is even a Trap Music Museum in Atlanta.

Where we come from is who we are.

Play It Again, Sam

Art can be initially deceiving. Did you ever buy an album or CD for the one song you love, take it home and play it, only to find you hate the rest of the music? BIG disappointment and an expensive one. Since you are stuck with it, you played it a few more times, and lo and behold, it began growing on you. After a half-dozen or more plays, your big dud purchase became one of your favorite records. The music did not change; you did. A listener transformation occurred because you made the effort by taking the time to play it again, Sam. The listener reaches a deeper listening level of understanding and appreciation through this creative process. The jazz pianist Bill Evans was right: you can't get there without effort and exposure.

Depending on your point of view, whether you think it's cool or nerdy, you might even go further into the music. What do the lyrics mean and what story does it tell? Most of the time, people go for the beat and don't pay attention to the words. I have made that mistake. Lyrics are a big part of the story *if* the artist is really trying to say something. (Emphasis on the word *if*.) In my high school rock band, Mirrors Image (band names were not our strong suit), we, a bunch of suburban white kids, played Neil Young's "Southern Man" not having a clue what it was about.

Blame it on my youth.

America, a Country of People Wearing Bizarre Masks

Words matter. Lyrics can lead us to the land where the artist discovered the inspiration to make the music. By absorbing influences from great songs and artists of the past, writers like Bob Dylan could turn "No More Auction Block for Me," a 1873 Negro spiritual, into "Blowin' in the Wind," an anthem for the 1960s. That is the past coming forward. Everybody borrows and steals from someone else, at least a bit, but the term *influence* is a nicer word. The courts are full of copyright cases facing the difficult problem of parsing out musical influence as opposed to thievery. The music business was made for lawyers and accountants who don't dress like Elton John, Lady Gaga, or Steven Tyler.

Music illustrates the contrasts and paradoxes of American life. The '20s jazz age of F. Scott Fitzgerald was a time when flappers and their dates, drunk and falling out of Studebakers, were rebelling against their parents' generation in orgy-like style, with jazz as their liberating soundtrack. Sorry, Gatsby, they didn't really get the music at all, knowing even less about the Black men and women who created this art form in the first place. In America, we learn these truths much later. Teaching these lessons—that is another matter.

Go back even further to the nineteenth-century minstrel shows, whites in blackface were imitating African American songs and dances. This was followed by Black minstrel shows where Black people corked their face black yet again, performing in tent shows on a rough touring circuit through the South. We are a country of people wearing bizarre masks in a strange dance where the music doesn't stop. Americans defy definition.

Imitation may be perceived as flattery, but as minstrel shows became America's most popular form of entertainment from 1830 to 1900, the Ku Klux Klan and Jim Crow laws were just getting started. It was the ultimate irony and injustice of whites loving the music while refusing to respect and acknowledge the people who created it. The '50s rock and roll craze caused white teenagers to dance to rock and roll (really rhythm and blues), and the music forecasted a new era. B.B. King said, "If it weren't for music, civil rights would have come much later." Folk and rock of the '60s gave voice to change and protest as draft cards burned, Vietnam raged, and the Doors droned, "This is the end." It turns out, they were right. By the late '60s, the music was, in a sense, over, turn out the lights. Dialing up '70s rock, we find that all that altruism had hitchhiked back to suburbia, where young people were becoming the very thing they had been rebelling against: their parents. Rebelling Kerouac- and Ginsburg-reading hippie becomes a dentist.

You gotta love it.

You Could Feel the Road Miles Dripping Off Their Leather Jackets

Deeper listening considers an artist's stance and attitude. It is in their onstage presence at a live event before they make a sound. A performer's image has always been important, long before people used the dreaded "branding" term. Album covers that reflected the music were essential to the listening process. It was a portrait of the artist as a young rock star. I remember hanging out with some high school friends, poring over the Allman Brothers album cover, *Live at the Fillmore East*, while listening to the album. Who are these guys? What was it in the Georgian water that makes them sound like this? What is the Fillmore East, and where is this alley they are standing in on the back cover? (Answer: It is now a bank on New York City's Lower East Side.) You could feel the road miles dripping off their leather jackets. They were the Allman Brothers and they came to play. There was no talk about keeping it real; they lived it. To paraphrase Dylan, those albums had "stature." Later, when I played with the Allman Brothers drummer, Jaimoe, and asked him about the classic Fillmore record, he shrugged and said, "It was just another night." After a pandemic, we could use more nights like that.

The Beatles' first album made an impact not just by its sound but by the way it looked. Most American album covers were corny depictions of white suburban scenes of Mommy and Daddy with their 2.5 kids gathered around the stereo for a night of family fun. Blah. The "Meet the Beatles" album featured a creatively lit, iconic album cover photo that said, this is cool and different. Bruce Springsteen said it best: "I remember running in and seeing that album cover with those four headshots. It was like the silent gods of Olympus. Your future was just sort of staring you in the face."[1] I know what he means. As a nine-year-old, I saw the

Beatles on the *Ed Sullivan Show*. The next day, I got a guitar, my hair got longer, and my father was not amused. Carrying around that guitar case was my passport to being a cool ten-year-old hipster.

Right.

"They left and took the air with them."

As a young music student, I recall seeing Miles Davis in 1973 at Paul's Mall in Boston with his raucous, disjointed fusion band. Music to some and a fire in a pet shop to the less open-minded. He emanated a mysterious aura, particularly to those who did not know him. Miles was, indeed, the Prince of Darkness—danger ahead. The night was memorable not just for the music but also for a music student schoolmate of mine, critical of his performance, who was bold or crazy enough to go up to the living legend and tell him. Miles told him where he could go to with the epitaph, "Fuck off, white boy."

Miles doesn't care what you think.

The Beatles, though I never met any of them, radiated an energy and excitement that was magnetic. I read a story of the time they walked into the famous London jazz club Ronnie Scott's at the height of their fame. Sitting at the bar in the back of the club, it didn't take long for the audience to shift their attention from the jazz quartet on the bandstand to the four famous lads. They finished their drink, got up, and left, and as a writer commented, "They left and took the air with them."

I turned pro, and one day the phone rang. It was the contractor Joe Malin inquiring if I was free to back Frank Sinatra on a Monday night for the reopening of Carnegie Hall in 1987. This is one of those life moments when time stands still and you feel you are levitating over Schenectady or someplace like it. "Yeah, I guess I'm free," I murmured in shock. What else would I be doing on a Monday night—playing whiffle ball? So there I was, rehearsing with Frank Sinatra and his orchestra at Carnegie Hall, just another day in New York. It was an experience to see this rather diminutive man walk out on stage to thunderous applause. Sinatra was larger than life. He could have been seven feet tall that night, all before he had sung a note. The *man* embodied a command and mastery of his art that radiated outward. What he lacked in vocal abilities at that point in his life, he more than made up for in his presence, vocal phrasing, and musicality. It was like witnessing an athlete past their prime but still knowing how to persevere by outwitting a younger opponent. Sinatra owned it all, air included.

He also scared the hell out of me.

The good news in music is there are no rules. Listening is a very personal experience and there are no directives to what you should or should not like. A listener makes a vivid inner connection by identifying with the music on a personal level. We must see ourselves in the music. This defies words and technical description. I have found that music carries hope and inspiration and helps us find our identity. Your appreciation can increase by knowing more about the music, artist history, lyrics, and stance, but I have found that excessive analysis can take the fun out of it. I love the stories around and through the sound.

There is a striking similarity between performing music and listening or dancing to it. A dancer physically becomes one with beat. Terrible dancers become two with the beat, but they have fun anyway. It is a feeling of elation on the dance floor that harkens back to African ring shout roots. If the night and the moment are right, a magical spark occurs between the musicians and dancers. They become possessed by a joy that transcends our daily issues. Freedom is experienced in a personal way. It is, as author Robert Farris Thompson called it in his landmark book, *The Flash of the Spirit*. The great jazz drummer Art Blakey said, "Music washes away the dust of everyday life."

Seize the beat.

"That don't move me, fellas. Let's get real gone for a change."

Art reminds us of how lucky we are to be alive. Elvis once said in a recording studio, "That don't move me, fellas. Let's get real gone for a change." It is the inner freedom that music can bring, a release from the daily challenges that keep us going back for more.

Another great American, Frank Zappa, remarked, "Americans hate music, but they love entertainment." Good old Zappa had a point there. People love the packaged, hyped-up image and glitter of pop but have little patience for in-depth musical works that require focus, not to mention repeated listening. Most people are first-level listeners, driving an industry that delivers the appropriate product without challenge. Subtlety and nuance tend to get left out as well. Loud becomes louder, and dynamics take a back seat.

I come from a pre-digital, -internet, and -computer age when dinosaurs walked the earth (they were quite messy). We walked to the Sinclair gas station with the big dinosaur out front, past Woolworth's five and dime store, over to the Monroe Elementary School ice-cream social (I can still hear them playing "Green Onions" by Booker T. and the M.G.'s). It was the age of vinyl records, black-and-white, then color TV, and John F. Kennedy, Lyndon B. Johnson, and Martin Luther King Jr. Necessity forced us to put the needle down on the LP's side one until it was finished. Random play was impossible without adding more ticks and pops into the grooves—that would cost you another $6.95. Most of my students have never even touched a record player tone arm. So I demonstrate one in class to show how the thing works. They look at me like I had just found a 2,000-year-old fossil. When I bring in a 1929 Victrola I bought at a tag sale, they really think this guy has lost it, but they remember the moment. One student even cited this classroom experience in a job interview ... and got the job. I'm sure you can find these visuals on YouTube, but you'll miss my scintillating presentation.

No wonder vinyl is having a bit of a comeback. Music was tactile; you held the record, the tone arm, and the album cover jacket in your hands. Touch gives us a connection. A big part of the reason I love playing the upright bass is how it feels in my hands, next to my body. The strings under my fingers vibrate and run through my arms. I can even feel the whoosh of air as the note escapes through the sound hole. As a fourth-grader, I chose the bass not for its size—I stupidly didn't make the connection that I would have to carry the thing—but for the way the string felt when I plucked that low E. Love at first sound. Boing.

No, I didn't figure on carrying it onto planes, cars, trains, subways, and horse-drawn carts. I never was any good at planning ahead. I would wait at the airport curbside baggage check-in with my seven-foot-high fiberglass bass trunk that looked like a coffin that had seen hard times. It had my name on the outside and strangers would come up to me and ask, "Is Brian Torff in there?" Then I knew how the Peanuts cartoon character Charlie Brown felt.

What was the result of hearing music on that antiquated technology? We were impressed by the LPs—*Pet Sounds, Sgt. Pepper's, Aretha Live at the Fillmore,* Dylan's *Blonde on Blonde,* and James Brown's "*Sex Machine,*" hearing them as complete works that must be experienced with the songs in succession, as the artist had intended. Playing individual favorite songs in random order would have been disconcerting, like starting a movie in the middle, then skipping to the end, followed by the beginning. A band constructs a live performance set list with carefully considered songs in sequence for maximum effectiveness and impact.

In a digital world, instant gratification through random play is easy. Aren't we lucky, right? Right? You can skip over a lot of music by only playing your favorite tracks. It's easy to miss the story. Listening is fun, but it is also a skill that can be infinitely developed.

Concert audiences have changed over the past sixty years. They have less patience for improvisation, nuance, development, and subtlety; just skip to the good part, will ya? For all of digital music's convenience, I have to agree with Dylan: it lacks stature, and most of it does not last very long.

"I should be sorry if I only entertained them; I wished to make them better."

This is not to disparage the modern generation—these kids today blah, blah, blah. It has always been this way between musicians and the general public. Mozart and Beethoven struggled mightily with an audience who demanded simple musical entertainment, not uplift. Handel's famous quote rings true today: "I should be sorry if I only entertained them; I wished to make them better." Good luck with that, George Frideric. Yet, I agree with him. Art makes us think, and that can only make us better.

I am a card-carrying idealist, a professional dreamer who believes that music is a gift that illuminates our life and tells our stories.

It is the artist with the flashlight in the dark who points and says, **It's over there. Look!**

If you're open to having a transformative experience at a concert, music festival, art gallery, museum, theater, film, or blues club, then many gifts may await. It is impossible to describe, but you know when that feeling of discovery happens. Art can do this. I never got that from a spreadsheet, but I'm open to anyone who can convince me. Duke Ellington once said about composing music, "All I do is dream." Listeners dream inside the music.

I have realized one thing over many years of performing, teaching, and writing music: Real learning is about discovery. That's it. I love teaching, but only a fraction of learning comes from classes, test taking, and grades. I realize people paying enormous amounts of tuition would rather not hear this. Who can blame them? Real and lasting learning usually comes from self-initiative, the need to know more. When I hear from a student many years after graduating, and they tell me they listen to Bill Evans, Son House, Bessie Smith, or some obscure rock and roller, I think to myself, "Mission accomplished."

We can't shovel culture down one's throat, but we can encourage personal discovery by illuminating the darkness. Music is a gift, and as Dizzy Gillespie once said, "You can't steal a gift." The joy is passing it on to someone else.

High school was hard for me. My father died suddenly during my sophomore year, and I felt lonely and filled with self-pity. Suddenly, life shattered, and I had never known that was possible. One afternoon, my high school English teacher, Mr. Gill, played us a record of Son House, the Delta blues master, singing "John the Revelator." It blew my mind. It was a message from another world that hit me like a lightning bolt. I realized that day, America was many different countries with groups of people that I did not see in my little Illinois town. The power of art was revealed to me in that classroom on that gloomy Tuesday afternoon. I knew from that moment on I had to enter a bigger, wider world someday. I'm glad I did.

You should go listen to it, right now.

A Juke Joint for the Twenty-First Century

Life and its many curveballs are upon us. I have spoken to therapists who see troubled patients with no developed interests other than work and watching TV. The 2020 pandemic has caused untold stress on millions of people. We are burned out on multiple levels with no end in sight. The millennium blues are upon us, and like hard-pressed sharecroppers on the Mississippi Delta, we will need healing art to help us make it through the day, a juke joint for the twenty-first century. Our minds need a spark. Who will bring the matches? I consider myself lucky to make a living doing something I love. I try to share that feeling; just don't ask me to fix anything around your house.

Music of all kinds

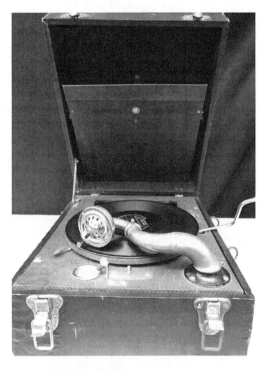

The author's Model 255 Victrola record player that sold for $35 in 1929.

await your discovery. You don't have to play an instrument or be a terrific singer. Associate Justice of the Supreme Court Oliver Wendell Holmes commented on living a life without the arts: "Alas for those that never sing but die with their music in them." I can attest to this. After my father's death, it was music that pulled me through. I know that was the same for Paul McCartney, who at age fourteen, lost his mother to cancer. He did all right for himself. Inspiration and the strength to go on is there if you look for it.

In her book on writing, *Bird by Bird*, Anne Lamott writes, "Lighthouses don't go running all over an island looking for boats to save; they just stand there shining."

Get on with it. Put this book down.

Go find a lighthouse.

Listen.

2

Listen Up, Africa!

Maybe you should sit down for this one. When it is all said and done, the fact is we all come from Africa. It has been proven since the early 1950s; civilization evolved from a single, female African embryo. What does that mean to you and the music that lives in your cell phone? Everything.

The ripple effect of African culture that was transplanted in the New World through slavery resulted in the hip-hop beats you dance to today. Our appearances and skin tones may vary, but a common musical soul remains. Human beings are drawn to music, and those impulses resonate in our body like a drum.

Think about it for a minute. Our hearts beat in rhythm as we walk through the day, breathing in our own individual tempos. Our voices are musical instruments that move up and down in pitch as we speak, from high, loud, and excited to a low whisper. Our speech makes musical accents by emphasizing syllables and words that convey meaning. No one speaks in a monotone; if you do, chances are you're not very interesting. Never mind that Ms. Clinkscales, your childhood piano teacher, hit your fingers with a ruler and said you had no talent, or your choir teacher declared that you couldn't carry a tune in a bucket. Talent aside, though Carnegie Hall may not be an option, humans are musical beings.

Americans have trouble with foreign musical sounds. African music can sound repetitious and strange to Western ears accustomed to three-minute pop music. We may become bored by all those drums and chants—it is the root of our music, yet it seems far away. The connections of past to present are undeniable. The three primary elements of African music are drums, dance, and song. Drums provide rhythm for the dancers, while voices sing in call-and-response style. Hmm, sounds like popular music to me. Our dance music has always been drum, dance, and song—from ballroom to hip-hop.

In an African village, music establishes community by bringing

Globe, William J. Clinton Presidential Center, Little Rock, Arkansas.

people together to celebrate life. Someone beats on a drum, a village dances, and everyone sings songs that proclaim their identity and heritage. A rock concert does a similar thing. It gives people a connective, live experience that surpasses any recording.

European classical music is generally led by a conductor. The music is usually notated carefully, emphasizing melody, harmony, and motivic development. In an African drum group, there is no conductor; the drums and bell patterns (large metal bells) take the lead as other instruments fall into the groove. Rhythm is there for one specific purpose—to engage, inspire, and converse with the dancers and the spirits. Aché, the inner spirit, lights the fire in each dancer, musician, and singer. The sound makes for a thrilling experience. African drummers know they are not performing a concert for well-heeled patrons. If the village stops dancing, the drummers pack up and go home.

The ring shout ritual that engages an African village and begins my class invites everyone to join a communal circle, creating unity. The European concept of the demure, reserved concert hall with a well-dressed, passive, seated audience does not exist here. The Western world has fallen for the star system. We have made icons out of musical superstars, making us passive yet hungry, an insatiably star-struck audience. We literally look up to the giants on the stage, seeing them on large-screen monitors. African music keeps the musicians and dancers on the same level, down here on the ground. In time, America encountered the beat, and we have been living in that world for generations.

Let me give you an example. During jazz clarinetist Benny Goodman's 1938 Carnegie Hall concert, young swing fans jumped out of their seats and began dancing in the aisles to the shouting swing band. It was an upheaval that signaled a new era. The African-derived jitterbug dance had just entered a European-style concert hall. Once the pounding African American beat, later to be called swing, entered the bodies of American youth, that was it. There was no way to put the genie back in the bottle. If you have been to a rock or hip-hop show, you get it. The beat, later aptly called big beat during '50s rock and roll, unearthed the excited natural rhythms of the body. Why not? Music was the gateway to a newfound personal freedom. No wonder conservatives condemned the music; they were losing control and they knew it. In their minds, it was the downfall of the America they had known. We were only getting started.

There are numerous stereotypes regarding Black people and rhythm. The rich environment of rhythm from African drums to popular music is clear, but there is more to it than that. Africans taught us new ways to sing. The human voice is an expressive musical instrument. Any culture with an oral tradition passes along information through call and response. Children learn how to speak from copying their parents' voices. It is a natural way to learn and is perhaps the most enduring.

This African oral tradition was imbued with creative vocalizing, free and improvisational, which stood in sharp contrast to the more formal European singing voice. The Black voice bent the note, later to be called the blue note. It was soulful expression of the deepest kind that became the language of America's twentieth-century popular music. This extemporaneous singing could mine the vastness of human emotion, from joy to sorrow.

America is a twisted and complex land where few of us realize our tangled roots. Indeed, as Ralph Ellison surmised, whites are blacker and Blacks are whiter than they can imagine. Our culture has been shaped by the diversity that built the United States, despite the cruelties and injustices that went along with it. In this rich land we must wonder, why is America the musical source of blues, gospel, jazz, rock, country, hip-hop, and much more? Numerous world cultures were far older and more developed. How did such a relatively young nation of brash upstarts create so much art in a few hundred years?

Creation sometimes comes from unpredictable places; the human spirit endures. Once manifest destiny was determined and the slave trade grew, a strange course was set for America. When warring African tribes used their captives as bounty for sale on the Gold Coast, a worldwide industry was set into place. Slave labor was deemed essential to a vast country that needed workers. The profits would be great and the ultimate cost is still being tallied to this day. It is an astounding human achievement, where great art evolves from horrific times, turning into a thing of beauty. There is no denying that slavery would map a cultural path that influenced us from the first slave ship to the latest songs we hear on the pop charts. Time, and the past, move forward.

The first slave ship, arriving in August 1619, carried human cargo that planted cultural seeds and transformed a nation. Few suspected that Africans, seen as heathens and subhumans by many whites, could contribute anything more than hard labor, yet culture is a powerful sword that can never be taken from the captured. You may change a person's name and language and attempt to erase their spiritual beliefs, but you cannot take their culture. It is an enduring memory that has been passed down through the oral tradition for thousands of years. No auction block could diminish the need to retain heritage; it only grew stronger. Music and dance meant hope and, ultimately, survival.

There is obviously an enormous difference between voluntary immigration and displacement by enslavement. On the deck of slave ships crossing the Atlantic, some Africans played drums. Inevitably, the three basic elements of African music were transplanted to American soil, shaping us forever. The modern beat and rhythm was forged in the past under unspeakable conditions. Hundreds of years later, American music would be a driving and compelling force in the civil rights movement. Its power is limitless.

Enslaved Africans knew they would never return to their native land. The only way to survive was to hold on to their identity through tradition. The ring shout was a common West African ritual that moved into the Deep South coming through slave routes from South America and the Caribbean. It became a powerful outlet of spiritual expression, an underground stream that would carry enslaved people for centuries. As slaves danced in counterclockwise motion to pounding drums and vocal chants, a sense of community was established among a broken race who would never see their loved ones again. Africans are a spiritual people who believe in the concept of *ubuntu*—a person is only a person through others. The power of African culture comes from the concept of village strength, the unity of people working and singing together. This communal strength is largely lacking in modern industrialized society.

Heritage can define a life identity. In a West African tribe, a male elder taught the young how to make a drum, demonstrating the rhythms and dances while instilling a sense of pride, history, identity, and integrity in the children. These teachings defined what it meant to be a Wolof or Bantu person. The griot was the tribal storyteller, musician, and historian who passed on traditions to the younger children. Africans saw the oral tradition as a gateway to learning morals, culture, and worldview. What was heard, imitated, and absorbed became permanent, to be passed on and delivered to future generations.

Music in Africa is so common that there is no word for it. African field-workers sang in rhythm, creating a unified work energy that expressed their heritage and got the job done. It belies the plantation myth that enslaved people sang because they were happy and content. African women making dough would sing for three beats as they worked their hands in a large wooden pot. They would pull their hands out on the song's fourth beat while another woman pushed the dough into place, then the sequence would start again. The African oral traditions settled in America as stories were told, dances were created, voices sang, quilts were sewn, and drummers played rhythms that spoke in a language emanating from the dun-dun, a "talking drum" that changes pitch like a human voice. African music would not die in America; enslaved people needed it as an essential expression of their dignity, identity, and heritage. America was introduced to musical elements that would modernize and transform virtually everything that came in its path. Enslaved people have always sung when they are oppressed; their song signifies an inner freedom and worldview.

Slaves were valued for their physical labor and musical talent. They provided the entertainment for dances, socials, barn raisings, and other plantation functions. Drums were accused of starting slave uprisings and were outlawed in some southern states, but the driving rhythms persisted. Their musical abilities carried over from ring shout drumming to syncopated rhythms that were applied to the banjo, fiddle, Jew's harp, bones, and later, guitar and harmonica. Rhythms that were no longer permitted on outlawed drums were transferred to the feet, hands, and body, resulting in the mid-nineteenth-century stardom of William Henry Lane, known as Master Juba, an early tap-dancing innovator. Slave musical talent transferred drum rhythms to European instruments such as the piano. Brass instruments would not be far behind in this musical connection between Africa and America.

The contribution of the African drum is widely known, but what is often forgotten is the unique, innovative beauty of the African voice. Unlike the European trained opera singer who expresses a pure singing tone, Africans took an entirely different approach. The voice of the griot does not strive for European tonal purity but relies instead on a gritty, soulful, personal, and heartfelt realism that embraces cries, moans, yells, whispers, sliding notes, and other spontaneous improvisations. Whereas Europe embraced the tempered scale, or do-re-mi system, Black Americans sounded the African bent note "dirty" tone in the fields, work camps, docks, levees, and church. The field holler's sliding, bending voice defied European musical history. Rather than singing a fixed pitch, the African voice emotionally shaped the note, delivering a personal form of expression that could not be duplicated in a score or notated on music staff paper. It is impossible to transcribe Jimi Hendrix's version of the "Star-Spangled Banner" for the same reason.

The field holler birthed new musical possibilities. The African voice improvised with a controlled freedom that sharply contrasted with structured white church vocalizing. Their use of the African-derived pentatonic scale created a unique mood and feeling that stood in direct contrast to European diatonic tempered scales. The bent note of the past would become the signature sound of blues guitar, jazz saxophone, and the soul singer of the future.

Few Americans are aware of this historical impact on modern music. There is hardly a pop, jazz, blues, soul, gospel, or rap artist who has not been touched by these past musical influences. When the first slave ship arrived, it released the tremendous power of Blackness from that day forward. It would be a reckoning force in American life. In order to survive, slaves found in the words of E. Franklin Foster, "a motive for living under American culture or die." Their survival and propensity for cultural memory, the valuing of ancestral traditions, and the spiritual force they brought to the present resulted in a worldview that would impact a new nation.

Who knows more about freedom than the enslaved? It is a staggering irony that a country allegedly based on constitutional freedom could support a slave industry from 1619 until the end of the Civil War in 1865. Immigrants arriving willingly to America sought self-destiny, with the option of choosing assimilation. Enslaved Africans needed their music and spiritual beliefs to assure future generations that they would not be erased, marginalized, or homogenized. The griot, a singer and historian in an African village who delivered lessons through story and song, became the African American preacher, blues singer, jazz sax-ophonist, soul man, and rapper. A common African expression says, "When you play it, say it."

In a country of constant change, Americans might have trouble understanding why slaves continued this ring shout tradition in the New World. It would have been far easier for the slave to relinquish their past by simply following their white master's orders. Missionary work attempted to convert slaves to Christianity, but transformation took hold, not conversion. It is essential to realize that although you can rob someone of their name and country, displace their family members, and scatter their lives like seeds in the wind, their culture can never be erased. Slaves held on to things past, a cultural memory that is the last currency of human dignity. It would have been easy for slaves to forget cultural beliefs by adopting European values. This did not happen, and America is all the better for it. Instead of erasing their heritage, African Americans brought the past forward into a new land and time. Duke Ellington was a progressive musician who knew the value of cultural evolution when he said, "The memories of things past are important to a jazz musician."

People under hardship and duress turn to art as a release from pain. It is a celebration of humanity in a bewildering and often insane world. Holocaust concentration camp prisoners formed choirs and orchestras, South African mine workers protested their squalid conditions by sing-ing, and World War II female prisoners vocalized excerpts from sym-phonies and operas.

Far from savages, Africans brought to America a sophisticated, cultural worldview that loved not only beats but also words and stories. Whereas most Europeans saw music as either for church or leisure, Afri-cans regarded it as an essential element for daily life. There were rhyth-mic work songs for picking cotton, baking bread, and washing clothes and a song given to a newborn baby at birth. African-language concepts began finding their way into the English language. Slang expressions such as "OK" became commonplace. African words such as *dega*, mean-ing to understand, became "dig it." *Hepi*, meaning "to be aware," found its slang in "hip."

Drum, dance, and song connect past to present. These musi-cal principles are the foundation of gospel, jazz, rock, blues, country, hip-hop, and Latin music. These musical styles are based on drum-beats, followed by melodic singing or rapping. Contemporary music is largely an interactive dance where the audience plays a role in the heat of the moment. From integrated Harlem nightclubs and dancehalls of the 1930s to house and techno music, African traditions show their face and influence. You can see social change on almost any American dance floor.

Europeans valued a written heritage of books and notated music to be sung in church, but Africans brought an oral tradition that committed knowledge to a deep place in the human soul. I inform my students that memorization is not the same thing as "knowing," which is a deep and permanent personal experience. African slaves carried their knowledge inside, concealing its power. The famous bop innovator Dizzy Gillespie once said, "I know more than they think I know." It is sadly ironic that a genius like Gillespie once had to hide in the New York subway to avoid a drunken, violent group of sailors who resented his walking with a light-skinned woman in the middle of Manhattan. I was fortunate to work with him a few times, his outer fun-loving demeanor contrasted with a brilliantly analytical mind.

Whereas whites danced waltzes, ballroom dances, and jigs, Africans in America combined their native dance with the styles they witnessed through plantation windows. America is a land of hybrids that merge distinctly separate styles into a new, organic whole. Without syncretism, there can be no jazz, rock, hip-hop, and beyond. American culture is a mixed-race story that endures due to artistic perseverance. It remains astounding to me how few people realize this. Our educational system has done us a disservice in this area.

Culture is a measuring stick for past and future civilizations. One generation passes their creations on to the next, and in the end, we look to art, architecture, music, books, and film to tell the story of a past era. It provides insight into human evolution and indicates commonalities and differences from past to present. By better knowing past roads, we derive new directions into the future.

Perhaps the greatest African gift and concept given to America was aché, the inner life force that drives all human action. European-style church services in America seemed somber and alien to Africans, perceiving them as strange and misguided. How could there be God without shouting? How could the gods hear you without the drum, without dance, without a shouting exclamation of joy and spiritual possession? For an African, there could be no God without rhythm. Slaves sat obediently in white churches, waiting for the moment to take hymns and psalms into their own hands. They required a musical language that resonated in their heart, mind, and soul.

There was drum, dance, and song outside of the sterile Anglo church environment. The open field and market called Congo Square in New Orleans became a musical laboratory that brought people from various parts of the world together, primarily for the first time.

Drawings and writings from the 1700s reveal the excitement of a ring shout where anyone, regardless of race, could hear and absorb new music as cultures collided. We can only imagine an Italian violinist, a French accordion player, and a German brass player interacting with an African American ring shout. This was the frenzied beat of the New World, a phenomenon that could not have occurred in Europe, Asia, or Africa; Congo Square was a musical ground zero that would be the key to future sounds in music. Through the concept of syncretism, America would slowly start to find its musical voice, despite institutionalized slavery. When musical instruments were not readily available, African Americans crafted their own, making something out of nothing. History views New Orleans as the birthplace of jazz. But more than that, it was the city's mixed-race diversity and joyful spirit that made Congo Square possible. No northern city with its strict geographic segregation would have ever allowed such an experience inside city limits. Whether it's 125th Street in Harlem, Michigan Avenue in Chicago, or 8 Mile Road in Detroit, this is a sordid history.

New Orleans is key to our understanding of America's deep musical culture. Once owned by the Spanish and the French, it was a steaming cauldron of every musical style imaginable in the eighteenth, nineteenth, and twentieth centuries. Walking through the city streets, a person could encounter opera, symphonic orchestras, academies of music, ring shouts, spirituals pouring out of Baptist churches, street vendors singing in bent note style, brass bands, string groups, and the sound of piano professors pounding out the latest popular minstrel show song, drifting from a brothel window. New Orleans with its incredible diversity was far more artistically advanced than any other American city of the nineteenth century.

America's racial complexities enabled a musical chemistry to occur that was heard in churches, cotton fields, or at the downtown market. African Americans could be heard in spirited singing while selling their wares. This either impressed or revulsed a white Anglo culture accustomed to modest decorum in most public places. The passionate commitment in the Black singing voice was attractive and infectious. African Americans exemplified the idea of showing your feelings in song, not hiding behind the words in a hymnal. Jazz trumpet legend Louis Armstrong taught us to show our feelings and not live in muted silence. It was letting the soul fly freely.

White and Black churches eventually encountered each other in religious revival meetings and gatherings during the Second Great Awakening of the early 1800s. The shouting, moaning, bending, and sliding vocal style of Black congregations, accompanied by hand clapping and foot stomping, demonstrated to white churches the possibilities of an expressive manner of worship. The Black church employed elements of improvisation that were rarely seen in an Anglo religious service. Instead of singing the spiritual "Amazing Grace" literally from the church hymnal, the Black church lined the melody, swooping up and down in a moaning style that inferred slavery's grim legacy while instilling hope. "I Been in the Storm so Long," "Wade in the Water," "Sometimes I Feel like a Motherless Child," "Go Down Moses," and many other spirituals described this experience. This singing style could not be reproduced; it had to be experienced firsthand. Like blues, jazz, rap, and other styles, the performer must live the music, not merely imitate it.

Black music culture put expressive nuance and feeling ahead of technical prowess and tonal singing perfection. Telling your story with a passionate and believable commitment, a sense of deep knowing and singing inside the song, not above it, were the valued elements of Black music. In call-and-response style, there was no doubt when a preacher or singer got their message across; it was the sound of conviction, later to be known as signifyin'. It was a loud, declarative voice that indirectly states there is more to "The Signifying" Monkey than merely entertainment.

What would this mean in the future? The sanctified church would provide an immersive, Black cultural experience, from early childhood until death. It would be a place of confirming identity, tradition, soulfulness, and dignity in a country that had denied those things. The church would be the training ground for the major gospel, blues, jazz, country, rhythm and blues, Motown, soul, pop, disco, and rap performers of the twentieth century and beyond. Learning their Sunday morning lessons well, gospel vocalists utilized a dazzling array of colors that would lead the way to contemporary vocal styles.

As America grew into a powerful nation, the infrastructure was built on the backs of enslaved people and poor immigrants. They built the railroads, raised white children, provided plantation entertainment, and performed in minstrel shows. European melodies and African American rhythms would fuse to form musical styles that were authentically American in sound.

The talking drums are the center of an African village. They unite people by inspiring the dancers, providing the driving rhythms that are the center of any occasion—from marriages to births, praise songs to funerals. Those drums continued to speak in America. Slaves designated certain drumbeats to signal escapes and uprisings. These syncopated rhythms would be transferred to the fiddle, banjo, bones, and piano. European instruments in America were seeded by this rhythmic sensibility that made for joyful dancing. Like a cascading river too strong to stop, rhythm went undeterred around restricted barricades. Art can never be confined by convention.

White slave owners feared that by allowing their slaves attendance at Anglo church services, they were becoming overly educated and thus, desiring of their freedom. As a result, African Americans broke away from white church domination in the late 1700s by forming their own churches. The First African Baptist Church in Savannah, Georgia, was founded in 1773, making it older than the United States. Free from white control, the church was a safe haven and sanctuary where Black people could freely worship. Taking the syncopated rhythms of the ring shout and combining it with the European hymns and psalms that they had learned, a new syncretism was occurring.

The spirituals were born in the Black church. Combining African rhythm with European melody, harmony, and form, this would be one of the first original American musical forms, after Native American music. African Americans used their feet, hands, and shouting voices to convey the ring shout rhythms that had been forbidden in the Anglo church. The European melodies and song forms that African Americans had sung in white churches could now be utilized in new ways. By combining these melodies with the syncopated rhythms and improvisational spirit of the ring shout, a new syncretism was born. Shout spirituals, also known as jubilee spirituals, such as "Goin' Shout All Over God's Heaven," were examples of the ring shout moving inside the church. It was rhythmic music without the drum. The congregation would stomp their feet, clap their hands, and shout-sing to the rafters. The contrasting sorrow songs, such as "Soon I Will Be Done," conveyed the somber reality of a life without freedom. Spirituals gave strength, hope, and an identity that seemed to convey "You will not take this from me." Determination lived in the music. The spiritual's influence evolved into modern gospel music in the 1920s, becoming an essential ingredient in blues, jazz, soul, Motown, and beyond. In order to understand contemporary music, one need only look to the past where seeds were once planted. The spirituals, like an African ring shout, proved that rhythm could be front and center as the most important musical element, unlike many Europeans forms that emphasized words, melodies, and harmony. Listen to Benny Goodman's classic jazz recording of "Sing, Sing, Sing." It is Gene Krupa's up-front drums that drive the sound, similar to a drum machine-driven hip-hop track.

The African American singing voice introduced a rough, "dirty" tone into the American musical landscape. Instead of the pure tone style of most European vocalizing, Black people emphasized the rough, expressive, and soulful voice. Rather than a pretty sound, importance was placed on telling a story, making the audience feel the music in a deeply personal way. It was an African griot-influenced singing voice that made contact by not merely singing the note but by bending, sliding, growling, and expressing melodic feeling. Later, the growling, bending trumpet of Louis Armstrong and Ray Charles's soulful voice would gain worldwide prominence.

Secular music, performed outside of church, was another essential ingredient. Africans, like many European cultural identities, combined work with song. Listen to a recording of postal workers at the University of Ghana as they cancel stamps in a rhythmic groove, while whistling a harmonized melody at the same time. Music has a functional role in daily African life, as opposed to the Western notion of music as an add-on, optional entertainment subjected to school board budget cuts. Whether working in the fields or preparing dough for baking bread, present-day Africans sing in a rhythmic call-and-response style that keeps the work flowing in musical time.

In the Deep South, where there was work there was song, as there had always been in Africa. African Americans carried on the tradition of the work song, a functional part of African life. Dockworkers sang as they unloaded cargo, as did railroad work gangs whose call-and-response chants such as "Rosie" kept the sledgehammers synchronized, landing on the beat as they laid miles of track. Farmworkers sang haunting and expressive field hollers as they toiled alone in the burning Delta sun. Street vendors turned their sales pitch into an improvised chant to lure potential customers. Work songs distanced the chain gang from their oppressors, standing over them with shotguns and bloodhounds—a hell hound on your trail. A railway work song leader calling out, "Rock and roll it!" had no idea that this would be a musical style of the next century. Timeless art comes from dark and brilliant corners.

As European folk songs found different words and meanings in America, they merged with African roots to form songs. "John Henry," part African American blues, part English folk ballad, is an example of the rich, creative American musical voice as it emerged in the late nineteenth century. Bob Dylan once said, "If you sang 'John Henry' as many times as me...."[1] John Henry was steel-driving man, driving with a hammer in his hand, John Henry said a man ain't nothing but a man. "If you sang that song as many times as I did, you would have written 'How many roads must a man walk down, too." A visionary is an individual, an entrepreneur who sees a market before it exists. The minstrel show that began in the 1830s turned various musical strands into a spectacle that would become the most popular entertainment of the century. Suddenly, plantation music was on stage, accompanied by racial stereotypes that would haunt twentieth-century American stage and screen. It was a strange double mask of whites blackening their faces with burnt cork in order to portray African Americans in comedic depiction, but it was the African American minstrel shows that layered an additional blackface mask to put on, and down, white performers. It was as if to say, "This is what you look like when you try to sound like us, but here is how it's done."

Black and white children growing up on plantations and towns where Blacks and whites lived side by side were an active part of this cultural fusion. They played rhythmic jump rope games, combining call-and-response singing and hand clapping. It is a misconception to think that white and Black children lived in separate social conditions. Not only did they play together, but mixed-race children, white and Black, often formed deep friendships, soon to be broken apart during their teenage years. A racist society would not permit public interracial friendships. Whites have always been deeply involved in the lives of the Black race. Our culture is a shared human experience, despite Jim Crow laws that attempted to keep people apart in an economic and social need to control and dominate. The constant white fear of miscegenation has existed for hundreds of years.

By the late nineteenth century, music's potential as a profitable industry was clear. The popularity of minstrel shows and vaudeville resulted in audiences being exposed to music they now wanted to sing and play at home. The sheet music industry was born, and the ever-popular piano and pianola, a player piano, was a staple of middle-class life. Ragtime piano performances created a demand for sheet music, and the piano roll industry grew. The parlor became the center of home entertainment. At the turn of the century, people read music out of necessity, far more than in modern eras. Without television, radio, or the internet, self-creativity was essential.

The nationally popular minstrel shows introduced mainstream America to Black culture for the first time. Famous songs by Stephen Foster—"Oh! Susanna," "Beautiful Dreamer," and "Old Black Joe"—were rife with racial stereotypes, and the cakewalk dance moved off the plantation and onto the international stage. White Americans were drawn to the excitement of Black music and dance, a direct contradiction to the prejudicial views taught by their parents. They were drawn to a musical form by a group of people disdained by polite society. Music does not preach or lecture; it illuminates, exposing our strengths and shortcomings by drawing diverse people together.

With the music came racist songs that were accepted as commonplace in their day. The musical category "coon songs," clearly indicate America's racial consciousness in the late 1890s. While spreading the excitement of Black music, these racial stereotypes were sung with great gusto by whites and Blacks in minstrel and vaudeville shows and in the early stage of recordings. Music has the ability to function as a societal bookmark, revealing the views of a particular era.

The turn-of-the-century boom music was ragtime, pounding forth on upright pianos at county fairs and on bar room spinets. It was American syncretism at its best, right on the keyboard. Pianist composers such as Scott Joplin played European march time in the left hand, while the right hand played banjo-like dance rhythms. These two contrasting rhythms, as different as Europe and Africa, worked to form a new sound that was American in character—brash, young, and the sound of a faster-paced new century. Music would move to the tempo of twentieth-century technology. Many conservative parents and high-society aristocrats hated ragtime, which made it sound even better to their children. This music spread across the world, gaining fame in the high-class salons and ballrooms of Paris, London, and New York. The musician's union detested it, requesting that their members refrain from playing it in public. America's youthful rebellion would be a key ingredient from this day forward. These young patrons loved ragtime's brash attitude because it wasn't their parents' waltz, minuet, and polka. Little did they know, the cakewalk to which they shimmied was a Black plantation dance of minstrel show origins. Ragtime represented a new nation coming of age at the beginning of the twentieth century. America would become a world leader in a century of cars, planes, skyscrapers, motion pictures, and morals that would make your grandparents shudder.

The ghostly slave ships of the past played a role in the future as America pulled away from its European cultural ties. It was not a country of kings and queens but a nation that demanded music to fit its restless spirit—a revolution that made us dance. The cultural seeds were sewn from the day diverse people interacted. Despite race laws that attempted to protect and preserve white control, music would provide a meeting ground that pointed to a common soul. James Baldwin once wrote, "Nothing is ever escaped." That is true, not only of social problems but of culture as well. With this sense of heritage, the past never dies. Post–Civil War America would find new ways to express emancipation and freedom. America moves to a revolution between the beats.

Teachers who pay attention can learn a great deal from their students. Yvette Lumor was a former student of mine who came from

African dresses at a street market, Memphis, Tennessee.

Agbozume in West Africa. In her musical background paper for our class, she wrote that tribal history is taught to young children through singing songs. Yvette noted that music is used for virtually everything—ceremonies, rituals, births, deaths, spiritual worship, and storytelling. This is communicated through drum, dance, and song.

Music is so essential to her tribe that each child is given a special song at birth, depending on the day and month. These special songs point the way to the child's destiny and, most importantly, the roles he or she must contribute to the well-being of the universe.

Yvette went on to write, "Now I understand the music that has played an important role in all stages of my life."[2] Reading her paper, it became clear to me that music brings people closer together for Yvette and her Ewe tribe, despite the absence of sophisticated technology. Live music was all around Yvette Lumor, and it shaped her upbringing.

The Western world, starving for community, could use more of this.

In the words of Nikole Hannah Jones, "When the world listens to quintessential American music, it is our voice they hear. The sorrow songs we sang in the fields to soothe our physical pain and find hope in a freedom we did not expect to know until we died became American gospel. Amid the devastating violence and poverty of the Mississippi Delta, we birthed jazz and blues. And it was in the deeply impoverished and segregated neighborhoods, where white Americans forced the descendants of the enslaved to live, that teenagers too poor to buy instruments used old records to create a new music known as hip-hop. Our speech, fashion, and the drum of our music echoes Africa, but is not African. Out of our unique isolation, both from our native cultures and from white America, together we forged this nation's most significant original culture."[3]

You may take my drum, but you can't steal my thunder.

The ring shout continues.

3

Framing a Jazz
and Blues Century

Art must have a foundation to grow. The blues is a springboard, a wellspring for artistic inspiration. Its modest sound is a musical legacy that began in the early twentieth century. Originating around the same time, jazz has been the evolutionary powerhouse twin that has given American music unlimited resources. Blues and jazz represent the trunk of a cultural oak tree that has spawned new branches over a century. It is perhaps Black Americans' foremost contribution to American culture. "Without the presence of Negro style, our [U.S.] jokes, tall tales, even our sports would be lacking in sudden turns, shocks and swift changes of pace [all jazz shaped] that serve to remind us that the world is ever unexplored, and that while a complete mastery of life is a mere illusion, the real secret of the game is to make life swing."[1]

Ragtime was the overture to the twentieth century. It was America's musical shot heard around the world—change was in the air. Ragtime's brash, syncopated rhythms heralded a vibrant music that broke free from past European traditional dances. Soon, high-society youth in major metropolitan cities around the world were dancing the cakewalk to ragtime's persistent beat. Cross-cultural wheels were set in motion as whites moved to a Black plantation dance that had originated from the minstrel shows. I'll bet they didn't even know it.

Ragtime's popularity caught on, resulting in sales of player pianos and sheet music—the birth of the music industry. By the 1920s, wind-up Victrolas blasted the latest recordings and most middle-class families had to have one. Suddenly, home entertainment was now possible. Records would serve as a learning tool for young musicians in a country that refused to acknowledge the importance of this new native-born music. No music school would teach blues or jazz; you were on your own. The launching pad was ready for a musical liftoff and explosion. It would be an American musical century.

50

Blues and the Abstract Truth

The blues is America's bedrock music, but no one truly knows who first started it. Female vocalists featured the blues in traveling minstrel show acts, usually accompanied by a jazz band. The popularity of the banjo, African in origin, and later the guitar enabled musicians to be a self-driven band. The sound of the blues, with its moaning, bent note, dirty-tone vocalizing, reminiscent of Negro spirituals and work songs, became a driving force. Little did blues musicians realize how influential that style would become.

The blues, counter to public notion, is not a sad form of music. They may express hard times, but it is always with a sly smile that indicates not self-pity but ultimate triumph over life's obstacles. Blues expressed hardship mixed with hope—"The sun will shine in my back door someday." We are all waiting for the sun—maybe not today but someday. The blues juxtaposed grim reality with life's quest for a good time, line by line. Poetry and song were happily married to the accompaniment of juke joint whiskey and dancing. Despite a hard life, those southerners knew how to live.

The music industry in the '20s was male dominated but not the blues. Ma Rainey and Bessie Smith transitioned from minstrel and vaudeville shows to establish themselves as blues artists in their own right. They didn't merely sing to an audience; they left them spellbound. Ma Rainey and Bessie Smith, among other female blues vocalists, were astoundingly ahead of their time.

The author's Nicola Gagliano double bass, made approximately 1775.

Instead of singing the typical pop material of the day, filled with escapism and romance, displaying a woman as a shrinking violet, African American blues women sang forthright, sexually charged songs with unapologetic lyrics, filled with a woman's strength, determination, and independence. These legendary blues divas bridged cabaret-like vaudeville shows, largely for a white audience with the down-home, gritty realism of authentic Black southern folk expression. With a jazz band in tow, they established what is known as the classic urban blues style, music for a steamy night in Memphis, Chattanooga, Jackson, or New Orleans.

Women's blues in the 1920s forecasted, decades before its time, a women's movement that would reshape American thought. In her book, *Blues Legacies and Black Feminism,* Angela Davis wrote, "The representations of love and sexuality in women's blues often blatantly contradicted mainstream ideological assumptions regarding women and being in love. They also challenged the notion that women's 'place' was in the domestic sphere."[2]

The race record market of the 1920s exploded with blues recordings, some selling over half a million copies. Originally conceived as appealing to the Black record-buying public, race records—Black singers and instrumentalists playing for an African American market—crossed over to the majority-white audience from the first release of Mamie Smith's "Crazy Blues" in 1920. This was followed by Bessie Smith's "Down-Hearted Blues," selling over 800,000 copies in 1923. Who knew a white audience would not only buy but also learn to love this music? It offered them something cool, dangerous, and provocative, elements largely missing in white Victorian-influenced life. On the dark side of town, the other side of the tracks, there was mystery in a forbidden territory, occupied by a different race. Intrigued young whites began crossing that line against their parents' wishes. That which is forbidden is desired.

It was another country. From the rest of the United States, a different life occurred in the Deep South, hundreds of miles from major cities. Slavery gave way to sharecropping, one unjust travesty followed by another, a farming system that was slavery by another name. It left Black and white farm workers in perpetual debt without legal recourse or justice. Poor tenement farmers living in corrugated shotgun shacks found the only available entertainment, turning their modest home into a juke joint nightclub on weekends. Make some moonshine, find a blues singer, and you were in business.

How do you make music when instruments are scarce, even nonexistent? The countryside had no access to musical band instruments until Sears Roebuck, of all things, inadvertently had a hand in the blues. Sears distributed the first mail order catalog in the late 1800s, eventually adding the Stella acoustic guitar, a popular instrument in the early 1920s. Now poor white and Black country blues singers could buy a guitar, learn a few chords, and provide a musical response to the call in their voices. The style was called country or Delta blues.

Numerous musicologists have attempted to trace the blues to Africa with mixed success. It is an American music that borrows certain elements from Africa. The call-and-response communication between African drums and dancers became a conversation between a blues singer and their guitar. Imitating the bent-note voice, heard in the cotton fields and country churches, blues guitarists used a broken-off glass beer bottle neck to slide on the strings. Blues musicians entertained a drinking, dancing, and often drunken juke joint audience on a Mississippi night, no electricity required. They removed the furniture and replaced them with floor-to-ceiling mirrors along the walls. Lit candles were put in front of the mirrors, making the juke joint a glowing sight in the dark Delta night.

There were many country blues masters—Charley Patton, Son House, Robert Johnson, Skip James, John Lee Hooker, Howlin' Wolf, Blind Lemon Jefferson, and Leadbelly, among others. They were the pioneers who would inspire Jimi Hendrix, Eric Clapton, Jimmy Page, Keith Richards, Bonnie Raitt, Janis Joplin, and more in future decades. Country blues artists had stories to tell, drawn from living a rough and often dangerous life, dusty roads in a hostile land. The dark lyrics of Robert Johnson, with references to the devil, revealed there were other countries within America, existing beyond the idealized, typically Hollywood ending on the silver screen.

To be a Black man in the South was to live in a lawless terrorist country. Listen to the lyrics in a Robert Johnson song; it is a voice from another world. The great jazz bassist Milt Hinton, my friend and mentor, told me a story about growing up in Vicksburg, Mississippi, around 1915. His grandmother would regularly put pepper in his socks to throw off the scent of the bloodhounds. He said, "If something bad happened in our town of Vicksburg, something got stolen or vandalized, they'd send out the bloodhounds and if they came up to you and started barking, they'd lynch you on the spot."[3] I often tell this story to my students, who are astonished to realize what a different country America once was. These geographical regions were like a veritable wilderness, with the white southern majority and the terrorist Ku Klux Klan disregarding the Constitution, resulting in violent lawlessness based on racism. These horrific stories are the yardstick dramatically measuring the long struggle in the ongoing process toward American democracy.

The blues singers all knew this. They didn't have to "keep it real"; they were real. You can hear it in the music.

Blues developed off the radar of mainstream American culture until the Great Migration. Poor African Americans and sharecropping whites began heading to points north from 1918 to 1960. They brought their songs, hopes, and traditions with them in search of a better, more just life. Memphis, Kansas City, Chicago, Gary, Detroit, Cleveland, Pittsburgh, Philadelphia, Baltimore, Harlem and Washington, DC, were among the cities seeded by the blues. The southern juke joint was now modernized into the city blues bar but with one problem: how could a transplanted southerner with an acoustic guitar, from a quiet country town, compete with a raucous urban bar?

It was perfect timing—enter the newly invented electric guitar. By the early 1940s, this shiny amplified instrument became the key weapon in projecting the guitar as a solo lead instrument. The electric guitar cut through a band of rhythm section and horns, stepping forward as never before. T-Bone Walker pioneered the electric guitar by combining virtuosity and showmanship. He played it with his teeth, between his legs, and behind his back. Sound familiar? As he barnstormed through the chitlin circuit, the African American touring venues, T-Bone Walker was doing Jimi at Monterrey before Hendrix had any idea.

Music enables a person the ultimate dream of imagining their future. In the late 1930s, McKinley Morganfield was a Mississippi farmer by day and blues picker at night. He built a small local following in the area known as Stovall Plantation, a few miles outside Cleveland, Mississippi, when musicologist Alan Lomax from the Smithsonian ventured south in 1941 to record and interview him. That did it. Inspired upon hearing his voice on record, Morganfield decided to set out for Chicago in early 1943, following his dream of becoming a blues singer. He became his nickname, Muddy Waters.

Upon arriving in Chicago, Muddy realized he would need more musical ammunition and volume than his acoustic guitar could provide. His uncle bought him an electric guitar. Muddy Waters went on to form the prototypical blues band, assembling electric, lead, and rhythm guitars, bass, drums, piano, and harmonica. His legendary tracks for Chess Records, run by Polish immigrants on Chicago's Southside, would be heard on radio and greatly supported by Black transplanted southerners who yearned for the sounds of home. These were the early days of do-it-yourself in the independent record label business. Test pressings would be played out of speakers, strategically placed in windows pointed at people waiting at a bus stop. If the people moved to the music, the records were distributed from the trunk of a car to record stores and radio stations. Songs by Muddy Waters, Howlin' Wolf, Willie Dixon, and other Chess artists such as "Hoochie Coochie Man," "Rollin' Stone," "Got My Mojo Workin'," "You Need Love," "I'm Ready," and "Mannish Boy" were exported to seaports around the globe. The world was waiting for the sunrise, and in the United Kingdom, the British were ready. The Rolling Stones, named for the Muddy Waters song, and a multitude of other soon-to-be famous bands would follow his lead.

Muddy is to the blues what Picasso is to modern art. They were artists who created a form, a signpost and blueprint for future generations. There is a distinction between popularity and artistry. The commercialized Western world is overly enamored with fame. Popular success in the arts is wonderful, fortunate, and fleeting with fame usually leaving as quickly as it arrives. It is the rare artist who creates a form that lives forever. More than a hit song, they draw a blueprint serving as a springboard for future musicians to utilize toward creating their own sound. Influence is the path to finding an authentic voice. You can't have the Rolling Stones without Muddy Waters. Nor can you have Muddy without Son House and Robert Johnson. The past comes forward, always. David Samuels writes that genius is "a word that can be usefully defined as the ability to create and realize an original style that, in turn, can for decades generate its own genres of music containing the DNA of deeply original songs by other extremely talented, original songwriters and musicians, all of whom owe something to him."[4]

Blues, Rhythm and Blues into Rock and Roll

Boogie-woogie was the engine that put blues into high gear. Originating from the southern honky-tonk style on beat-up pianos that were used to entertain rowdy crowds in rough bars, this barrelhouse piano music sounded like a midnight train rolling over the tracks. Never underestimate the importance of a train to poor southern folks. It represented a symbol of freedom, an escape route out of dire poverty to the promised land, wherever that was. Whether boarding a train to freedom or watching it leave with a loved one never to return, the train's whistle conveyed hope and sadness. Like the train's rolling rhythm, this lonely sound would be imitated by blues harmonica players. In the South, the harmonica was known as the Mississippi saxophone.

Lower- and middle-class African American families sang spirituals in church Sunday mornings. At times their children covertly played boogie-woogie on the parlor piano when their parents weren't within earshot. To an older generation, the blues was decadent—the devil's music, and God forbid if you were caught getting anywhere near his fire. Boogie-woogie was blues with a faster tempo, an irresistible dance beat. When she was young, jazz pianist Mary Lou Williams was a driver for the Andy Kirk Band, a top-notch African American territory band of the 1930s. "I'd wait outside the ballrooms in the car, and if things were going bad and people weren't dancing, they would send somebody to get me and I'd go in and play 'Froggy Bottom,' or some boogie-woogie number and things would jump."[5] Mary Lou Williams soon became the only female band member and went on to become the first major woman jazz instrumentalist.

The southern boogie-woogie piano professors migrated north with their audience, and by the 1930s, the beat had caught on. Dance and swing bands performed the music with full horn sections and it was an instant dancehall success. Mary Lou Williams scored her classic boogie-woogie piece, "Roll 'Em," for Benny Goodman's big band in 1937. I played "Roll 'Em" with her in the mid–'70s. It was a joyful boogie that set the soul free. It was also a rock-of-the-ages music that put the beat into the modernized rhythm and blues genre of the 1940s. Vibraphonist Lionel Hampton furthered boogie-woogie, featuring it with a big band sound. Complete with a shouting horn section, animated singing, and a driving rhythm section, boogie-woogie became rhythm and blues, building the bridge that led to the term *rock and roll* by the early 1950s.

In 1948, "rhythm and blues" was the new genre term that replaced the racist "race records" category for Black music. Vocalist and saxophonist Louis Jordan and his Tympany Five understood that entertainment value was essential to attracting a general public. Jordan sang colorful songs combined with choreographed dance moves and instruments that lit up for visual effect. Blues was moving to the big city with overalls cast aside in favor of zoot suits. A few years later, they would call it rock and roll.

All of this musical, social, and cultural development occurred in the shadow of distorted race relations. In the so-called separate but equal climate of apartheid America, Jim Crow remained in power from the late 1870s until well into the 1960s. This impacted everything including music. Bands were strictly segregated until the late 1930s. Black bands were paid less, if at all, and were denied accommodations in most white sections of American cities. They toured the chitlin circuit, consisting of rough bars and roadhouses found on the Black side of town or in the outskirts of the countryside. This was where the gritty real music of the Black experience could be heard, but few whites went into those areas.

Mary Lou Williams recalled how the Black bands were occasionally required to play behind a screen at dances so the white patrons would not have to see them. When the music became so exciting that they couldn't resist, the white dancers would put gloves on and go around the screen to shake the performers' hands. Miss Williams laughingly recalled on one occasion, "The music got so good one time they came from behind the screen and didn't have the gloves on!"[6]

It would take radio playing rhythm and blues recordings in the late 1940s to send the message to the masses. Television was the exciting new technology that swept America in the 1950s. It spelled competition for radio with its obvious visual appeal. Afraid of losing their sponsors, various southern radio stations, such as WDIA in Memphis, switched to an all-music format, playing rhythm and blues and hiring Black DJs, a first on American radio. On a clear night, the music could be heard across the country, garnering both a young Black and white audience. Radio airwaves did not segregate.

"The Blues Had a Baby and They Named It Rock and Roll," once declared a song by Muddy Waters. African American artists who recorded on small independent record labels struggled to get on mainstream radio. It would be a young white boy from Memphis who would "pep up" Black music, becoming the mid-century superstar game changer. His name was Elvis Presley. He did not invent rock and roll, but he possessed the total package—talent, looks, sex appeal, charm, and charisma—to bring it into an explosive mass acceptance. Presley himself knew the origins of the music that made him a superstar: "The colored folks been singing it and playing it just like I'm doin' now, man, for more years than I know. I got it from them."[7]

Blues reached its peak popularity in the 1960s when it merged with rock. A strange cultural transition was taking place, as a young Black audience began rejecting jazz and blues as old and irrelevant. Blues master B.B. King, once booed by a Black audience, noticed a change as whites began attending his performances in record numbers. As young African Americans turned to soul and Motown, the Rolling Stones, Jimi Hendrix, Cream, John Mayall, Johnny Winter, Paul Butterfield, Janis Joplin, and the Allman Brothers Band introduced a young, white, hippie audience to this ageless music. By the mid–'70s, the popularity of disco and pop music would diminish the awareness and exposure to the blues.

Where are the blues today? Standing in the shadows. Drum machine and synthesized pop music has distanced itself from this great American musical form, for better or worse. As some pop stars display

hollow, prefabricated images that are hell bent on branding and marketing, popular music rarely has much in common with past traditions.
Goodbye old, hello new, past forgotten. There are some who may say
that jazz and blues are museum pieces, but musicians with depth and
an extensive toolbox know it remains as viable and vibrant as ever. Eric
Clapton has referred to the blues as a "battery," a place to return for
energy and inspiration.

Cultural amnesia is dangerous. The record producer T-Bone Burnett once said, "I think the dilemma is that we can move into this future
so rapidly that we can leave the past completely behind, but would be
impoverished by it. We could move into the matrix if we wanted to. If
we're not moving backward at the same time and keeping that in check,
I don't think we'll make it out of the century. That's my view. I'm interested in the people like Bob Dylan and the Coens, who are able to go
backward and forward at once. This is about understanding where we
come from so we can end up in a better place."[8]

There is much truth from this perspective. Take the blues out of the
cake and it seems to fall flat—a lifeless plastic thing. There is a spontaneous joy in a Chicago blues bar when the music, the band, and the audience start cooking. It is the sound of humanity at its best—joy, humor,
love, sadness, ecstasy, and triumph all blended together in a simmering
stew.

I hope you taste that someday.

Jazz: A Misunderstood National Art Form

America loves a marching band. Brass and drums blaring down the
street or performing in an open-air pavilion are a long-standing tradition. Out of that cacophony of melody, rhythm, and sound came jazz,
an American art form and musical style that has evolved for over one
hundred years, from the early 1900s to the present. The elements of jazz
have influenced the majority of musical styles we hear to this day. The
Allman Brothers drummer, Jaimoe, once told me, "Everything I play is
jazz." It is the combination of form and in-the-moment improvisation
that establishes jazz as a major achievement in Western culture.

We lead an improvised life, never knowing what will happen next.
Jazz, as in life, is filled with the random and unexpected. The '20s Chicago jazz cornetist Bix Beiderbecke said it best: "One of the things I like
about jazz, kid, is I don't know what is going to happen next. Do you?"[9] It
is a call-and-response conversation resulting in music of the moment. A
typical misconception of improvised jazz is that it is without structure,

totally free and chaotic. Jazz is improvised music built on a melodic and harmonic form that allows the soloist the freedom to create a new melody in real time. A composer writes with pencil and eraser, shaping and editing the work; an improvising musician creates on the spot. Jazz is an explorative music, risk without a safety net.

Most art forms are collective movements comprised of numerous risk takers. The major evolution of early jazz can largely be attributed to one man—Louis Armstrong. The legendary New Orleans trumpet god rose from a detention home in the New Orleans "Battlefield" ghetto. He became one of the twentieth century's most famous artists. Armstrong was the American dream personified, rising from poverty to superstar status. He was exactly as Duke Ellington described him, an American original. His improvisational genius enabled jazz to become an improvising soloist's art form. Armstrong's elastic, rubber band–like phrasing against a steady rhythmic pulse taught us how to swing. We have been living in that feeling ever since.

Armstrong's charisma mixed with his genius for swinging made him a popular artist with a common touch that appealed to all types of people. Ralph Ellison said, "In 1929, Louis Armstrong had been playing in Kansas City and when he came down to Oklahoma City the bandstand in our segregated dance hall was suddenly filled with white women. They were wild for his music and nothing like that had ever happened in our town before. His music was our music but they saw it as theirs too, and were willing to break the law to get to it."[10]

Armstrong's legacy is felt in today's music, though few realize it. Press play and you'll discover how popular music, from rock to hip-hop, perpetually accents beats two and four. Louis Armstrong started that movement of playing off the backbeat, changing the way dancers moved and musicians thought about music. Armstrong was an international superstar, appearing on landmark recordings with the Hot Five, performing on film, television, and touring the world for over forty years until his death in 1971. Louis Armstrong's recordings established a new standard in Western music. He inspired the big bands of the 1930s, sometimes billed as "orchestrated Armstrong," to put a swinging rhythmic feel to set arrangements with sections for improvisation.

Louis performed for kings, queens, and presidents and was loved by the common man and woman, who saw him as one of their own. The audience always came first for Louis Armstrong, a man who never forgot his humble New Orleans roots. There are many stories that attest to Armstrong going out of his way for his adoring fans. The documentary filmmaker Ken Burns once told me, "Listening to Louis Armstrong makes my day." I wish I had met the man.

The second major jazz giant, Duke Ellington, took Armstrong's revolutionary musical ideas to new heights by composing and arranging for a big band in innovative ways. A big band is an American invention. It expands the small jazz group to an enlarged ensemble consisting of brass, reeds, and rhythm section. Ellington did not invent this classic musical staple, but he demonstrated that jazz could be as sophisticated as classical music, yet swing a Harlem dance floor. As the Depression of 1929 gradually lifted by the middle to late '30s, big bands ruled and jazz reached the greatest mass popularity it would ever know. It symbolized freedom to European audiences terrorized by the onset of a growing Nazi regime. What Bob Marley's reggae was to Jamaica in the '70s, jazz was to Europeans seeking freedom in the '30s and '40s.

Jazz groups were strictly segregated by race; there was both a Black and a white musicians' union in many cities. The segregation color line affecting jazz bands was broken when a white Jewish clarinetist named Benny Goodman performed with an interracial group at Carnegie Hall in January 1938. Goodman was a swing-era superstar who put the music first, and to his considerable relief, so did his adoring fans. Dancing to swing was the antidote to Depression-era blues, and the enormous popularity of jazz elicited a sense of hope. Whether on radio or recording, swing was impossible to ignore, garnering around 70 percent of all record sales. Amid the gaiety, a dark shadow lurked around the corner. Hitler and World War II ended that celebration in the early 1940s.

World War II, from 1941 until 1945, signaled a period of great uncertainty and the end of the classic jazz era. The cost of the war imposed a tax on dancing. The draft drained many big bands of their talent pool, and the need for shellac meant manufacturing bombs, not records. The jitterbugging days were ending.

Music is a barometer of life in constant upheaval. Art is forward looking by nature. Bop in the early 1940s would be the next era in jazz, a brash, risk-taking sound with seemingly chaotic textures. Although Louis Armstrong was a revolutionary in his time, alto saxophonist Charlie Parker, trumpeter Dizzy Gillespie, and pianist composer Thelonious Monk expanded the jazz improvisational language, employing new harmonic and melodic ideas. Bop rebelled against the formulaic confines of commercialized swing, challenging the listener while refusing the appeal to the dance floor ritual. It was a hip, beat-era listener's music; squares stay home. The beat movement of the 1950s was a social and literary movement that embraced bop's seemingly spontaneous creativity.

When people stop dancing, a musical style is usually relegated to a cult following. Popular music depends on an audience that listens with their feet. Bop appealed to suburban white kids who were reading Kerouac and Ginsburg, rebelling against a '50s emphasis on consumerism and the conservative refuge of suburbia. This is a recurring theme in American life. Music, like theater, must have its set and character changes. Enter Miles.

The young trumpet talent from East St. Louis, Illinois, Miles Davis conjured a dark, haunting, and melancholy-cool sound that provided a more melodic alternative to the frenetic and sometimes disjointed bop style. He had a cult following as opposed to a pop success. Armstrong's worldwide fame was due to his musical brilliance, and to a larger degree, the New Orleans trumpet vocalist was a heartwarming entertainer. He was internationally adored, but the postwar pre–civil rights African American youth saw him as an ingratiating Uncle Tom–like figure. Viewing Armstrong's film roles of the past, this can be somewhat understood, but in retrospect, he was unfairly judged by modern standards. It was bop innovator Dizzy Gillespie who wrote, "Later on, I began to recognize what I had considered Pop's grinning in the face of racism as his absolute refusal to let anything, even anger about racism, steal the joy from his life and erase his fantastic smile. Coming from a younger generation, I misjudged him."[11]

Miles Davis fit the image of the modern Black entertainer who refused to bow to white pressure and decorum. His cool approach left improvisational space between fewer notes and longer tones, a "less is more" direction after the note-filled sound of bop. Davis was a sound innovator who gave the trumpet a darker, lonelier tone as opposed to the bright, happy sound of Louis Armstrong. His music served as a perfect soundtrack to the existential solitude experienced in modern city life, as epitomized by the famous 1942 painting *Night Hawks* by Edward Hopper. He represented the epitome of hip with a glamorous, sexy, dangerous demeanor that became iconic. Music, fashion, and style were essentials in an outward image that said, "Don't mess with Miles."

Miles Davis was a visionary musician who uncannily realized new jazz styles before they occurred. His series of landmark recordings—*Sketches of Spain, Kind of Blue,* and *Bitches Brew,* among others—spanned vast musical territories that broadened the range of jazz expression. He could make his trumpet sing like a romantic Sinatra ballad, resulting in his reaching a mainstream audience. I recall a *New York Times* magazine cover ad for Absolut Vodka titled "Absolut Miles." The image was the album cover of Davis's landmark recording *Bitches Brew.* We don't even need the guy's last name. Miles lived by the Shakespeare edict, "To thine own self be true."

Miles Davis found a way to impose his style on bop, cool, hard bop, fusion, and even hip-hop before his death in 1991, stating, "I have to change; it's like a curse." Gerald Early concluded, "The major overarching context that, I think, explains him better than most is that he came of an age when jazz music ceased to be popular commercial music. Thus, he was faced with the dilemma of trying to make a living, of being something of a personality, in a music that had a dwindling audience and lacked the cultural and artistic presence it once had."[12]

The jazz boundaries continued to expand in the turbulent 1960s. Saxophonists Ornette Coleman and John Coltrane introduced new elements of the avant-garde that paralleled the abstract expressionism art movement—Jackson Pollack in sound. America, a torn nation, was immersed in the horrors of Vietnam abroad, the growing civil rights movement, the assassinations of major political and spiritual leaders, and rioting in the streets at home. Protest became the order of the day. The Eurocentric curriculums of public schools and universities were challenged by students believing they were not being given a carefully considered, balanced education. From the musical point of view alone, they were correct. American popular music, largely created and influenced by Black Americans, was glaringly absent. American education would need to take a hard, honest look at itself.

People choose their symbols and icons based on their needs and desires. Coltrane veered away from social intensity by creating a spiritual serenity in his music. His classic 1964 album, *A Love Supreme*, created a melodic, searching, avant-garde music, a perfect soundtrack to this explosive era in turmoil. His composition "Alabama," set to the rhythm of Dr. Martin Luther King's speech following the Birmingham church bombing, sets a sad, longing, and spiritual tone that sounds like a man praying through the saxophone. John Coltrane died in 1967 at the age of forty. His music would become, similar to the late '60s, a hurricane force of dissonance by the end of his short life. It was a decade of social change, and artistic creativity and growth, all coming at a very high price.

Many musical stars aligned in the 1960s due to not only the musicians but also the open-minded audience who were willing to venture into uncharted territories. "Young audiences were very open to highly experimental pop music in the late 60's and to a kind of jazz-rock sound or a sound that expanded the idea of a popular song."[13] This audience embraced the musical journey of Davis and Coltrane as well as jazz-rock-oriented groups such as Chicago, Traffic, Frank Zappa, and Blood, Sweat & Tears.

Unlike blues, which stands as a classic form that resists sophisticated transformation, jazz has proven itself to be a flexible and adaptable style that can be grafted onto almost any musical element. The 1940s Latin jazz innovations of Dizzy Gillespie, Mario Bauza, and Chano Pozo proved that modern jazz improvisation could sit atop a foundation of hot Afro-Cuban rhythms. Decades later, Miles Davis would improvise over James Brown–inspired funk beats with electric instruments in a style known as fusion. Musical hybrids illustrate the dynamic flexibility of jazz; the experimenting continues. Today, DJs regularly sample bits of classic jazz tracks, adding loops, beats, and rapping over it. The haunting voice of a Billie Holiday vocal sample lives again in a modern age, telling a story, hanging like an apparition in midair.

Even American dance and performance venues deliver renewed versions of themselves. The big band swing ballrooms of a past heyday, boarded up in the late '40s and '50s, were reinvented as rock venues. Where Ellington performed, Jimi Hendrix followed. Jazz has fallen in popularity, slipping from everyday context, moving to the margins. This happened to blues and rock as well. Time marches on, and styles become classic, giving way to the new. Although jazz is no longer part of mainstream popular culture, the music never dies. Every summer the world fills with jazz festivals that celebrate the music, carrying on forms old and new. Jazz education from middle school through university has more talented young players coming forward than work opportunities can accommodate. They determinedly perform the music with commitment and purpose. Duke Ellington once said, "We're not the kind of band that folds up shop just because business isn't very good." This is American music's enduring strength.

I would be hard-pressed to think of a musical style that offers more inspiring tools to a young musician than jazz. Combined with classical training for developing technique and tone production, it gives students the ability to express themselves in almost any future genre they choose. I came out of blues, rock, and soul and stumbled into jazz. It has enriched my life in more ways than I can possibly say, traveling to places and meeting exceptional people along the way.

The faster the world moves, the more fragmented we become. We hear critics who speak of a culture that is now "fractured." This may be true, but the fact remains, blues and jazz of the twentieth century is our story; it is as soprano saxophonist Sidney Bechet once said that jazz tells what happened to us. These forms will continue to influence the future and evolve, despite its separation from pop culture. The art forms of jazz and blues had to grow or risk being caught in a corporate branding and marketing game it could never win. That is the reason why we are still talking about it, listening to it, composing and playing it.

People young and old continue to discover the music every

day. Young artists must adeptly use social media and other creative resources as the bottom has fallen out of the music industry. It is the day of do-it-yourself. May the twenty-first century yield great gifts in art, and most importantly, may we learn to value our culture with greater depth, appreciation, and commitment.

Music old and new is a matter of language. It must move forward while retaining the best elements of its past. The great American writer Toni Morrison has written about the value and fragility of language. Jazz and blues are musical languages that must be preserved. They have much to teach us. She once wrote that "language can never live up to life once and for all. Nor should it. Language can never 'pin down' slavery, genocide, war. Nor should it yearn for the arrogance to be able to do so. Its force, its felicity, is in its reach toward the ineffable."[14]

I have on occasion seen my students walking into class with a Howlin' Wolf, Muddy Waters, Bill Evans, or John Coltrane album under their arm. These artists are not gone; they live on, as do Rembrandt, Picasso, Monet, and Michelangelo. That is the gift of art. It lives on for future generations to discover in their own way.

I know this to be true.

4

The South, Elvis, and the Dawning of Rock and Roll

Elvis Presley is one of the most famous and thoroughly misunderstood people of the twentieth century. Even since his death in 1977 at age forty-two, he cannot rest. He is analyzed, prodded, and torn apart in hopes of solving some sort of musical mystery. Elvis remains an elusive figure in a puzzle where few pieces fit.

I will admit that he didn't much matter to my generation of the late '60s and early '70s. We were the era of the Beatles and Stones, and to us, Elvis belonged to a distant past. Who knew or cared about the 1950s? He was only a name to us and little more, but when John Lennon recalled, "Elvis was a religion to me. Before Elvis there was nothing," we had to take notice. Every American generation is reborn and naive to the recent past. What music teacher ever taught about Elvis or Muddy Waters for that matter? No wonder we were ignorant. We had no idea of America's musical roots.

Southern Culture and Music

It all started in the South. American music evolved from the blues and country music of the cotton fields, juke joints, roadhouses, and churches where gospel songs rang out. It is a place where music is fundamental and functional in everyday life. As Robbie Robertson of the Band has said, "It's the only place in the country I've ever been where you can actually drive down the highway at night, and if you listen, you hear music.... The South is the only place we play where everybody can clap on the off-beat."[1]

The diverse southern racial mix enabled social opportunities causing considerable musical and human impact, unlike the geographic racial bigotry of northern and midwestern regions. Sam Phillips, producer of Elvis Presley, had a family friend, "Uncle" Silas Payne, a Black field-worker. "It was admiration for those same qualities of imagination, creativity and invincible determination that he had first noted in the black field workers on his father's farm-that and the kind of emotional freedom, the unqualified generosity and kindness that he himself would have most liked to be able to achieve."[2]

It is a fact that southern blues, country, and gospel has been shrouded in mystery and romanticism by the media, from *Gone with the Wind* to the racist *Birth of a Nation*.

"The Delta, with its vast cotton plantations, devastating floods and grueling poverty, has become the stuff of myth, and not only because of its music. It has been called the most Southern place on earth, and whether that phrase conjures up images of beautiful old mansions, cotton aristocracy, home style cooking and Elvis Presley, or the extremes of racism, isolationism, and a social system so archaically unjust as to invite comparisons to medieval feudalism, there is some truth to it."[3]

There can be no denying that the deep roots of American music originate in the South, and almost all the branches and tributaries of modern music flow from that point.

Whether it is B.B. King, Jimmy Reed, Elvis Presley, Bo Diddley, Muddy Waters, Johnny Cash, Mose Allison, Louis Armstrong, Ray

Statue of B.B. King at the B.B. King Museum, Indianola, Mississippi.

Baptist Town storefront, Greenwood, Mississippi. This area was the final residence of legendary bluesman Robert Johnson.

Charles, or Robert Johnson, our Mount Rushmore of American music stands there.

It is a glorious and brutal place where beauty and terror live side by side. Racism falls into a "gentleman's agreement" even to this day. "We were used to the smiling and subservient black, because the Southern police customarily arrested any black who even wore a sullen look.... At some county lines in the South, there were signs that read—NEGRO, DON'T LET THE NIGHT CATCH YOU IN THIS COUNTY. KEEP MOVING."[4]

Yet through this violent haze, some saw through it and heard the music being created. "My conviction was that the world was missing out on not having heard what I heard as a child.... I've just got to open me a little recording studio, where I can at least experiment with [some of] this overlooked humanity."[5]

We are eternally grateful that this vital American history was not overlooked. The recordings are the pillars of an American culture nearly lost. Writer Nelson George states, "The most fanatical students of blues history have all been white. Blacks create and then move on. Whites document and then recycle."[6] To tell this story with a modicum of accuracy, we must look to the seeds that were planted long before Elvis Presley.

Architects on the Road to Rock and Roll

By the late 1940s, Black music, formerly referred to as "race records," was called rhythm and blues. The driving, boogie-woogie-inspired music took on increased volume and weight by the advent of horns, drums, bass, and the electric guitar. It has been contended that the first rock and roll record was recorded by Sam Phillips at Sun Studio in Memphis by a group from Clarksdale, Mississippi, the Kings of Rhythm, featuring pianist Ike Turner. "Rocket 88" was a boogie tune inspired by the new Oldsmobile model of the same name. The fuzz tone–like guitar, the result of an amplifier falling out of a car before the session, was the symbol of things to come—volume, distortion, and excitement in popular music. "It was a combination I had never heard before and it got my ear right off."[7] "Rocket 88" became number one on the Billboard charts, sold over 100,000 copies and sent rock and roll on its way—a speeding car down the newly constructed American highway.

Little Richard always exclaimed loudly, in his inimitable way, that he was the real king of rock and roll. It is hard to doubt him. His exciting voice-on-the-edge vocal and boogie-woogie piano style, combined with a showmanship that included dancing on top of his piano, transferred the cutting-up southern preacher on the pulpit to the nightclub bandstand. "Of all the churches, I used to like going to the Pentecostal church, because of the music."[8] Little Richard's cross-dressing image, culled from working in New Orleans clubs featuring transvestite performers, was an image from outer space in the button-downed, conservative 1950s. "They were exciting times. The fans would go really wild. Nearly every place we went, the people got unruly.... It would be standing-room-only crowds and ninety percent of the audience would be white. I've always thought that rock and roll brought the races together."[9] His flamboyant image and lifestyle proved to be in direct conflict with his strict, southern church upbringing. The battle between holiness and the devil would force Little Richard to straddle both worlds, as a rock and roll star and as a preacher. This struggle would be carried on in many musical careers.

John Lennon once contended, "If you tried to give 'Rock and Roll' a name, you might call it 'Chuck Berry.'" As a lyricist, songwriter, virtuoso guitarist, and electric performer, Berry is in a class by himself, the poet laureate of rock and roll. Similar to other rock performers, Chuck

Berry was a synthesist, combining pop, country, and rhythm and blues. His lyrics showed a deep understanding of the teenage world, as illustrated in "School Days," "Johnny B. Goode," and "Sweet Little Sixteen." Often overlooked are the lyrics to "Brown-Eyed Handsome Man" and "Promised Land," songs of depth veiling racism in the United States at a time when radio would never play a more explicit statement. "There was nothing you could do to keep Chuck Berry's spirit down.... He had that abandon. You listen to the lyrics, man, [and] you want to do a little bit of everything that he talks about in his songs."[10] In many ways, Chuck Berry is seen as the first true rock and roller, a pioneer who stands alone. "I felt that all the others took after him.... I can give you a little insight into why Bill Haley and Elvis Presley got all the credit for beginning rock and roll. Chuck was in one vein of the blues and some radio stations got it in their minds they didn't want the black man's music to move and blues is the black man's music."[11]

Bill Haley was a rockabilly star, a mixture of country vocals fired by a rhythm and blues beat. The slap bass, minimal drums, swing feel, and a country twanging voice made "Rock around the Clock" a hit and the first rock soundtrack to the movie, *Blackboard Jungle*. The impact was enormous. For the first time, teenagers who had been listening to thin-sounding transistor radios could now hear rock and roll blasting out of large movie theater speakers. They not only heard the music; they felt it, music as a sensory experience. "It was the loudest sound kids had ever heard at the time. I remember being inspired with awe. In cruddy little teen-age rooms across America, kids had been huddling around old radios and cheap record players listening to 'dirty' music of their lifestyle.... But in the theatre, watching Blackboard Jungle, they couldn't tell you to turn it down, I didn't care if Bill Haley was white or sincere.... He was playing the Teen-Age National Anthem and it was so LOUD!... They made a movie about us, therefore, we exist."[12]

The world could only handle one Jerry Lee Lewis. His powerhouse talent mixed with brash egotism and charm brought boogie-woogie and gospel to the rock and roll stage. Lewis epitomized rebellion and, like Little Richard, suffered from the inner conflict of his religious background. He was a publicists' nightmare, and the bad press came at a time when it could seriously damage a career. Jerry Lee Lewis approached "Great Balls of Fire" with an intensity and recklessness rarely seen in music. He was "as deft as a concert pianist," according to his producer, Sam Phillips, and he could "discourse with equal authority on the music of Gene Autry, Bing Crosby, Frank Sinatra, Al Jolson, and Fats Waller."[13] Like almost all '50s rock stars, Lewis could not make the transition to the shifting musical trends of future decades, yet his legacy lives on.

Buddy Holly was a dream deferred. He may have been the greatest rock and roll talent of the '50s, only to die in a plane crash in 1959 at the age of twenty-two. He was a musical innovator who combined rural American styles into a visionary pop music vernacular. His boy-next-door image and Fender Stratocaster guitar are reminders of rock's biggest loss during this decade. It was Buddy Holly, assisted by Norman Petty at Petty's Clovis, New Mexico, recording studio, who showed the future of rock music would be largely determined by the palette of colors available through recording innovations. Listen to a Holly recording. It could have been made last month; it is not dated the way many '50s recording can be. His two guitar, bass, drum lineup would influence the Beatles and move rock into a guitar band orientation. His influence on their songwriting and the future of rock makes his loss all the more profound. One wonders what impact he would have had on music in the 1960s.

The Early Years of Elvis Presley

In his landmark work *Mystery Train,* the author Greil Marcus points out the essential concept of a creative artist imagining their own destiny. It is not only having the dream but also the confidence, talent, and fortitude to make it a reality. That is the struggle. It is creating a better life, the individual as the playwright in their own destiny. Elvis, like Little Richard before him, did just that. "The earliest picture of Elvis shows a farmer, his wife and their baby, the faces of the parents are vacant, they are set, as if they cannot afford an unearned smile. Somehow, their faces say, they will be made to pay even for that."[14]

Never underestimate the impact of the Deep South on American culture. From its writers to musicians, the region has largely shaped the nation's voice. Race is constantly discussed, but the subject of class is mostly avoided. Elvis Presley was raised a poor boy in Tupelo, Mississippi, followed by his family's move to Memphis when he was thirteen years old. "Elvis grew up a loved and precious child. He was, everyone agreed, unusually close to his mother."[15] Being in the South gave him a cross-racial, cross-cultural exposure that most of the country had not yet experienced. Elvis had Black friends, bought his clothes on Beale Street where they shopped, went to the areas where Black musicians performed, and entered the back doors of churches in order to hear the singing. He absorbed everything. When Presley listened to a record, he played it over and over again until he had extracted the essential elements, tools for a later date. "He was serious about this work.... He found him with a stack of records ... that he studied with all the avidity that other kids focused on their college exams."[16]

The African American gospel revival meetings that he attended would impact his future wild onstage performance style. His earliest musical experience was the Pentecostal services of the First Assembly of God. "The preacher was cutting up all over the place," he said, "jumping on the piano, movin' every which way.... I guess I learned it from them." His biographer added, "Gospel music combined with the spiritual force that he felt in all music with the sense of physical release and exaltation for which, it seemed he was casting about."[17] Little Richard and Elvis Presley would put that intensity into their performance style and influence a future generation of performers.

It is one thing to be influenced by numerous musical styles, but it is something far greater to synthesize them into a unique new whole. Elvis Presley utilized his innate, instinctive ability in combining gospel, country, blues, and voices from the cotton fields into rock and roll. He was not an inventor; he was an architect, a painter with many brushes.

Elvis was an unpolished talent, a shy high school boy with an unsettled voice and a guitar. His future lead guitarist, Scotty Moore, once said, "He was a rebel without making an issue of it." Throughout high school, Elvis Presley was a social misfit with a guitar under his arm, a young man in search of a musical talent that would ultimately require guidance.

Sam Phillips was a white man who opened a recording studio in Memphis because he saw a musical and cultural need. "Negro artists in the south who wanted to record just had no place to go," said Phillips. "I set up a studio just to make records with some of those great Negro artists."[18] Phillips made dynamic records at Sun Studio only to face the constant frustration of slamming into America's segregated racial divide. Selling Black artists to mainstream America in the 1950s was nearly impossible. Separate but equal was in force from 1896 until *Brown v. the Board of Education* in 1954 struck it down. It was a country divided, racially, socially, and culturally.

It has been said that a genius is someone who can see a market before it exists. Sam Phillips clearly had a vision. "If I could find a white man who had the Negro sound and the Negro feel, I could make a billion dollars," he said in perhaps the most important quote in rock history. Born in Alabama, Sam Phillips knew and loved the Negro sound, the singing in the fields. "I listened to that beautiful a cappella singing— the windows of the black Methodist church ... even when they hoed, they'd get a rhythm going ... and then the singing, especially if the wind happened to be in the right direction—believe me, all that said a lot to me."[19] He would remember that music in his approach to record production. He was looking for something different, as Greil Marcus wrote, "for something that didn't fit."[20]

Fate smiled on Sam Phillips when the nineteen-year-old Elvis Presley walked into Sun Studio in 1954. His polite and shy manner contrasted with what his biographer Peter Guralnick would observe: "By his dress, his hair, his demeanor ... he was making a ringing declaration of independence."[21] Yet on the surface, he was, as Phillips's associate Marion Kesker said, "He had all the intricacy of the very simple."[22]

A few months after their first meeting, Sam Phillips found a song for Elvis, recording him at Sun Studio with Scotty Moore on guitar and Bill Black on bass. At the end of a disappointing session, Elvis Presley suddenly cut loose, blasting out a cover of Arthur "Big Boy" Crudup's "That's All Right, Mama." They had struck gold. "That damned thing came through so loud and clear it was like a big flash of lightning and the thunder that follows," said Phillips. "We thought it was exciting," said Scotty Moore, "but what was it?"[23] They had discovered a sound that did not fit, but one thing was for certain: Elvis Presley had found his authentic musical voice.

"That's All Right, Mama" by Presley, Moore, and Black was recorded in July 1954. It sounds as fresh today as when it first thundered through Sun Studio. With only two guitars and acoustic bass, no drums, it is an amazing display of raw energy and power that sounds like spontaneous combustion. One year later, Elvis Presley was on multiple national charts.

The local impact was immediate. Memphis DJ Dewey Phillips said, "Sam brought the record by the other night and I played the sonofabitch fourteen times and we got about five hundred phone calls."[24] Even though it was a mixture of previous styles—rhythm and blues, country, and pop—the record sounded new. Elvis Presley's easy, unforced, high-energy delivery was seemingly unattached to past musical traditions. Upon hearing "That's All Right, Mama," many people thought he was Black. Sam Phillips had realized his vision.

Elvis had the natural ability to do deeply into the feeling of a song and deliver that message to his audience. Great singers do not merely sing a song; they get inside it. In addition, Elvis was down to earth and personable in his early years. Nat Williams, a favorite African American DJ at WDIA in Memphis, said, "Elvis Presley on Beale Street when he first started was a favorite man.... He always had that certain humanness about him that Negroes like to put in their songs."[25]

He was on his way.

Onstage: Singing the Body Electric

"I went with the idea that an artist should have something not just good, but totally unique,"[26] said Sam Phillips. In Elvis Presley, he got even more. From the moment he started performing on flatbed trucks in grocery store parking lots, Elvis lit up a stage so much that his guitarist, Scotty Moore, asked, "What is going on? During the instrumental parts he would back off the mike and be playing and shaking, and the crowd would just go wild, but he thought they were actually making fun of him."[27] Presley's natural stage style, influenced by southern preachers and Negro rhythm and blues artists, delivered a one-two punch. It would virtually eliminate the past of demure, detached pop singers who stood idly at the microphone, crooning softly.

Elvis Presley's uninhibited sexually charged moments created a hysterical frenzy among fifteen-year-old southern girls who had been raised in genteel ways. The southern belles became emotional A-bombs during an Elvis performance, only to return to their polite selves when the music was over. Offstage, Elvis was shy and extremely introverted. It was a Jekyll and Hyde experience. "It was the girls who went wild, and Elvis gave them more of what they obviously wanted, the movement of his body. This was the beginning of a phenomenon that determined his early career, an amazingly intimate relationship between Elvis onstage and the women in his audience."[28]

Presence in the arts is an indefinable thing. We know it when it is there and can feel it, but it is indescribable. Elvis Presley had that magic when he walked into a room or onto a stage. Reporter Fred Danzig describes "a tall lean young man ... wearing a shirt the likes of which I have never seen before ... just for the face alone, if you saw him on the street you'd say, 'Wow, look at that guy.'"[29]

Elvis Presley represented a cultural shift in America that exploded when he reached the masses through television. In September 1956, he appeared on the massively popular *Ed Sullivan Show*. It was the biggest break that a performer could have at a time when there were only around twelve channels. By 1959, there were 40 million American homes with televisions. Bruce Springsteen best describes the impact of Presley's televised performance: "In the beginning, every musician has their genesis moment.... Mine was 1956, Elvis on the Ed Sullivan show. It was the evening I realized that a white man could make magic, that you did not have to be constrained by your upbringing, by the way you looked or by the social context that oppressed you. You could call upon your own powers of imagination and you could create a transformative self."[30]

Springsteen's insightful observation goes right to the heart. Music's ability to transform both the performer and the listener make it one of humanity's greatest achievements. The Elvis Presley performance on *Ed Sullivan* made Bruce Springsteen conclude, "There was a red-hot rockabilly forging of a new tomorrow before your very eyes."[31] The Beatles appearance on *Ed Sullivan* in February 1964 would have the same impact on millions of others, changing America in ways that Presley did in the previous decade.

Like seismic waves traveling through the earth's layers, everything shifted. Radio became the way music was delivered to American youth. The transistor radio and the jukebox were now geared to the invention of the American teenager and their disposable income. Countless performers after him adopted Elvis's performance style. Jimmy "C" Newman said, "What he did was he changed it all around.... Elvis could do it, but few others could."[32]

Big success is followed by a dramatic shift in supply and demand, usually to the detriment of the performer. It is a cycle that starts with the starving artist and tilts to a merry-go-round that spins out of control. Presley's grueling tour schedule took its toll: "I don't know where I am going from one day to the next. It's all happening so fast, there's so much happening to me ... that some nights I just can't fall asleep. It scares me you know; it just scares me."[33]

Elvis Presley increasingly became withdrawn from conflict and uncomfortable situations by pretending ignorance. He fell out with Dewey Phillips and began to lose trust in people close to him. The death of his mother, Gladys, in 1958, shattered him more deeply than most could imagine. He felt like he had lost everything in this world and was uncertain what lay ahead.

He was a millionaire by his twenty-first birthday, but his misery remained. Seeking spiritual guidance, he said, "Pastor, I am the most miserable young man you have ever seen.... I want someone to understand."[34] The star of Elvis Presley was rising and so was the price he would have to pay for his platform.

Assimilating into the Mainstream

"I've never written a song in my life.... It's all a big hoax,"[35] exclaimed Elvis Presley. This inability to compose and generate songs, giving him a potential musical direction put Presley in a continued state of musical dependency. His artistic direction and repertoire would have to come from others. In Sam Phillips, Elvis had the perfect producer who knew how to extract the best from his young client, but Phillips and Sun Studio was in debt, resulting in Phillips selling Elvis Presley's contract to a major label, RCA records, with the huckster "Colonel" Tom Parker taking over as Presley's manager. Parker took 25 percent, an amount that only grew as Presley requested loans and advances throughout his life.

Parker reasoned that major label exposure would maximize profits for the first major rock and roll star. "Elvis was the Colonel's dream, the perfect vehicle for all the Colonel's elaborately worked out and ingenious promotional schemes. Elvis was the purest of postwar products, the commodity that had been missing from the shelves in an expanding marketplace of leisure time and disposable cash."[36]

"Colonel" Tom Parker's dubious character was not a mystery to most. Gabe Tucker observed that "he lived in a world of mirrors—he never really left the carnival world.... All of them just like the Colonel, they'll cut your throat just to watch you bleed. But they've got their own laws, it's a game with them, to outsmart you, you're always a pigeon to them."[37]

One has to wonder if Elvis himself ended up a pigeon, easily manipulated by the cunning Parker. If so, he never let on. "He's the one guy that really gave me the breaks. I don't think I would have ever been very big with another man. Because he–he's a very smart man."[38]

Managing Elvis Presley was not without risk. Elvis had many detractors from the conservative right and the media. Jack Gould wrote that Presley had "no discernible singing ability." The *New York Journal American* stated, "Popular music has reached its lowest depths in the 'grunt and groan' antics of one Elvis Presley." *Variety* magazine concurred: "Elvis Presley, coming in on a wing of advance hoopla, doesn't hit the mark here."[39] Sensitive to any criticism and shocked by the negative backlash, he countered, "I don't feel like I'm doing anything wrong."

His manager called for an image change by booking Elvis on the *Tonight Show* with Steve Allen. He appeared wearing formal white tie and tails, singing "Hound Dog" to a dog on the set. It was a calculated attempt to tone down the rebel image and make Presley appear innocent and nonthreatening. The prophetic parting words from Sam Phillips to Elvis upon releasing his contract was, "Don't let them tell you what to do. Don't lose your individuality." It was seeping away, like a tire with a steady leak.

You can't knock success, but success at what price? Parker's strategy called for total media saturation as RCA records sought to increase Presley's fan base by adding lavish pop production to his records. The rawness of his rockabilly Sun Record recordings gave way to pop records that were filled with strings, crooning background vocals, and songs with innocent lyrics such as "Let Me Be Your Teddy Bear" and "Love Me Tender."

It was all a commercial success. "Heartbreak Hotel" was in the top five of the pop, rhythm and blues, and country charts simultaneously. Presley proved he could sing any material, from ballads and spirituals to lowdown blues and rock and roll. As his success grew, his vocal style took on ever-increasing mannerisms, a sign of ego and self-absorption that Phillips would have never allowed.

Manager Parker turned Presley from a rockabilly star into an all-round mass entertainer. He was concerned that if rock and roll faded, it would take his boy with it. After Presley served in the army from 1958 to 1960, making Elvis into a Hollywood movie star became the priority marketing strategy. If you have ever seen an Elvis Presley film, it is far from great cinema and even Elvis knew it. Films such as *Love Me Tender, Loving You, Jailhouse Rock,* and *King Creole* were basically showcases for furthering his mainstream image and selling Elvis Presley records. It was a long way from Elvis singing rock and roll in a black leather jacket to playing a ukulele and crooning insipid love songs to young women on a Waikiki beach.

Performing is the lifeblood of a musician. It is that vital connection between performer and audience that keeps the engine of inspiration running. Hollywood and Elvis's manager had such a hold on his career that he gave no public performances from 1961 through 1967. Elvis lived a reclusive life, hiding from a famished and insatiable audience waiting to tear him apart at any public appearance.

Despite his millions, Elvis's wild spending and continued fueling of his excesses put him in constant debt to his manager. This resulted in a further dependency, creating an overseer-sharecropper relationship. The more Presley owed, the more he looked to his manager for future earnings. Success can be an addiction.

1968 Television Comeback

Elvis Presley's 1968 TV special, titled *One Night with You,* has often been heralded as one of his greatest performances. For Presley fans, it brought hopes of a comeback for his flagging career. That night he returned to the old form of his rockabilly days, performing with a fire that hadn't been seen in a decade. It was a performance of a lifetime and still worth watching to this day. Yet perhaps the most revealing and saddest moment in the evening comes from a short speech that Presley makes before launching into Jimmy Reed's "Baby, What Do You Want Me to Do?"

With a visible sadness in his eyes, Elvis Presley alludes to the many changes that have occurred in popular music of recent years. He is clearly a champion who is past his prime. The Beatles, the British invasion, and a new generation of American rock bands have stolen his thunder, leaving him a memory, a relic of a bygone era. Elvis begins speaking about the roots of rock and roll, then abruptly cuts himself off with "I don't know what I'm saying. I'm just mumbling." Who knew more about the origins of rock and roll than Elvis Presley? He no longer believed in what he is saying, and one wonders if he had ceased believing in himself. "There was a way in which virtually his whole career has been a throwaway, straight from that time when he knew he had it made and that the future was his."[40]

Peter Guralnick writes in *Last Train to Memphis*, "Each man is doomed to stumble in their own darkness." Despite the bright lights of Las Vegas, Elvis Presley had stumbled and fallen into an abyss of his own making.

Sadly, this would not be a comeback, and Elvis Presley would retreat further into a darkness of pills that would eventually end his life.

"My voice is God's will, not mine."

Pills and Throwaway Years

His later years were grim. Elvis Presley lost all control of his personal and professional life while the world watched. His multiple personal problems and character flaws as both a womanizer and drug abuser put him in a paranoid orbit. This does not reduce his importance, but it clouds and detracts from his body of work. As Presley biographer Dave Marsh wrote, "You don't need to be a great man to be a great artist."[41]

What went wrong? There are more factors than we can count. Some blame his manager's influence, but we must look to Elvis himself, a man who could not possibly fathom his place in American culture and society. The curious young artist who strove to improve his art gave way to depression; he was lost, and his lack of any semblance of a private life was certainly not his fault. Elvis became a caged animal. There is no regulating success of this magnitude, no faucet that controls how much or how little. He lacked personal vision and self-awareness, key components essential to an artist. Not being a songwriter and never attempting to obtain those skills diminished his ability to be a creative force in rock music's development.

"Presley's art no longer stood for or belonged solely to him. It also became whatever we made [and remade] of it."[42] The fact that he made an album titled *Something for Everyone* speaks volumes. His artistry lost all focus and musical identity. Many of Elvis Presley's performances of the 1970s were similar to watching an ex-champion boxer teetering in the ring, getting knocked down again and again. His dependency on countless pills throughout the day made Elvis into a different person. I once spoke to a man who saw Elvis onstage during his last years. "Don't ask me about Elvis Presley," he said with both anger and disappointment. "I spent a lot of money to see him in Las Vegas. He fell down twice and had to be helped back up. Elvis Presley can go to hell."

In his brilliant *Mystery Train* chapter titled "Presliad," Greil Marcus pulls no punches. Reviewing a Presley performance, Marcus writes, "He closes with an act of showbiz love that still warms the heart, but above all, he throws away the entire performance."[43]

Elvis Presley was either unwilling or unable to take direction of his life and career. Complete musical assimilation into the mainstream brought him an inconceivable success, but it left him without the musical identity that he and Sam Phillips had nurtured in the mid–'50s. In his essay, "The Spirit of Place," D.H. Lawrence writes, "Men are not free when they are doing just what they like. The moment you can do just what you like, there is nothing you care about doing."[44]

There is a segment during the last concert of Elvis Presley where he sings the ballad "My Way." It is a song that has been done to death and parodied by comedians, but this song is delivered with such feeling that it is a truly transcendent and moving performance. The sad irony is the fact that he did not live his life his way. The story might have been different.

Sam Phillips knew that "no matter what happens to you in this world, if you don't make it your business to be happy, then you may have gained the world and lost your spirit and maybe even your damned soul."[45]

Cultural Shifts

Elvis Presley was the first major, worldwide rock and roll star, a revolutionary who changed the times. People in remote regions around the world knew his name and image, an American symbol. He stole the limelight from Frank Sinatra, making everything before him seem obsolete. Before Presley, Tin Pan Alley and the great American song from composers such as Irving Berlin, George Gershwin, Cole Porter,

Richard Rodgers and Lorenz Hart, and others were the soundtrack to American musicals and pop songs, setting the standard for the recording industry. Rock and roll and Elvis came with a tidal wave force—the modern era had arrived. For an older generation shaking their heads, it seemed bad was now good, and what had been good was considered bad, or at the very least, irrelevant. Presley was more than a rock star; he became a total entertainment entity wrapped in a handsome, sexy, innocent, boy-next-door package.

We don't have the Elvis phenomenon today and we probably never will. In one of the most astute observations ever made in the history of rock journalism, the wonderfully insightful and eccentric *Village Voice* critic Lester Bangs wrote upon Presley's 1977 death, "We will continue to fragment in this manner ... but I can guarantee you one thing: we will never again agree on anything as we agreed on Elvis. So I won't bother saying goodbye to his corpse. I will say goodbye to you."[46] Bangs had that one right. After Elvis, rock fragmented into countless pieces, styles, genres, and categories, and so did the media that amplified it. The range of sounds would multiply with the advent of new technology and the mainstream that Elvis once waded through would never be the same. Music producer Brian Eno was accurate in seeing this as a situation of no more sunlike stars, only constellations.

Elvis remains a fascinating figure of stature because he reflects his audience. "He was like a mirror in a way, whatever you were looking for, you were going to find in him."[47] Indeed, Elvis reflects the American dream at its best and nightmare at its worst. We look at his legacy and we see ourselves.

His great talents mixed with driving ambition brought him an unfathomable success, moving him into myth. Elvis Presley paid the price for his legacy.

Conclusion: A Mystery Train Lost in the Fog

The distance between genius and fake, real and farce is a thin line. There is more confusion about Elvis Presley than one can comprehend, but biographer Peter Guralnick sees his legacy broken down into factions:

1. Audience loyalty for the early rocker period
2. An audience attracted to his "emotionally scarred music of the 1970s"
3. An audience that views Elvis Presley as an overrated cultural joke.

The gas station in front of Dockery Plantation, Cleveland, Mississippi, where Charley Patton and others created a blues culture that has had worldwide influence.

In his Presley biography *Last Train to Memphis,* Guralnick admits, "I wanted to rescue Elvis Presley from the dreary bondage of myth, from the oppressive aftershock of cultural significance."[48] Those aftershocks may be over, but the imprint on the land remains.

We know that Elvis Presley was a revolutionary with lasting influence. He impacted the culture by giving us a new musical language, a revitalized version of America. He could have never done this without the profound influence of African American roots music. This fact must never be overlooked and should be taught in every American grade school.

Elvis Presley is easily lost in the fog of myth. When I show my students a video of his final performance, there is a heavy sadness in the room and even a few tears among my students.

They get it.

5

Say It Loud: Black Music in the 1960s

Out of the fire came the music. The '60s, heralded as the turbulent decade of the twentieth century, yielded America's dynamic new sounds. The nation's temperature was taken by the songs heard on radio. Being a passive observer was almost impossible. With draft cards lodged in their wallets, young men knew the score but not the game. Vietnam was no longer on the other side of the world; it was right around the corner.

Sweetie Pie's restaurant and music venue, Jackson, Mississippi.

If you were young and Black in the '60s, there was a feeling that perhaps, after hundreds of years, your time had finally come. Activism, self-help, economic independence, respect (Sing it, Aretha!), and above all, freedom as promised by the Constitution, all long overdue, seemed to be within an African American's grasp. Beyond the sheen of pop music, a question remained—how could contemporary music adequately express the tumultuous, destructive, and creative times? From "Blowin' in the Wind" and "Street Fightin' Man" to "A Change Is Gonna Come" and "Respect," American youth would look to music, not political speeches, as a place they could trust. More than ever, for better or worse, art meant truth.

The '60s are forever trapped between liberal idealization and conservative disdain—the reality lies in the middle. Realizing the vastness of this musical decade, this chapter examines Black music as represented by soul, Motown, and John Coltrane. The '60s were an incredible period to be young and alive in America. Looking back, we can either sigh in nostalgic reverie or despair, realizing we will never see those times again, yet it remains a decade of many lessons.

Soul Messengers

By the late 1950s, the lines were clearly drawn. Black music meant gospel, rhythm and blues, and in the hands of Ray Charles, soul. Pop music, and the newly labeled rock and roll, were marketed to the white teenage mainstream. Drawing from deep church roots, African American singers pointed the way to a deeper vocal and musical expression. The pulpit transformed its way to the nightclub bandstand. Radio, now forced to compete with television, delivered new sounds and messages. Despite the rule of separate but equal, music on uncensored airwaves would become a common denominator.

Soul has a double meaning. It is a musical style, heavily influenced by gospel yet laced with a secular, often sexual, message. It is a sensibility and display—a style of dress, swagger, display of cool, and most importantly, a pro–civil rights consciousness. Soul was an essential musical element that had always existed in Black music, but "the word 'soul' has taken on a connotation of social identity."[1]

By 1965, "soul had come to define a special quality that blacks possessed and whites didn't, a different way of talking, walking, and looking at the world."[2] The roots of soul music recall the African ring shout, brought forward into a modern era. "It should always be remembered that soul music in all its forms is the aesthetic property of a race of people who were brought to this country against their will and were forced to make drastic social adjustments in order to survive in a hostile environment. This black experience provided the foundation for the popular art of today."[3]

It has been said that on a compass, north, east, and west are directions, but the South is a place. Its historical complexities and paradoxes are almost unfathomable, yet when it comes to music, the South is second to none for its cultural impact. This environment exposed both Black and white races to a mélange of country, gospel, hillbilly, blues, rhythm and blues, boogie-woogie, Cajun, and numerous folk styles that proved to be the ingredients for future musical syncretism. The music existed within the paradox of prejudiced southern whites who openly loved Black music, while failing to make the human connections with the people who created it.

It was an expression of humanity. Soul's strength was the fact that it transcended race. Booker T. and the M.G.'s drummer, Al Jackson, once said, "It's my belief that soul comes from a cat's folk roots, regardless of what color he might be. He has his own soul.... When it comes to this soul thing, people have to remember that whites, particularly in this area [Memphis, Tennessee], have their own kind of soul roots in country and western music, while we as blacks have ours in blues, gospel, R&B, or whatever you want to call it."[4]

Getting the music heard wasn't easy. Radio and the record industry were as racially biased as the multitude of white-controlled industries. By the late '50s and early '60s, vocalists Nat King Cole, Johnny Mathis, Sam Cooke, and eventually Ray Charles were the few African American artists to gain major label exposure. Radio enforced musical segregation until southern stations such as WDIA in Memphis broke the code, featuring African American DJs who played Black rhythm and blues. Pop music and rhythm and blues stood on different sides of the fence as "there is a definite difference between the type of music programmed for R&B and soul radio stations aimed at black audiences and featuring black deejays, and that played on the 'Top 40' and 'underground' rock stations towards whites."[5]

Soul, rhythm and blues, and rock all evolved parallel to the civil rights movement. By the mid–'60s, radio and television slowly began presenting African American performers, largely because it was good business. "One of the effects of the Civil Rights movement had been to condition a generation of white children to seeing evidence on television of qualities in Negroes that seemed heroic."[6] Indeed, growing up in the Chicago area, when I saw James Brown perform live on a local station, I was mesmerized. My favorite baseball player was Ernie Banks of Chicago Cubs fame. Greatness is always obvious.

Memphis Soul Stew

Music at its best is an emotional capturing of history. Perhaps better than any other medium, it revealed the social temperature of America. Although soul was a collective movement, one man stands out as its rhythmic genius—James Brown. From the beginning, he was a man working and dancing alone. James Brown taught the world that by turning every instrument into a drum, you could open new musical doors. While the Beatles were singing romantic ballads like "Michelle" and "Yesterday," James Brown wrote hard, scaled-down songs with one or two chords that contained the hottest grooves imaginable. Songs like "Papa's Got a Brand-New Bag" and "Sex Machine" took blues songs to a soulful, funky place. It was music that forced you to dance.

He put the '60s Black identity on stage for all to see, conveying a bold, forthright pride unusual in a music industry that was reluctant to make space for African American performers with a message of Black pride. "James Brown was a solo man who forged ahead on his own, who far from renegotiating any kind of compromise solution to reach a broader audience, demanded that that very audience sit up and listen to what he had to say."[7]

James Brown had much to say about being Black in America. In the heat of the civil rights movement, after the assassination of Dr. Martin Luther King, his 1968 recording "Say It Loud, I'm Black and I'm Proud" was an anthem for African Americans. The song seemed directed to a nation embroiled in war on city streets and in Vietnam. What Dylan's "Blowin' in the Wind" was to white youth, "Say It Loud" was to Black America. It came at a cost. "Say It Loud, I'm Black and I'm Proud" united James Brown's Black audience while the white mainstream recoiled, resulting in fewer television appearances and general media exposure. Mass acceptance would never come to the Godfather of Soul.

His records and, in particular, his rhythmic grooves are musical achievements that live in hip-hop samples to this day. James Brown was no fan of disco, a style that borrowed heavily from him, locking his beats into drum machines without the pliable give of his great rhythm sections. The dance floor got crowded with a simplified mechanical beat. Brown saw what other soul artists in the '70s experienced, a vanishing career and a legacy left behind. His difficult, defiant personality and legal escapades eroded the iconic soul man hero stature that James Brown once represented in the 1960s. His beat remains eternal.

A collective soul movement grew from the red clay of Memphis, Tennessee, a city historically rich in blues and jazz. A main hub for southern Black and white blues musicians and sharecroppers fleeing the terrors of the Deep South, Memphis was the first stop toward the promised land. "Memphis inherited the spontaneous musical expressiveness of newly freed slaves who made their way north from plantations further down the river, after the Civil War."[8]

Important cultural movements generally start by accident. When something truly great occurs, it is an alignment of the people, the environment, and the stars. Jim Stewart, a local Memphis banker and fiddle player, assisted by his sister Estelle Axton, founded Stax Records in the early 1960s. They rented an old movie house, the Capitol Theater, in South Memphis, converting it into a recording studio. With its slanted floor, the acoustics would enhance the magic soon to be created. Stewart admitted, "Stax Records was born by accident at the intersection of a particular time and place."[9]

Without any preconceived intent, Stax would symbolize Blacks and whites working together, side by side, in one of America's most racially torn cities. "We didn't even know what rhythm and blues was then. We just happened to move into a colored neighborhood."[10] Soon after opening Stax, young local Black and white Memphis musicians came by, curious to see if this might be an opportunity. Estelle Axton said, "We didn't see color, we saw talent."[11] Stax opened an adjoining record shop, run by Estelle, that allowed the label to determine what young listeners on the street wanted to hear. "The record shop was a magnet that drew young black dream-chasers in Memphis as powerfully as Motown's early digs on West Grand Boulevard had in Detroit."[12]

The Memphis soul sound that was born at Stax and a few other local recording studios was based on an intangible, inexpressible, musical feeling. Soul sprang up from the ground in an organic way that could only happen at this time and place. It was a case of musical feeling over technique and instrumental prowess. "The technical ability possessed by Memphis musicians can be acquired, but their feeling of affinity with the music seems to be inbred."[13]

The premier star of Stax Records, Otis Redding, once said, "If you got the feelin', you can sing soul. You just sing it from the heart, and there's no difference between nobody's heart."[14] No one knew this better than Otis Redding, but there were misconceptions about soul, similar to the notion that blues and jazz originate solely out of African American suffering. It was not that simple. "You hear soul music explained in terms of oppression and poverty, and that's certainly part of it—no soul musician was born rich—but it's more than that. It's being proud of your own people, what you came from. That's soul."[15]

Unlike the slicker productions of Berry Gordy at Motown Records, Stax offered a free-wheeling, creative environment that encouraged

individual input and inspiration. Jim Stewart understood the art of getting out of the way by trusting and believing in his label's talent: his "ability to surround himself with people not simply of talent but of character,
people on whom he could rely, individuals who were capable of growth."[16]

Stax's distinct sound and success came quickly. The 1961 single
"Last Night" was followed by the mixed-race band Booker T. and the
M.G.'s, selling 1 million copies of "Green Onions" in 1962. The irony of
this legendary million-selling group was the fact that they could record
and perform together but could not congregate together in a Memphis
bar or restaurant without social unease should be lost on no one. "Green
Onions" was recorded in an hour and has been heard around the world
for over half a century, the epitome of Memphis soul.

By 1965, Stax hired Al Bell, a Black DJ, placing him in an upper-level
executive position, something virtually unheard of in the music industry. Bell shared the same office and phone with Jim Stewart and was
hired to make Stax into a national brand. "This makes Stax one of the
very very few record companies—they number fewer than the fingers on
one hand—to have a black man in a top administrative position."[17] The
integration at Stax, from bands, staff, and studio musicians to executives, was remarkable in the midst of American race rioting and assassinations. Stax was clearly blazing its own musical and social trail. "For
any business that doubt that black and white people can work together
with ideological differences and at the same time, be productive, we've
proven that it can be done."[18]

The record industry smells success. Stax attracted the attention
of the New York–based indie label Atlantic Records. After successfully
recording and eventually losing Ray Charles, Atlantic needed a boost.
Tired of the New York City environment, record producer Jerry Wexler said, "I lost interest in recording with the same arrangers who were
out of ideas. Musicians were out of licks [and] the songwriters didn't
have any songs."[19] Wexler found inspiration in the Memphis music
scene. Atlantic entered into a business deal with Stax, one that would
have dire consequences in the future; Jim Stewart signed a contract
without consulting a lawyer. At this point, Stax and soul lacked the
crossover superstar who would reach the mainstream. She was about
to arrive.

The Summer of Aretha Franklin

There is but one queen of soul and that is Aretha Franklin. The
daughter of the famous African American preacher C.L. Franklin,

young Aretha absorbed her father's sermons, providing a foundation for her phrasing and vocalizations. "Most of what I learned vocally came from him, he gave me a sense of timing in music and timing is important in everything."[20] Discovered by John Hammond, who claimed she was the greatest voice since Billie Holiday, Aretha would struggle throughout her recording career at Columbia Records from 1960 to 1966. She and her numerous producers failed in focusing her musical identity. With only nominal success, the promise of her remarkable talent remained unrealized.

Her troubled personal life—conceiving children during her teenage years while enduring abusive male relationships—created an inner sense of turmoil. Aretha Franklin had grown up lonely and seemed to only come alive in performance. Her later producer, Jerry Wexler, referred to her as Our Lady of Sorrows. Even Aretha herself was unsure of her true musical identity until she left Columbia Records to move to the smaller, independent label Atlantic in 1966.

Everything suddenly changed. Jerry Wexler astutely realized that Aretha had not been musically taking her audience to church, her greatest strength untapped. Gospel singing was at the core of her identity, something her Columbia recordings had largely ignored. From the dramatic moment of her historical recording session in Muscle Shoals, Alabama, Aretha had "at last cast off the confining stays of her long apprenticeship and was once and for all ready to give herself over to the unbridled secular ecstasy of her music."[21]

The subsequent explosion of hits for Aretha Franklin resulted in *Ebony* magazine declaring the civil rights movement of 1967 as the "summer of 'Retha, Rap [Brown] and Revolt." Her taking over of Otis Redding's song "Respect" exemplifies the power of music when set against the context of the 1965 Watts rebellion, rioting in Newark and Detroit, and the idea of Black Power. It is more than a song in the way her voice carries the words; "Respect" is an anthem—for women, Black people, and all humanity. In her long career, there would be many hit records for Aretha Franklin, who died in 2018, though her later years are uneven, marked by inconsistent performances. The musicologist Henry Pleasants noted that her later music was "the depressing sound of an insecure adult who wants only to be loved."[22] Fame and fortune could never remedy this.

Unlike the flood of future music stars, known for their popularity and tabloid celebrity status, Aretha Franklin stands as a beacon, a seminal artist who contributed mightily to American culture in countless ways. Her legacy was best summarized by President Barack Obama upon her death: "American history wells up when Aretha sings, because it captures the fullness of the American experience, the view from the bottom as well as the top, the good and the bad, and the possibility of synthesis, reconciliation, and transcendence."[23]

Otis Redding was the dynamic soul singer of the Stax catalog. His delivery of a song was like none other. "Otis Redding was the real soul messenger and I think that's when they [a white audience] really began to become oriented as to what soul was."[24] Redding was more than a star vocalist; he was a visionary who led his Stax sessions by molding the horn section into what became the "Memphis soul sound." Booker T. Jones recalls, "He was just like Leonard Bernstein.... He was the same type of person. He was a leader. He'd just lead with his arms and his body and his fingers. That place had its own soul."[25] Indeed, Otis Redding was seen as a good, hardworking man you wanted to be around. He wouldn't be around for long.

Like Aretha Franklin, success came big and suddenly for Redding in 1967. The Stax spring European tour, followed by his breakthrough success at the June Monterrey pop festival illuminated soul's worldwide impact. "We had never had acceptance from a white audience in the United States.... There was a new feeling.... History was changing at that moment and we knew it."[26] From this point on, in contrast to the British invasion lead by the Beatles and the Rolling Stones, Otis Redding and Stax were perceived as the personification of soul with a strong tie to the blues. Southern soul music was rising in popular consciousness.

White performers such as Janis Joplin would come to admire and be heavily influenced by Otis Redding and the soul movement. Similar to Elvis Presley, the Black music–white face syndrome was a perpetual pattern in American popular music, but as the critic Nat Hentoff warned, "With regard to the young white performers, they will not only have to write much more of their own material, but they will also have to confront the present and the future as themselves."[27]

Soul's demise began with the plane crash of Otis Redding and his band in the icy waters of Lake Monona, outside of Madison, Wisconsin, on December 10, 1967. Although all commercial flights had been grounded due to weather, Redding, on tour, pressed on, determined not to miss a concert date. A stunned music world seemed to halt in its tracks. Jim Stewart lamented, "I think the death of Otis took a lot of heart out of Stax, it really did." The guitarist and producer Steve Cropper agreed, "If Otis had lived, everything would have been different."[28] At age twenty-six, Otis Redding, a former well driller and high school dropout from Macon, Georgia, now a world-famous celebrity with considerable wealth, was gone.

Stax's end was on the horizon. Corporate takeover resulted in

Atlantic Records being sold to Warner Brothers, while Stax was purchased by Gulf and Western. The effects were felt as dissension and animosity infiltrated the Stax ranks. Booker T. Jones recalls that "things had become quite corporate," and Steve Cropper said, "The whole air ... and feeling had changed."[29] More than any other single world event, the assassination of Dr. Martin Luther King in Memphis on April 4, 1968, affected soul, the music industry, and American life. An atmosphere of rage and public distrust grew, resulting in permanent damage to many interracial working relationships across the country. Stax came apart at the seams, the integrated bonds forged in the past now broken. "That was the turning point," said Booker T., "the turning point for the relations between races in the South. And it happened in Memphis."[30]

American racial progress was a far-off dream by the late 1960s. After hundreds of years of slavery, minstrel shows, Jim Crow laws, and white supremacy, a seemingly impenetrable wall of hate had been erected. "You see, there's one thing about the South of America, and that is that there are certain structures that are there, probably will always be there, that you just can't change. And one of them has to do with just how much power a black can have."[31]

Soul's steady demise came from internal and external forces. As the record industry consolidated through corporate takeover, the smaller independent record labels found that survival was next to impossible. "The revenue from four-fifths of the top-selling records in the early 70s passed through the counting houses of six multinational corporations. As raw materials—the performing talent got pricier, the infrastructure that made it possible for twenty-five years to distribute goods independently of major companies was crumbling."[32] Stax, once a multimillion-dollar independent label, was bankrupt by 1974, with a few hundred dollars left in their bank account. Rather than establishing partnerships with the musicians and the employees, essential to a soul record label's success such as Stax, the smaller record companies were sold for capital gains, leaving out the creative people. Speaking of Stax, Jim Dickinson, record producer for the famous Ardent Studios in Memphis, concluded, "They never understood what they had, they always wanted something else."[33]

The Stax recording studio was eventually torn down, only a vacant lot remained, later to be reconstructed as a museum. This is typical of America's tendency to ignore or undervalue its culture, only to realize it far too late. Yet the legacy of Stax and soul music live on. Representing an example of Blacks and whites working together through adversity, Estelle Axton said, "I imagine all those kids still admire Jim and myself for what we did for them in those early years. I doubt if you'd find any of them that would say we didn't do as much as we could have."[34]

The New York critic Pauline Kael once wrote of Aretha Franklin that she seemed to be looking at her audience as her audience gazed at her.

So too does soul and its enduring legacy.

Under the Wheels of Motown

Motown is to soul music as polished glass is to coarse sandpaper. Musical styles are generally conceived by large groups of people, but Detroit's Motown Records was the vision of one man—Berry Gordy. It is a complex and perplexing story of the rise and fall of the most successful Black-run independent record label in history. Motown produced Black music that appealed to the masses by successfully crossing over into the white mainstream. "At no other time in record industry history has an independent label been better organized to capitalize on its talent."[35] It became more than a label; it represented a musical style.

Berry Gordy's incredible drive and work ethic enabled his assembly of an array of raw talent that became Motown's foundation. Set in the context of America's racial struggles, Quincy Jones wrote that Motown let "everyone see the beauty of black music despite the barriers Motown had to overcome."[36] The label boasted a song catalog of astounding success. "The Motown hits [and quite a few of the misses] of the sixties may stand as the most impressive and enduring book of pure pop for people that rock and roll will ever produce."[37]

Yet there is an undeniably dark side to this story. Robert Christgau states that Motown represents "the paradox of power for black people in America undermine their temporary triumphs.... For Gordy, not only did he act like any other boss and treat the talented people who worked for him like peons, but he ended up where the American entertainment industry always ends up—in Hollywood."[38] It is sobering to realize that the majority of hardworking, dedicated, and talented people who made Motown finished with little more than a scrapbook of memories. It is yet another example of the American dream gone wrong, "a testament to the power of black music and an example of how soul-stifling success can be when its fruits are not shared."[39]

The Vision

Detroit was a city of historical importance with a deep culture, an important stop on the Underground Railroad during slavery. It was here that Berry Gordy, a struggling songwriter and Detroit automotive assemble line employee, began his career. A jazz enthusiast, Gordy opened the 3-D Record Mart in 1953, featuring bop and other forms of modern jazz. By 1955, the store went out of business. Gordy began to realize that Detroit African Americans, many working nightshifts at the Ford Motor plant, wanted danceable, feel-good blues that spoke to their hard lives, not hip, esoteric jazz. This surprising failure had an impact on Gordy's songwriting approach. "He'd learned the hard lessons of John Lee Hooker well, and all his songs would tell a story, directly and concisely, yet with a distinguished flair."[40]

Berry Gordy wrote songs for soul singer Jackie Wilson and began recording songs that sought to achieve a rhythm and blues sound that would appeal to white and Black America. At the urging of Smokey Robinson, Motown Records was formed with the idea of having as much freedom in the record industry as possible. "All Motown is the result of one thing leading to another and Berry Gordy saying, 'I'll do it myself,' when he could not get something to his liking."[41]

Motown was a Black-owned label that employed whites in key positions. From its inception, the label's business affairs were kept private with an air of secrecy, never giving outsiders access to their talent or their accounting books. This prevented outside organizations from auditing or questioning Motown's internal affairs. Talent in Detroit was plentiful—there was music in the churches, in the schools, at Cass Technical High School, and in the bars and nightclubs. Gordy signed young, naive talent to contracts that favored Motown, not the artists, charging them with promotional expenses against their unclear record royalties. Innovative to a fault, Motown supported their touring revues, making them "the first record label in history to tap directly into income generated by its entire roster."[42]

Motown carefully developed their talent in a tightly controlled environment. Berry Gordy was determined to make hit records and prepare his young talent for stardom, crossing them over from the Black chitlin circuit to the white mainstream of radio, records, Las Vegas, and television. In order to do this, he would need a catalog of great songs.

A Musical Production Line

Bob Dylan called him "America's greatest living poet." Smokey Robinson contributed the classic Motown songs "My Girl," "You Really Got a Hold on Me," and "Two Lovers," a song of breathtaking depth. Robinson used the songwriting format to demonstrate the highs and lows of adult relationships. He was not alone. The songwriting team of Brian Holland, Lamont Dozier, and Eddie Holland turned out two or three songs per day under the constant pressure to create hit songs. The exceptional gifts of this legendary songwriting team were simply that they "did possess an innate gift for melody, a feel for story, song lyrics, and an ability to create the recurring vocal and instrumental lines known as hooks."[43]

Like an automotive plant turning out cars, quality control was enforced at monthly Motown meetings when the new recordings were played and analyzed. All who attended voted to either release the record or remake it if it was deemed substandard, later to be rearranged and rerecorded, or scrapped altogether. The key was Motown's consistency. More than its individual artists, Motown sold a trademark sound, teaming Holland, Dozier, and Holland with the Supremes, signed in 1961 at the ages of sixteen and seventeen. This collaboration would yield five consecutive number one hits, pushing the elegant, polished, straight-hair wigged Supremes into the American mainstream. It was musical crossover and cultural integration through music resulting in a sense of racial pride.

Once recorded, Motown artists went through a rigid finishing school. The young, hard-knock talent took etiquette classes with Maxine Powell, an important step toward polishing an artist and refining them before they engaged the public. The groups worked with the musical director Maurice King and the staff choreographer Cholly Atkins. It was a long way from the chitlin circuit to the showrooms of Las Vegas, and Berry Gordy knew this. In addition, Motown artists were "trained not to give interviews of substance; for years, almost nothing about Motown—from the roles of its executives to the names of its musicians—was general knowledge."[44]

As Motown's success grew, the artists and songwriters, despite the thrill of fame and notoriety, began wondering when they would reap the financial rewards as they were kept at modest weekly retainers. It was the beginning of questioning Motown's true intent.

Funk Brothers in the Orchestra

They worked in the shadows, making records so America could dance. The Motown studio band, known as the Funk Brothers, brought a distinctive rhythmic groove to the songs that turned young vocalists into stars. They toiled in the Motown recording studio basement at 2648 West Grand Boulevard, known as the snake pit, and not until years had passed were they ever credited for their work on the albums. Session musicians like pianist Earl Van Dyke, legendary electric bassist James Jamerson, drummer Benny Benjamin, and many others played on countless Motown hits for five, seven, and ten dollars per session, far less than the fifty-two-dollar union scale in Detroit. Through their inventiveness, the Funk Brothers discovered the bass lines, grooves, riffs, and melodic hooks that made the Motown sound and brought the music alive. The Funk Brothers were an essential and unsung group in the Motown musical assembly line.

Motown's musical synergy of drums, bass, tambourine, guitar, keyboard, and horns was topped off with a sweetening process, adding orchestral strings, woodwinds, and brass from the Detroit Symphony, giving the records a crossover appeal. Seeking commercial success, Berry Gordy realized that the white pop mainstream related to the smooth string sounds on a Frank Sinatra record. By combining that with a rhythmic underpinning, Motown created a sound that young Blacks and whites would buy—the sound of young America.

Despite the massive popularity of the Beatles, Rolling Stones, and other British invasion groups, their music was generally not ideal for dancing. Motown and soul *seized* the beat, bringing the groove forward, mixing the records to sound impressive on car and transistor radios. The Funk Brothers took potentially great songs to a new level. If you were a live band playing for dancing in the '60s, you had to play Motown; even the Beatles did. By 1970, the Funk Brothers finally began to receive album credit, but it was too little too late. Berry Gordy, without notice, moved to Hollywood, stranding his employees. The 2002 documentary *Standing in the Shadows of Motown* rightfully told the Funk Brothers stories—greatness revealed.

Padlocks and Legacies

Success often turns back on itself, sowing the seeds of its own destruction. By 1967, after seven years of hit records, "the old Motown family began to wither away, as dissension, over-blown egos, lawsuits, and pressure from an industry that began to exploit Motown's own methods, hacked away at its roots."[45] Stars such as Martha Reeves and Mary Wells, along with the Holland, Dozier, and Holland songwriters who gave Motown its sonic identity, left the label with litigation following in their wake, feeling underappreciated and economically unrewarded. Berry Gordy's statement that "some of these artists would be waiting tables somewhere if there hadn't been a place in Detroit to recognize their talents"[46] remains revealing. Over time, recognition had turned into exploitation. Motown's total artistic and contractual control produced massive profits with little risk. "In this respect, Berry Gordy was not a black business innovator, but with obvious forethought, maintained the unbalanced relationships between black artists and record companies Whites had already established."[47]

With the door padlocked and a note indicating an abrupt move to California, Berry Gordy, accompanied by Diana Ross, was gone. There would be great Motown records in the future from Marvin Gaye, Stevie Wonder, Michael Jackson, and others, but the label would never be the same. Even Gordy's attempts at breaking into the Hollywood film industry fell short over time. The magic was gone.

Musical legacies in the recording industry often end up as either vacant lots or padlocked doors. Soul, Stax, and Motown are stories of people working together, creating something far greater than any one individual could possibly imagine. Their legacy is a pillar of America's music culture.

We may remember that as we hear Otis Redding singing "Sittin' on the Dock of the Bay."

John Coltrane: Soul Explorer

Music connects the spirit and the soul. Jazz composers Duke Ellington and Mary Lou Williams wrote their masses with the idea that music is a healing force for good. Although jazz had initially been a dance music, a few musicians explored a higher realm. John Coltrane was the ultimate jazz explorer and an inspiring musical giant, a soul man cut from a different cloth.

Since the 1930s swing era, the saxophone had become the sexy lead instrument of jazz. The instrument's stature rose with the evolutionary work of Coleman Hawkins, Lester Young, and the modern innovations of Charlie Parker. The tenor saxophone spanned a range of color and emotion, and like Lester Young himself, it was cool. "A saxophone has always been a symbol of power with me ever since the days I first sat chilling and rocking to things like John Coltrane's Africa/Brass while staring in awe at the pictures of the man on the jacket, awash in yellow and purple lights blowing the truest testament in history through that big bonking horn."[48]

John Coltrane was a rising jazz star in the '50s who was hindered by his addictions, and he knew it. His 1957 spiritual awakening led him to a clean life at age thirty and, along with it, the clarity of mind to envision his ultimate purpose. Coltrane said, "The main thing a musician would like to do, is give a picture to the listener of the many wonderful things he knows of and sees in the universe."[49]

Although his life would end prematurely at age forty in 1967, John Coltrane became a towering musical figure in the turbulent context of American life, offering music to heal the soul. A quiet man, Coltrane spoke forcefully in his compositions such as "Afro Blue" or in a meditative state in "Alabama," composed after the 1963 Birmingham church bombing that killed four young Black girls. "In the day, not so long ago, when he played, he stood before his audiences like an earnest black knight intent on blowing away evil spirits with an unrelenting sound that seared the consciousness of those who came to listen."[50]

A creative artist confronts the stark challenge and reality of either forging their own path or following those made by others. It is clear that John Coltrane, in his younger years, a disciple of Charlie Parker, made many critical realizations in his work with the bop innovator Thelonius Monk. Coltrane likened the experience to "falling down an elevator shaft." "Monk kept insisting that musicians must keep working at stretching themselves, at going beyond their limitations, which were artificial limitations that came from having standards of what can, and what cannot be done on an instrument."[51] Working with Monk taught Coltrane the importance of seeking his own way and thus, to find himself. Coltrane's musical legacy is documented in his recordings which are astonishing for their breadth over less than a decade. Critic Nat Hentoff wrote, "It is clear that Coltrane was one of the most persistent, relentless expanders of possibility—all kinds of possibility: textural, emotional, harmonic, and spiritual—in jazz history."[52] He practiced incessantly and went at his music, as drummer Jimmy Cobb once said, "like a man who knew he didn't have much time." The Coltrane quartet's bassist, Jimmy Garrison, recalled, "He was the sort of man who was always learning, always practicing between sets. He was one big piece of music and he knew there had to be more roads to cover."[53]

In his 1964 landmark recording *A Love Supreme,* John Coltrane expands song forms and boundaries by the sheer persuasive force of his preacher-like tone. The work sounds like a man praying through the saxophone, similar to his dramatic '63 recording of "Alabama." Coltrane united his spirituality with the notes that burst forth, leaving a lasting impression on the listener. "'A Love Supreme,' an extended four-part jazz 'prayer' without words that became one of his most famous recorded works, grew out of his nonsectarian spirituality and was dedicated to the God in which he believed."[54] Unlike many modern jazz musicians, Coltrane, during his middle period, was concerned with establishing a connection with his audience. "I never even thought about whether or not they understand what I'm doing.... The emotional reaction is all that matters—as long as there's some feeling of communication, it isn't necessary to be understood."[55]

Coltrane's exploratory music provided a new horizon and served as inspiration for musicians of diverse styles. "'My Favorite Things' and then 'A Love Supreme,' in particular, turned rock musicians on to Coltrane."[56] The Allman Brothers drummer, Jaimoe, once told me that he "brought two jazz albums for the band to hear—'My Favorite Things' and Miles Davis's 'Kind of Blue.'" Taken and inspired by the music, the recording changed the Allman Brothers' direction by turning them toward extended, jazzlike improvisation. Without premeditated intent or calculation, John Coltrane now connected with the world of rock. "Certain qualities of Coltrane's playing spoke to the intensity of rock music—the force of his playing in long, legato lines could be more easily approximated with an electric guitar and amplifier on a high-gain setting."[57]

Like the Allman Brothers, the San Francisco–based Warlocks, later to be named the Grateful Dead, were a rock band open to jazz and world music influences, and it was their bassist, Phil Lesh, who introduced them to the music of John Coltrane. "In 1964, the Warlocks, Lesh and Garcia's electric blues band, started playing elongated jams in performance. Lesh had urged the band members to listen closely to Coltrane's music to see how he took songs like 'A Love Supreme,' reduced them to a one-chord vamp for a long middle section, then exploded them into a long-form performance."[58] It should be noted this was a considerable simplification of the Indian Hindustani classical music form, but it undeniably opened new possibilities in rock.

John Coltrane, influenced by the music of his friend, master Indian sitarist Ravi Shankar, was having a spiritual impact that extended to live rock band performances and their audiences. The long jam in-the-moment improvisations of rock groups, heard on FM radio, were unlike the Beatles and other pop groups who performed their mainstream hit singles like their recordings. David Crosby, then a member of the Byrds, was also mesmerized by the strength and velocity of Coltrane's approach. "Eight Miles High," recorded twice by the Byrds in December 1965, and January 1966, intimated Coltrane's modalism—both in its introduction, a short twelve-string guitar solo over a drone, and its frequent middle section solo. Later in 1966, the Doors extrapolated from Coltrane's "Olé" when they recorded "Light My Fire."[59] Even the Stooges singer Iggy Pop was influenced by the physical force and magnitude of John Coltrane.

The 16th Street Baptist Church, site of the 1963 bombing that killed four African American girls. This inspired the song "Alabama" by jazz saxophonist John Coltrane.

His death left a considerable hole in the music world. John Coltrane's art, though it became extremely dissonant toward the end of his career and was summarily dismissed by many critics as being "anti-jazz," left an enduring legacy that resonates to this day. "I think that like all real artists, he spoke of matters of the spirit, of those things by which the soul of man survives."[60] The program for a Coltrane-themed 1975 town hall concert in New York City stated in its program, "But beyond the technical explorations is the soul. It was the soul of the man and his music that came through then and will continue to reach out forever."[61]

Desiring to be a force for good, the ever-searching jazz explorer John Coltrane completed his mission. Churches in San Francisco and in the suburbs of Paris worship to his music.

Over a half century later, in equally divisive and cynical times, his sound, like a beacon from a far-off lighthouse, shines on.

6

Bob Dylan
and the American Voice

A young nation struggles to find its identity. Folk music is an all-encompassing art that includes hillbilly, Appalachian Mountain music, rural and urban blues, cowboy, pro-union, hobo, military, and left-wing propaganda. The music appealed to a college-age audience in '50s postwar America. The natural, acoustic sound of groups like the Weavers stood apart from a decade of plastic advertising and consumerism, providing a countervoice to the politics of Joseph McCarthy and the Communist scare. Out of the folk group the Weavers came Pete Seeger, who led the music into a newfound popularity, an antidote to Elvis and rock and roll.

Coffeehouses emerged in Greenwich Village, Cambridge, Massachusetts, Dinkytown in Minneapolis, and Old Town in Chicago. Through the '50s, jazz gave way to folk singers. Up-and-coming folkies signed up to perform a short set, tried out new material, and passed the hat for tips, oftentimes their only compensation. The folk scene offered "espresso and existential doubt."[1] There was no glitter, glamour, or show business involved.

Music of the small-scale folk community emphasized lyrics, stories, and ideas in song, sans the big beat drums of rock and roll. "By 1960, the folk music revival that began in the fifties had expanded into an all-inclusive smorgasbord, with kitschy imitation folk groups at one end, resurrected cigar box guitarists, and Ozark balladeers on the other."[2] The legendary folk singer Woody Guthrie was a godlike figure for folk inspiration, while Pete Seeger served as an organizer and guiding light. Folk venues expanded nationwide with the inception of the Newport Folk Festival in 1959, Club 47 in Cambridge, and the breakthrough success of Joan Baez in 1960. The blues singer Lightnin' Hopkins could be heard in Greenwich Village bars and coffeehouses. The opening of Israel Young's Folklore Center, at 110 MacDougal Street, provided

The confirmed gravesite of Robert Johnson, Little Zion M.B. Church, Money Road, Leflore County, Mississippi.

a community of folk musicians with a place to sing, swap songs, and belong. Musicians sang for free in Washington Square Park, a scene where both artists and the audience were engaged in a process of musical discovery. Pop and rock music addressed teenage concerns—dancing, cars, and romance; folk songs were viewed as authentic, genuine, bohemian, and counterculture. Songs such as Woody Guthrie's "This Land Is Your Land" and Pete Seeger and Lee Hays's "If I Had a Hammer" were standard repertoire, but in the air was a creative tension, something was about to break. He would go by the name Bob Dylan.

The Midwest is more than flyover country. It was in the American heartland that Bob Zimmerman was born on May 24, 1941, in the mining town of Hibbing, Minnesota. It was a typically small midwestern town, with a main street filled with privately owned businesses on both sides that thrived until years later, the internet and shopping malls would drive many of them out. His father, Abraham, ran a furniture and appliance business, while his mother, Beatrice, held a clerical position at a department store.

He was a stranger in a strange land. Growing up in Hibbing, Bob Zimmerman never seemed to fit in. "My father was the best man in the world and probably worth a hundred of me, but he didn't understand me. The town he lived in and the town I lived in were not the same."[3] I met a woman from Hibbing who knew the Zimmerman family, and she told me, "Bob was rather strange."

It was clear from the beginning that Bob Zimmerman was a reader, thinker, and above all, an intense listener. His diverse musical interests included Woody Guthrie, Odetta, Leadbelly, Duke Ellington, Charlie Parker, Thelonius Monk, Hank Williams, and Homer and Jethro. But it was the analytical, meticulous way that Bob listened which ultimately made the difference. "I took the songs apart and unzipped it," he once said of Robert Johnson's music. "It was the form, free verse association, the structure that gave it a cutting edge."[4]

When rock and roll began a stagnant period in the late '50s, an interest in folk music grew as an authentic and genuine musical expression. It was here that Bob Zimmerman sought his inspiration from Buddy Holly and Hank Williams to the rebellious film image of James Dean. "Young Bobby Zimmerman was bad enough, though, stealing folk records from a collector friend in the name of being a 'musical expeditionary.'" Television host Steve Allen asked Dylan if he sang his own material or other people's. He replies, "They're all mine now."[5] Seeking a new identity, he changed his name to Bob Dylan.

The writer Ellen Willis noted that "so skillfully had Dylan distilled the forms and moods of traditional music that his originality took time to register."[6] The mark of an artist is their ability to be a sponge, absorbing diverse influences while turning them into a personal toolbox. Dylan, enamored with Woody Guthrie's autobiography, "Bound for Glory," realized the nomadic life was the one he sought, the road ahead. It changed his life. "For me it was an epiphany, like some heavy anchor had just plunged into the waters of the harbor. A voice in my head said, 'So this is the game.'"[7] By January 1961, the road for Bob Dylan led to New York City.

It was an exciting time to be young. In the early '60s, Greenwich Village was a place of low rents that offered an affordable bohemian lifestyle budding with opportunity for newly arrived folk singers. Gerde's Folk City opened in 1960 and numerous other coffeehouses followed. In that same year, California's Joan Baez had the first major folk hit recording by a woman; the future looked promising. Folk clubs offered singers an opportunity to perform traditional repertoire and original compositions, providing a place to get your act together and find your voice.

The traditionally tight-knit folk community welcomed the newly named arrival Bob Dylan. There was an innocent, quirky, worldly, and mysterious air about a young man who changed his stories regarding his origins with the shifting of the wind. "Not since Rimbaud said, 'I is another,' has an artist been so obsessed with escaping an identity."[8] Bob

Dylan arrived in town, slept on various folk musicians' sofas, and began sitting in at various Greenwich Village nightspots. He remained elusive but compelling, a young artist with an indefinable presence. Dylan visited Woody Guthrie, suffering from Huntington's chorea, at Guthrie's hospital bedside. The concept of writing topical songs to traditional folk melodies was passed along from mentor to student—a future vehicle for Bob Dylan.

He approached music first as a writer. Dylan's research at the New York Public Library indicated his ink blotter method of absorbing influences, then transforming them into his singular voice. This started him on the path to a new level of lyric writing. Like a modern-day Walt Whitman, Dylan said, "I started reading articles in newspapers on microfilm from 1855 to 1865 to see what daily life was like.... After a while you became aware of nothing but a culture of feeling, of black days, of schism, evil for evil, the common destiny of the human being getting thrown off course."[9] He began performing at the Village Gaslight in 1961 for sixty dollars per week. Word spread about his fresh songs and unique point of view. Listening to English folk songs, he wrote, "Girl from the North Country," the melody from the traditional folk song "Nottamun Town" became Dylan's "Masters of War." "Maybe I'm nothing but all things I soak up."[10]

Many white folk singers became enamored with Black, country blues artists such as Son House, Skip James, Big Bill Broonzy, Robert Johnson, and the Rev. Gary Davis, among others, and they often fell into the trap of emulating them. Bob Dylan wisely stayed with his drawling, Guthrie-like sound. "When he sang about lynchings and assassinations, he was joining the movement, but in this period and in these performances, he avoided phrasing out of African-American vernacular. It would have been an untoward imitation."[11]

Dylan's most popular song, "Blowin' in the Wind," was written in 1962, an adaptation of the Negro spiritual "No More Auction Black for Me." Far more famous at the time, the folk trio Peter, Paul, and Mary recorded Dylan's song, setting a major success in motion. "Their recording sold a million copies, inspired more than fifty other versions, and established topical songs as the most important development of the folk revival."[12] Decades later, Dylan would explain that "if you sang 'John Henry' as many times as me—'John Henry was steel-driving man, driving with a hammer in his hand, John Henry said a man ain't nothing but a man,'" he said. "If you sang that song as many times as I did, you would have written 'How many roads must a man walk down,' too."[13]

Dylan's early work continued to be heavily influenced by Woody Guthrie, William Blake, and his girlfriend at the time, Suze Rotolo, a civil rights activist. His work displayed a "dark tone, rhythmic verve, a mercurial point of view, carelessness and verbosity."[14] "He soon grew out of using other writer's melodies and conceptual ideas. He was still learning from Woody Guthrie, but he often substituted despair for Guthrie's resilience."[15]

Like a phantom, Bob Dylan would soon slip away from the Greenwich Village scene, outgrowing everything around him. "Bob Dylan as an identifiable persona has been disappearing into his songs, which is what he wants. This terrifies his audience.... Instead of an image, Dylan has created a magic theater in which the public gets lost willy-nilly."[16] Dylan's ambitions were apparent; he was ready to move on. "I was greatly influenced by Dave van Ronk. He'd tower over MacDougal Street like a mountain but would never break into the big time."[17] Bob Dylan would become that mountain.

There are few who are blessed with the gift of discovery. John Hammond was easily popular music's foremost talent scout of the twentieth century. Coming from Vanderbilt family wealth, his liberal views pushed him into a lifelong agenda: finding authentic American artists and championing unsung Negro talent, while facilitating racial integration whenever possible. Hammond's discoveries read like a who's who in popular music, from Billie Holiday and Aretha Franklin to Bob Dylan and Bruce Springsteen. Robert Shelton's favorable *New York Times* review of Dylan led Hammond, a record producer at Columbia Records, to the young folk singer. Columbia Records had regretted missing the opportunity of signing Joan Baez. Hammond was determined not to make that mistake again. Far more than a record executive motivated by profits, the easygoing Hammond was both a mentor and friend to Dylan, giving him a copy of Columbia's 1961 release "Robert Johnson: King of the Delta Blues." Dylan, in his typically analytic manner, took Johnson's haunting, visionary songs apart, dissecting them to see how they worked. "I copied Johnson's words down on scraps of paper so I could closely examine the lyrics and patterns."[18]

Signing Dylan to a major label contract was a gutsy move on John Hammond's part. After hearing his singing voice, Dylan was mocked at Columbia Records as being "Hammond's Folly." Conservative musical tastes leaned toward pretty-sounding vocalists in the early '60s. A "singer" meant Barbara Streisand, Joan Baez, Andy Williams, and Johnny Mathis, not the twang of Bob Dylan, who even admitted, "My style was too erratic and hard to pigeonhole for the radio, and songs, to me, were more important than just light entertainment."[19]

In the air hung a sense that things were about to be blown apart. Bob Dylan moved beyond the folk music expectations of standard songs like "If I Had a Hammer," "This Land Is Your Land," and "Waltzing Matilda." Dylan was armed with something else. "I always thought that one man, the lone balladeer with the guitar, could blow an entire army off the stage, if he knew what he was doing."[20] Taking his cue from Woody Guthrie, Dylan combined modern-day issues (civil rights, the Bay of Pigs, etc.) with new melodies and chords in his songs. They would be labeled "protest songs," but Dylan disagreed with the term. "I tried to explain that I didn't think I was a protest singer."[21]

By his second album, Bob Dylan set a course that would impact American popular music, eroding the walls that had traditionally existed between literature and popular song. "In the course of writing and performing them, he has changed everyone's expectations of the kind of complexity and meaning that popular songs could deliver."[22] Bob Dylan's formidable talent, driving work ethic, and considerable ambition would lead modern music in yet untold ways. "I did come from a long-ways off and had started a long ways down. But now destiny was about to manifest itself. I felt like it was looking right at me and nobody else."[23] Walking down MacDougal Street and out into the wider world, his time had come.

That world was spinning faster than ever between fall of 1962 and summer of '63. Like cards stacked on each other, the Cuban missile crisis, civil rights, the women's movement, ecology, and the '63 March on Washington presented a need for music that would define the times. Bob Dylan songs such as "Blowin' in the Wind," "The Times They Are A-changin'," "Only a Pawn in Their Game," and "Masters of War" resonated with a young, anxiety-ridden audience deeply concerned for the country's future and the impact on their personal destiny. Dylan was either passionately singing about world issues or making a calculated effort to meet public demand. In an interview with Nat Hentoff, Dylan said, "I have to make a new song out of what I know and out of what I'm feeling."[24] Dylan felt an ever-increasing pressure from the poet-prophet mantle pushed on him by the media and adopted by his avid, demanding fans. Ironically, Dylan privately "proclaimed to his friends that he was non-political, and that he was flabbergasted as the rest of us by his newfound fame and growing reputation as a guru of the coming counter-culture."[25]

By the '63 Newport Folk Festival, Dylan's prophet pedestal was in place. The onstage introduction/proclamation was, "And here he is.... Take him, you know him, he's yours.... Bob Dylan." It was the start of a merry-go-round success that was spinning out of control. His understandable reluctance in becoming the spokesperson of a generation and the immense weight that went with it was deeply resented by his loyal folk audience. "Many people hate Bob Dylan because they hate being fooled ... for Bob Dylan has exploited his image as a vehicle for artistic statements. Phil Ochs had predicted that Dylan might someday be assassinated by a fan.... Alan Lomax had once remarked that Dylan might develop into a great poet of the times, unless he killed himself first."[26] It was Ochs who committed suicide in 1976. Despite his growing popularity, Dylan found gigs hard to come by in the early stage of his career. He would need a boost from somewhere. Before establishing himself as the greatest songwriter of his generation, he would need a little help from his friend and future lover Joan Baez.

It was a powerful image. The performers locked hands onstage at the 1963 Newport Folk Festival, singing, "We Shall Overcome." The photo image became a symbol of the connection between the civil rights movement and the soundtrack provided by folk music. Bob Dylan and Joan Baez became the musically and romantically linked prince and queen of their era. Dylan wrote the songs that were uplifted on the wave of Baez's great success. "Finally, the Old Guard must have thought, a brilliantly talented and creative and charismatic youngster who could bring their own message of social justice to a larger audience."[27]

Joan Baez brought Dylan on her concert tours, championing his music and message at a time when the general public was still unsure of the rough-hewn sound of his voice: "My audience didn't like it, they didn't want this scruffy little guy out there, singing off key."[28] Dylan sounded better when he sang duets with Baez. "Baez gave Dylan class, and Bob gave Joan sex appeal.... They both sounded like teenagers again."[29]

Baez was responsible for Dylan reaching a wider audience by offering her seal of approval. Without that support, he might have remained a first-rate composer and a performer of midrange notoriety. There is a lot to be said for glamour. Comedian Mort Sahl referred to the couple as the "Liz Taylor and Dick Burton of the self-righteous set."[30] At their 1964 Philharmonic Hall concert in New York City, they were at the top of their game, but the strings that held Baez and Dylan would slowly come apart. Ironically, Baez began moving to songs of social issues, while Dylan moved away from them and the poet-prophet moniker that came with it.

Robert Shelton, in the *New York Times*, called Bob Dylan the "brilliant singing poet laureate of young America."[31] But the ever-restless poet, playing harder and more rhythmically on his acoustic guitar, was tiring of being a solo artist. He was hearing something else—the sound of an electric troubadour.

It was an interesting scenario. The compositional process that

Bob Dylan used for his album *Bringing It All Back Home* included his spreading dozens of images from newspaper and magazine clippings on the floor as he gazed down on them, seated on a chair with his guitar. Bernard Paturel observed that "Bob would start with a simple musical framework, a blues pattern that he could repeat indefinitely, and he would close his eyes—he would not draw from the pictures literally but would use the impression the faces left as a visual model for kaleidoscopic language.... When something came out that he liked, he scrawled it down hurriedly, so as to stay in the moment, and he would do this until there were enough words written for a song."[32] Dylan's intuitive way of songwriting enabled a spontaneous, creative process. Later on, he observed that "as you get older, you get smarter and that can hinder you because you try to gain control over the creative impulses.... If your mind is intellectually in the way, it will stop you."[33]

Bob Dylan composed "Mr. Tambourine Man" on a cross-country driving trip, influenced by Mardi Gras in New Orleans. Listening to the radio as he traveled, Dylan was stunned by the electricity of hearing the Beatles' first American releases. Feeling trapped by the folk audience's need to hear songs of social justice from voice and acoustic guitar, the impact would jolt him. Barry Kornfeld said, "All people wanted to hear from him were finger-pointing songs. He didn't want to do that anymore."[34] Dylan had tired of his role as a solo folk performer. He saw the Beatles as a major new musical development; it was time for a change. He turned away from topical issues and began writing songs that dealt with his own life. Some would view this as the beginning of the singer-songwriter trend that would gain traction in the 1970s.

After hearing the Beatles and seeing them perform live, Bob Dylan began experimenting with an electric guitar, desiring to hear his music in a bigger, louder, and fuller group context. Working quickly without rehearsal and often recording in one or two takes, his new brushstrokes were quick and in the moment. Similar to Miles Davis, who four or five years later would combine jazz with funk beats laden with electric instruments, Bob Dylan pursued a hybrid of folk mixed with rock elements, saying, "The folk music scene had been like a paradise that I had to leave, like Adam had to leave the garden. It was just too perfect."[35] Stylists in music work within defined margins; innovators disrupt by breaking through a wall of perceived limitations.

Dylan moved from refined folk songs to a rough, electric energy with all its sharp edges. His legendary 1965 performance at the Newport Folk Festival, viewed by 15,000 people, was widely misjudged due to an inadequate sound system. It was a landmark event in American music, a changing of the guard. Suddenly the hyphen between folk and

rock, formerly worlds apart, was in place and a new form had been created. Dylan belted out "Maggie's Farm" as a send-off to a folk world that
had demanded conformity and loyalty. He had closed the gap between
poetry and the electricity of rock, worlds colliding. Many would harshly
disapprove, seeing Dylan's new style as sloppy, disorganized, and a sellout. He was despondent after the reception to his Newport performance, yet determined. "He didn't look like a guy who thought he had
very much to celebrate."[36] Bob Dylan would hit the road hard and musically press on. In doing so, he would reach a wider audience, influence
a generation of folk musicians to form bands, and pay the cost of fame.

Popularity breeds contempt. Dylan began working with the Hawks,
later to become the Band, and his feeling regarding the folk scene
became clear: "Folk music is a bunch of fat people."[37] His song "Positively
4th Street" is a put-down in song, a goodbye to a past life in Greenwich
Village. Bob Dylan was thrown into the turbulent and chaotic world of
rock stardom and all its perils. D.A. Pennebaker's documentary *Don't
Look Back* portrays Dylan as rock star, hunted by U.K. press and aggressive fans. They are dark images. Dylan looks sickly, sullen, and somewhat fearful of all that surrounds him. The distance between him and
former lover Joan Baez is palpable. "Bobby's rise had happened so fast
that he was hotter than I was, and he didn't need me anymore. It was a
big slap in the face."[38]

The folk community that had supported Dylan was, for the most
part, irate concerning the "new" Bob Dylan. Irwin Silber, editor of
the folk magazine *Sing Out,* criticized him for turning his back on the
folk scene that had been instrumental in his rise to stardom. Dylan
explained that "what I did to break away was to take simple folk changes
and put new imagery and attitude to them."[39] Baez was incredulous: "I
have never understood how he could suddenly change, as if everything
he had done before had never really happened."[40] With his many gifts,
Bob Dylan was caught between his alleged "betrayal" from folk purists
and an expanded audience attracted to his electric and more accessible
sound. "Dylan was like, 'Look all you want, you'll never see me,"[41] said
the folk musician Mitch Greenhill.

Performing live, the audience responded intensely to his new direction. Robbie Robertson of the Band noted, "They booed, chanted, and
hissed, sometimes they even charged the stage or threw things at us.
We were in the middle of a rock and roll revolution, either the audience was right, or we were right."[42] Dylan was uninterested in becoming a polished performer. He strongly disliked the "folk-rock" label that
was applied to his music. Most musical genres are labeled by writers and
critics, not by the artists who birth them. He had shocked an audience

who thought they knew him. "Then Dylan yanked the rug, he renounced political protest." "My Back Pages" scoffed at his previous moral absolutism; Dylan had been older, but his new self was younger than he had previously been.[43]

As Dylan toured relentlessly with the Hawks, his fame and ego rose. "He has become so unbelievably unmanageable that I can't stand to be around him,"[44] said Joan Baez. The former couple had grown in opposite directions: Baez turned outward, embracing themes of social justice; Dylan moved inward toward cynicism. "I asked him [Dylan] what made us different, and he said it was simple, that I thought I could change things, and he knew that no one could."

Returning from his triumphant U.K. tour, Dylan, ill and exhausted, wrote "Like a Rolling Stone," a number one hit. Now everyone around the world could sing along, which they did, to his distinctive snarl. "Every day it seemed that Bob's fame was growing exponentially. A lot more people were trying to get a piece of him."[45] The halcyon days would soon be over. By the mid–'60s, the folk music movement dwindled and musicians moved from Greenwich Village to Laurel Canyon in Los Angeles and San Francisco. Instead of solo acts, they became bands— Buffalo Springfield, Flying Burrito Brothers, Crosby, Stills, Nash and Young, and the Byrds. Bob Dylan, who had grown up on '50s rock, had led music in a new direction. Richard Farina said, "Folk music, through no fault of its own, fooled us into certain sympathies and nostalgic alliances with the so-called traditional past."[46]

As Dylan's fame grew, he pushed himself into a grueling tour schedule while his health spiraled downward. His manager, Albert Grossman, did little to curb Dylan's increasing drug use. "Albert's benevolence was insidious, he was not into excess himself, but he encouraged it in his clients.... He made sure his clients had anything and everything they wanted, which made them all the more dependent on him."[47] This is a sadly typical form of music entertainment management practices. Running from his clinging fans, Dylan and his young family moved to Woodstock, New York, but there was no place to hide and little peace. "Goons were breaking into our place all hours of the night. Everything was wrong. It was backing me into a corner.... Whatever the counter-culture was, I'd seen enough of it."[48]

Bob Dylan's July 29, 1966, motorcycle accident kept him off the road for a year and a half. In some ways, it may have been a lifesaver. His accident enabled him to collaborate with the Band and forge ahead in new musical directions. *Bringing It All Back Home* (1965), *Highway 61 Revisited* (1965), and *Blonde on Blonde* (1966) are considered masterworks of Dylan's best period. "As a composer, interpreter, most of all as a lyricist, Dylan has made a revolution. He expanded the folk idiom into a rich, figurative language, grafted literary and philosophical subtleties on the protest song, revitalized folk vision by rejecting proletarian and ethnic sentimentality, then all but destroyed pure folk as a contemporary form by merging it with pop."[49]

An artist's choices make all the difference. When the Beatles' *Sgt. Pepper's Lonely Hearts Club Band* album was released in 1967, it was played everywhere—you could hear it coming from car radios, stores, apartment windows, and local bars. Popular music turned right toward a sophisticated, thematically conceived art rock. Seeing the pretension in this, Bob Dylan turned left, rejecting pop's slick, excessive production. His music became more rural, basic, and country in his December 1967 release, *John Wesley Harding*. Dylan knew when to be influenced by the Beatles and when to walk away. "Dylan's basic rapport with reality has also saved him from the excesses of pop, kept him from merging, Warhol-like, into his public surface."[50] As the world searched for another Sgt. Pepper's, Dylan's album, named after a Texas outlaw and misspelled, was critically acclaimed and a commercial hit.

Conclusion

It has been a long, never-ending road for Bob Dylan. He was awarded the Nobel Prize for Literature in 2016 for "having created new poetic expressions within the great American song tradition." This award was greeted with controversy and discussion. In his autobiography, Dylan writes, "I really was never more than what I was—a folk musician who gazed into the gray mist with tear-blinded eyes and made songs that floated in a luminous haze."[51]

His art is full of contradictions. Sean Wilentz explains that "Dylan, an artist, steals what he loves and then loves what he steals by making it new."[52] Joni Mitchell has stronger views: "Bob is not authentic at all. He's a plagiarist, and his name and voice are fake. Everything about Bob is a deception."[53] Controversy aside, it is the way Dylan merges words and music that stands out. "His strength as a musician is his formidable eclecticism combined with a talent for choosing the right music to go with a given lyric. The result is a unity of sound and word that eludes most of his imitators."[54]

He remains a cultural presence long after his mid–'60s fame due to his constant artistic growth. Dylan is part of the American experience he read about in newspaper clippings from the 1860s. "By combining African-American blues, white country music, rural folk music,

Road outside of Po Monkey's Lounge, Merigold, Mississippi, one of the few remaining juke joints.

imagist poetry and rock and roll, Dylan created a new musical and literary form, both popular and serious at the same time."[55] This form is a panoramic, cross-country view of America, created by living up to individual, not audience, expectations. Ian Bell writes, "The music's enduring effect on the culture was in precise parallel to American literature's long struggle to find itself, to escape the grip of English tradition, to speak of America with an American voice."[56] His work spreads like the open road where he remains. "His has been an example not only to songwriters but to fiction writers, playwrights, poets, and filmmakers, constant proof that this culture in all its contradictions, is still there to be claimed yet again, seen anew, through the agency of the human heart and imagination."[57]

In his 2012 South by Southwest keynote address, Bruce Springsteen said, "If you were young in the '60s and '50s, everything felt false everywhere you turned. But you didn't know how to say it. There was no language for it at the time. It just felt fucked up, you know? But you didn't have the words. Bob came along and gave us those words, he gave us those songs. And, and the first thing he asked you was: 'How does it feel? Man, how does it feel to be on your own?' And if you were a kid in 1965, you were on your own, because your parents, God bless them, they could not understand the incredible changes that were taking place. You were on your own. Without a home. He gave us the words to understand our hearts."[58]

Unlike many '60s pop and rock icons who burned out like shooting stars, Bob Dylan remains, a survivor who understands his journey as a marathon, not a sprint, as Woody Guthrie did before him.

"The road would be treacherous, and I didn't know where it would lead, but I followed it anyway. I went straight into it. It was wide open."[59]

7

Beatles, Stones, and Cultural Amnesia

When the times get ready, you've got to move. After World War II, British and American youth sought a separate identity from their parents. The need that burned in the newly invented concept of the teenager would move mountains. American middle-class families enjoyed unprecedented prosperity that powered the '50s into the dream of owning a suburban home. Dad went to work. Mom maintained the house, while the kids took off on their Schwinn bicycles and returned for supper.

Britain was not so lucky. The country had been decimated by the war and the Nazi Luftwaffe. In the United States, the children played in a park; in England, it was a former bombsite, rubble by another name. Poor diets due to persistent postwar rationing resulted in skinny, underfed children with bad teeth, lacking adequate fruit and vegetables. Everything was scarce—meat was a luxury and anything acquired was precious. George Harrison recalled that getting a cup of sugar was difficult and so too were rock and roll records. "There was also the sense, particularly in Europe, that things needed to be new.... The old world had destroyed itself in 1945, so there was no point looking at the past, kids weren't interested in their parent's ideology and taste."[1]

Never underestimate the cultural power of a seaport. Liverpool, like New Orleans, reached out to diverse, imported influences. "It was a cosmopolitan port with musical advantages [American R&B records could be heard in Liverpool whatever the metropolitan industry's successes in cleaning up white rock and roll] and unique material opportunities. Liverpool had clubs where groups were employed to play grown-up *gutsy* music."[2]

Geographic isolation can create a distinct character. Liverpool stood apart from cosmopolitan London, allowing for the growth of a separate musical scene. "Liverpool, too, felt itself segregated from the privileged Midlands and the South."[3] It was here that John Lennon, Paul McCartney, George Harrison, and Ringo Starr developed into working-class musicians. They were hearing something else. Liverpool had taste and an ear for music that made contact. "While Britain listened to Adam Faith and pop music, Liverpool listened to rhythm and blues. The Cunard Yanks were bringing over records, now to be heard outside the segregated circuits of his own country. His name was Chuck Berry: the songs he sang were wry and ragged, vividly pictorial eulogies to girls and cars, the joys and neuroses of big city American life. Those songs broke like anthems on the young of the northern city still gripped by the Victorian age, which had no truck with black people since the slave hulks set sail from Liverpool Bay."[4]

Childhood was a challenge. John Lennon lost his uncle; then his mother was killed by a drunk driver. Ringo Starr (originally Richard Starkey) suffered from poor health, while Paul McCartney's mother died suddenly of cancer when he was fourteen. George Harrison had the more stable situation—his father was a bus driver. Boyhood skiffle bands such as the Quarrymen sprouted and musical friendships began.

The timing was perfect to be young and creative in the early '60s with the emergence of British art schools. "In 1960, the kindly Macmillan Government abolished National Service. For those between sixteen and twenty-one, no obligation remained save that of spending their ever-increasing pocket money on amusements demanded by their ever-quickening glands."[5]

The English guitarist John Etheridge recalled, "It's very difficult for people now to imagine the emotional suppression that working class children in England were brought up with after the 2nd World War. Yet at the same time with the arrival of the 60s, the postwar political settlement had given these

The microphone used by Elvis Presley, Sun Studio, Memphis, Tennessee.

children [historically deprived] access to education, funding and the arts."

Art school enabled members of the Beatles, Stones, the Who, Led Zeppelin, and Eric Clapton the luxury of time to develop an artistic sensibility and awareness. This stood in stark contrast to the American educational system which offered nothing remotely similar. Art school provided time to write songs, paint, draw, act, practice guitar, and copy records of American artists who became influential teachers. To the importance of art school, Paul McCartney said, "Without that there could have been no Beatles."[6]

Musical movements start in bunkers and trenches. The Beatles performed in the seedy clubs of Liverpool and Hamburg playing covers of American artists they admired. Playing six to eight hours per night for four and a half months in Germany, the band, though green and unpolished, exhibited an onstage charisma and electricity that would take them to superstardom. Early recordings of these live performances reveal a diamond in the rough. Through the din and musical naïveté is a center—a forcefield indicating something special was there.

While in Hamburg, it was their open personalities and character that drew them to the beautiful young German photographer Astrid Kirchherr. Her iconic band photos capturing the early phase of the Beatles are famous worldwide. "I became deeply impressed by their intelligence, their civility, their charm, and their immense curiosity and open mindedness.... They attracted us like magnets."[7] Her moody black-and-white shots reveal the influence of Richard Avedon's lighting but most importantly, the marrying of rock and roll to an artistic image. Her studio portraits "were big, grainy prints conjured by the girl herself from the recesses of her black satin room and showing the five Beatles as they never imagined themselves before.... Each image held its own true prophecy."[8] This European aesthetic would soon make American record album covers look embarrassingly trite in comparison. This artistic sensibility had an immense impact on rock visuals by the middle to late '60s.

You don't make it alone in music. In 1961, the Beatles met record store manager Brian Epstein, and life would soon change. It was a beginning—an assembly of smart, sensitive, and hardworking individuals behind the scenes enabling the Beatles' creativity and popularity. Here lies a distinction between American and English music management. Generally, U.S. managers, such Elvis Presley's notorious "Colonel" Tom Parker, sought dollar signs, commercial exploitation, and media saturation without a thought to artist development. Epstein, a closeted gay man at a time when homosexuality was illegal in Britain, believed in the Beatles and never interfered with their creative direction. "They weren't a business to Brian: they were a vocation, a mission in life. They were like a religion to him."[9] Brian Epstein, unlike many American talent managers who took large percentages from their artists (and some English ones as well) was "always worried that he might be taking advantage of them. He came to me once and said he wanted to give them a piece of his company. He gave them ten per cent of it, so they would get back some of the twenty-five per cent they paid him.... He was a decent, honest, average human being."[10]

So too was the Beatles producer, George Martin, who auditioned the band for Parlophone Records in June 1962. Martin, a classically trained musician, heard their rough edges and was attracted to the Lennon–McCartney vocal sound, but above all, it was their individual charm, wit, and irreverence that sold George Martin on signing them. He approached the Beatles as a facilitator who would enhance and draw out their talents, as opposed to many American pop producers who took full control, both artistic and financial, of their artists' careers. Rather than pushing tunes by other writers, Martin creatively interacted with their original songs, ultimately exploring new sonic colors and textures. The Beatles were far too creative and independent to work with an American pop music producer.

George Martin drove the Beatles in their recording debut, grinding through fourteen tracks in a thirteen-hour session. Over time, the more confident they became in the studio, the more the Beatles pushed Martin into exploring new ideas in an expanded sound spectrum. It was the fact that "the workmen taking over the factory were also the children taking over the playroom, determined to find effects that no one had thought of pulling out of the drawer before."[11]

Not since the Buddy Holly recordings of the late '50s had rock and roll been so expansively documented. Pop music in the early '60s largely consisted of sound-alike girl groups and teen idol vocalists accompanied by large orchestras. The music was homogenized, white, safe, light on the beat, while heavy on innocence, teenage romance, and sentimentality. It is little wonder that various American record labels turned down the option of distributing the Beatles, a mistake that lives in infamy. Record executive comments ranging from "You guys don't know how to make pop records" to the laughable, "Guitar groups are on the way out"[12] should be carved on a Beatles monument.

In the midst of the early '60s payola scandal, rampant institutional racism and musical snobbery prohibited the American record industry from the realization that something fresh could originate beyond their grasp. Listening to the 1962 Beatles release, "Love Me Do," displays strong '50s rock and roll influences—a rockabilly beat, Everly Brothers–style vocal harmonies, a bluesy harmonica, all driven by a Chuck Berry and Little Richard energy played with a Buddy Holly and the Crickets instrumentation. Less than a decade past, these "old," seemingly out-of-date influences sparked the early Beatles sound. They were understood by an American pop industry wanting to return to business as usual—white pop singers with orchestra in assembly line fashion.

This is why my English friends have said to me, "You Americans invented rock and roll, but we perfected it." Screaming British fans mobbed the Beatles' appearances, while the band remained unfazed by their success. Their Royal Variety Show concert in London, with the famous stage banter from John Lennon—"People in the cheaper seats, please clap. The rest of you just rattle your jewelry"—charmed Queen Elizabeth the Queen Mother, who found them "young, fresh, and vital."

Although not known as a rock critic, the Queen Mother was right. The Beatles' universal appeal to all classes would resonate beyond Britain to the wider world. "Never again would pop music be considered the prerogative only of working-class boys and girls. *With the Beatles* [the first album] was played not only in Council Houses but in West London flats, in young ladies finishing schools and in the blow-heated barns where country debutantes held their first Christmas dances."[13] Capitol Records relented in December 1963, releasing *Meet the Beatles* in America. The impact was swift and immediate. Beatles biographer Phillip Norman recalls a scene of Brian Epstein, sitting on a chair with the Beatles seated on the floor around him. "He had said the news had come through that the single, 'I Want to Hold Your Hand' was number one in the American Top Hundred. The Beatles couldn't even speak—not even John Lennon. They just sat on the floor like kittens at Brian's feet."[14] The world would soon be at their feet.

The Beatles were massive stars in the United Kingdom, while the United States hibernated in a state of stunned mourning after President John F. Kennedy's assassination in November 1963. They were painful days of disbelief. Adults with ashen faces gazed blankly into black-and-white television screens. I recall my grandmother Charlotte and I, age nine, watching in horror as Kennedy's accused assassin, Lee Harvey Oswald, was gunned down on live television. It felt as though the nation was coming apart. The air grew thick and grim. "We had been brought together in horrified spectatorship, and the sense of shared public mourning seemed to go on forever, yet it was only a matter of weeks that the phenomenally swift rise of a pop group from Liverpool became so pervasive a concern that Kennedy seemed already relegated to an archaic period in which the Beatles had not existed."[15]

They never saw it coming. When the Beatles landed at JFK Airport on February 7, 1964, their 10,000 screaming fans did. On the flight to America, George Harrison wondered aloud, "They've got everything over there. What do they want us for?"[16] Wherever the Beatles went from here on, they would take the air with them. Rock critic Lester Bangs called it "not simply a matter of music but of event."[17] Not since the appearance of Elvis Presley on the *Ed Sullivan Show* in 1956 had America experienced such a cultural explosion.

The gloom lifted when the four young men exited the plane into their first American press conference. They hadn't played one note, yet one could sense a new order emerging. Life before the Beatles would soon look dated; the world was changing from black and white to Technicolor. A harsh reality of American life is that in order to obtain the new, you must sacrifice the old. Elvis and Sinatra became legends of a bygone era, marking an older generation's youth. What was once cool is transformed into something different, if not less. The "four young men seemed more alive than their handlers, and more knowing than their fans ... professional in so obtrusive a fashion that it looked like inspired amateurism. ... When you looked at them they looked back, when they were interviewed, it was the interviewer who was on the spot."[18]

Their presence and appeal was remarkable. Combining charm, wit, naïveté, humility, and humor, the Beatles quickly won over the press. "The sum of the Beatles was greater than the parts, but the parts were so distinctive and attractive that the group itself could be all things to all people, more or less."[19] Despite the explosion of their instant fame, few Americans realized the irony. A group of British youth were returning the influence of American music to the country that had first created it. At their first press conference, the Beatles "made clear that African-American musicians were among their major influences," while the Motown star Smokey Robinson said, "The Beatles were the first white artists to ever admit that they grew up on black music."[20] The blues master Muddy Waters wisely noted of Americans, "Now they've learned it was in their backyard all the time."[21]

The Beatles knew what few Americans did—their musical roots were the catalyst that propelled their songs. Startled by their immediate success, John Lennon explained that "all they were doing was crossing the ocean to sell America's homegrown music—Chuck Berry's rock and roll, Little Richard's twist and shout—back to it."[22] The raw musical elements that pop music had eliminated in the early '60s, replaced by a homogenized sound, came alive when America met the Beatles.

Predictably, the older establishment music critics were dismayed by their success, an ominous changing of the guard. It meant a diminishing of the great American song, show tunes, and the classic work of Tin Pan Alley composers. Broadway would turn from Gershwin and Rodgers and Hart songs to *Hair* and *Godspell*. John Horn, in the *New York Herald Tribune*, wrote of the Beatles, "They're really a magic act that owes less to Britain than to Barnum." Dismissed by adults as a passing fad, it was the Beatles evolution over the next six years that proved the naysayers wrong. Their film director, Richard Lester, who worked with them on their first two full-length movies, said, "I think they're on to something, they are more inclined to blow away the cobwebs than my contemporaries."[23]

When Hollywood called, previous superstar Elvis Presley was coerced into trite roles that degraded his rock and roll–rebel image, turning him into a pandering pop star for the masses. This was not the case with the Beatles. Their 1965 film, *A Hard Day's Night*, enhanced their charismatic qualities, despite a weak plot. What the '50s movie *Rock around the Clock* was to teenagers, *A Hard Day's Night* was to '60s youth. The audio and visual impact of this movie in a theater equipped with a large sound system, instead of small TV, record player, or transistor radio speakers, made for a sensory experience. "I emerged from *A Hard Day's Night* as from a conversion experience.... I came out as a member of a generation, sharing a common repertoire with a sea of contemporaries, strangers who suddenly felt like family."[24] This artfully done, film noir release once again exhibited the European aesthetic. Instead of Elvis reciting stilted dialogue, singing with a ukulele on a beach to bikini-clad girls, you got devil-may-care Brits delivering a one-two musical and comedic punch.

The film critics were impressed. Andrew Sarris, in the *Village Voice*, wrote, "The open field helicopter shot sequence of the Beatles on a spree is one of the most exhilarating expressions of high spirits I have ever seen on screen.... I like the Beatles in this moment in film history not merely because they mean something but rather because they express effectively a great many aspects of modernity that have converged inspiredly in their personalities."[25]

One thing leads to another. Although the media had taken favor with them, the Beatles, as the most popular touring act in the world during their middle period of 1964–1966, encountered an unprecedented degree of chaotic public attention. They toured the world, usually not seeing it or realizing where they were due to the elaborate escape routes required to elude mobs of hysterical fans. Every day was spent between limos, hotels, and stages—constantly running to escape being torn apart. "It was cops and sweat and jellybeans hailing in dreamlike noise; it was faces uglied by shrieking and biting fists."[26]

Their mammoth-like popularity turned the group into hunted animals, running from an audience that seemed intent on devouring them. "The spectacle was not tender but warlike.... The screams that were like chants and bouts of weeping that were like acts of aggression, the aura of impending upheaval that promised the breaking down of doors and shattering of glass, this was love that could tear apart its object."[27]

Pop innocence turned to bomb threats; altercations between fans and police were commonplace. Something was in the air that was far bigger than rock and roll. The Beatles, now world celebrities, met boxer Cassius Clay (Muhammad Ali) in 1964, training for his first championship fight in Miami. Ali biographer David Remnick wrote, "The country was in the midst of an enormous change, an earthquake, and this fighter from Louisville and this band from Liverpool were part of it, *leading* it.... The Beatles blend of black R&B and Liverpool pop and Clay's blend of defiance and humor was changing the sound of the times, its temper; set alongside the march on Washington and the quagmire in Viet Nam, they would, in their way, become essential pieces of the sixties phantasmagoria."[28]

The Beatles constantly composed new material, churned out two records per year and toured exhaustively. Their remarkable development and succession of hit records was due to their relentless quest for new sounds, styles, and musical colors. They generated the ideas, but it was producer George Martin who shaped their inspiration. Considered the "fifth Beatle" by some, it is hard to imagine a more perfect producer for the biggest group in musical history. "He took the raw songs, he shaped and pruned and polished them and with scarcely believable altruism, asked nothing for himself but his EMI salary and the satisfaction of seeing his songs come out right.... The importance of George Martin cannot be over-emphasized."[29]

He clearly saw the Beatles' direction and evolution, stating, "Until recently, the aim has been to reproduce sounds as realistically as possible. Now we are working with pure sound. We are building sound pictures."[30] Their 1966 release, *Revolver,* paved the way for the album as a large-scale canvas, a medium that conveyed unified sonic ideas. Their album covers remain iconic. "The Beatles eventually ruled over time itself.... Their album covers are the portrait of an age."[31]

It was inevitable that their live stadium performances, often carried over baseball public address systems to 50,000-plus screaming teenagers, could not possibly live up to the craftmanship of their recordings. By August 1966, their touring life would end. George Harrison said, "We had to help break the Beatle madness in order to have some space to breathe, to become sort of human."[32] Bob Dylan's influence on the band, particularly John Lennon, emphasizing lyrical substance, contributed significantly to their songwriting evolution. Gone were the pop boy-girl lyrics, replaced by the existential "Nowhere Man," "Tomorrow Never Knows," and "Eleanor Rigby." Without touring, manager Brian Epstein found himself without a role to play, adrift and unneeded. "With all else to be heard in their brilliant new music, Brian could hear the sound of his own doom."[33]

The June 1967 release of *Sgt. Pepper's Lonely Hearts Club Band* was a pop culture shot heard around the world. The Beatles had done it. They raised pop and rock music to the level of undeniable "art." *Sgt. Pepper's* arrived one year after Brian Wilson and the Beach Boys landmark *Pet Sounds* recording; these two albums expanded the past boundaries for what could be heard and expressed in popular music. "There are to this day, thousands of Britons and Americans who can describe exactly where they were and what they were doing at the moment they first listened to Sergeant Pepper's Lonely Hearts Club Band."[34]

The album impacted musicians around the world. Critic Kenneth Tynan called it "a decisive moment in the history of Western civilization."[35] Even the conservative classical music world had to admit this was a major breakthrough. Pop music had graduated from cars, girls, and love songs to a realm never before imagined. More than songs, it was artistic innovation. The concept album came into prominence as FM radio opened doors for creative, hybrid-filled music; it was new air. Classical composer Ned Rorem said of the Beatles, "They have removed sterile martyrdom from art, revived the sensual."[36]

The *New York Times* critic Richard Goldstein became a standout dissenter of *Sgt. Pepper's*: "Like an over-attended child, Sergeant Peppers is spoiled. It reeks of horns and harps, harmonica quartets, assorted animal noises and a 41-piece orchestra."[37] Goldstein had a point. The instantly acclaimed record was recorded over a four-month period for an approximate cost of $100,000, an indicator of coming trends. Soon artists attempted to make their own Sgt. Pepper's, mostly falling short. Rock would become increasingly complex, elaborate, and highly technical, a case of something gained, something lost.

Ironically, the wheels came off at the time of the Beatles' greatest creation. The troubled Brian Epstein died of an overdose on August 27, 1967, just over two months after the release of *Sgt. Pepper's*. The Beatles manager, who had once said, "I am determined to go through the horrors of this world,"[38] had been a stabilizing force in the complex Beatles empire. His death resulted in business disorganization and group dissension, leading to the Beatles' breakup in 1970. It all ended on a rooftop concert on a cold, windy day in London. Like a Beatles lyric, it was all too much for them to take. "In the end, it was not the music that wore out but the drama, the personalities, the weight of expectation and identity."[39]

It was a dream, fairy tale, and nightmare all wrapped together, one that the Beatles themselves had difficulty grasping. Paul McCartney said, "We gave everything for ten years. We gave ourselves."[40] Ringo Starr saw it from the perspective of personal evolution: "From 1961, 1962, to around 1969, we were just all for each other. But suddenly you're older, and you don't want to devote all that time to this one object."[41] For John Lennon, the '60s dream was over, only now everyone was older and had long hair. George Harrison, undervalued until the Beatles later stage, said, "Being a Beatle was a nightmare, a horror story. I don't even like to think about it."[42] The effect of being the most wildly popular band in the world for a six- or seven-year period was one of shell shock and withdrawal.

Through the haze, their legacy grows. The Beatles' creativity, work ethic, insatiable curiosity, and drive to evolve, combined with their retiring at the top of their profession, are a tribute to their integrity and resulting longevity. Unlike rock stars and athletes who have stayed too long at the party, the Beatles are fixed in our memories to a time and place when the world was young. They stretched the boundaries of popular music, transforming the record industry for better or worse while altering the cultural landscape. The Beatles didn't predict the times, but their music was a societal soundtrack that moved throughout the decade. From their inception in 1960 to their end in 1970, "the Beatles opened the door for harder, more provocative bands like the Rolling Stones, the Who, and the Animals, and began the process of questioning that made the counter-culture possible."[43] The late Astrid Kirchherr recalled their humanity: "It was such a joy meeting them and becoming close friends with them. They gave me so much in return as far as love and affection was concerned, they always cared about me and looked after me."[44]

The Beatles were simultaneously mainstream pop stars and countercultural agents, instigators of change, but their colleagues, the Rolling Stones, like the ghost of Christmas future, would icily point to darker places.

Rolling Stones in Our Passway

They gave you a choice—love or hate them. The Rolling Stones, billed as "The Greatest Rock Band in the World," have influenced future musical generations in ways contrary to the Beatles. Following Beatlemania, they wisely set their own course. Rather than appearing as another British invasion Beatles' clone, their "being first means being free to invent and go it alone. Being in any place but first means riding the wake. It means being defined in comparison."[45] Charting their course through American blues, the Stones attracted an audience through provocation, a gang-like contrast to the wholesome Beatles image. "There grew up an odd fascination between the Beatles, who owned their success to reassuring the adult world, and the Stones, who got rich by outraging it."[46]

The Beatles and Stones grew from similar roots. They were the postwar generation raised on food rationing, economic despair in a black-and-white existence. America seemed to have it all in the '50s; suffering from the devastating effects of World War II, Britain had little. English youth sought hope and excitement by looking to music and art as salvation. The mid–'50s rock and roll explosion had dimmed by the decade's end, withering in a timid, bland, pop crossover sound. Rebellion, as usual, had given way to commercialism.

British youth headed to art school, discovering a creative world that offered a chance of finding one's identity through the creative process. Time spent drawing, painting, writing plays, practicing guitar, and copying blues records would pay vast dividends for future rock stars like the Rolling Stones. Rich Cohen wrote that it was "the joke that this generation played on fate, which had them marked for lives of quiet desperation in factories and insurance firms but instead set them up like medieval princes."[47]

A fateful meeting of Mick Jagger and Keith Richards, two teenagers waiting on the platform of the Dartford train station, led to a common bond—Black American music. Jagger was carrying mail-order Chess record albums by Muddy Waters, Chuck Berry, and Little Walter. The fact that they were both drawn to this music speaks volumes. Even in their youth, they could perceive the authenticity, grit, and realism of Chicago blues and Chuck Berry's rock and roll energy. "Taste is more important than knowledge. Anyone can learn, only a few can *know*."[48] This deep sense of knowing drove English bands, providing a gateway to their own future voice.

Similar to the Beatles, the Rolling Stones fully and respectfully acknowledged their musical influences. "All we've ever done," said the drummer Charlie Watts, "is play a version of Chicago music. In other words, you [Americans] have had to travel musically speaking, all the way to England just to hear your own music."[49] It is easy and inaccurate to dismiss the Rolling Stones as imitators. Emulation serves as an art world bridge, a key to finding new sounds while taking them past their origins. "In trying to imitate their heroes, they infused the songs with their own experiences and personalities and invented something new.... The breakthrough came not from imitating the blues but from emulating the approach of blues musicians, whose lyrics achieved power by including the particulars of their lives."[50] Even the Rolling Stones were surprised by the results.

The question "Why England?" continually arises. Britain's detachment from American racial issues allowed for a greater freedom to explore Black life, music, and culture. It was a safe place to discover, champion, and respect the blues masters. In America during the 1950s and '60, this was socially problematic. Growing up in Port Arthur, Texas, Janis Joplin had a different experience. "Not only did she not 'hate Negroes,' but Janis stood up for desegregation in an environment particularly hostile to African Americans that pretty much resulted in her being picked on for the rest of the time in high school—call her names like "nigger lover."[51] Thus, the Rolling Stones, Beatles, and others would beam America's musical culture back to the United States. The blues represented cool music in England that was youthful and free of racial intolerance. "Whereas for Elvis and those natives who followed him the blues bore an inescapable load of racial envy and fear, Mick's involvement was primarily aesthetic."[52]

For the Stones, the blues was a religious obsession, a failed salvation in the short life of their guitarist, Brian Jones. Like Elvis before them, the Rolling Stones and the notion of cultural appropriation is ever present. Ellen Willis wrote, "As white exploitation of black music, rock and roll has always had its built-in ironies, and as the music went further from its origins, the ironies got more acute.... Rock was too superficial, blues too alien. The Stones music was the perfect blend."[53] Jagger, in the words of Robert Christgau, "simply customized certain details of blues phrasing and enunciation into components of a vocal style of protean originality."[54]

The songwriting of Jagger and Richards, combined with their careful observation of live acts—Little Richard, the Everly Brothers, and Bo Diddley—enabled the group's transition from blues to rock. They were students who gave full credit to their masters. Although the Rolling Stones did much to support the careers of Muddy Waters, Chuck Berry, Howlin' Wolf, B.B. King, and others, the cultural impact on American audiences, more focused on entertainment, remained limited. "It reminded the love crowd that in their naïve rapacity they had taken what sustenance they needed for black music, and the black outlaw culture without much thought about what they could give back."[55]

The Rolling Stones meant front man Mick Jagger, who commanded attention as an entertainer and sex symbol, catapulting them to fame. Despite his limited vocal instrument, Jagger is a classic example of doing more with less. British bluesman Alexis Korner recalled that from his early beginnings, "he had a feel of belting a song even if he wasn't.... Mick always had that, and he had this absolute certainty that he was right."[56]

Blues and rock put an emphasis on feeling and communication over technique and vocal brilliance. Jagger, like Dylan and others, could make up for any shortcomings. "Imperfectionism made him interesting.... Good voices are a dime a dozen; what a front man needs is distinction."[57]

In any genre, great singers manage to inhabit a song, acting it out and living it as opposed to a surface performance. Jagger's vocal performance came from within, pushed out by a forceful ego mixed with an erotic power capable of arousing and provoking an audience to often violent and deadly consequences. "Jagger's male power trip is alienating, and the fact that he obviously doesn't take it all seriously only makes it worse."[58]

From the moment the Stones first manager, Andrew Loog Oldham, realized that youth loves what their parents despise, the direction was clear—the Beatles go high, we go low. Even many of their musical peers resented their public stance and bad-boy charades. David Crosby said, "I think they have an exaggerated view of their own importance; I think they're on a grotesque ego trip."[59]

The Beatles spanned ten years as a band, the Rolling Stones, for better or worse, have lasted over a half century. The relentless drive and ego of Mick Jagger is a primary reason for their longevity. The Rolling Stones are equally loved and scorned; there has never been a middle ground. "Mick is not Lucifer. He's showbiz, a pop version of the classic Hollywood diva for whom the show must go on, for whom obscurity is even more terrifying than death."[60]

The Glory of Chaos

Music brings out an intuitive response in an audience, stirring emotions that few realize. The Beatles' audience reacted to their live performances with an elated fervor and electric excitement, the Stones, with aggression and violence. Keith Richards felt this audience behavior was forcedly put on the group, but Ian Stewart, the band's sometimes keyboard player and roadie, said, "It wasn't pleasant to see what the music did to people."[61] The band's simmering hostility permeated the audience, and Mick Jagger realized this was "physical violence.... That's the kind of trouble we get into."[62] From their earliest Rolling Stones' performances, fame and fan adoration would be linked with a fury of confused feelings. "It was always a classic outcome for the Stones. The choice was always a tricky one for the authorities who arrested us. Do you want to lock them up, or have your photo taken with them and send them a motorcade to send them on your way?"[63]

Darkness followed them. Drug arrests, run-ins with authorities, court appearances, and the death of Brian Jones, followed by Altamont. A Rolling Stones concert represented danger itself. "The whole building was jumping; I thought it might collapse like a bridge from lock-step marching.... When the show ended Sam told me he had been backstage rescuing kids from cops who were beating them on the feet with clubs.... In Hamburg also there were police on horses with clubs and hoses keeping out the kids who were trying to get into the Stones show. Cars were overturned, and kids were trampled by horses."[64] The Beatles-Stones comparison became a good cop–bad cop scenario. The Stones' sullen demeanor as agents of darkness, combined with their drug and sexual exploits made the Beatles good chaps. Even in their songwriting approach, a Beatles song was a polished composition; the Stones made music out of free-form chaos.

Fame made things worse. "The band was tapping the energy that had driven rock from the start.... Beatles fans tended to behave, but the Stones summoned the dark angels."[65] A rock concert releases audience emotions. It was a time characterized by *Vogue* editor Diana Vreeland as a "youthquake." The kids were now in charge—making the music, creating the industry, shaping the culture while defying past conventions and institutions, or so they thought. By the late '60s, rock audiences attending live events became increasingly hostile and contemptuous, resenting rising ticket prices while insisting that music should be free, storm the gates. They even began to heckle the expensive rock stars they had worshipped and paid to see. Ellen Willis, reviewing a 1975 Rolling Stones concert in Madison Square Garden, noticed that "the crowd was unaccountably hostile. All night, people kept throwing things on to the stage, and the objects were relatively benign—flowers, frisbees, toys of various sorts—the feeling was not."[66]

Charmed by the Beatles, the mainstream press took aim at the Stones. *Newsweek* called them "tasteless and leering," and another critic, with unveiled racism stated, "Never before has there been a sound to rival this—except, perhaps, in the jungle of darkest Africa."[67] In the mid-1920s, Duke Ellington's orchestra, performing at Harlem's exclusive whites-only Cotton Club, was described as playing "Jungle Music." As Vietnam raged on, the Stones' conduct was resented by an older generation while over a hundred American soldiers died daily in the jungles of Vietnam. War correspondent Martin Goshen stated, "We've got kids dying out there without a sound and we've got punks here who dress up like girls and make millions of dollars doing it."[68]

The Rolling Stones felt both the pressure and hypocrisy of their audience's political agenda that claimed rock stars should be committed to their fan's expectations. Keith Richards noted, "These kids at the press conferences want us to do their thing, not ours. Politics is what we were trying to get away from in the first place."[69] During their first American tour in 1964, the Stones were shocked by two things—America's ignorance regarding Black music's importance and the racial prejudice exhibited by intense segregation across the country. One thing explained another.

Mick Jagger was an astute lyricist and societal observer who foresaw the shifting audience attitude. Comparing the Stones' American tours of 1964 and 1966, "they were all satisfied by convention.... They never thought about whether politically anything was right or wrong," but by '66, Jagger noticed "a lot of young people saying my country should be right, not wrong."[70] Led by the music, the audience dynamic reflected the rising temperature of a nation torn apart by the war in Vietnam and the civil rights movement. "He [Jagger] wrote more hate songs than love songs, and related tales of social and political breakdown with untoward glee."[71]

Paint It Black: Altamont and Its Remains

Three days after the July 1967 drowning death of Brian Jones, recently fired from the band, the Stones put on a bizarre send-off concert in London's Hyde Park. It was a premonition of dark days to come. Instead of focusing on the death of Jones, a talented but troubled person, the Rolling Stones turned inward. "There was a schizophrenic element in the rites of mourning performed by Jagger in Hyde Park. Wearing cosmetics and a little girl's party dress, and flanked by Hell's Angels bodyguards, he read a passage of Shelley that seemed less a memorial to his dead companion than one further medium for his own primping narcissism.... With a corpse, a man in make-up, and hundreds of dead butterflies, the Hyde Park concert held too many prophecies for the decade at its turning point."[72]

The winds were changing. Rock performers and their followers seemed caught in a web beyond their comprehension. Mick Jagger fore-saw a rising angst and frustration from young audiences who were deeply worried about the world and their place in it: "I see a lot of trou-ble coming in the dawn."[73] No longer comrades in a youth culture revo-lution, it was a "Street Fightin' Man" crowd that had become demanding consumers—unwilling to pay for music, feeling ripped-off by rock stars and their affiliation with corporate recording industry greed. Little did they know it was only the beginning. Without announcement, rock had become big business with soaring egos and profits.

It would only get worse. A love-hate idolization of rock stars turned to fanatic obsession where an audience felt ownership of their favorite artists and their music. There is the story of a man coming backstage after a Bob Dylan performance, dominating the small dressing room and exclaiming, "You've done your thing. Now it's time for me to do mine." What was once communal had become self-centered. The times, indeed, were changing.

In rock, you get what you give. The Rolling Stones' stage presence and dark energy became a ritual. At the end of their 1969 American tour, a free concert had been badly and hastily arranged, set finally at the Altamont Speedway in Northern California. If it was an attempt to upstage the Woodstock event of a few months prior, it would not only be a failure but also a disaster. The Albert and David Maysles documentary *Gimme Shelter* resulted in Altamont and the Stones living in infamy. On the day of the event, an ominous black sky hovered over an exhausted audience, frustrated and lost. "Bad drugs were flooding the grounds, yellow acid tabs laced with chemicals, possibly strychnine."[74] When the Stones arrived by helicopter, Mick Jagger disembarked and was punched by a young man, yelling, "I hate you! I hate you!" The anxious and trip-ping audience were at the end of their communal rope, waiting for the Stones to perform. "That kid punched Mick Jagger because the Stones had put him and everyone in an untenable position, squeezed between the landscape and the Angels."[75]

The Hells Angels had been allegedly recommended by the Grateful Dead and informally hired as concert security. They couldn't have been more wrong. Under the influence of drugs and alcohol, the Hells Angels turned violent—keeping the audience in line by beating them with pool cues. Jefferson Airplane lead vocalist Marty Balin tried at one point to intervene and was knocked unconscious. "Michelle Phillips of the Mamas and Papas came into the trailer bearing tales of how the Angels were fighting with civilians, women, and each other, bouncing full cans of beer off people's heads.... The expression on the cops' faces said they didn't like this scene at all but they're not scared, just sorrowful-eyed like men who know trouble and know that they are in the midst of a lot of people who are asking for it."[76]

Gimme Shelter is a terrifying portrayal of a decade's demise, a revolution gone awry. In the film, the largely hippie audience appears confused, desperately trying to have a good time, hoping something will happen to release them from their fear. The documentary illustrates that rock and roll and its megastars are helpless in finding solutions. Things were too far gone. At one point, presumably after the stage-left murder of Meredith Hunter, the Rolling Stones, incredibly, carry on with the concert. The camera pans to a young woman in tears, sitting on the edge of the stage, hoping that the music might erase the horrors she has just witnessed. Like looking into the sun, it is an impression that lasts a lifetime—a modern-age Devil's Den at Gettysburg.

What went so terribly wrong? "The Stones' music was strong but it could not stop the terror. There was a look of disbelief on people's faces wondering how the Stones could go on playing and singing in the bowels of madness and violent death.... How are we gonna get out of here? I wondered. Will we get out, or will we die here?"[77] At the end of *Gimme Shelter,* the frightened yet callous reaction of Mick Jagger as he views the murder on film is chilling. His stare is empty and emotionless. One wonders what the Rolling Stones allowed themselves to feel after Altamont. According to writer Stanley Booth, directly after Altamont, Keith Richards "sounded like an English public school boy whose fundamental decency and sense of fair play had been offended by the unsportsmanlike conduct at soccer of his peers."[78]

The era of optimism was over. The tide of potential change ran out, leaving hollow fashion and consumerism in its wake. The youth movement would leave San Francisco, returning to school and resuming their lives in conservative ways similar to their parents. Altamont was a tragic end with many lessons to be learned. It was "the product of diabolical egotism, hype, ineptitude, money, manipulation, and, at base, a fundamental lack of concern for humanity."[79]

Controversy would not stop the Rolling Stones, but the collateral damage would be irreversible. A rebellious image is one thing, but seeming indifference to human plight is another. "Mick Jagger had long pretended to be the devil. Then one night he threw a party and the real devil showed up.... What did the Stones see at Altamont? Their own demise, the fate of all those who held the grenade too long."[80] The Stones had always been Mick Jagger, but that image and what it represented would never be the same. They would retain a large, nostalgic fan base as the "world's greatest rock and roll band," but their power would erode. "Jagger's 'demonic' persona was not enhanced by the death at Altamont, as some people supposed; it was destroyed. In the face of one man's real death, Jagger's '*demonic*' posture was shown to be merely perverse."[81]

It still haunts us. The eerie image at Altamont of the audience, stumbling and groping in the dark after the Stones set was over, attempting to find their way out … somewhere, anywhere.

Gimme Shelter is a portrait of a nation trying to find the long way home.

Conclusions and Cultural Amnesia

The revolution died, harder drugs entered the '70s, the Beatles broke up, and we walked through the ruins. Rock became a corporate industry, bloated and mainstream with greed as the usual culprit. "America had been completely about music, politics and the war. That's the air everybody was breathing. Then the publicists arrived. After that, all the excess was choreographed, for show."[82] The business of rock and its superstars became so engorged by fame and the "sex, drugs, and rock and roll" syndrome that it was bound to affect the creative process and its end result. "After Altamont, all that was shut down and order was imposed…. In the age of corporate rock, every encounter is tagged with a price gun."[83] Rather than music focusing on outward communication, it shoots inward—a sonic selfie.

The Beatles knew when to quit. Rock concerts of the '70s, elaborate as Broadway musicals, were staged in stadiums with often horrible results—poor sound and sightlines, expensive ticket prices, expensive concessions and merchandising, mollified by tremendous profit. Keith Richards observed, "When you play these big stadiums, you're hoping that when you first hit it, it fills the room…. Something you played yesterday in a little rehearsal room sounded fantastic, and you take it out on the big stage and it sounds like three mice caught in a trap."[84]

The Beatles escaped the mythical 1960s with their legacy preserved. The Rolling Stones pressed on in stop-and-go form, crashing from one decade to the next, dinosaurs in a roller derby. It is not a pretty sight "when you see Mick and Keith onstage, leaning together like Butch and Sundance, you're seeing actors. It's heartbreaking…. At the beginning, they imitate blues musicians. At the end, they imitated themselves."[85] Professionalism can be an advancement or a compromise.

They are a tale of contrasting legacies. The Beatles opened the door to harder sounding bands inspired by Black American Delta and Chicago electric blues artists, ranging from Robert Johnson and Leadbelly to Muddy Waters, Howlin' Wolf, and the rock and roll of Chuck Berry. America, with its institutionalized racism, rarely gave credit, respect, or industry support to its African American innovators. It took the British to accomplish that, a crime scene of American cultural amnesia. The irony of the Rolling Stones, according to Keith Richards, was that "the most bizarre part of the whole story is having done what we intended to do in our narrow, purist teenage brains at the time, which was to turn people on to the blues, what actually happened was we turned American people back to their own music. And that's probably our greatest contribution to music."[86]

The Beatles were cultural pied pipers who responded to the times by transforming rock music into an art. Their multitude of sonic innovations, aided by George Martin, including George Harrison's recognition of world music, blazed a path to a period of mythic imagination and experimentation in popular music. The Beatles were unique as a band and as individuals. "With their wonderful, distinctive personalities, they taught youth to be different, how to stand apart from the crowd, and how to dare, to experiment, and to assert themselves with humor, intelligence, and tolerance—this and more."[87] The Rolling Stones maintained an outlaw stance in the Delta blues tradition that influenced rock bands of future generations. They still sound like a

The last stop for Buddy Holly, Richie Valens, and J.P. Richardson, Clear Lake, Iowa.

Saturday night, Southside Chicago blues band while representing proof of rock's dynamic power.

You can enlighten your audience only up to a point. Despite their efforts, the Beatles, Stones, the Who, Led Zeppelin, and other British bands could only do so much. Over a half century later, few Americans understand the importance of Black music and its impact on American culture and the world. Students encounter an educational system that barely, if ever, mentions it in passing. Lacking this basic knowledge, popular music suffers—a tree without roots. The unique, authentic character of regionalized music scenes from Liverpool to Muscle Shoals, Alabama, have taken a hit. "The fire that lit early rock and roll and passed like a torch from Buddy Holly to the Beatles, from the Stones to the Clash, had gone out by the late 1990s.... The energy that powered music scenes in Chicago and Detroit and Alabama and London has moved to Silicon Valley."[88]

Identity is the moral of this story. If you don't know and value your own culture, you don't know who you are, but you can bet someone else does. They will use those influences for their own artistry and take it to the bank. After World War II, people in Europe were forced to reevaluate their lives. Who knew that the imported records blasting from U.K. jukeboxes would resonate and stir a generation? Perhaps a worldwide pandemic will jolt us into new ways of thinking about music, culture, the world, and ourselves.

Until then, one constant remains—when the times get ready, you've got to move.

8

Pistols at Dawn:
Janis, Jim, and Jimi

True story. Our scene opens in late 1960s New York City at The Scene, a nightclub on West 46th Street. Jimi Hendrix, rock guitarist extraordinaire, is jamming away when a drunk and belligerent Jim Morrison, lead singer for the Doors, yelling something obscene, suddenly jumps onto the small stage, wrapping his arms around Hendrix's legs. Witnessing this nearby, Janis Joplin, another iconic rock celebrity, begins fighting with Morrison, hitting him on the head with a bottle. The three superstars fall to the floor, scuffling until their handlers pull them apart—peace, love, and rock and roll.

Fantasy. Now imagine this happened during the eighteenth century and to settle the matter, the three musicians gather for a duel the following morning. Half-serious and still hung over, they aim pistols at each other. At the count of three, they fire them, unsure if they are loaded. Although only a fantasy, this scenario might represent our confusion regarding the demise of Hendrix, Morrison, and Joplin over a half century after their deaths at age twenty-seven. They remain musical and cultural icons, alive on posters, album covers, on film, larger than life, reflecting the glorious and broken ending of the 1960s—sunny days turning to darkness. The memory of these artists reminds us that the smoke never really cleared.

What happened to these talented, intelligent people? What can we learn from their brief, fast lives now that we live in a modern era where technology is the rock star?

Days of Love and Rage

The '60s were a great age to be young and an unfortunate one to be a parent. The generational gap was a divide resembling the Grand

131

Canyon. Rock critic Ellen Willis wrote, "Young Americans were in a sense, the stars of the world, drawing on an overblown prosperity that could afford to indulge all manner of rebellious behavior."[1] The creative art world blossomed in a decade fueled by the spirit of excess and experimentation under the guise of revolution. "Other aspects reflect youthful self-indulgence more than revolutionary transformation. But beneath it all was the notion that how one lived one's life and the power of art in the world were as crucial to an emerging social transformation

Statue of country music star Hank Williams, Montgomery, Alabama.

as any political activity—and more important, that they were all alone."[2] The role of art shifted to an emphasis on consciousness-raising. A musical event previously considered entertainment potentially became a political act. "Art, they came to see, should not only reflect the changing political realities, it should influence them.... Artists had always believed that their work could tap the deepest recesses of the human unconscious and touch lives profoundly."[3] American youth saw artists as spokespersons for their generation.

It was a decade of hope and disillusionment, spurred on by assassinations, race riots, and the war in Vietnam. There was the overarching sense that authoritarian lies were putting America in a dark and terrifying place. As the decade wore on, distrust grew to the point of violence and despair. "The discovery, thanks to Michael Herr's *Dispatches*—that American fighter pilots could machine gun Vietnamese farmers for sport while listening to Dylan and Hendrix on cockpit headphones finished off what remained for me."[4] American youth celebrated the "Summer of Love" in San Francisco and at the Monterey Pop Festival, but that elation would be short lived. "In 1968," wrote Greil Marcus, "dread was the currency ... dread was why everyday could feel like a trap."[5] Joan Didion saw Los Angeles change dramatically in 1968 and '69. "A demented and seductive vortical tension was building in the community." After the horrific Charles Manson murders in 1969, Didion recalled, "I remember that no one was surprised."[6]

In the twentieth century, youth's power was never greater than in the 1960s. Like all social, political, and cultural movements, it was a shooting star moment in time. "It is unlikely that American society will ever be eager again to allow adolescents the kind of dominion that they briefly enjoyed in the 1960s and 1970s. Instead, youth's power today is largely confined to a marketing power."[7] The widening distance between youth and their parents created havoc in the personal lives of Janis Joplin, Jimi Hendrix, and Jim Morrison, as well as most of the audience who followed them.

Rock became an essential social barometer that rallied people together. "There was a connection that people had through music," said Electra Records founder Jac Holzman. "The temperature of the country could be taken through its music."[8] Rock was evolving from having been teen innocence centered on romance, girls, boys, and cars to worldly concepts calling for societal change. Record producer Phil Spector said, "Whoever can create a song that is both an idea and a record can rule the world."[9]

Artists became more important than statesmen to young America. Joplin, Hendrix, and Morrison were idols from mid–1967 until the death of Joplin and Hendrix in 1970, followed by Morrison in 1971. Janis Joplin represented the past coming forward, "the only sixties culture hero to make visible and public women's experience for the quest for individual liberation."[10] She embraced the work of blues giant Bessie Smith, a towering figure of female independence long before the feminist movement, merging her style into the music while providing inspiration for women.

Jimi Hendrix was the epitome of guitar mastery, sonic innovation, sexuality, and cool in rock—a Black musical style previously dominated by white artists for many years. "Hendrix came along at a time in world history when only white boys were supposed to be handed rock star badges and the loudest, angriest Black folk around were bent on getting whitey off the planet."[11] Similar to Bob Marley in the subsequent decade, Hendrix took the middle road, embracing all people. He formed the Jimi Hendrix Experience with two white English musicians.

Hendrix and Joplin delivered the blues-rock influence into the love generation's orbit, but Jim Morrison and the Doors were far from the love crowd. "The Doors were different, the Doors interested me," wrote Joan Didion. "The Doors insisted that love was sex and sex was death and therein lay salvation."[12] Led by Morrison's poetry, the Doors music foresaw the encroaching darkness after the dawn of hippie optimism and utopian vision. Their first album closed with "The End." "It was the first major statement of the Doors perennial themes: dread, violence, guilt without the possibility of redemption, the miscarriages of love, and most of all-death."[13] Later, the Doors' music would be placed in the film *Apocalypse Now*, a soundtrack to the carnage of Vietnam. Darkness never goes out of style. Hendrix, Morrison, and Joplin walked the plank without hesitation.

Father Knows Best ... or Does He?

Janis Joplin was born on January 19, 1943, in Port Arthur, Texas. She came from a close family, but upon adolescence, Janis grew increasingly strong-willed, independent, and rebellious, resulting in a widening distance between her and her parents. "She was so outspoken ... a liberated female.... If somebody irritated her, she'd let them know!"[14] Joplin's persistent guilt regarding being a disappointment to her parents would cast a shadow over her life.

Jimi Hendrix was born on November 27, 1942, in Seattle, Washington. His mother died when he was young; his father was loving but often overly stern. Jimi's polite, shy, and quiet demeanor was a contrast to the louder, boisterous personality of Janis Joplin. "The princely mannered and charming Hendrix was read as 'somebody you could take home to your Mother,' says drummer Mitch Mitchell."[15]

Jim Morrison was born on December 8, 1943, in Melbourne, Florida. Of the three rock stars, his detachment from his parents was the most extreme. "Like everyone back then, Jim hated his parents, hated home, hated it all. Jim Morrison had it worse than a lot of kids. He was fat. And his father was a naval officer."[16] Doors drummer John Densmore noted, "With a naval officer for a father, Jim was sensitive to receiving criticism and interpreted any suggestions as orders from an archetypal father figure."[17] This was not uncommon in the '60s, where a typical parent's (particularly a father's) lament was, "You have no talent, get a job, stop wasting time." Having lived through World War II, the older generation was hard-pressed to understand American youth, appearing self-indulgent, irresponsible, and aimless. Sadly, Jim Morrison's father, George, would later admit, long after his son's death, "I was a poor interpreter of his talent.... He was a good man ... true to his own destiny."[18]

Youthful rebellion was the driving force fueling the lives of Morrison, Hendrix, and Joplin. Curious, open, and ambitious, upheaval provided inspiration for their work and colored their offstage life. Contrary to their sensationalized images, Joplin and Morrison read constantly. Janis read Billie Holiday's autobiography, *Lady Sings the Blues,* and Morrison devoured Nietzsche, Blake, Kafka, and Rimbaud. Both would make their own interpretations of how those works addressed their art and lifestyle. Jim Morrison, who once said, "Critical essays are where it's at," was noted by Jac Holzman as being "serious and extraordinarily well-read."[19] Jimi Hendrix was an intense listener who absorbed musical styles, studying them closely.

Similar to the heroes they absorbed, the three musicians were steeped in the audio and oral tradition, learning by ear. They were deeply serious about their art. Powell St. John, a friend of Janis, remarked, "She had a frivolous side, but she was a very intelligent girl."[20] Jimi Hendrix possessed an overly trusting trait that would later complicate his life and career. All three attempted making their lives fit their personal values. For Joplin (and perhaps Morrison and Hendrix), "much of her life would be colored by the attention of wanting to be loved and getting the attention she missed, while knowing that the best way to honor her family's unspoken creed of singularity was to set herself apart."[21]

Joplin, Hendrix, and Morrison embraced a distinctive stance that challenged the status quo, driven by a search for authenticity propelled by a sense of rebellion. "Jim Morrison didn't really challenge authority.

Rather he conveyed an unlimited, instinctive, but dramatized contempt for authority."[22] Add heavy, sustained drug and alcohol abuse and you have a Bermuda triangle of danger. Upon the deaths of Joplin and Hendrix, Jacob Brackman wrote, "Both were too passionate, too excited, in need of cooling out…. Both were willing to try anything…. Intoxication was their muse and their refuge."[23] A '60s misconception was the notion that being under the influence unlocked the gateway to unrealized creativity. Although it occasionally opened doors of the imagination, it often rendered temporary passion and inspiration helpless and unharnessed, resulting in an inability to mold the vision into a coherent form.

The Roots of Talent

Some artists have the spongelike ability to reach back into the past, extract the essence of an influential artist or style, then transport it into a modern age. As a teenager, Janis Joplin was struck by the power of blues vocalist Bessie Smith, a star of "race records" from 1923 until her death in 1937. She was attracted to the fiery independence and commanding voice of Smith, a fearless Black woman ahead of her time. Hard-drinking, bisexual, outspoken, and elegantly dressed, Bessie Smith led her own touring company—singing, dancing, and performing comedy skits at a time when men dominated public and private life. She was a woman who had single-handedly scared off a group of Klansmen threatening to burn down her tent show.

Janis was mesmerized by Smith's recordings, her spirit, and the power of her persona. "Janis listened over and over and over, and soon she was singing Bessie Smith songs."[24] To any knowledgeable blues fan, Joplin was a voice from the past, but to a young rock audience she appeared astoundingly new. From her troubled youth in Port Arthur to joining Big Brother and the Holding Company in 1966 during San Francisco's Haight Ashbury days, Janis, like her heroine, was a star the moment she took the stage. "The most dynamic of the musical performers is a granny-gowned Janis Joplin…. She sings everything as a blues and bases her style on the Ma-Rainey-Ida Cox tradition of the 1920's with a bit of Bessie Smith thrown in."[25] Shortly before her death, Janis Joplin helped fund a headstone for Bessie Smith's unmarked grave—a gift to the woman who inspired her to sing.

Joplin's total musical immersion exhibited a voice ranging from a shout to a whisper, putting a spell on her audience. It wasn't long before she emerged as the star of Big Brother, causing friction in her relationship with the band, often disparaged by critics and industry figures. "She had more talent than they and I can't help suspecting that that was good for her not only emotionally and socially but aesthetically."[26]

Like Joplin, Jimi Hendrix was influenced by Delta and electric blues. His mastery of the guitar is, in many ways, unparalleled to this day. The jazz-rock guitarist Larry Coryell once told me this story: "I was jamming with Jimi at The Scene in New York City when he suddenly broke a string in the middle of a solo. Most people would stop and get off the stage at that point, but not Jimi. He continued playing with one hand while keeping the song's form, and with the other, he reached into his open guitar case, pulled out a new string, then uncoiled the broken one, replaced it with a new string and tuned it up without missing a beat."

Jimi Hendrix bridged old and new musical styles. "Hendrix merged blues, modern soul, avant-garde jazz, and English rock and roll derivatives."[27] Jimi's talent was no accident but the product of hard, intensive work, similar to jazz masters Charlie Parker and John Coltrane. With extravagant showmanship, he developed his virtuosity into a style he referred to as "science fiction rock and roll." Ironically, many young Blacks in the '60s saw the blues as old fashioned, outdated, and irrelevant. It was embraced by white English rock musicians as the Bible, the key to teaching the essential elements of musical expression.

Jimi Hendrix was discovered performing in Greenwich Village by Chas Chandler, former bassist with the Animals turned manager. Hendrix went to London in 1966 and immediately stood out from the English musicians. Organist Brian Auger said, "The difference between him and a lot of the English guitar players like Clapton, Jeff Beck, and Alvin Lee, was that you could still tell what the influences were ... but Jimi wasn't following anyone—he was playing something new."[28] Hendrix was expanding the sonic boundaries with a kaleidoscope of colors that only he could create—utilizing distortion, feedback, and a wah-wah pedal. "Jimi's special gift was his ability to harness these distortions, before him—and usually after him, for that matter—it was primarily a game of chance.... Few others have been able to duplicate his sounds live or in the studio.... Most of the explosions and other sound effects were arrived at through ingenuity and experimentation."[29]

His artistry was an exhibition of sound and light. Eric Clapton said, "He was very flashy, even in the dressing room.... It was just, well, he stole the show."[30] Jimi Hendrix wielded his Fender Stratocaster like a western gunslinger, leaving no doubt of his mastery. Renowned blues guitarist Michael Bloomfield recalled a Hendrix performance when "he just got right up in my face with that axe, and I didn't pick up a guitar for the next year."[31] Hendrix was a dual personality—quiet and soft-spoken offstage, yet screaming and bombastic on his instrument.

Jim Morrison's primary vocal influence was Frank Sinatra, especially noticeable when he sang softly. He drew less on blues and soul for his inspiration; literature and poetry was his muse. Morrison was an accidental vocalist, a film student with an ability to draw melodies from the poems he had written. "And there is something to be said for singing in tune, Jim not only sang in tune he sang intimately—as Doors producer Paul Rothchild once pointed out to me, Jim was the greatest crooner since Bing Crosby. He was Bing Crosby from hell."[32] Morrison needed the Doors to transform his poems into a musical form. Many vocalists throughout popular music have lacked musical knowledge, an area of insecurity. Drummer John Densmore said, "Jim was a guy with a natural instinct for melody but no knowledge of chords to hang it on, the combination of Robby, Ray, and me was perfect for orchestrating Jim's words."[33]

Whereas Hendrix and Joplin had a dynamic onstage presence, Jim Morrison was a theatrical performer emphasizing the music's dramatic moments. He was the front man for an unusual band. "The Doors were fashioning music that looked at prospects of hedonism and violence, of revolt and chaos, and embraced those prospects fearlessly."[34] Their power lay in suspense, tension, darkness, and uncertainty—light years from the euphoric '60s flower-power slogans. The hit "Light My Fire" created a mainstream success while their performances were anything but middle of the road. "If 'Light My Fire' hadn't made the Doors into stars," wrote Greil Marcus, "you can hear how their music could have curdled into artiness."[35]

Black and White Lightning

Underappreciated in America, Jimi Hendrix stood out the moment he landed in London, England, in 1966. With the guidance of Chas Chandler, they formed the Jimi Hendrix Experience with Noel Redding on bass and Mitch Mitchell on drums. "There were so few musicians who were black on the scene, and so many fans of American blues, that he was afforded instant credibility.... In one single day in London, it felt like his entire life had been permanently recast."[36] Hendrix was soon a sensation as word spread quickly around the city, no one in England had ever seen anything quite like him.

Hendrix was a logical choice to play the June 1967 Monterey Pop Festival. The contrast between his reserved demeanor and stage manner became apparent. "It was at Monterey that I first met Hendrix," said Steve Katz, singer, guitarist, and songwriter with the Blues Project, and Blood, Sweat & Tears. "Jimi was a sweetheart, a very gentle person who I immediately took a liking to. Later, when he got on stage, I didn't think it was the same guy, aggressive and brilliant. To this day, I will never forget it."[37] In front of an audience who had barely heard of him, Hendrix exploded onto the Monterey stage with virtuosity, sexuality, and outer-space chitlin circuit showmanship that concluded with him famously burning his guitar, one of rock's most enduring images. The Jimi Hendrix Experience had landed and instantly burst into stardom, but the visual aspect of the performance overrode the artistry. "He played exhilarating music throughout, but when it was over everyone buzzed about nothing but the *show*."[38]

Without realizing it, Hendrix had inadvertently branded an image leading to future expectations of showy pyrotechnics. Although he considered himself a musician first, he had set a trap that would forever bind him. The irony was that "the boy who had waited so long for this first guitar was now onstage destroying them."[39] No one at Monterey knew that only three years and three months later, Jimi Hendrix would be gone.

One is easily overtaken by Janis Joplin's presence, forgetting the real person underneath. Her blues-mama persona, with a bottle of Southern Comfort in one hand and a cigarette in the other, is a dominant image she promoted. Joplin was conscious of the fact that the blues divas of the past dressed in style. "I want the audience to look at me as a real performer, whereas now the look is 'just-one-of-us-who-stepped-on-stage.'"[40] Steve Katz recalls her as "always a lady to me, honest and elegant.... I was on the side of the stage at Monterey when Janis sang 'Ball and Chain.' I was mesmerized as was everyone else there."[41] Like Morrison and Hendrix, Janis was intensely theatrical, sexy, and uninhibited, but credit must go to Little Richard a decade before, who transformed rock and roll performance into a gospel-like, frenzied, healing, uplifting, and liberating experience. Janis Joplin was more than the typical performer. "She was also the only woman to achieve that kind of stature in what was basically a male club, the only sixties culture hero to make visible and public women's experience of the quest for individual liberation which was different from men's."[42]

Like Hendrix, Janis had conflicting sides—her personal life was at odds with the one she led in the public eye. Her lustful, joyous character contrasted with a lingering self-doubt, something that fame could not eradicate. "Janis always had this thing of total insecurity and total power at the same time," according to Big Brother and the Holding Company's guitarist, Sam Andrew. "It was really something to be confronted with both of them."[43]

There may have never been a more confused and conflicted rock star than Jim Morrison. The Doors' producer Paul Rothchild said, "You never knew whether Jim would show up as the erudite, poetic scholar or the kamikaze drunk."[44] You couldn't be sure if he would show up at all. Morrison thrived on chaos, loved revolt, and brought disorder to everyone around him, but his sexual magnetism was undeniable—appearing half man, half lion. "Jim made it cool to be a poet," wrote Eve Babitz. His poetry turned melodious, but his song lyrics were hit and miss. When he was on, he invoked a shaman-like power to the words he composed, but when he missed, he sounded sophomoric and amateurish. "If being stupid is not that bad, then Jim's poetry would be okay, but it's not, fortunately Jim had looks.... By the time Jim left L.A. everyone thought he was a fool.... Underneath his mask, he was dead."[45]

The Doors, unlike Hendrix and Joplin, didn't perform at Monterey, but by the summer of '67 they were the number one band in America. "Light My Fire" was second only to the Beatles' *Sgt. Pepper's Lonely Hearts Club Band* during the summer of that year. From their ascent to Morrison's rapid descent soon thereafter, it became clear that "this man is more damaged, his speech slurred, his demeanor distracted, someone screaming at himself, tearing at his clothes."[46]

Only he could understand his mission. Joan Didion accurately called it a "suicide pact."

The Sticker Price of Adulation

Janis Joplin felt she represented something more than a rock star; she was a continuum of female singers. "Janis saw herself as a part of a sisterhood of song from her early influences of Ma Rainey and Bessie Smith, both of whom influenced [Big Mama] Thornton to Odetta, Nina Simone, Etta James, Billie Holiday, and eventually, Aretha Franklin and Tina Turner."[47] Similar to her idols, she felt the blues deeply, delivering it with power, drama, and conviction. B.B. King once said that Janis Joplin sang the blues harder than any white person he had ever heard.

Jim Morrison's performing stance partially derived from a place of anger and resentment stemming from childhood. His lyrics were dreamy and romantic, contrasted by verbally lashing out at his audience.

As his fame grew, he berated the audience who had placed him in an anointed position. Morrison's lyrics were "a recognition that an older generation had betrayed its children, that this betrayal called for a bitter payback."[48] Fame's pressures were relentless. Rock promoter Bill Graham observed that although there had always been major stars in popular music, celebrities' intense flame in the modern era was unlike the past. "Adulation came on such a level, but it wasn't bobby soxers screaming at Frank Sinatra." "People followed him [Morrison] across the country like the crusades—and how do you deal with the responsibility of being an involuntary leader?"[49] Bob Dylan encountered the same problem and ceased performing for a number of years. Jim Morrison's way was to dismantle, destroy, and obliterate his fame. When Morrison and the Doors performed, "he could get away with it because his audience was all college kids who thought the Doors were cool because they had lyrics you could understand about stuff they learned in Psychology 101 and Art History."[50]

Jimi Hendrix had been a frustrated sideman performing on the rhythm and blues circuit, limited by the restraints of band leaders wary of being upstaged by his antics. A stage is, among other things, an ego-driven place where people stake their territory, but the chitlin circuit was a proving ground, a place to learn. Hendrix observed the moves of star performers from Little Richard to Jackie Wilson (two of the best ever) which he successfully merged into his own stage identity. By the time he began performing at Café Wha? in Greenwich Village for young white audiences who had never even heard of the chitlin circuit, the impact was startling.

Success took its toll. Hendrix became exhausted from constant touring and his performances grew increasingly erratic. Frustration with his life and career eroded the enthusiasm once so apparent in his early days. After Monterey Pop, "his reputation for being a showman was already causing him problems; the crowd wanted to watch a spectacle and were impatient when they didn't get the display they had read about in the papers."[51] The burning-the-guitar mask of shock theater had come to haunt the Jimi Hendrix Experience. Once established, it could not be dismantled. Folk singer Bob Neuwirth said, "If you wear the mask long enough, sooner or later you become the mask."[52]

Fame has no faucet; it cannot be controlled. Joplin, Hendrix, and Morrison hadn't bargained for sacrificing their privacy when they were struggling young artists. Janis remarked, "You give up every constant in the world except music, that is the only thing in the world you got."[53] As their celebrity grew, so did audience resentment of high artist fees, rising ticket prices and perceived rock star elitist attitudes. The same audience who had adored them were now feeling "screwed by their heroes." The notion that "music should be free" didn't start with Napster.

Rock and Race

American life has been perpetually entangled in race issues. The middle to late '60s brought rioting in American streets as it would a half century later. It has been said that history does not repeat itself; people do. As a teenager, Janis Joplin was an outspoken supporter of racial integration, but racism and high school peer pressure exacted a high price. After the blues divas, she was drawn to Memphis soul singer Otis Redding. His dynamic vocal delivery and the tight sound of his Stax recordings influenced Joplin's future endeavor after Big Brother—the Kozmic Blues Band, followed by Full Tilt Boogie. She once told a friend that "she wished she were black because black people had more emotions, more feelings, and more ups and downs than white people."[54]

The racial views of Jim Morrison are unclear. He admired Black blues artists, yet in the heat of a drunken rampage he allegedly was heard screaming the N-word. The Doors' dark music avoided the racial question that fell hardest on Jimi Hendrix. A Black artist in America faced constant racial pressure to stand with African Americans exclusively, but Hendrix had been raised in Seattle and spent time in Vancouver. Being exposed to a racially diverse climate where he was often in the minority found him wishing "to be in a place where his ethnicity and music were embraced for their essence and not their oddity."[55] Thus, Hendrix was an introductory bridge to a white audience's discovery of Black music. Similar to jazz giant Louis Armstrong, Hendrix steered clear of the race question, stating, "Music is stronger than politics. I feel sorry for the minorities, but I don't feel part of one."[56] Hendrix was pressured by Black activists who took issue with his having two white men in his band and for his relationships with white women. His response when confronted by a Black Nationalist was, "You got to do what you have to do and I have to do what I have to do."[57] His music was never accepted by a Black audience while he lived in Harlem. It wasn't until he brought his electric style downtown to the Village that Jimi Hendrix found a supportive white audience who embraced his style.

On multiple levels, he was a man without a home. As a result,

"Jimi remained a man torn between two musical cultures: the strict, regimented tradition of uptown Harlem R&B and the loose amalgam of folk and rock that was developing in the Village."[58] Similar to the hip-hop era that followed him, Jimi Hendrix's music was neither heard nor initially accepted by Black radio. Although he received extensive critical and popular praise, the critic Robert Christgau once referred to him in minstrel show terms as an "Uncle Tom"—pandering to a white audience. A Black artist working in white-dominated rock during the '60s found it impossible to escape racial tension. Hendrix paid a price for being visually unique and an anomaly. In 1969, Hendrix played a benefit in Harlem where "nobody knew him ... and the audience replied with an egg.... He started playing like he'd never played before," said his friend Arthur Allen. "That was his first communication with Black people and they dug him."[59] He never gained Black audience acceptance, something that pained Jimi Hendrix in his short life. Perhaps the best take on Hendrix came from fellow blues guitarist Michael Bloomfield. It took Bloomfield, white and Jewish, to see that in reality, Jimi Hendrix was "the Blackest guitarist I ever heard." His music was deeply rooted in pre-blues, the oldest musical forms like field hollers and gospel melodies.[60] Being a Black artist in America has always been a long, hard road.

There is a dramatic moment in Joe Boyd's 1973 documentary of Hendrix. Playing and singing "I Hear My Train A-Comin'" in a studio, Jimi sings softly, strumming an acoustic twelve-string guitar with a timeless soul that embodies the history of Black music. You can almost hear the night crickets singing in the Mississippi cotton fields. "A profound irony of Hendrix's career is that even after shredding racial shibboleths by the dozens he discovered a gate at the country's color-obsessed edge he was not able to bust wide. This being the same gate that has kept Black people from embracing him as one of their own to this day."[61]

Where and how does one draw the lines between a public and private life? This was a major problem that contributed to the early demise of Joplin, Hendrix, and Morrison. Janis said, "A lot of artists have one way of art and one way of life, but they're the same for me."[62] Between constant travel and the pressures of maintaining a career, the inability to develop meaningful relationships resulted in a lack of perspective. Hendrix biographer Charles Cross noted, "The very traits that had made Jimi a star—ambition and talent—made it impossible for him to step back from his career and have a life offstage."[63]

The more famous the Doors became, the more Jim Morrison reeled out of control. His volatility in combination with heavy drug and alcohol use became tiring and destructive for the band. "Jim's pranks could be clever but there was an undertone of ugly aggressiveness, usually vented at the wrong time and place."[64] Morrison realized this, but he couldn't or wouldn't see himself as his own worst enemy. "I think of myself," he once said, "as an intelligent, sensitive human being with the soul of a clown which always forces me to blow it at the most important moments."[65] Eve Babitz's sister noticed that Morrison was always "a very dark presence in the room.... I'd say it was of a person who was severely depressed. Clinically depressed."[66] Steve Katz recalled, "In retrospect, I now think of Morrison as just another fucked-up kid."[67] Morrison's self-destructive ways reflected a late–'60s American society careening toward a dark and destructive place, brought on by Vietnam, civil rights rioting, police brutality, heroin and harder drugs, and the Manson murders. "In effect, the Doors were asserting themselves as the archetypal band for an American apocalypse that we didn't even know was creeping upon us."[68]

Janis Joplin admitted being unable to control her feelings, a youthful backlash to the emotionally reserved atmosphere of most American families. Her friend Jim Langdon said, "She just did what she felt like doing ... with anybody."[69] Joplin was resigned to a "Kozmic Blues" fate—that life would shoot you down no matter what you did. Her biographer wrote, "She could never escape a fundamental darkness created by loneliness and a bleak fatalism bequeathed by her father. Choosing alcohol and drugs as painkillers just made everything worse."[70]

Jimi Hendrix's unresolved feelings about this mother, combined with a difficult, conflicted relationship with his father, placed him on unstable ground. His gentle manner shifted into a resentment of his fans, viewing him as a freakish spectacle while failing to embrace his dedicated musician side. Neither Joplin, Hendrix, nor Morrison could be prepared for the accelerating merry-go-round success. The responsibility of stardom means dealing with your audience's expectations. Jac Holzman observed of singer-songwriter Tim Buckley that "he saw the audience as an animal that might gobble him up, expecting the same songs year after year after year. Jim Morrison—I think he came to the same point too."[71]

As fame increased, so did their drug and alcohol use. For Jimi Hendrix, combining both altered his personality. His friend Herb Worthington said, "You wouldn't expect somebody with that kind of love to be that violent.... He just couldn't drink, he simply turned into a bastard."[72] Like her idol Bessie Smith, Janis Joplin could handle heavy drinking, but her habits turned to heroin. "Better than anything else, heroin briefly cured her loneliness, anxiety, insecurity and sense of dislocation."[73]

After leaving Big Brother for a solo career, her drug use compromised her abilities as a band leader, rendering her unable to lead and fully articulate ideas to collaborating musicians.

Alcohol helped Jim Morrison gain confidence without control. Remarking on his love of "scotches," Eve Babitz wrote, "I myself didn't drink, get drunk, and then jump out of windows, get busted, stick my fist through plate glass, show up three days late for an interview with Joan Didion from Life Magazine, drunk, unshaven, and throwing lit matches in her lap."[74] Morrison made life difficult for all around him, especially his girlfriend, Pam Courson. "She was devoted to Morrison, but just couldn't deal with his abuse and the drugs."[75] An environment for hangers-on and bad company ensued. Hendrix and Morrison began trailing an entourage of drug dealers, hustlers, and questionable characters. Morrison's crowd began encroaching on the Doors' recording sessions and often had to be removed. "The Doors lead singer, who only two years before had been one of rock's smartest, scariest, and sexiest heroes was now a heartrending alcoholic."[76]

As Morrison's performances deteriorated, his audience continued buying tickets to a show of self-destruction. Lester Bangs wrote that "the whole nightmare easily translated into parody—and there was a supremely sad irony here ... because in time he became a true clown, picking up the Lizard King cartoon and wearing it like a bib to keep the drunk drool from rolling down to stain his shirt."[77] Joplin, Hendrix, and Morrison were ground down by the rock and roll touring machine, recording deadlines, and drugs. The end was in sight. Ellen Willis noted of Janis Joplin's four encores at the Fillmore East that "finally she came backstage. 'I love you honey,' she said, gasping, 'but I just got nothing left.' Someday, we were sure, it would certainly be true."[78]

Fame breeds a demanding audience claiming rock heroes as personal property. In a Doors concert review, Liza Williams compared Jim Morrison to "the Ultimate Barbie Doll." The crowds want the doll to "do her thing which is our thing because we own her/him/the ticket/the poster/the record/the idol."[79] There is a spectators-at-the-Roman-Coliseum aspect to all of this. "The Doors made the myths and were instantly the victims.... Already in 1968, the Doors were performing not freedom, but its disappearance."[80]

Mass acclaim brought an eerie sense of personal detachment, a feeling of possibly fading away. "Jim sensed the distance between who he really was and his public persona."[81] Janis Joplin's fame changed her as well. Her star rose with Big Brother and the Holding Company, the band who had first launched her, but the bassist Peter Albin said, "I started noticing Janis believing all her publicity. Janis started to become a phony, a caricature of herself."[82] Her sister, Laura Joplin, wrote in her book, *Love, Janis,* the hurt Janis caused when she lied about being kicked out of the house at age fourteen. "Not only was Janis flouting most of the morals that their [parents'] generation prized, but she was lying about her relationship to her family in a very public way. They felt powerless and wronged."[83]

Jimi Hendrix's hunger for success proved to be a double-edged sword. His great talent, virtuosity, and musical commitment "also caused Jimi to act on his immediate desires or urges, with reckless-ness at times."[84] With his rising fame and relentless touring schedule, critics noticed Hendrix's loss of passion for the joy of making music. "I am so fed up with playing. They want me to do all these shows. I just want to move to the country. I'm so sick of burning my guitar."[85] At a Madison Square Garden peace benefit, he stopped mid-performance, unhappy with himself and his post–Experience band. He walked off the stage, "seemingly lost in his own world."[86] A shadow of futility had replaced the fire in the Jimi Hendrix Experience. Despite his recent musical exchanges with Miles Davis, his desire to record with arranger Gil Evans, and his interest in recording with the Blood, Sweat & Tears horn section, Hendrix told Melody Maker, "I'm back right now where I started. I've given this era of music everything. I still sound the same, my music is still the same, and I can't think of anything new to add."[87] The enormous expenses Hendrix incurred building his Greenwich Vil-lage recording studio, Electric Lady, kept him working constantly. Time off for reflection never came to Jimi Hendrix.

The practically overnight superstardom of Joplin, Hendrix, and Morrison was followed by personal and artistic dissatisfaction. In the documentary *Echoes of the Canyon,* David Crosby says, "Bands evolve until they devolve." The Jimi Hendrix Experience began falling apart in 1968, partially due to bad business arrangements driven by youthful naïveté. "Jimi was more than happy with his fifteen pounds a week.... He signed his contracts with Jeffreys and Chandler without reading them and was concerned with the cash he was getting up front."[88] Artists hun-gry for a break often make a common music industry mistake—trusting the first interested manager to come along while failing to examine con-tracts with a reputable lawyer. Chas Chandler appeared to be honestly dedicated to Jimi's best interests, Michael Jeffreys less so. "Chas was one of the only people who told Jimi a straight story," said his English girl-friend, Kathy Etchingham. "When Jimi lost him, he was then only sur-rounded by yes men."[89] Joe Boyd agreed. "I think of Jimi Hendrix, whom I knew only on film but about whom I learned so much, a man whose dreams lead him into a life surrounded by pressures and people who meant him little good."[90] The Grateful Dead drummer Mickey Hart once said of Hendrix, "He didn't have anyone at the end of the day to tell him, 'This is what you really look like.'"

Dynamic contrasts often create great music. Keyboardist Ray Manzarek explained the Doors were "a beat Southern gothic French symbolist poet who joins with a classical jazz-blues keyboard player, a jazz marching band drummer, and a bottleneck American folk-blues Flamenco guitarist. Take those disparate types and play Bertolt Brecht and Kurt Weill, Willie Dixon, plus our own songs. The Doors combine those elements."[91] From their first album on, they created something that "did not sound of its time: it was a timeless sound."[92] The Doors recording engineer Bruce Botnick agreed. "The Doors paid no attention to any prevailing sound.... They had none of the identifiable 60s crutches.... That really set them apart."[93] From their aborted New Haven performance in December 1967 where Jim Morrison was arrested, it was downhill, leading to "four years of diminishing tolerance of each other ... which is sad."[94] While the Doors' audiences demanded "Light My Fire," the band's unraveling met with surprising crowd hostility and contempt. "People are screaming parodies of the lyrics that Morrison isn't singing ... but the huge, godlike voice is nothing compared to the more powerful mocking crowd."[95]

The interplay between Jimi Hendrix and the drummer Mitch Mitchell created a unique sound rarely heard in rock. Mitchell's driving contrapuntal rhythms, similar to the Doors' drummer John Densmore, came from a jazz background that dramatically impacted the music. Jazz drummer Warren Odze noted that "the drummers who were prominent in what has now been called 'classic rock' were mostly born in the 1940's to early 50's. There really weren't any 'rock' drummers at that time, what musicians heard were big band and jazz drummers, with a looser feel and higher pitched drum tunings. Mitch Mitchell, born in 1947, was one of those players and his early influences were Tony Williams and Elvin Jones. Mitch Mitchell was the gateway for drummers born in the 60's to Elvin Jones, who Mitch was channeling with Hendrix. It's hard to imagine 'Manic Depression' with a simple rock type beat keeper. Hendrix's group had the real jazz spirit of interplay as opposed to the drums laying down a repetitive beat."[96]

Janis Joplin's voice was sparked by the psychedelic high volume of Big Brother and the Holding Company, providing a contrast of old and new, Bessie Smith–inspired vocals with a rock band. The problem was the group could not compete with the media attention that focused solely on their lead singer. "We weren't strong enough to get in her way," said Sam

Andrew.[97] "Janis' voice would be the key to the struggling band's success and the reason for its eventual demise."[98] Joplin's manager, Albert Grossman, pushed her to leave Big Brother and form a band of more highly skilled musicians. Her future bands had more individual talent but with mixed results. The effective contrast between Janis and Big Brother disappeared as Joplin's sound transitioned to the soul textures of Aretha Franklin and Otis Redding. Ironically, higher musicianship in Janis Joplin's Kozmic Blues Band would diminish the uniqueness she had previously established. "For the elitist concept of 'good musicianship' was alien to the holistic, egalitarian spirit of rock and roll as the act of leaving one's own group, the better to pursue one's individual ambition was alien to the holistic egalitarian pretensions of the cultural revolutionaries."[99]

In many ways, rock has been a counterintuitive art. In the literary world, an author writes a book, embarks on a promotional tour, then returns to work on the next project. In rock, the road is continuous, supporting band members, managers, agents, roadies, and more. When the tour stops, so does a major part of the income. For Hendrix, Morrison, and Joplin, the physical exhaustion of a nomadic life left few opportunities to compose new material. This is a typical problem in rock, leading to the "third album syndrome," where the library of original songs has run out, leading to makeshift composing in the studio spurred on by pressure to release a new album. The result is weaker material. This shortsighted business plan drains the artists who oftentimes aren't helping themselves physically or mentally. The horse burns out in a few years, causing the permanent business of managers and record companies to look for new stallions. In retrospect, this highlights the Beatles' ten-year song catalog of brilliant music as an astounding feat. Even they stopped touring after six years.

Conclusion: Posters Curled and Grayed

> "Can you hear me?
> Twenty-seven
> Like a morning
> With barely a sunrise."

It all ended in a puff of smoke. Jimi Hendrix died of an overdose in London on September 18, 1970, almost four years since his solo career began in that city. Three days after his funeral, Janis Joplin died of a heroin overdose in room 105 of the Landmark Motor Hotel in Hollywood. Nine months later, Jim Morrison would succumb to a heart attack in a Paris bathtub. All were twenty-seven years old. Their passionate disregard for the future met a predictably tragic end. They had their vulnerabilities. "Perhaps Jimi's biggest weakness was his inability to say no to anybody.... Nobody with a vested interest seems to be able to speak authoritatively about Hendrix, and so his death has only deepened the mystery and confusion."[100]

Jim Morrison's legacy is crowded out by his sensationalized image, like litter strewn across his Père Lachaise grave in Paris. The Byrds' leader, Roger McGuinn, said, "Morrison has this iconic image about him, but I think that has tended to be at the expense of the music. His musical talent gets overlooked."[101] His melodic gift and the expansive musical abilities of Krieger, Manzarek, and Densmore remain underrated.

The '60s died along with them. There would never again be a decade of such creative turmoil. For rock legends, the past is never past, "but the funeral never seemed to end, and the burial never seemed complete."[102] The era of passionate utopian ideas was followed by a predictable backlash of conservatism, calming the waters but not without its drawbacks. "For the truth is that anti[-]utopianism also has its price," wrote Ellen Willis, "which is the inability to feel our deepest longings and ultimately feel much of anything at all."[103]

It is a musical and cultural legacy that is easily distorted, overrated by some, summarily dismissed by others. "The ideal of the sixties were visible mostly in fun house-mirror form. Today when the mode of music changes, the walls of the city are covered in corporate ads sponsoring specifically subversive artists."[104] Even the Doors had a billboard on Sunset Boulevard; many more would follow. Today, '60s protest songs are packaged and sold for nostalgic consumers, far from the original intent. Rock has become "Dad music."

Joplin, Hendrix, and Morrison were among the millions of confused and searching youth in a volatile, exciting, and frightening era. "I don't think Janis and Jimi suffered from anything that was any different than what most of us were going through at the time, they were just unlucky. With Janis, I don't think her problems were that long-term. We were all on self-destruct to one degree or another, but Morrison was on serious self-destruct and the outcome was predictable. Janis had some romantic and self-image problems. Jimi died by accident, not because he wanted to."[105] Writing of Morrison later in the 1970s, Eve Babitz found "I began running into women who kept Jim alive—as I did—because something about him began seeming great compared with everything else that was going on. He may have been a film-school poet, but at least he wasn't disco."[106] It is a legacy that casts a long shadow over a great deal of commercial music that follows it.

Would they have gone on creating and evolving? It is a difficult question to answer. They may have thrived or been swamped by the '70s, only to be obliterated by the '80s MTV era. We will never know. "The best information indicates that towards the end of his life, Jim Morrison lapsed into severe depression over his inability to reinvoke his poetic music."[107] His last notebook contained page after page of the words "God help me." His death relieved him from a suffering only he could comprehend. "Death proved to be Morrison's most rewarding friend. It halted the singer's decline before he might have gone on to even worse behavior or art."[108]

Janis Joplin would have undoubtedly developed into a versatile vocalist of American song. She had the capacity to sing jazz, blues, pop, rock, country, and more. "She was a better singer than the world or even she knew," said Paul Rothchild.[109] Janis Joplin, claiming she was from "pioneer stock," felt she was invincible. She lived by the words she uttered four days before her death: "You are only as much as you settle for."[110]

Jimi Hendrix remains untouched as a master of rock guitar and the sound spectrum he created, seemingly descended from another planet. His influence on contemporary music spans multiple genres. "The advent of hip-hop MC's (hands down the most musically intelligent interpreters of lyrics today) has made Hendrix's own conversational way with a line sound like even better singing than ever we fans originally thought."[111]

Janis, Jim, and Jimi did what most important artists do—they brought past influences forward into a new light, expanding boundaries in a modern language. We should remember, like the title of Patti Smith's book, they were just kids. Success turned

Front Porch Post, Greenwood, Missi sippi.

Fountain opposite the Rosa Parks Bus Stop, Montgomery, Alabama, where she boarded a city bus on December 1, 1955, and refused to give up her seat to boarding whites.

them into brands against their will. Today, it is a desirable goal. All were searching into their past for something they had lost while hurdling at rocket speed into the future. Alas, "Whitman's open road is not finally the Hollywood freeway, and in any case neither stardom nor prosperity could deliver what they seemed to promise."[112]

Despite our digital world a half century later, the castles made of sand they molded have not fallen into the sea.

And those pistols keep on firing.

9

Rebels: The Authentic Lives
of Women in Music

The story is undervalued and rarely told. The dynamic contribution of women in American popular music is an inspiring example of a struggle for personal and artistic freedom. James Baldwin once wrote, "It is only in his music, which Americans are able to admire because of protective sentimentality limits their understanding of it that the Negro in America has been able to tell his story."[1] This can also be said for our limited awareness of women's achievements in a male-dominated music industry.

They are musicians, vocalists, band leaders, composers, and arrangers who have defied convention from Bessie Smith to Beyoncé. Female artists have sought a daringly risky life path, not marrying for security while enduring the challenges of a volatile career. The notion of women in the arts has been scorned since Shakespeare's time when aspersions were cast on "loose women" who endeavored to be artists, painters, actors, or musicians. Fast-forwarding to the 1960s, the pop vocalist Lesley Gore remarked, "Nobody in the business really took female performers too seriously back then. The system just wasn't open to women."[2]

The strength of female musicians comes from an inner determination, often beginning in their formative years with the notion of creating an art capable of equaling or surpassing their male counterparts. Some were encouraged by an English or music teacher who inspired them to take the helm of their artistic dreams. There would be many obstacles. Male egos were fearful of the additional competition, finding collaboration uncomfortable with women in what had been traditionally male-dominated roles.

Similar to other marginalized groups, women in music had to doubly prove themselves. Not only was their music being judged, so was their gender. Recording engineer and producer Susan Rogers said of this proving ground, "If a woman's work is great, she'll be helping herself and the

152

women who come after her. If it's not great, it will be more difficult for the next woman which is not the same for men, who are more apt to be judged as individuals."[3] Men's lack of respect for women in music spans genres from blues, country, jazz, and pop to female rappers in hip-hop.

Labels are an odd thing. The many genres and musical categories from jazz to punk are vague, revealing the interpretation of writers and fans more than the artists who created them. African American musicians have been confined to "race records," "rhythm and blues," and "urban" monikers that are neither useful nor accurate. The term *women's music* almost screams, "Look at this: an all-female band. Isn't that cute?" or worse, "She's so good. She plays like a man." In her book *She's a Rebel,* Gillian G. Gaar writes, "Women in rock are still by and large defined in that order, as women first, and rock performer second."[4] No one called the Beatles, the John Coltrane Quartet, or N.W.A. an "all-male band."

The women's music label became increasingly problematic "as the network grew into a movement, straight women became marginalized, and the term became a virtual euphemism for lesbian music."[5] Categorizing music drives industry marketing while creating misunderstanding and confusion by their descriptions. The Ramones never called their music "punk"; Charlie Parker and Dizzy Gillespie didn't name their music "bop," but someone else did.

Despite this, female musicians set a course without concern for what it might be called or by whom. Their music is more than a statement of identity; it is a larger artistic vision. As Emmylou Harris said, "It wasn't about country music or folk, or Americana, or even just sheer beauty, it was my pulse and breath."[6]

Bessie Smith: Defiantly Herself

She was the Empress of the Blues. A major star during the 1920s and part of the 1930s, Bessie Smith broke through gender barriers long before the women's movement arrived decades later. She once said, "If you can't keep up with me, you better get out of my way."[7]

Bessie meant business. Whereas the typical 1920s female white pop singer delivered romantic ditties of fragility and submission, Bessie Smith, as an independent Black woman, was having none of it. When she sang "I Ain't Gonna Play No Second Fiddle," it was a no-holds-barred order to a cheating man to pack up and go. Her big sound and church-influenced phrasing required no microphone. She projected a larger-than-life image that left her audience spellbound.

A major star on the Theater Owners Booking Association circuit, the vaudeville for African Americans in the 1920s, Bessie Smith was in charge. She led her own troupe, arranged dance numbers and comedic skits, and sang her blues her way. Had she been born a half century later she would have been a multimedia celebrity. Her terrifying version of "Send Me to the 'Lectric Chair" was a declaration of a woman admitting guilt without feeling guilty.

The story of her scaring away a Ku Klux Klan posse is legendary. At her July 1927 tent show in Concord, North Carolina, with stubborn courage, "she ran towards the intruders," wrote her biographer, Chris Albertson, "stopped within ten feet of one of them, placed her hand on her hip and shook a clenched fist at the Klansmen." "I'll get the whole damn tent out here if I have to. You just pick up them sheets and run."[8]

They did.

Bessie Smith was a free woman before the notion barely existed. Bisexual and proud, she burned down the facade of subservient feminine fantasy. She was true to herself, no matter what others thought. Her sexual freedom ignored pretension and Victorian rules. Her roughness and coarse language created a hard exterior that future generations would emulate.

Her life and musical career was a series of highs and lows, yet nothing stopped her. If she was ever discouraged, it never showed. Her voice beams across generations that follow her, being picked up like short-wave radio. It was a signal discovered by a young Janis Joplin in Port Arthur, Texas. It changed her life and made her want to sing.

The life of Bessie Smith, cut short by an automobile accident in 1937, "had to be the story of a woman who was black and proud long before that became the acceptable thing to be."[9] Her unmarked grave finally received a headstone in 1970, made possible by contributions from Juanita Green and Janis Joplin, just months before Joplin's death. That headstone reads: *"The Greatest Blues Singer in the World Will Never Stop Singing."*

Even in death, Bessie Smith defies the ages.

Billie Holiday: Singing Her Life

America's most popular entertainment form, the minstrel shows of the nineteenth century, took more than it gave. It enabled African Americans the opportunity to display their singing, dancing, and comedic talents while instilling racist caricatures of buffoonery and clowning in negative stereotypes. Those stigmas live on in black-face incidents on college campuses, major network television shows, and the closeted past of government officials.

Billie Holiday, America's preeminent jazz singer, with a bullshit detector sharper than the Hubble Space Telescope, put an end to all manners of such foolishness. Her innate talent—the ability to turn a lyric and melody into her own meaning—stood in contrast to her troubled personal life. Elizabeth Hardwick wrote that Holiday's life "had taken place in the dark" and that she "was always behind a closed door—the fate of those addicted to whatever."[10] Typical of the public's voyeuristic tendencies, her demons provided entertainment for an audience unaware of her artistry.

Tragedy attracts and sells. To this day, Billie Holiday's downfall and death at age forty-four receives excessive attention. She was a genius musician who listened closely to the jazz musicians who surrounded her. Billie sang with the band, not in front of it; she lived inside the song. Her lyrical phrasing, sounding like an instrument, influenced Frank Sinatra, Miles Davis, Mel Tormé, Etta James, Erykah Badu, Nina Simone, and many others. Her voice was a human cry that redefined popular song. Composer Ned Rorem noted, "She made you accept her song on her premises, and then you got caught up in her content."[11]

As a beautiful, light-skinned Black woman, Billie endured countless episodes of racism while traveling the road with the big bands. For squeamish ballroom owners, she was too dark to sing with an all-white band (Artie Shaw) and too light for the all–Black Count Basie Band. It is no wonder she quit and headed for Café Society and the New York City club scene in the late '30s. Her version of the graphic, anti-lynching song "Strange Fruit" was a bold move, confronting and shocking an audience oblivious to southern life's realities. It increased her reputation while driving her toward a torch-singing style.

More than anyone, Billie stirred the cauldron of distortions and inaccuracies about her life. She would fight any drunken heckler on 52nd Street who threw stones in her passway. She dealt with life through self-medication; heroin was a constant companion. Her downward trek of sorrows continued through the '40s and '50s as "her work took on, gradually, a destructive cast as it so often does, with the greatly gifted who are doomed to repeat endlessly, their own heights of inspiration."[12] Intelligent and sensitive creative artists such as Billie Holiday engage in a crash course with the reality of a cold and indifferent world. It offers no surrogate parent or remedy for a painful childhood.

Walking through a clothing store one day, I heard her voice, a sample embedded in a hip-hop track, fading in and out of the music while people shopped.

Her ghostly warning laughs and says, "I'm not as far away as you think."

Steamrollers

I performed at the Cookery in Greenwich Village during the fall of 1975, playing bass six nights per week for three months with Mary Lou Williams. One night during a break between sets, we sat in a booth near the piano, close to where they threw the dirty dishes into a large, gray plastic bin. She began telling me this story. "When I was with the Andy Kirk Band during the 1930s [she was the only female], my husband would drive us through the night as we went from one one-nighter to the next. I was learning on the job how to compose and arrange big band scores. I would take out a flashlight and blank manuscript paper and go to work as we rode through the night. That's how I learned."

I was struck by this story of self-determination. Here was a brilliantly talented woman in a male-dominated field, her mind set on learning no matter what it took. I could see the car headlights on the highway and the lone flashlight, a beacon in the night. The fact that Andy Kirk and His Twelve Clouds of Joy encouraged and performed her soon-to-be-classic works was compelling. They made room for her immense talent.

There were other important female pioneers. Lil Hardin, the pianist, bandleader, and composer of "Strutting with Some Barbecue" and "Just for a Thrill" recorded by Ray Charles, was a forceful role model for women. It was not easy. Lil Hardin, the former wife of Louis Armstrong, was also a French teacher, seamstress, tailor, and piano teacher. Alice Randall wrote of "Strutting with Some Barbecue" that "every time I hear it, I think of Lil empowering generations of listeners. Show yourself, inhabit yourself, with pride."[13]

Women like Mary Lou Williams and Lil Hardin rolled into every town with determination. It went beyond their passionate love for music into a quest for self-realization. They changed their lives with the music that ran through their veins. Like Mary Lou, the image of country singer Maybelle Carter, "riding on the running board of a Model T used for touring, because the lights were out,"[14] is similar to a sailor in the crow's nest, leading a ship between the rocks.

Kitty Wells felt that opening doors for women in country music was her greatest achievement. Wells, June Carter Cash, Wanda Jackson, and Bobbi Gentry, among others, fought both male chauvinism in a one-sided industry and the limited role for women in society before the 1970s. Female performers generally found greater acceptance in folk music. Sheila Weller wrote that folk "in the 1950s allowed young women to use deceptively ultra-traditional vessels [high, pure, trilling voices, long skirts and hair; imagery of hearth, heart, and childbirth] to social and cultural limits."[15]

The Decca records recording star Sister Rosetta Tharpe was a fiery singer and electric guitarist who trailblazed a path for women. Combining gospel, blues, and jazz, she was peerless, recording "Rock Me" and "Strange Things Happening Every Day." Her aggressive guitar playing style was perceived as being "masculine" by some as she outplayed the male guitarists who tried her in "cutting" contests. Inez Andrews said, "She was the only lady that I know who would pick a guitar, and the men would stand back.... Men don't give her no credit because she was competition. You know a man's not gonna sit up and say a woman can beat him doing nothing!"[16] Like Mary Lou Williams, Sister Rosetta Tharpe never saw herself as a "woman" musician or guitarist. If you could play, that was all that mattered.

The early female folk icons from Jean Ritchie to Odetta were inspirational to the modern generation of singer-songwriters who soon followed. "When Carly Simon saw Odetta in the audience, she was so awed, she passed out. When she came to, there was Odetta, fanning her with a menu."[17] The symbolism is striking.

Despite societal pressure for females to conform to the good housewife and home-keeper roles during the 1950s, women musicians broke through constricting barriers. Similar to the generation of Bessie Smith, Billie Holiday, and others before her, rhythm and blues vocalist Etta James stood in stark contrast to the wholesome white pop singers dominating the charts in the '50s. She "was the original bad girl of rock whose defiance has inspired and underwritten singers as diverse as Janis Joplin, Salt-n-Pepa, and Polly Jean Harvey."[18]

Etta James sang with confidence at a time when Black singers were undermined by the music industry. A white face potentially meant better sales for a major label who feared conservative backlash, resulting in cover song versions of Little Richard and Etta James among others. These musically inferior, bland renditions (with the exception of Elvis Presley) generally outsold the original recordings due to superior mass marketing, advertising, and distribution. Despite the 1954 striking down of the "separate but equal" law that had previously ensured racial apartheid, Black artists found it nearly impossible to gain access and exposure in the white-controlled world of radio and television.

Southern country blues evolved into a louder, faster rhythm and blues when it traveled north with the Great Migration, enabling Koko

Taylor the opportunity to make a name for herself in Chicago and beyond. Koko sang with intensity and heartfelt conviction that rang through the blues clubs on the south, north, and west side of the city. "I'm showing men," she said, "that they're not the only ones.... I can do just as good a job as they can at expressing the blues and singing the blues and holding an audience with the blues."[19]

It was artists such as Sister Rosetta Tharpe, Koko Taylor, and Etta James who inspired the singer, blues guitarist, and songwriter Bonnie Raitt. She has continued the blues legacy and has "outlived, out sung, and outplayed every walking rocker-babe-blues-mama cliché."[20] Raitt supports the new generation of women musicians from sales of her signature-model guitar.

The art of singing is a process of digging deeply into one's own feelings while expressing those emotions in real, believable terms. It is a matter of going beyond technique and tone into human realism, storytelling through sound. The song's message resonates inside the heart and mind of the listener, enabling these women to become leading artists in their field. Singer-songwriter Patty Griffin was first inspired by the songs her mother sang. "It's not the words she's singing, it's the feeling."[21]

Taking the trials, joys, sorrows, and hardships from their lives, these women have adeptly turned those life lessons into a universal art. As Dolly Parton once said, "If you don't like the road you're walking, start paving another one."[22]

Making Their Own Rules

In order for women's careers to evolve, it requires more than breaking sound barriers; they need to redefine preexisting parameters. In the early 1960s, a young woman's average age for marriage was just under twenty-one. Actress Jill Clayburgh, star of the film *An Unmarried Woman*, noted that at that time "ambition wasn't cool or feminine."[23] Betty Friedan wrote her 1963 groundbreaking work, *The Feminine Mystique*, seen as feminism's second wave, by tirelessly working in the New York Public Library while raising her children.

Whether female musicians read Friedan's work or not, her influence had great impact on the arts in general. In a male-dominated environment, "women have survived in the music industry since rock and roll's birth by rising to the challenge of setting their own rules."[24]

Mary Lou Williams once told me she had trouble understanding a woman's movement that seemed alien to her experience. "Men always helped me," she once told me. "I would ask a question about arranging music and they would show me." Tina Weymouth, bassist with the Talking Heads, felt that overfocusing on the feminine musician's role was detrimental and excessive. "One thing I did that I'm glad about in retrospect is that I've never talked about the problems of being a woman. I didn't want to discourage anyone who had the same idea."[25]

Busy Being Free: Joni Mitchell

Joni Mitchell, one of Canada's (and America's) greatest songwriters and performing artists, stands as an example of a woman who persevered past boundaries and stereotypes. Moving beyond the typical parameters of folk music, she has evolved by showing her restless spirit as Picasso and Miles Davis once did. Sculptor Morton Rosengarten observed that Joni Mitchell in the fall of 1967 "was driven, she clearly had a path; she was ... on the trail of her creative truth."[26]

Such a bold route means certain risk, pain, self-doubt, and societal pressure. Lindsay Zoladz noted that "very often, women who live as freely and hedonistically as the average man are criticized by outside forces for not behaving correctly."[27] History either rewards or scorns those who do not behave. It has taken many decades for female musicians to break through, to live and work on their own terms, and to find an audience who openly accepts them. Liberate the listener and you free the music as well.

Jimi Hendrix referred to her as a "fantastic girl with heaven words."[28] Joni Mitchell is in a class of her own. Her ability to paint with a brush transferred into painting with words. She escaped her background by quickly learning "the lesson that any ambitious, talented girl in the Canadian prairie might draw from the matriarchs seems clear: having babies in poverty and desperation, and remaining in the provinces will destroy your dreams almost before you can dream them."[29] Joni sensed an adventurous life beyond her upbringing.

Recovering from polio in her youth, she learned how to play open chords on the guitar while discovering unusual open tunings. "I lost my speed," she once recalled. "I turned to grace."[30] The beautiful colors she discovered made her music unique and were widely marveled by musicians.

Joni Mitchell's pursuit of greatness came with the realization that her young marriage would be a detriment to her dreams. In order to create, she would need to be free. In the '60s, this was a drastic contrast to the norm, requiring a woman of considerable strength, conviction, and idealism. Joni's life of creative freedom influenced future female artists. She befriended Georgia O'Keefe, one of the noteworthy artists of the twentieth century, who made a lasting impression. Joni said, "After 1965 was really the first opportunity that women had in history to be accepted as creative artists."[31]

Inspired by a passage in Saul Bellow's book *Henderson the Rain King,* she composed "Both Sides Now." It reached anthem-like status for young women connecting with her message. Joni Mitchell's deeply personal lyrics were a breakthrough, revealing women's hopes, dreams, doubts, and triumphs. From a female perspective, it was a new day. Her lyric writing equaled Bob Dylan and Leonard Cohen, possibly surpassing them both. "It was the detailed precision of her lyrics—that teetering on the edge of sharing—that made listeners connect so intimately with her."[32] Joni's "Circle Game" addresses time and aging in a lyric of poetic wisdom. Her ability to encapsulate the 1969 Woodstock Festival in song prompted David Crosby to say that "Joni contributed more towards people's understanding of that day than anybody who was there."[33]

Joni Mitchell's *Blue* album became an enduring example of a woman's brilliance while outshining her male peers. Like the writer Eve Babitz, she was a fearless female adventurer who cleared hurdles and criticism. Despite commercial success, Joni had the temerity to musically go her own way, even if it meant risking her popularity and confusing her audience. In a *Rolling Stone* interview with Cameron Crowe, she said, "You have two options. You can stay the same and protect the formula that gave you your initial success. They're going to crucify you for staying the same ... but staying the same is boring. And change is interesting. So of the two options, I'd rather be crucified for changing."[34]

Carly Simon: Music without Apology

She had to live down the privileged-rich-girl syndrome. Coming from the Simon family of Simon & Schuster, the third largest publisher in the United States, with intelligence, talent, and integrity, Carly Simon has persevered. *Rolling Stone*'s Jon Landau wrote, "Carly Simon never apologizes for writing about herself or her well-to-do background that has been so gratuitously criticized."[35]

Rich or poor, the blues finds its way in the door. Carly's home life was darkened by a detached and distant father, giving it a sense of abandonment. Loneliness and creativity are close companions.

Well-educated, well-bred women who were strikingly independent often resulted in high-powered female achievement. Along with the actresses Diane Keaton and Jill Clayburgh, Carly Simon "represented those brainy, likeably neurotic women who just learned to stop taking crap from men, while other women cheered them on."[36] Jacqueline Kennedy was attracted to Carly's freedom, resulting in a longtime friendship. As a public figure, she must have longed for a similar freedom she had once had.

Carly Simon proved to be a great songwriter and vocalist with a magnetic sensuality. Her song "That's the Way I Always Heard It Should Be" became, according to the biographer Sheila Weller, "the first anti-marriage pop ballad written by a woman."[37] The song was a declaration against convention and the idea that a woman's worth was somehow determined by her relationship with a man.

Being successful, attractive, and independent was difficult for a woman such as Carly Simon in a relationship with a celebrity, her now-former husband, the singer-songwriter James Taylor. There were times when Carly Simon's records outsold her partner's. Simon's manager, Arlyne Rothberg, said that Carly "always, always minimized her success in front of others, especially when James was around."[38] Some marriages are unable to make room for dual successes; an unspoken rivalry became the elephant in the room. Writer Jake Brackman (later to become Carly Simon's husband) noted that "James was not at all delighted with Carly's creativity."[39] Men and women are never free trying to be smaller in life than who they truly are.

Whether it is *Blue* by Joni Mitchell or Carly Simon's "You're So Vain," these artists built a distinct musical legacy. It is, as Ann Powers wrote, "the clearest and most animated musical map to the new world that women traced, sometimes invisibly within their daily lives in the aftermath of the utopian, dream-crushing 1960's."[40] Their legacies are complicated by the double standards of aging. Allegedly, older men stay vital and vibrant while senior women are relegated to their past image and accomplishments, a media misconception. Joni Mitchell's and Carly Simon's standout work shadows many of the female pop music stars of the glittery '80s and beyond. "It was the era of Madonna and Cyndi Lauper. Carly and Carole [King] and Joni's generation—their bulging emotional dossier, all those lessons learned—was irrelevant."[41]

Great art is lasting, while pop music clings to branding, image, and social media manipulations.

Art, like a distant sun, endures.

The song remains.

Craft and Mastery: Carole King and Laura Nyro

The American popular songbook was largely composed by men—Irving Berlin, George Gershwin, Cole Porter, Jerome Kern, Rodgers and Hart, Harold Arlen, and many more. In the hands of Carole King and Laura Nyro, that tradition expanded and evolved. John Lennon and Paul McCartney credited Carole King and her songwriting partner, Gerry Goffin, as major influences. King and Nyro crafted songs that were masterpieces of lyric and melody. Carole King said, "I loved taking simple melodies influenced by classical compositions and Rodgers and Hart and Hammerstein—taking those melodic influences and putting them in context of rhythm and blues styling, phrasing and rhythm."[42]

A wife and mother, her major hit in 1960, "Will You Still Love Me Tomorrow?" recorded by the Shirelles, was a liberated message resonating across America. This was beyond Tin Pan Alley traditional songwriting; it was a sexually wise statement for a new generation. Transitioning from behind-the-scenes songwriter to solo artist, her landmark album, *Tapestry,* was one of the biggest selling records in music industry history, establishing Carole King as a major force for women as singer-songwriters. It was a commercial and artistic pinnacle that would be difficult for her to match. Jon Landau wrote that *Tapestry* "is an album that takes a stand, is an album of surpassing intimacy and musical accomplishment."[43]

Laura Nyro remains the dark horse genius of her generation. Her brilliant songs shine like diamonds, including "And When I Die," "Eli's Comin'," "Time and Love," and "Wedding Bell Blues." Fellow musicians were awed by her talent. Steve Katz proclaimed that Nyro's "Stoned Soul Picnic" should be the national anthem, while Stephen Sondheim said, "In economy, lyricism, and melody it is a masterpiece."[44] A Jewish New Yorker from the Bronx, Laura Nyro emanated a world-weary sadness, partially accounting for why she lacked sufficient popular acclaim during her lifetime and after.

Like her mother, she died of ovarian cancer at age forty-nine. Her ashes were scattered under a maple tree, close to the brook that ran under her home in Danbury, Connecticut. It is a beautiful and sad place. Her songs live on.

Aretha: You'd Better Think

She stands alone. Aretha Franklin's face appears on America's musical Mount Rushmore as an inspiring symbol of her artistry, race, and gender. Coming from gospel roots, she is one of the twentieth century's magnificent voices, a tidal wave–like sound that projects and overpowers the listener. "The church provided one place where black women could command authority and respect."[45] Aretha knew what her singing voice could do to people.

Had she never recorded anything beyond her version of Otis Redding's song "Respect," we would still be talking about her. It was an anthem, a cry for freedom on multiple levels—racial, as a woman, as a human being. The sheer force of her vocal presence changed the song's meaning, giving women the strength to rise in the morning and carry on. In 1967, you heard this record everywhere, many times in an hour. It is arguably the most dynamic two minutes and twenty-eight seconds ever recorded. Her album, *Live at the Fillmore West*, backed by a band led by the saxophonist King Curtis, with Bernard Purdie on drums, is one of the greatest soul albums ever made. It sizzles.

Her career surpassed mere popularity, largely because she dedicated herself to the civil rights movement. Aretha took charge, as witnessed in her scene-stealing role in the 1980s Blues Brothers film. Like her famous preacher father, C.L. Franklin, from whom she learned her gift of phrasing, Aretha spoke out loud and clear, never hiding behind a publicist's manufactured image. Aretha Franklin is remembered quite differently from many of the female divas who followed her. Her career transcends hit making; it is a musical portrait of America from slave ships to church, stage, and the world. She sang while race riots exploded, Detroit burned, and Dr. Martin Luther King was buried. "Aretha's songs, like the novels of Toni Morrison and the memoirs of Maya Angelou, illustrate how the struggles and growth of one woman could talk back to the whole of American history."[46]

Of all the music critics, it was perhaps President Barack Obama who best summed up the life and work of Aretha Franklin: "Nobody embodies more fully the connection between the African-American spiritual, the blues, R. & B., rock and roll—the way that hardship and sorrow were transformed into something full of beauty and vitality and hope," he wrote through his press secretary. "American history wells up when Aretha sings. That's why, when she sits down at a piano and sings 'A Natural Woman,' she can move me to tears—the same way that Ray Charles's version of 'America the Beautiful' will always be in my view the most patriotic piece of music ever performed—because it captures the fullness of the American experience, the view from the bottom as well as the top, the good and the bad, and the possibility of synthesis, reconciliation, transcendence."[47]

It is her ability to capture American history in sound that makes Aretha Franklin's legacy as enduring as the faces on Mount Rushmore. Gentlemen, kindly move over.

Pedestals and Prisons

The music industry's star-making machine is largely based on flash, image, and branding. By placing stars on a pedestal with a fabricated image, a product is bought and sold at a price. Regarding the ill-fated pop singer Karen Carpenter, it was "as Gloria Steinem once wrote of pedestals, 'as much a prison as any other small space.'"[48] The female star faces a carnival house of mirrors while catering to male fantasies. Janis Joplin fought back against what the media and, as a result, her fans ultimately demanded of her. She told the Associated Press that "interviewers don't talk about my singing as much as about my lifestyle."[49] Even Bob Marley encountered a similar problem in his short life, artist as zoo exhibit and spectacle.

Although rock and roll was a male-dominated, chauvinistic club, it nevertheless provided an outlet for female strength and independence. It gave women musicians a platform for self-discovery. Grace Slick, former model and lead singer for the Jefferson Airplane, said, "What we took for granted seems remarkable now: a fearless, authoritative, frankly female voice, claiming rock and roll as a political force."[50] Surely the spirit of Bessie Smith must have been smiling.

Selling a female pop or rock star is largely beyond the artist's control. Blondie was first and foremost promoted as a sex symbol. "The media," she said, "just promoted me as a female body. It's like I had to prove that I'm an artist in a female body."[51] The singer-songwriter Liz Phair, creator of the acclaimed *Exile in Guyville* album in 1993, found the same pressure to be "gregarious, social, cute, and fun than for me to be a great musician. I think that is sexism."[52]

Being taken seriously is an ongoing issue for women in music. The condescendingly "cute" aspect has resulted, as I have witnessed as a professional musician, in male musicians dismissing females as unimportant and irrelevant. Courtney Love once lamented, "I put as much thought in the way we sound as Pavement or Sonic Youth do, but no one ever asks about the music. It's like my persona—boom! Knocks everything else out."[53]

Even the classical music world has biases. Double bassist Orin O'Brien was hired by Leonard Bernstein as the first full-time female, regular member of the New York Philharmonic in 1966. "I had a lot of experience and I think that a lot of the publicity was just that, suitable publicity." Ms. O'Brien, a gifted educator (I was one of her students), expressed embarrassment due to the sudden notoriety of her hiring. "The articles [in *Time* magazine] all stressed that I was 'cute' and silly things like, 'what a tour was like with only one female, etc.' It was basically pretty frivolous and I also did not like being the center of attention [no matter how brief]."[54]

Ultimately, it is the work that matters, not the stereotypes. Singer Marianne Faithfull's recording career was hindered by her star couple relationship. She found that being involved with Mick Jagger, "I didn't understand that it was very important for me to work, whatever happened in life."[55]

Rock and Sexism

The majority of male rock singers and instrumentalists have delivered predictably sexual roles in their song lyrics. In the 1950s and early '60s, young female vocalists were largely pawns in the hands of male record producers who controlled virtually every aspect of their careers. "Like most women in music [and as with Black artists in general]," wrote Donna Gaines, "the girl groups story is a typical one of under-recognition, exploitation and disappointment."[56] Ronnie Spector Greenfield had to sue her ex-husband, the renowned record producer Phil Spector. The Ronettes claimed they were taken advantage of after receiving only one $14,482.30 check for their million-selling hit "Be My Baby." They were awarded $2.6 million in royalties and interest, but it took them thirty-seven years to get paid.

It wasn't until the groundbreaking work of Aretha Franklin and others that female solo artists and "girl groups" were given the opportunity to produce, write original material, and play instruments on their recordings. In the music industry power struggle, men have been reticent in giving female artists control over their careers. "Their ambivalence toward power-sharing with their female colleagues manifests itself in a kind of willful ignorance, aggressive indifference, and, sometimes, even sabotage."[57] When auditioning guitarists for her band, Patti Smith found that "almost to a man, none of them warmed up to the idea of a girl being the leader."[58]

Despite their struggles in rock and popular music, women have used the genre as a key to freeing themselves. The self-realization of being an independent artist leads to discovering who you are and how best to say it. Beyond imagination, it becomes a human reality.

Punk and Liberation

It isn't surprising that punk in the mid–'70s began primarily as a man's game. Following the virile rock acts of Mick Jagger and others, most punk bands set their course with a low consciousness toward women. "The Sex Pistols and the Clash, twin figureheads of punk, were testosterone-steeped bands [can you imagine a woman in either group?] whose lyrics generally ignored women, or else treated them with disgust."[59] While eschewing tradition, the male punk bands projected an atmosphere of suppressing and oppressing women in general. Ellen Willis recalled seeing the Ramones at CBGB on New York City's Lower East Side. "I was also put off by the heavy overlay of misogyny in the punk stance." Willis viewed the rock community as a "male monopoly, with women typically functioning as more or less invisible accessories, around male musicians, I've often felt as out of place as a female sportswriter in a locker room."[60]

Despite its primitive outlook, punk inspired women musicians to cast off the typical folk singer image and claim a bolder, convention-free stance. Patti Smith emerged in this light while influencing many who would take her lead and form their own bands. "She either inspired or improved the climate for a generation of women in rock whether they actually got somewhere or remained so minor you've never heard of them."[61]

Women utilized punk by expressing it as a social critique, liberating them from traditional conventions. They provided an assertive voice that assumed a truer identity, getting into what Congressman John Lewis once called "good trouble." Punk influenced music, fashion, and the MTV image but did not sell as successfully as pop records. From the '80s on, a generation of gifted women vocalists were signed by major labels to make pop hits. This was achieved by heavy production followed by image making, branding, and extensive marketing. Hits build careers, grow audiences, and create income streams. That is how the game is played.

The '80s and '90s pop singers erected careers that contrast with Aretha and Joni Mitchell. Multiple songwriters crafted material that the divas would sing (not unlike Motown in the '60s), who then performed and sometimes strangled the song into submission (*American Idol*). The result was commercial success at artistic cost. Remember Elvis? Hello? The *New York Times* critic Jon Caramanica wrote that "something deadening is at play on these records.... There is no play for authenticity.... [They are] impressive singers fighting against the technology and algorithms designed to flatten them into a homogenized whole."[62]

These muted recordings stood in sharp contrast to the indie label–driven music of the past. Although no one doubted the immense talents of Whitney Houston and Mariah Carey, they "constitute a sort of twin towers of Adult Contemporary soul, a shining, corporate, colorless [as opposed to more benign color-blind] take on black music."[63]

Major labels with a high overhead require massive hits. These are corporate choices, not accidents. Gritty soul singers experienced diminishing sales during the '70s and '80s. That singing style offered little chance for crossover success in an industry dominated by pop, disco, hip-hop, and country music. Yet there is a price to be paid. Whitney Houston's commercial success serves to diminish her artistic legacy. Many of the songs she sang were unworthy of her talent. Bright tabloid lights shine on her personal difficulties, while her catalog fails to truly represent her. There is no "Respect" we can turn to, and that is troubling and sad.

Pop crossover can mold a performer's character. Dismayed by the newer generation of "rock stars," Joni Mitchell lamented, "The childish competitiveness, the lack of professionalism—I don't have a peer group," she told the biographer David Yaffe. "All of them, these spoiled children. It's not what I'd expected in an artistic community."[64]

In the end, we are judged by our body of work *and* our character … always.

Conclusion: Writing Women's History

Women have made monumental gains through the arts. In 1992, Gloria Steinem wrote in *Revolution from Within* that getting a man to fall in love with a woman had been, in those days, "alarmingly easy providing you're willing to play down who you are and play up who he wants you to be."[65] With almost monastic focus, women musicians have written their true destiny by tuning out the surrounding criticism. One wonders how many countless women never wrote, sang, or realized their artistic selves due to these restrictions.

A question remains: What impact do the past female artists have on the present? Since the '80s, this is difficult to determine in a vastly changed culture. Ted Gioia wrote that *Billboard* editor Bill Werde stated, "It's a sign of the times that celebrity trumps actual culture."[66] These words fall like thunder. Do millennials value the work of past female musicians, many of whom seem boldly out of step with current times? It is, as an Australian friend of Gioia's said, "You Americans represent the best of the best, and the worst of the worst, all hopelessly mixed together."[67]

The constructed canons of music are predominantly male. The result is that "it follows that the masculine forces of canonization are stacked up against female artists as they age."[68] This doesn't stop women musicians from supporting one another. Unlike their male counterparts, women as a general rule have created a nurturing atmosphere and kinship as opposed to envy and competition.

The female musicians who will be remembered strove for a distinctive voice that remains authentic, bold, and forthright. In the book *Woman Walk the Line,* Amy Elizabeth McCarthy writes that she and Canadian country artist Terri Clark are "not quite what the world wants in a woman. But I know that women like us, the ones who recognized the power of our emotions and being completely, sometimes painfully honest with ourselves, are the ones who get to live a life that is wholly authentic."[69]

This is the house they built.

Piano keyboard, similar to the upright piano of jazz master Mary Lou Williams.

10

No Time to Get Cute
in the '70s

When I arrived in New York City in 1973, the Big Apple had turned into Dante's inferno. The city was over $5 billion in debt; garbage was piled high like snowbanks on the street. Bruce Springsteen said from the stage one night at Max's Kansas City, "It's midnight in Manhattan; this is no time to get cute."[1]

I was nineteen, young, ambitious, naive and being oblivious helped. I was in the eye of the hurricane and didn't even realize it. You never know you are living in a historic time and place until it has passed you by. I lived on the Upper West Side, then moved to Carmine Street in Greenwich Village where the cockroaches defeated me. With a friend's help, I found a loft at 55 Mercer Street between Broome and Grand. I was now a struggling SoHo musician, arriving at a time when most people were desperately trying to leave New York City, like the Kliban cartoon of Houdini escaping from New Jersey. "An executive recruiter from Chicago told a reporter that he had been handling an alarming number of résumés from people who were willing to go anyplace but New York, and that was before the blackout."[2]

The '70s was a terrible time for public education. Music and art programming were almost nonexistent; art class became a "study hall." In *Love Goes to Buildings on Fire,* Will Hermes wrote that "back in the late 60s, there were around 650 art teachers in New York City public schools. By '77, there were fewer than 250, roughly one for every thousand students."[3] Through the creative arts, marginalized people proved they knew how to make something out of nothing, the legacy of New York in the 1970s. Kurt Vonnegut once declared, "Manhattan Island, at its center, inspires utterly baseless optimism—even in me, even in drunks sleeping in doorways and in little old ladies whose houses are shopping bags."[4]

Rents were cheap (yes, you heard that right), enabling artists the

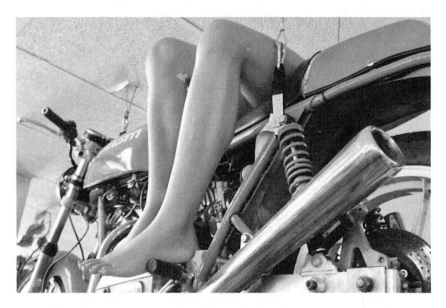

Manikin on a motorcycle, Speaking Volumes record store, Burlington, Vermont.

freedom of existing through part-time employment. Living in SoHo meant ekeing out a living in a quest for an arts life. The once-proposed-then-failed Lower Manhattan Expressway project kept rents low through the '60s and early '70s. My loft was 2,500 square feet with brick walls, wood floors, and huge windows that barely caught the eastern sun ... all for $350 a month.

SoHo (being south of Houston Street) was "where the inhabitants of a roughly one-square mile area of Lower Manhattan changed the way we think about music, art, performance and human sexuality."[5] I practiced my eighteenth-century double bass looking out on Mercer Street with the bustle and noise of delivery trucks parked helter-skelter on each side of the street. It was bedlam during the day and a ghost town at night. Manhattan was illuminated in color, but to me, SoHo was in black and white.

Chaos brought creative possibility. Despite the city's fiscal decay, "designers, artists, musicians and filmmakers formed collaborations, making art and meeting at rock venues."[6] The walls between diverse art forms collapsed like the Mercer Arts Center, beauty among the ruins. Guitarist and writer Lenny Kaye said, "There was a lot of interweaving between the literary and the cinematic worlds, and musical performance, and it didn't seem to have many boundaries."[7]

All I knew was that I had more space to live, work, rehearse, and dream. Few realized that SoHo would have a worldwide impact. Being only a few miles from New York City's center, this cultural movement "helped circulate cutting edge ideas and innovations."[8] I wasn't aware of the magnitude of all this; I simply loved being there. Being in close proximity to free-thinking artists rubs off and affects your work. As the musician Chris Stein said of the ever-present art guru Andy Warhol, "He taught us not to be bogged down by the past, or nostalgia, and to be open and ready for the next thing that comes along—the newest music of fashion or technologies."

The '60s were over. It was time for something else.

Cast-Iron Bohemia

SoHo had geographic, not artistic, boundaries. Houston (pronounced How-stan) Street was the northern boundary; Canal Street, with its eclectic bric-a-brac stores, was the southern end. West Broadway was brilliantly placed west and Lafayette Street was east. It made for a defined area that represented the largest concentration of full and partial cast-iron facades in the world. Knowing these buildings were constructed between 1840 and 1880, I wondered what people of that era would have made of colorful characters such as the Ramones, Patti Smith, Television, Suicide, and theater at Café La MaMa.

Most of these historic buildings had serviced the textile industry. I occasionally discovered small wooden thread spools in my loft, messages from the past. Over eighty years later, this industrial area, for a brief, magical time, became an artist colony, made possible by urban pioneers who converted these buildings into homes, art studios, art galleries, rehearsal spaces, and recording studios. SoHo was a work of art in itself, having fully evolved by the mid–1970s. What these creative artists did was a process of "taking received culture and violating it, breaking it up, transforming it into something funnier, weirder, fresher, more exciting—and one's own—this was the aesthetic engine of 70's art."[9]

It wasn't luxurious. In 1976, I was youthfully ignorant and would put up with anything. Climate change came to New York City first, the summers were exceptionally hot, and between the thick air and cigarette smoke in bars, it is a wonder I am still around to type this. The garbage smelled worse each day, and the rats got as big as small cats. I remember the New York Police Department cordoning off a city block and going in with shotguns. It wasn't for the faint-hearted. The biggest fireworks display in the city's history was for the tall ships celebration on July 3, 1976. The intense heat turned my girlfriend's tuna sandwiches she had planned on selling at the event into a biology experiment. She was quite disappointed.

New York is not for everyone.

Loft Martyrs

At first glance, SoHo seemed bleak. There were no public schools, no supermarket, and the few children raised in the area didn't realize that most of the world doesn't live a life dedicated to art. The people on the streets were mostly in their twenties and thirties, trailblazing and improvising their lives. In 1975, Laurel Delp of the *SoHo Weekly News* described the area as "'a land of hazards, true pioneer stuff' instead of Indians, there were fire inspectors, instead of cowboys, artists, and no one knew where to put his trash."[10]

Each new day began with the street noise of delivery trucks filling my second-floor loft; at night there was silence and empty streets where I parked my Volkswagen Rabbit in a nearby garage for $40 per month. I retreated to the back of the loft where there was an old gas stove with a washer and dryer in the bathroom. It was freezing cold in the winter. The front windows were tall and wide and "had previously made daytime industrial work possible without the expense of light."[11] I covered the windows in plastic sheets that billowed like sails on cold, windy days. The place was dark and tomb-like, but it was a refuge from the city. The vintage tin ceilings were cool looking, but sound resonated like a Harlem air shaft.

Bars, clubs, and restaurants with live music were steadily appearing. I wheeled my double bass out of the subway (you haven't lived until you've schlepped a large instrument on the IRT), plowing my way through Manhattan like a nuclear icebreaker. Late one night, I came upon two men, drunk and tumbling out of Oh-Ho restaurant onto West Broadway, like cowboys flying through a saloon door. Laughing hysterically on the ground at my feet were Elton John and Divine, the transvestite star of John Water's films. In SoHo, you never knew what would happen next. A 1974 *New York Magazine* article called it the "most exciting place to live in the city."[12]

When the limousines pull up and the hair salons start appearing, you know you're in trouble. Demand increased, my rent rose to $500, and in 1977, there was plenty to complain about throughout the city. SoHo artists pressed on. Edmund White noted that "face to face encounters are essential to a city's vitality ... for the exchange of ideas and to generate a sense of electricity.... In the 70s, creative people could meet without plans,"[13] like Elton John falling at your feet. Collaboration of diverse, converging disciplines made SoHo into what Greenwich Village had once been. The real question was how long would it last?

I survived on tours with major jazz artists Cleo Laine, Stephane Grappelli, and George Shearing, among others, and by working local venues such as WPA, the Cookery, Greene Street bar, the Bitter End, and the Bottom Line. SoHo wasn't ideal; it was a visionary place where "in most cases, they reveal people taking the lousy hands they'd been dealt and dreaming them into music of great consequence.... Sometimes the worst situation produces the deepest beauty, and the most profound change."[14]

Until SoHo became unaffordable for the artists who pioneered it, "this was the last period in American culture when the distinction between highbrow, and lowbrow still pertained, when writers and painters and theater people still wanted to be [and were willing to be] martyrs to their art."[15] I'm not sure we saw ourselves as martyrs; we were too determined and immersed in our work to notice. Like a slow, steady invasion, the gentrification tanks were closing in. One day I came upon a wall covered in graffiti art where someone had written, "Soho Sucks, Bring Back the Trucks."

I wished Stephen Sondheim had put that title to music.

Dirty Yet Alive

Surviving New York City in the '70s meant being in a constant state of heightened awareness. You never knew when a hand grenade might be tossed your way. The high crime rate became a comedian's punchline, and a person had to be careful not to wear anything that someone might want to steal. I never worried about that, believing that carrying an enormous double bass around Manhattan acted as my invincible shield. Muggings were so common that "Allen Ginsberg was attacked while walking near his apartment on East 12th Street at seven o'clock on Halloween night."[16] Ghosts and goblins weren't intimidated by New York City.

The subways had a stench from a mélange of rain and garbage, a fragrance beyond description, Eau de Subway. The trains were heavily adorned with graffiti, later to be recognized as art as opposed to a crime. I remember one elderly lady getting on the subway train and exclaiming in her most critical voice, "The subways in Montreal and Paris certainly don't look like this." True, and they weren't innovating there like New York City.

The trains rarely ran on time and patience was required. We waited forever at 2:00 a.m. on the platform in the summer heat. Will Hermes wrote that in the subway alone, there were "2,971 purses snatched in '76, 5 rapes, 5 homicides, 145 felonious assaults" (and a partridge in a pear tree). In addition, there was the city sanitation workers' strike. They eventually returned to find "about fifty-thousand tons of rotting trash to collect from city curbs."[17] The Bronx became an inferno. Slumlords torched their buildings for insurance money rather than maintain them. There were "5,500 arson cases in the South Bronx alone in seventeen months."[18] Thirty fires per day was typical for the Bronx.

You get the picture.

I played jazz at the West End Café near Columbia University with some ex-Basie and Ellington musicians, including the legendary drummer Jo Jones, who could swing the world with brushes on a *New York Times* newspaper or bang out a solo on the shutters behind the bandstand. With his wild-eyed look, he would admonish me, "Young talent, you will never know about life until you make a baby." Their glory past, time had been unkind to these veterans, some of whom were mail carriers, bathroom attendants, and minimum-wage day laborers. Music is an unforgiving business once the dance is over.

No one leaves the music business; the music business leaves them.

A serial killer added to the festivities. The Son of Sam murders began in July 1976, attacking young women and couples parked in cars, spreading terror throughout the five boroughs. Times Square street vendors began selling Son of Sam T-shirts emblazoned with the killer's police sketch and the warning, "Son of Sam: Get Him before He Gets You."[19] Terrified young women attempting to hide their gender cut their hair short. They got him on a parking ticket, issued to one David Berkowitz of 35 Pine Street in Yonkers, New York. He had parked his cream-colored Ford Galaxy sedan near a fire hydrant. He was arrested the evening of August 10, 1977, and received six life sentences. It was a deadly, endless summer.

While New York City was sinking under imminent bankruptcy, the beautiful and glamorous danced the night away at Studio 54, drinking and consuming large quantities of cocaine and weed laced with angel dust. "Yet at the same time, Studio's Rome-in-the-twilight-of-the-empire feel seemed very much in keeping with this moment in the life of New York."[20] The sheik disco crowd contrasted with the homeless living on the streets of SoHo and the Bowery. Returning from a late-night gig, I was frightened out of my wits by a pile of cardboard on the sidewalk that suddenly rose with a human being underneath. New York was the Roman Coliseum and the lions weren't hard to find.

Despite all of this, I, like most people in the arts, felt hopeful. For something special to happen, creativity must slow dance with risk. "It's always right before a storm that the air is filled with dangerous possibilities."[21] Being in the city meant taking chances, and attempting a career in music was a gamble. Neil Young once said about the process of making a record, "If it sounds dangerous, you're on the right track."[22] SoHo offered a place to experiment in front of your peers. It was "a place and time in which, rich or poor, you were stuck together in the misery and the freedom of the place, where not even money could insulate you."[23] I was too intoxicated by the air of unrestrained energy to fully realize the hazards. It all made for potentially provocative art, and for me, it certainly wasn't the Midwest. "Who's going to write a book about walking the safe streets of Manhattan?"[24]

Bronx Bombed

Baseball fans either love or despise the New York Yankees. It is an American tradition. The '70s team of manager Billy Martin and colorful players like Reggie Jackson, Thurman Munson, and Catfish Hunter were a motley crew who absorbed the atmosphere of those lean times. They were as volatile as New York itself. Pete Hamill wrote, "We are dirtier, less charitable, less grand, and less just. But we are here. We have survived."[25]

That certainly describes the late–1970s Yankees, owned by George Steinbrenner whose infamous love-hate relationship with the scrappy Billy Martin was legendary. The fires were not only rising from torched buildings in the Bronx; they were in the Yankee dugout. When Martin tried to fight Reggie Jackson in the middle of a game, it felt as though baseball, America's great pastime, was subject to the city's street temperature. The Yankees were fighting themselves while striking cops were handing out "Welcome to Fear City" flyers. You have to wonder what tourists from Iowa were thinking upon their arrival at LaGuardia Airport.

If those visitors from America's heartland figured taking in a Yankees game would be a pleasant family outing, they were wrong. Sportswriter Roger Angell, recalling a Yankees series, wrote, "During the third game a group of fans in the upper decks showered their fellow spectators with beer, hurled darts and bottles onto the field, and engaged in a near riot with stadium police."[26]

Fun for the whole family.

Like a clobbered baseball rolling on the ground whose cover had been knocked off, New York City was coming apart at the seams.

"Often," wrote Thomas Boswell in the *Washington Post*, "the Yankees cut too close to the bone. They resemble the suffering, everyday world far too much."[27]

Take me out to the ball game.

Gigs and Low Rents

I became so ensconced in the Village and SoHo that I avoided Midtown, Uptown felt like the North Pole. Downtown meant art, culture, ideas, and energy; Midtown was commerce, congestion; and Times Square, pornography shops, which numbered in the hundreds. It was not a place to go walking with your mother, although mine was amused by it. The relatively low cost of living meant a freelance musician could pick up club, bar, and restaurant work for $30–$75 per night and still make your rent. Those rates haven't changed much in the past fifty years and there are fewer gigs around town, but rents, that is another story.

Venues were everywhere: punk at CBGB, rock at Great Gildersleeves, Kenny's Castaways, Café Wha?, Max's Kansas City, and some remaining folk clubs like the Back Fence on Bleeker Street. I played at the Bitter End with French jazz violinist Stephane Grappelli who liked the place because it had "an amusing little soup." There was jazz at the Village Vanguard, Village Gate, 7th Avenue South, Studio Rivbea, and the Tin Palace. Ali's Alley was run by the drummer Rashid Ali, formerly with John Coltrane. I played with him at Yale University and the students looked stunned, as if Martians had just landed with musical instruments. Because of city noise ordinance rules, drums were forbidden in many venues. It was a great way to learn how to play rhythmically without a drummer.

Experimental music flourished in SoHo. The Kitchen offered a performance space for Laurie Anderson and the always-innovative Brian Eno, who had a loft on Broome Street. We schlepped to the Grand Union on LaGuardia Place for our groceries and coffee at Café Reggio. Lenny Kaye worked at Village Oldies record store, and the avant-garde saxophonist John Zorn was a clerk at the Soho Music Gallery. It was a great time for off-off Broadway theater. "Ellen Stewart's Café LaMama was located in the East Village, and like Café Cino, was among the first to uproot theater from its midtown home."[28] I was cast there as a musician in a tuxedo with my face painted silver in a production of *La Bohemia Based on Trilby* with John Vaccaro, Richard Weinstock, and Ruby Lynn Reyner. It was the debut and finale of my theatrical career.

We didn't care about not making money. We got by. It was a rare opportunity to be in the middle of a lightning storm. Lower Manhattan was exciting, crazy, sensuous, fun, and dangerous, and besides, I would have never experienced any of this back in Hinsdale, Illinois, where a hamburger at the Piccadilly and ice cream at Dipper Dan's was a night out.

Punk and Other Scarecrows

The '70s was a time of beginnings and endings and the worst hair decade in human history. Jazz, salsa, and contemporary composition were on the wane; rock had become corporate and bloated. David Byrne, of the seminal band Talking Heads, said, "The days of naïve, primitive rock bands are gone."[29] The era of the Beatles, Stones, and Woodstock was over. It gave way to do-it-yourself energy that became "punk," a music that turned its back on fat cat rock, big hair, cocaine, Learjets, and limousines.

Personal ambition was the engine running the era. "You were working in a record store," said Lenny Kaye. "You're surrounded by music ... and then you think, 'Hey, it's not unreasonable for me to try to make that music and be one of a hundred million records that we're selling here.'"[30] Punk musicians were street people with little or no money, adopting their look by invading thrift stores, Salvation Army sites, and garbage cans. New York City has fascinating trash. Few punk bands made money; the point was to create, have fun, and experiment. "You're doing it for your peer group, essentially."[31]

As '70s rock grew into an overproduced monster, weighed down by technique and flash, punk headed in the opposite direction. The songs and instrumentation were stripped down to a basic three-minute song, excessive improvisation à la Grateful Dead was eliminated. Vocalist and eventual superstar Debbie Harry of the band Blondie said, "I approached the songs from a kind of an acting perspective.... With each song, I could be a new character."[32] This theatrical, as opposed to a technical approach, gave punk its fresh look and sound.

The values of underground theater influenced the music. Harry said of director Tony Ingrassia, "He was making us work very hard and not to sing technically, but to sing emotionally ... to make sure that you really had a connection with what you were saying or talking about, or singing about rather than just singing a nice melody with a good technique."[33]

Ground zero for New York punk was the Bowery. With its bombed-out buildings, flophouses, and homeless people on the street, the Lower East Side was the perfect setting for a new wave, just before gentrification's teeth set in. Musicians fit into the street's image like crows in a cornfield. Patti Smith's infusion of poetry and music echoed the beat poets who came before her. "She looked like a scarecrow in a garden of chick peas," wrote Frank Rose. "It was all very hard and furious."[34]

An enduring quality of great American art from Walt Whitman to Chuck Berry and Bob Dylan is the fact that it contains multitudes. Patti Smith's song "Piss Factory" represented "every musician and artist and hard-luck dreamer working their ass off in the urine stench of New York City in the summer of 1974."[35] Living a few blocks from the Bowery, I was aware of punk, but it was not my world. I must admit that I didn't get it at the time. I played free jazz and was open to abstract ideas, but punk sounded primitive compared to the jazz scene in which I was immersed. Years later, I realized what punk represented, and by that time it had come and gone.

The gritty noise of music blasting like jackhammers out of CBGB, all for a two-dollar admission fee, fit New York City in the '70s over more "sophisticated" musical forms. Punk was a product if its time. Much to the owner Hilly Kristal's credit, CBGB encouraged original music, not bland covers of pop songs. It was a small scene for the same thirty or so people; then it took off. "At Hilly's and later CBGB, the aesthetic similarly seemed less about escaping the nastiness of the city than reveling in it, amping it up to a cinematic scale, drawing a narrative in which artists could wage heroic battle."[36]

CBGB was a dump, complete with winos collapsed on the curb outside of 315 Bowery Street. It was the launching pad for the Ramones, Talking Heads, Blondie, and others. We rarely give credit to visionary entrepreneurs promoting cutting-edge art—in this case, punk. The mid–'70s was the time of commercial cover bands in orange jumpsuits playing Tony Orlando, Abba, and the Captain and Tennille. There are never enough promoters like Hilly Krystal or John Hammond to go around.

Punk got abrasively louder, while mainstream rock staggered like *Tyrannosaurus rex* into stadiums and large amphitheaters. Big business. Rock became an extravaganza complete with elaborate sets and special effects, as predictably staged as a Broadway show or Disney spectacular. "Led Zeppelin played Madison Square Garden.... At other points—like the familiar Whole Lotta Love/Rock and Roll closer—it felt stale, a remake of something that had lost its original meaning."[37] So goes the way of all things, including punk. Over time, musical categories become overripe and generic. By 1977, punk became "a useful catchall term for critics and journalists but one that flattened the nuance that existed among a diverse range of downtown musicians."[38]

Seize the Beat

Rock and pop of the '70s had a mainstream white audience, offering minimal representation of America's diversity. In order to love music, an audience must, in some way, identify and see themselves in it. The gutting of New York City public school music programs meant that necessity would have to be the mother of invention. Bronx, Brooklyn, and Queens youth seized the beat, creating a sound representing their lives and neighborhoods. Innovation in American music comes from the bottom up, not the top down. Throughout history, marginalized people have shown greater access to their voice. In the late 1960s, the Last Poets, a Harlem group of young Black men reciting militant messages over African drumbeats, jump-started a sound that would inspire a new genre: hip-hop. Traditional African drums had forecasted the future.

Technology was waiting. Turntables and towering speaker systems, popular in Jamaica, took form as "disco" in Europe. When this concept came to America, it created a musical sea change, dancing to records instead of a live band. The Gallery, at 126 West 22nd Street, opened as a gay-only dance club in June 1973. The modern disco age had arrived. Hundreds more followed and the DJ became the main focus. In the South Bronx, disco evolved into an innovative art. The Jamaican-born Kool Herc transported an island musical tradition of talking over records, resulting in "a party on the last week of August 11,1973 in the West Bronx rec room of 1520 Sedgwick Avenue."[39] It was the birth of hip-hop culture—emceeing, breakdancing, graffiti art, and a declaration of one's pride in their uniquely diverse cultural identity.

By 1975, discos were the most popular entertainment in New York City; rap took to the streets. DJs plugged their sound systems into nearby lampposts, transforming parks into an outdoor dance party. With a city unemployment rate of 12 percent, disco and rap made things bearable; every night was an excuse for a party. Music and dance have always provided social release. People dance and sing hoping to escape the worst of times, choosing music that best expresses their feelings. "If disco was euphoric, hypnotic, punk rock was assaultive, relentless, if discos like Studio 54 provided an escape from the ugliness of

New York, its punk analogy, a urine-stained dive on the Bowery called CBGB embraced and indulged it."[40]

Rock, like jazz before it, had grown too sophisticated for the dance floor crowd. People didn't dance to *A Love Supreme* or *Sergeant Pepper's Lonely Hearts Club Band*. It is a double-edged sword. Art must grow or risk stagnation, but when it evolves, inevitably, something is lost. Soul and funk, the engine for disco grooves, lost popularity in the '70s but the beats infiltrated drum machines. DJs advanced their craft despite negative reactions from critics and musicians. In the spring of 1977, "Kraftwerk's 'Trans-Europe Express,' which DJ's played into its pre-segued 'Metal on Metal,' sounded unlike anything else with its chugging mid-tempo synth drums, processed vocals, and zero-gravity vibe."[41]

By the fall of '77, disco was the biggest success story in popular music, fueled by the film *Saturday Night Fever*, a watered-down Hollywood version of the real thing. There were many critics of discos who scorned not just the scene but also the people involved. "Most white male critics turned a blind eye to disco's subcultural leanings, or were downright hostile to the music and its fans."[42] I was on tour in Brazil during the spring of 1979, where I witnessed Western culture's worldwide domination. Discos and posters of *Saturday Night Fever* were everywhere. It was difficult to find and hear real Brazilian music in Rio de Janeiro and São Paulo; discos had run most of those places out of business. The girl from Ipanema dressed in yellow polyester.

The backlash started with the July 12, 1979, "Disco Sucks" fiasco, engineered by the shock jock Steve Dahl. In front of 50,000 baseball fans, disco records were blown up on the Comiskey Park baseball field of the Chicago White Sox, and an unruly mob descended onto the field. Dahl would deny it, but the bedlam was more than a musical protest; most people don't care *that* much about music. It was an opportunity for young to middle-age white males to make a racist, sexist, and homophobic statement, protesting a changing country. Disco's popularity provided visibility to diverse groups of people that the major media had always ignored. Backlash remains a constant in American life.

The disco trend quickly faded. Hip-hop evolved, innovated, and endured. In the '80s, MTV, accused of racial bias in its programming, relented at decade's end with a show dedicated to hip-hop. The rest is history. Hip-hop became a worldwide phenomenon and a dominant art form, commercialized by many, yet instilled with a thread of searching, innovating, and testifying. Listening to Grandmaster Flash and the Furious Five's *The Message*, it is a social wake-up call resonating almost forty years later, from Sedgwick Avenue to the world.

You and the Night and the Blackout

Wednesday, July 13, 1977, started out innocently enough. With a heat wave lasting for weeks, garbage piled high, Beatlemania at the Winter Garden, and a city terrorized by the Son of Sam serial killer, what could go wrong? That evening I played the sheik SoHo restaurant, W.P.A., with the jazz pianist Richard Wyands. We had just gotten started when in the middle of "Autumn Leaves," it all went black. Boom. No one knew what had happened; without warning, the world's extension cord was unplugged. "Ten thousand traffic lights blinked off. Subway trains froze between stations. Elevators, water pumps, air conditioning—everything sputtered to a halt."[43]

I said goodnight to Richard, fumbled in the dark, picking up my bass and amp, and staggered down Greene Street. A light summer shower fell in SoHo. With few car headlights to guide me, I stumbled over street debris, soaked in rain and sweat in the ninety-degree humidity. All music stopped. Uptown, "Bruce Springsteen and the E Street Band had been recording at the Record Plant on Forty-fourth street when the power went out."[44] No more music, just uneasy silence. Things were about to get worse.

Somehow, I made it home, struggling to find the keyhole, I eventually unlocked the door and crawled up the pitch-black stairs to my loft, where another find—the keyhole battle—was to take place. I entered in total darkness. A few minutes later, I heard glass shattering outside and a woman screaming in the distance, a city in turmoil. This was no time for a night on the town or for getting cute. "According to one police report, the looting had started at 9:40 p.m., only minutes after the onset of darkness."[45] One thousand major fires would break out in the five boroughs. We were in for a long, hot night.

Looting was widespread. People of all ages smashed store windows, walking away with expensive suits, appliances, sound systems, and even refrigerators, gifts courtesy of the blackout. Some store owners with shotguns defended their stores, but most had gone home for the evening. It didn't matter what race or nationality of the store owner, all were targets. Little would be left of their businesses the following day. Many shop owners were without insurance.

The next morning, I walked out into the streets of SoHo. It looked like a science fiction movie the day after the world ended—broken glass, papers blowing in the wind, and desolation. I walked for many blocks without seeing another human being. Surveying the battlefield in the bright sunlight, instead of bodies, parts of manikins from looted stores were lying in the street.

The city was in flames. "More than twenty fires were still burning along Broadway come Thursday morning ten hours after the blackout had begun. The stifling heat was made more oppressive by the blanket of black smoke that hung over the neighborhood."[46] It was 100° the day after the blackout, 102° on July 19, and 104° on July 21. The devil had arrived as a tourist in New York City.

The power came back on Thursday at 10:39 p.m., twenty-five hours after our rendition of "Autumn Leaves" crashed and burned. The damage had been done; almost 4,000 people were arrested for looting. New York City became the place America loved to hate. It became hunting season for critics armed with their I-told-you-so rhetoric. *New Yorker* writer Andy Logan remarked, "Instead of comfort, what New York received in the first days after the disaster was often the punitive judgement that it had just got what it deserved, considering the kind of place it was."[47]

Some neighborhoods were permanently ruined, but the city eventually recovered. Time is elastic. I remember it all like it was yesterday, the eerie sight of New York City streets after the apocalypse, the blackout of 1977. In my mind, I see the shattered glass, a manikin's arm, and papers rising in the hot wind.

It is a reminder that even in darkness, hope is never abandoned.

Walking Backward into the Future

A light rain fell the morning of May 27, 1974. I put on a jacket and tie, walked east on 110th Street, and ascended the stairs of St. John the Divine Cathedral. I was there to attend the funeral of Duke Ellington, a man I would come to admire throughout my musical life. I realized much later that this beautiful service, attended by around 10,000 people, the music by Duke's orchestra with Ella Fitzgerald, was symbolic. Jazz had been on a steady decline in popularity since the mid–1940s. The passing of this legend meant uncertain days ahead.

The '70s was the last decade that young musicians could apprentice with classic jazz musicians of Duke Ellington's era. At the West End Café, my working with Paul Quinichette, saxophone, Jo Jones, drums, Ed Lewis, trumpet, Tiny Grimes, guitar, and Sammy Price, piano, was like looking through a tunnel connecting past and present. I wish I had asked them all more questions, youth wasted on the young. They were kind and supportive. I was lucky to learn my lessons on the bandstand. Future generations of jazz musicians would have to realize their craft in music conservatories.

Uptown, every rehearsal at Mary Lou William's Harlem apartment was a trial by fire, all the way down to the circular cigarette burns in her piano keyboard. She scorched me and I learned. My mentor, famed bassist Milt Hinton, gave me my first professional experience in October 1974, playing at Carnegie Hall with the British singer Cleo Laine and her husband, John Dankworth. While punk, disco, and rap were in flower, I had reverted to a past era.

I was an old soul.

The following year, my tour with the pianist Erroll Garner ended abruptly in Chicago due to his second bout with pneumonia. "Garner was an anachronism for he was a folk musician.... He was self-taught, he never learned to read music, and, like all masterly folk artists, he developed a style of such originality and presence that it became nearly autonomous."[48] Waiting to go on backstage in the kitchen of Mister Kelly's, at what would be his last public performance, Erroll told me, "I try to make every night like a party." His philosophy diverged from most younger jazz musicians who displayed detachment and a studied indifference on the bandstand. With a punk spirit, Erroll, seated at the piano bench on top of a telephone book, made up the music as he went along. He was one of a kind.

Mercifully, '70s styles and fashions did not stay around long. In '77, I had the honor of playing a jazz cruise with the Thad Jones–Mel Lewis Orchestra, with Dizzy Gillespie as the guest soloist. Dizzy and Charlie Parker were two of the principal architects of bop, a major contribution to modern jazz. On my desk is a photo of Dizzy and me, with a beard and enormous hair, standing on the dock by the SS *Rotterdam*. Looking at old photos of the band on that cruise to Bermuda and Nassau, it is now clear to me there are few things worse than white guys in dashikis.

The '70s jazz scene was still vibrant. I lucked into a three-night gig with Oliver Nelson's all-star New York–LA big band at the Bottom Line, followed by a record date with bop saxophonist Sonny Stitt, who glared at me, the young white boy, in between shots of whiskey. I was thrilled and scared to death. Restaurant gigs in Greenwich Village included piano-bass duos at Bradley's, one of jazz's last great communities. One night, Charles Mingus came in and was visibly frustrated with the chord changes the young pianist was playing. With his massive frame, Mingus leaned over the upright piano and showed us mid-song how it should go. The Village Vanguard's 1:00 a.m. set of the Bill Evans trio was like church for me and the six other people in the audience. By the late '70s, I was putting on my tuxedo and heading uptown to play at the Café Carlyle with Marian McPartland and George Shearing. Whether downtown bohemia or uptown high society, everyone had a story to tell.

Young musicians were hungry to learn jazz, an essential American art form no longer in the mainstream of American culture. Let's face it, I wasn't cut out for the Ramones. "As Confucius said: He who lives in the past walks backward into the future."[49]

That was OK with me. I kept on walking.

The World Ends, Not with a Bang but a Realtor

By '70s end, SoHo's creative fire began to flicker. Rents soared and the squeeze on the art community was on. "It seems in retrospect that from the moment I moved into SoHo, back in 1974, the art world residing there had been threatened.... In 1979 real estate prices went up."[50] As the New York City economy slowly improved, the art scene began its decline.

The AIDS epidemic began its devastation from the early '80s on, casting a shadow over the Village and SoHo. "1981 changed all that. Suddenly the glamour boys, with their showboat bodies and high-paying jobs, were Auschwitz skeletons covered with black spots, like Canova's unfinished marble statues."[51] The impact on the art world was felt worldwide. It was a dark time.

SoHo's pioneering advances as a creative center resulted in the area's ultimate demise. "The downtown's cutting-edge artists were ironically, at the vanguard of a process that stripped these neighborhoods of their diversity and vitality."[52] Nothing changes people or a neighborhood faster than money. The tourists descended.

It resulted in a withering music scene in the '80s, '90s, and beyond, replaced by a high-end playground for the wealthy and "artsy." A designer wrecking ball had hit SoHo. One by one, creative music venues went under. Just before I moved out, my loft was robbed, wedding clothes were stolen, and my hard-earned grand piano was vandalized, black spray paint on the white keys. I left the city in '81 and barely recognized SoHo upon returning. "The loft-jazz scene wound down as the cost of living downtown went up—the usual story of music bringing a neighborhood back to life and attracting people who make the place too expensive for musicians to live there."[53] The free jazz musician Ornette Coleman's performance loft became a Cartier jewelry store.

Jazz went in conservative and mainstream directions. The audience diminished and experimentation was largely written off. Everything seemed to be a salute to the past. Now you had to go to Europe and Japan in search of a supportive audience for an American-born art form. Jazz had become a forward-looking art that looked backward into its past. CBGB, punk's desolation row, became overrun by suburban youth seeking the thrill of a gritty atmosphere, far from their safe environs. Who could blame them? After all, Patti Smith and Blondie came from Jersey. CBGB eventually became a John Varvatos clothing store. SoHo was just another American mall, a fashion designer brush fire burning out of control.

"High end retailers just don't make aspiring artists."[54]

The urban theorist Jane Jacobs wrote, "We must understand that self-destruction of diversity is caused by success, not failure."[55] Like dominoes, gentrification went from Greenwich Village to SoHo, the East Village to Brooklyn, and on and on. All things must change, but SoHo remains light-years away from the night I helped Elton John and Divine up from their collapse on West Broadway. My Mercer Street loft is a commercial whatever. Standing on the street where I once lived, it now feels empty. We have all moved on.

Patti Smith, a distinguished author, feels little nostalgia for the 1970s. But as for the music, "I do actually appreciate it more now than when I was doing it…. Hearing it again, I feel affection for it because the one thing that comes through to me is that we had a lot of guts, we had a lot of bravado, and we had a lot of heart."[56]

SoHo's story fits musician Brian Eno's invented phrase "scenius." It describes the spontaneous intuitive genius of a cultural scene, a group of creative people who collectively generate the excitement of vital new art.[57] The legacy remains like a cast-iron facade.

The world ends, not with a bang

The author's 1987 Banchetti electric upright bass with Indiana Jones fedora.

but a realtor. What endures is the fact that at a time when the stars aligned, SoHo transformed popular culture, resonating around the world. On tour of Japan in 2000, I noticed the Tokyo kids on the street had the punk look, minus the Bowery Street theater.

Time moves on and fires die out. We carry the spirit of New York in the '70s inside us, and as each new generation finds its own way, hope for a new day, anytime, anywhere, anyplace.

> *"I used to chase Samo [artist Jean-Michel Basquiat] from my corner on West Broadway and Spring, where he sold hand-made postcards. He was a real brat. If I only had those postcards now."*[58]
>
> —*Steve Dalachinsky*

11

Post-Authentic World: Your CEO Rock Star

We're living in a post-authentic world
Everyone knows it's true
Maybe it's a post-authentic world
What's a poor boy to do?

I wrote these lyrics after hearing a speech by Bruce Springsteen. Rock once prided itself on being a game with few or any rules. It allowed the performer a path to self-discovery and maybe an audience would find them in the process. Notice I am using past tense here; the game has changed. Art is a process of finding out what is truly inside of you. It is an arduous process of grueling hard work. You dig like a miner to bring out the best you can deliver so it may be shared with an audience.

The famed record producer Sam Phillips, the man who first discovered and developed the talent of Elvis Presley, understood this well. In 1978, Phillips said, in his southern preacher-like voice, "My greatest contribution was to open up an area of freedom within the artist himself, to help him express what he believes his message to be." Notice that Sam Phillips uses the word *freedom* as a concept within the artist himself. This is not freedom in the sense of the right to vote but rather pursuit of an inner freedom. The artist and the audience have the need to experience and discover that freedom in music. A musical gathering provides not only community, but at its very best, an individual sense of liberation. "That don't move me," said Elvis in an early recording session. "Let's get real gone."

If art is to have lasting impact, it must disrupt. It provokes, often dividing a society into seeing and hearing in new ways. These exciting moments when the stars align in a creative burst are what we talk and write about for decades to come. They inspire both musicians and future audiences, but this is not the desire of an industry fixated on the bottom line and disinterested in a limited audience for their product. As

Lone guitar man, San Diego, California.

the cartoon character Pogo once said, "We have met the enemy and he is us." Show me the money.

Art invariably loses control when a mass audience discovers it. Look at the before and after stories and everyone knows that's true. The artist can be washed overboard by an increasingly demanding audience that can be, by contradiction, overly accepting at the same time. Do what we want and we will love and adore you. Disappoint us and we will walk away and find someone else.

Every great revolutionary period must come to an end. Author Mikal Gilmore notes in his important collection of articles *Stories Done* that "by the early 1970s, most of the significant components of the 1960s dream had come apart or had been subsumed."[1]

Rock star egos exploded as millions of dollars poured in. The rock star god figure loomed over stadiums filled with worshipping fans. The '60s idealism have given way to a sex, drugs, and rock and roll mindset. It all had to end. Success all too often turns music into formula.

In the early days of independent record labels, the criteria for judging music was based largely on originality. These small labels were comprised of people who loved the music, though they certainly took financial advantage of the artists. Two quotes that indicate this philosophy came from Sam Phillips of Sun Records—"Gimme something different"—and Jac Holzman of Electra Asylum Records—"Have I ever heard this before?"[2] This emphasis on authenticity resulted in the music's best moments, startling originality and works that endure in their importance to this day.

There have always been music industry models and formulas, not to mention gimmicks; "How Much Is that Doggie in the Window?" comes to mind. Despite that, the indies successfully broke through until the late '60s when they saw the writing on the wall. Competing with the major labels who were now sinking serious funds into rock would be far too risky; time to cash out, take the money, and run.

By the mid- to late '70s the corporatization of America would affect music and the recording industry. Steve Katz, renowned guitarist-singer-songwriter with Blood, Sweat & Tears and the Blues Project, became a record industry executive with Mercury Records in the late 1970s. He witnessed increasingly corporate practices in record companies and radio. In his memoir *Blood, Sweat, and My Rock and Roll Years,* Katz writes, "By now I was a firsthand witness to the death of rock and roll. The major contributor was a company called Burkhart/Adams. These guys came up with a formula for airplay that made rock radio uniform across the country based on demographics, and computerized without regard to locality.... Burkhart/Adams affected the cultural landscape of America. Most, if not all rock stations subscribed to their service and within a few years airplay in America became homogeneous. Radio was losing its soul."[3]

Walter Kirn concurs in his 2003 *New York Times* article "Signals from Nowhere." Kirn navigated his cross-country road trips by the "accents, news and songs streaming in from the nearest AM transmitter." He describes losing way when he discovered "the announcers all sounded alike, drained, disconnected from geography, reshuffling the same pop playlists and canned bad jokes." He found that Clear Channel with its 1,250 stations (at that time) was largely to blame for "a miserable trip. I heard America droning."[4]

Uniformity caused by corporate principles results in profits for a few, a flattened landscape for a nation. The concept of artist as rebel became artist as commercial commodity. Writer Carina Chocano in her powerful *New York Times Magazine* article "Revolution Blues" reveals the development of a depressing phenomenon. Chocano notes the traditional use of the term *rock star* was as an "artist/hero/rebel" with personal issues who can give rise to adolescent behavior to a "jack of all trades," master of marketing, branding, and social media manipulation.[5]

The very idea of branding and corporate sponsorship was viewed as abhorrent in the Woodstock generation. It was the ultimate sellout and any artist who wafted over to this action risked severe career damage. By the late '70s, this approach became de rigueur. Artists began appearing as image-focused entrepreneurs who suddenly began speaking in business tongue. Instead of revolting against "the man," they had become him.

Chocano observes how the term *rock star* has been co-opted to the point where it has lost all meaning due to overuse and misappropriation. With rock stars endorsing everything from luggage to butter, she writes, "The spirit of the music is devoured."[6] Rock's cultural impact has been diminished to the point where hip-hop and other forms have overtaken the music. Selling your brand has resulted in profits, at the cost of flattening the artist's effectiveness in influencing the culture.

Where does this leave music? Not in the best place. Bob Dylan has been quoted as saying of most modern music, "it should be free, it ain't worth nothing." Dylan refers to the loss of stature in music. Advertising and licensing of music by placing songs into film and television commercials are major goals in an era of shrinking record sales and a music industry breakdown. One wonders if record sales are down due to our current

Street art, Jackson, Mississippi.

perception of artist as phony image and brand. More attention is given to pop stars squabbling on award shows that spill into social media distraction than to the music itself. We hear music droning, not singing.

If selling out is cool, not all of us are buying. The middle school squabbling and trash talking of major pop stars is juvenile and compromises the view of women in the industry. The total dilution of the artists' image as a revolutionary rebel has been replaced by, in Chocano's words, a musician who is "compliant, controlled, image-focused, and customer-service-oriented."[7] The result is a dubious body of work that quickly vanishes and, over time, is mocked, not respected.

Beyond the music is a bigger issue. What is our present culture? Do we even have one anymore? What does it say about us? Who are we? The Beatles were viewed in their day as musicians, celebrities, and above all, artists. We still see them that way, with an ever-increasing respect for their body of work over a ten-year period. When big business company Nike moved in on the Beatles' catalog and used their song "Revolution" (more than a little irony here) in a commercial, the Beatles sued them for $15 million. Beatles records still sell; every year, books are written about their lives, and the story of their constructive sense of rebellion remains. They were inside and outside at the same time. It can be done. In a world where too many are temporarily famous for being famous, we yearn for authenticity and straightforward integrity in a music that is neither vapid nor self-effacing. We have distorted the lines between real and fake, and that costs a society.

Present pop sounds like someone singing into their own mirror.

That ain't no revolution.

12

The Music and Art Spirit

It is a book of monumental importance. *Art Spirit,* by the Ashcan painter and art educator Robert Henri, was published in 1923, yet it remains as relevant today as ever. Henri writes of life's most insightful moments when we see or hear beyond the ordinary. These peak experiences are, according to Henri, "moments of wisdom" and "signposts to a greater knowledge."[1]

I believe this applies to not only composing and performing music but to the art of listening as well. We can have insights as listeners that enrich and possibly change our lives. This is difficult to achieve in a distracted and noisy technological world of limited attention spans that appear to grow shorter with time. We express ourselves freely through social media in a clipped shorthand method of communication; genuine insight is rare.

What is music and what can it do? Music takes measure of the time in which it was created. It looks forward and backward at the same time. Music draws from the past while addressing the present. If it is visionary in scope, music can forecast the future and point the way to modern innovations. The boogie-woogie piano style of the 1920s provided the gateway to rhythm and blues, then rock and roll decades later. Virtually no one realized these piano professor–pioneers were blazing a trail that Chuck Berry, Little Richard, and Elvis Presley would mold into America's youth music. The seeds of the future are always planted in the past.

You cannot have the Beatles without Buddy Holly, just as there would be no Rolling Stones without Muddy Waters. Music captures the human spirit and records the time, context, and what the people value most. And we can dance to our story. Yet none of this is easy. Any work of art is a beautiful struggle that challenges the creator at the greatest depths. Anyone can dash off a song or quick sketch, calling themselves an "artist." It is not that simple. Only the artist or musician who sees deeply into the work, extracting the unnecessary and revealing the essential can achieve lasting art.

This constant process of examination has been overly romanticized. It is, as Alistair Cooke once said, "the great sentimental delusion of our time.... To have any quality, it still takes years of nursing and cultivating, not to mention a daily quota of simple drudgery." It is not a matter of talent, though we certainly need that, but of the ability to dig like miners as we uncover what is inside us. It is a lonely process that requires courage. It cannot be avoided. It is easy to understand how creativity challenges the depth of humanity, taking a personal toll. Amid the cacophony of life, it is exceedingly difficult to focus on your own song,

Taxi stand in the rain, Union Station, New Haven, Connecticut.

bringing out what is inside of you. How do we find this song? No GPS can help us in seeking our own life's direction. We must love the work process as the great reward. As Henri said, "The beauty of art is in the work itself."[2] We are usually happiest in the most exulted moments of creation. The final outcome of a finished piece can be a mixed blessing. We are relieved at the work's completion yet are often saddened that the creative battle is over, at least for today.

Inspiration is another misunderstood concept. It is a bad idea to wait for it, to not create until that magical feeling is upon us. Picasso once said, "Inspiration exists but it has to find you working."[3] Creative artists are craftsmen who do not wait for divine moments of inspiration. They seek and explore through doing the work itself.

Our moments of seeing are fueled by a tenacious desire to remove the hurdles that stand in our way. This cannot be a passive act that waits for outside encouragement.

If we did that, little would we ever accomplish. "I don't wait for someone to call a rehearsal," said Duke Ellington.[4]

It is a life's work to seek an original authentic voice, a process that has no end. Henri urges us to "be yourself today, don't wait for tomorrow."[5] The "Who am I?" question looms large for all of us in life and art. The greatest personal growth comes from self-discovery. We create art, read books, listen to music, and go to museums to find what life means to us. In this way, we educate ourselves beyond schooling. What is our true intent—to coast through life by seeking the path of least resistance or take the more challenging and difficult fork in the road? Do we have the courage to grow, as my wife, Sarah, says, "toward our better selves?"

Our intent drives everything. In the Western world we are prone to think of success as a number—massive sales, fame, praise, and status. Although desirable, these things come at a very high cost with many strings attached. Henri suggests that artists satisfy themselves first, as opposed to seeking only commercial satisfaction. We will always confront this problem. We make our life, in large part, by the personal happiness we derive from our work; ignore this and we risk the consequences.

Our personal and professional lives are driven by experimentation. The creative arts require a combination of a childlike sense of imagination with a master's craft. The ability to seize a moment of inspiration or seeing, then transforming it into a song, painting, or some work of art, is the challenge we face. We must face forward and backward at the same time. All artists learn from the past. That is where they develop the toolbox necessary for developing their own language. It is the path to new ideas and concepts, but we must have the tools for expression.

Knowing how the masters did their work is invaluable, but infatuation can go too far and lead to imitation's dead end. Henri wrote, "Today is not a souvenir of yesterday."[6] Originality depends on an artist's unique vision, their ability to see inside the work, then show us the way.

Although sounding romantic to some, this is a long and uncharted road. The typical signposts are countless rejection, criticism, and just plain being ignored. The artist must be painfully honest, revealing what they know and believe to be important. If they should opt to state less than what they know, perhaps by pressures of commercial constraints, much will be lost. Great art is often initially rejected in the present but thrives in the future due to discovery of its inherent worth. We just didn't know it at the time.

Repeating the past is a terrible mistake. Any attempt at reenactment can only result in a wax museum–type outcome. We are easily seduced by the comfort of nostalgia, but the residue is a cotton candy that sticks to nothing, devoid of stature. Do I really want to see four guys who vaguely look like the Beatles try to sound like them? I don't think so. If you know the real thing, there is never a substitute.

Art lives by starting from nothing, working upward. Imitation is essential but only to a degree. We learn to speak by copying the voices around us, just as we study a musical instrument. The oral tradition of call and response may be our most enduring form of learning. Unlike memorizing written text, oral knowledge seeps into a person with depth and longevity. Imitation is the beginning but never the end.

Like a baby bird pushed out of the nest or a young lion forced to hunt alone, the time comes for the artist to move out and up. Not everyone is cut out for this. It can be a lonely process where self-discouraging demons attack at will and doubt is an ever-present shadow. Questions plague the creative process—what happens if I am off-track and what if my ideas lead nowhere? These voices are hard to shake. The simple answer to overcoming these feelings is to tune them out. Play through it; keep going. Athletes do this all the time. In the middle of a game when they are underperforming, the mind takes over to regain control and get back on track.

There are no guaranteed outcomes. It would be safer to sing someone else's song, to paint a painting we have already seen. Masks are always easier to wear; they protect us. How easy it is to say, "Find your own voice," but what does that mean? It is setting out on an unmarked trail where the only option is to find you own way.

Conclusion

The spirit of music is everlasting. Trends come and go, genres form and fragment, but music that hits its target can tell us volumes regarding who we are and where we might be headed. In his insightful 2016 *New York Times* op-ed article "Don't Turn Away from the Art of Life," Arnold Weinstein reveals the interrogative nature of the arts that "trace the far-flung route by which we come to understand our world and ourselves. They take our measure. And we are never through discovering who we are."[7]

Music, when heard closely and carefully, is a personal experience based on our own lives. We grow with a work of art because we are shaped by it. Weinstein writes, "Art and literature are tried on.... We invest the art with our own feelings, but the art comes to live inside us, adding to our own repertoire."[8] Landmark recordings or musical performances mark our lives, making an indelible impression on our character. We are forever changed by music that hits us in deep places. As Greil Marcus once wrote, "Great songs shudder and break and explode."[9]

Our tastes and perceptions grow as we mature. The more we hear and see and take in, the more we derive from art. It becomes part of our very being. Listening to music, we find a solace and company, a oneness with sound. We are not alone for music speaks to our heart and soul. We never know to what unexpected places it will take us. Of course, this oftentimes does not happen. Music that misses its mark becomes a soundtrack of indifference, never landing, never hitting home. We must either see ourselves in the music or perceive a place we have never been. Music can guide us, providing a running dialogue where new discoveries can be made with each listening.

Of course, the process of listening has changed dramatically. The vinyl LP forced my generation into sequential listening. You heard the entire side of a record before turning it over. Thus, the album was perceived in a holistic manner. The songs were sequenced like chapters in a book. Rearrangement would have made no sense. But along came the digital world; random play, streaming, and the listening process received a radical change. There is more selection and flexibility than ever, but the listening experience is fragmented.

The resurgence of vinyl is an interesting phenomenon. First perceived as a "hipster" fetish, the numbers for vinyl sales indicate that this

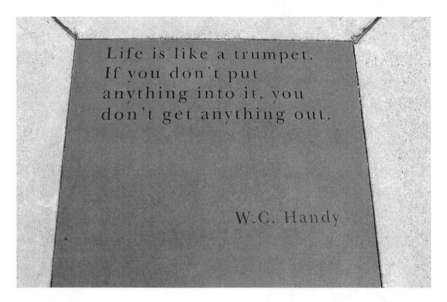

Wisdom from W.C. Handy, composer of the "St. Louis Blues," Montgomery, Alabama.

is no mere fad. There is a need for serious and enjoyable listening from a turntable-vinyl platform with good reason. The lost art of album cover design was too good to go away forever. It told a story by supplying a visual connection to the music—not a video but a still image that provokes the listener's imagination. Although the size of LPs may not be ideal for storage from a merchandising standpoint, the stature of vinyl is undeniable. With CD sales flagging and approaching obsolescence, the LP has returned for a mature, niche audience who no longer needs to buy singles, a young person's market.

We want to know who we are, and music has been key in that quest. Through discovery in the arts, we have a better idea of our own identity. We can listen alone or in a group, giving us a collective experience. We are alive in the world, in the rhythm of the saints.

Robert Henri recommended, "Paint like a man going over the top of a hill singing."[10]

I like to keep that image in mind.

We might consider living that way.

Epilogue

Behind every new musical era there is a wrecking ball. The seeds of the future were planted in the past. The dance goes on.

Sound is unavoidable. In the hospital, as I am waiting for a procedure in a rather compromised position, the nurse walks in and asks,

"Would you like for us to put on some music?"

"Sure," I reply.

Here's what follows:

- "Don't Fear the Reaper"
- "Highway to Hell"
- "Should I Stay or Should I Go?"

Music is always trying to tell us something.

Congo Square, New Orleans.

Chapter Notes

Chapter 1

1. Bruce Springsteen, "Keynote Speech," South by Southwest Conference, March 2012.

Chapter 2

1. Ben Sisario, "At Grammy Event, Bob Dylan Speech Steals the Show," *New York Times*, February 7, 2015.
2. Yvette Lumor, *Music Background Paper*, Fairfield University.
3. Nikole Hannah-Jones, "America Wasn't a Democracy, until Black Americans Made It One," *New York Times*, August 14, 2019.

Chapter 3

1. John F. Callahan, ed., *The Collected Essays of Ralph Ellison* (Random House, 1995), 797–798.
2. Angela Davis, *Blues Legacies and Black Feminism* (Pantheon, 1998), 11.
3. Brian Torff, *In Love with Voices* (iUniverse, 2009), 53.
4. David Samuels, "Neil Young's Lonely Quest to Save Music," *New York Times Magazine*, August 20, 2019.
5. Whitney Balliet, "Out Here Again," *New Yorker Magazine*, May 2, 1964.
6. Martha Oneppo, interview with Mary Lou Williams, Mary Lou Williams archives, Rutgers Institute of Jazz Studies.
7. https://www.brainyquote.com/authors/elvis-presley-quotes

8. Drew Fortune, "T-Bone Burnett on Inside Llewyn Davis," *Salon*, December 2, 2013.
9. https://www.musicwithease.com/bix-beiderbecke-quotes.html
10. Ralph Ellison, *Living with Music*, ed. Robert G. O'Meally (Random House, 2002), 28–29.
11. Robert Walser, *Keeping Time*, 2nd ed. (Oxford University Press, 2015), 154.
12. Gerald Early, *Miles Davis and American Culture* (Missouri Historical Society Press, 2001), 3.
13. *Ibid.*, 4.
14. Toni Morrison, *The Nobel Lecture in Literature* (Knopf, 1993), 2.

Chapter 4

1. Greil Marcus, *Mystery Train* (Plume, 1975), 122.
2. Peter Guralnick, *Sam Phillips: The Man Who Invented Rock and Roll* (Back Bay Books, 2015), 12.
3. Elijah Wald, *Escaping the Delta* (HarperCollins, 2004), 84.
4. Alan Lomax, *The Land Where the Blues Began* (Knopf, 1993), 61, 20.
5. Guralnick, *Sam Phillips*, 63.
6. Paul Oliver, *The Story of the Blues* (Random House, 1997), 195.
7. Guralnick, *Sam Phillips*, 106.
8. Charles White, Richard Wayne Pennyman, and Robert Blackwell, *The Life and Times of Little Richard* (Random House, 1984).
9. *Ibid.*
10. Guralnick, *Sam Phillips*, 405–406.

11. Willie Dixon, with Don Snowden, *I Am the Blues* (Da Capo, 1989), 91–92.

12. Frank Zappa, "The Oracle Has It All Psyched Out," *Life*, June 28, 1968.

13. Guralnick, *Sam Phillips*, 334.

14. Marcus, *Mystery Train*, 130.

15. Guralnick, *Last Train to Memphis*, 13.

16. *Ibid.*, 19.

17. *Ibid.*, 47.

18. Michael Bertrand, *Race, Rock, and Elvis* (University of Illinois Press, 2000), 63.

19. Guralnick, *Last Train to Memphis*, 5.

20. Marcus, *Mystery Train*, 15.

21. Guralnick, *Last Train to Memphis*, 49.

22. *Ibid.*, 120.

23. *Ibid.*, 213.

24. *Ibid.*, 102.

25. *Ibid.*, 206.

26. Marcus, *Mystery Train*, 137.

27. Joel Williamson, *Elvis Presley: A Southern Life* (Oxford University Press, 2015), 25.

28. *Ibid.*, 25.

29. Guralnick, *Last Train to Memphis*, 248.

30. Bruce Springsteen, "Keynote Speech," South by Southwest Conference, March 2012.

31. *Ibid.*

32. Guralnick, *Last Train to Memphis*, 142.

33. *Ibid.*, 249.

34. *Ibid.*, 441.

35. Ray Connolly, *Being Elvis: A Lonely Life* (Orion, 2016), chap. 12.

36. Guralnick, *Last Train to Memphis*, 240.

37. *Ibid.*, 169.

38. *Ibid.*, 258.

39. "Hillbilly on a Pedestal," *Newsweek*, May 14, 1956.

40. Marcus, *Mystery Train*, 114.

41. Mikal Gilmore, *Night Beat: A Shadow History of Rock and Roll* (Doubleday, 1998), 18.

42. *Ibid.*, 19.

43. Marcus, *Mystery Train*, 114.

44. D.H. Lawrence, *The Spirit of Place* (Viking, 1964).

45. Elizabeth Kaye, "Sam Phillips: The *Rolling Stone* Interview," *Rolling Stone*, February 13, 1986.

46. Lester Bangs, "Where Were You When Elvis Died?" *Village Voice*, August 29, 1977.

47. Guralnick, *Last Train to Memphis*, 120.

48. *Ibid.*, xiii.

Chapter 5

1. Phyl Garland, *The Sound of Soul* (Regnery, 1969), 9.

2. Nelson George, *Where Did Our Love Go?* (St. Martin's, 1985), 127.

3. Garland, *The Sound of Soul*, introduction.

4. *Ibid.*

5. *Ibid.*, 31.

6. *Ibid.*, 239.

7. Peter Guralnick, *Sweet Soul Music* (HarperCollins, 1986), 220.

8. Garland, *The Sound of Soul*, 16.

9. Arthur Kempton, *Boogaloo* (Pantheon, 2003), 227.

10. Garland, *The Sound of Soul*, 123.

11. Kempton, *Boogaloo*, 232.

12. *Ibid.*, 231.

13. Stanley Booth, "The Memphis Soul Sound," in *Shake It Up: Great American Writing on Rock and Pop from Elvis to Jay Z*, ed. Jonathan Lethem and Kevin Dettmar (Literary Classics, 2017), 98.

14. *Ibid.*, 104.

15. *Ibid.*, 109.

16. Guralnick, *Sweet Soul Music*, 131.

17. Garland, *The Sound of Soul*, 127.

18. *Ibid.*, 134.

19. Kempton, *Boogaloo*, 230.

20. Garland, *The Sound of Soul*, 198.

21. Guralnick, *Sweet Soul Music*, 341.

22. *Ibid.*, 347.

23. David Remnick, "Soul Survivor," *New Yorker*, April 4, 2016.

24. Garland, *The Sound of Soul*, 129.

25. Guralnick, *Sweet Soul Music*, 131.

26. Kempton, *Boogaloo*, 241.

27. Garland, *The Sound of Soul*, 39.

28. *Ibid.*, 35.

29. Kempton, *Boogaloo*, 251.

30. Guralnick, *Sweet Soul Music*, 355.

31. *Ibid.*, 370.

32. Kempton, *Boogaloo*, 294.

33. Guralnick, *Sweet Soul Music*, 362.

34. *Ibid.*, 394.

35. George, *Where Did Our Love Go?* xvii.

36. *Ibid.*, xi.
37. *Ibid.*, xiv.
38. *Ibid.*, xvii.
39. *Ibid.*, xvii.
40. *Ibid.*, 20.
41. *Ibid.*, 28.
42. *Ibid.*, 45.
43. *Ibid.*, 116.
44. *Ibid.*, 58.
45. *Ibid.*, 149.
46. *Ibid.*, 122.
47. *Ibid.*, 86.
48. Lester Bangs, *Psychotic Reactions and Carburetor Dung* (Random House, 2003), 104.
49. Gary Giddins and Scott Deveaux, *Jazz*, 2nd ed. (Norton, 2015), 328.
50. Garland, *The Sound of Soul*, 217.
51. Nat Hentoff, *Jazz Is* (Random House, 1976), 210.
52. *Ibid.*, 208.
53. Garland, *The Sound of Soul*, 224.
54. *Ibid.*, 219.
55. Bill Cole, *John Coltrane* (Da Capo, 1993), 171.
56. Ben Ratliff, *Coltrane: The Story of a Sound* (Farrar, Strauss and Giroux, 2007), 167.
57. *Ibid.*, 190.
58. *Ibid.*, 168.
59. *Ibid.*, 169.
60. Hentoff, *Jazz Is*, 216.
61. Ratliff, *Coltrane*, 187.

Chapter 6

1. David Hadju, *Positively 4th Street* (Picador, 2001), 16.
2. Ellen Willis, "Dylan," in Ellen Willis, *Out of the Vinyl Deeps* (University of Minnesota Press, 2011), 4.
3. Hadju, *Positively 4th Street*, 108.
4. Bob Dylan, *Chronicles* (Simon & Schuster, 2004), 275.
5. David Yaffe, *Bob Dylan* (Yale University Press, 2011), 43.
6. Willis, "Dylan," 7.
7. Dylan, *Chronicles*, 244.
8. Willis, "Dylan."
9. Dylan, *Chronicles*, 84–85.
10. Hadju, *Positively 4th Street*, 121.
11. Yaffe, *Bob Dylan*, 69.
12. Willis, "Dylan."
13. Ben Sisario, "At Grammy's Event, Bob Dylan Speech Steals the Show," *New York Times*, February 7, 2015.
14. Yaffe, *Bob Dylan*, 119.
15. Willis, "Dylan."
16. *Ibid.*
17. Dylan, *Chronicles*, 263.
18. *Ibid.*, 285.
19. *Ibid.*, 34.
20. Tom Piazza, *Devil Sent the Rain* (HarperCollins, 2011), 116.
21. Dylan, *Chronicles*, 82–83.
22. Piazza, *Devil Sent the Rain*, 115.
23. Dylan, *Chronicles*, 22.
24. Hadju, *Positively 4th Street*, 203.
25. Steve Katz, *Blood, Sweat, and My Rock and Roll Years* (Lyons, 2015), 12.
26. Willis, "Dylan."
27. Piazza, *Devil Sent the Rain*, 120–121.
28. Hadju, *Positively 4th Street*, 203.
29. *Ibid.*, 171.
30. *Ibid.*, 201.
31. *Ibid.*, 232.
32. *Ibid.*, 233.
33. Edna Gundersen, "Dylan on Dylan, 'Unplugged' and Birth of a Song," *USA Today*, February 5–7, 1995, 12D.
34. Hadju, *Positively 4th Street*, 195.
35. Piazza, *Devil Sent the Rain*, 123.
36. Hadju, *Positively 4th Street*, 263.
37. *Ibid.*, 278.
38. *Ibid.*, 248.
39. *Ibid.*, 67.
40. *Ibid.*, 254.
41. *Ibid.*, 229.
42. Robbie Robertson, *Testimony* (Three Rivers Press, 2016), 191.
43. Willis, "Dylan."
44. Hadju, *Positively 4th Street*, 251.
45. Robertson, *Testimony*, 193.
46. Hadju, *Positively 4th Street*, 227.
47. *Ibid.*, 282.
48. Dylan, *Chronicles*, 116, 120.
49. Willis, "Dylan."
50. *Ibid.*
51. Dylan, *Chronicles*, 116.
52. Yaffe, *Bob Dylan*, 93.
53. *Ibid.*, 93.
54. Willis, "Dylan."
55. Piazza, *Devil Sent the Rain*, 115.
56. Ian Bell, *Once upon a Time: The Lives of Bob Dylan* (Pegasus, 2012), 562.
57. Piazza, *Devil Sent the Rain*, 117.
58. Bruce Springsteen, "Keynote

Speech," South by Southwest Conference, March 2012.
  59. Dylan, *Chronicles*, 292–293.

Chapter 7

  1. John Etheridge, Email to the author, April 15, 2020.
  2. Simon Frith, "Music for Pleasure: Essays in the Sociology of Pop," in *Read the Beatles*, ed. June Skinner Sawyers (Penguin, 2006), 224.
  3. Phillip Norman, *Shout: The Beatles in Their Generation* (Simon & Schuster, 1981), 67.
  4. *Ibid.*, 67.
  5. *Ibid.*, 189.
  6. Jon Wild, "Uncut Magazine, July 2004," in *Read the Beatles*, ed. June Skinner Sawyers (Penguin, 2006), 244.
  7. Astrid Kirchherr, foreword to *Read the Beatles*, ed. June Skinner Sawyers (Penguin, 2006), xv.
  8. Norman, *Shout*, 98.
  9. *Ibid.*, 252.
  10. *Ibid.*, 196.
  11. Geoffrey O'Brien, "Seven Fat Years from Sonata for Jukebox," in *Read the Beatles*, ed. June Skinner Sawyers (Penguin, 2006), 176.
  12. *Ibid.*, 174.
  13. Norman, *Shout*, 201.
  14. *Ibid.*, 214.
  15. O'Brien, "Seven Fat Years," 167.
  16. Norman, *Shout*, 220.
  17. Griel Marcus, "Another Version of the Chair," in *Read the Beatles*, ed. June Skinner Sawyers (Penguin, 2006), 79.
  18. O'Brien, "Seven Fat Years," in *Read the Beatles*, ed. June Skinner Sawyers (Penguin, 2006), 168–169.
  19. Greil Marcus, "Another Version of the Chair," in *Read the Beatles*, ed. June Skinner Sawyers (Penguin, 2006), 80.
  20. June Skinner Sawyers, introduction to *Read the Beatles*, ed. June Skinner Sawyers (Penguin, 2006), xlv.
  21. Christopher Porterfield, "Pop Music: The Messengers," *Time*, September 22, 1967, 107.
  22. Greg Kot, "Toppermost of the Poppermost," in *Read the Beatles*, ed. June Skinner Sawyers (Penguin, 2006), 323.
  23. Porterfield, "Pop Music," 109.
  24. O'Brien, "Seven Fat Years," 169.
  25. Andrew Sarris, "A Hard Day's Night," *Village Voice*, August 27, 1964, 57–58.
  26. Norman, *Shout*, 240
  27. *Ibid.*; O'Brien, "Seven Fat Years," 169.
  28. David Remnick, *King of the World* (Vintage, 1999), 158.
  29. Norman, *Shout*, 257–258.
  30. Porterfield, "Pop Music," 112.
  31. Norman, *Shout*, 14.
  32. Mark Hertsgaard, "The Breakup Heard 'Round the World," in *Read the Beatles*, ed. June Skinner Sawyers (Penguin, 2006), 163.
  33. Norman, *Shout*, 284.
  34. *Ibid.*, 292.
  35. *Ibid.*, xliii.
  36. Ned Rorem, "The Beatles," in *Read the Beatles*, ed. June Skinner Sawyers (Penguin, 2006).
  37. Richard Goldstein, "We Still Need the Beatles, But," in *Read the Beatles*, ed. June Skinner Sawyers (Penguin, 2006), 98.
  38. Azquotes.com
  39. O'Brien, "Seven Fat Years," 176.
  40. Norman, *Shout*, 13.
  41. Hertsgaard, "The Breakup Heard 'Round the World," 163.
  42. Mikal Gilmore, *Stories Done* (Free Press, 2008), 107.
  43. Anthony De Curtis, "Crossing the Line: The Beatles in My Life," in *Read the Beatles*, ed. June Skinner Sawyers (Penguin, 2006), 303.
  44. Allan Kozinn, "Astrid Kirchherr, 81, Friend Whose Photos Portrayed Beatles as Tough and Tender," *New York Times*, May 18, 2020.
  45. Rich Cohen, *The Sun & the Moon & the Rolling Stones* (Spiegel and Grau, 2017), 66.
  46. Norman, *Shout*, 277.
  47. Cohen, *The Sun*, 5.
  48. *Ibid.*, 66.
  49. *Ibid.*, 58.
  50. *Ibid.*, 105.
  51. Holly George-Warren, *Janis: Her Life and Music* (Simon & Schuster, 2019), 36.
  52. Robert Christgau, "The Rolling Stones," in *The Rolling Stone Illustrated History of Rock and Roll*, ed. Jim Miller (Rolling Stone Press, 1976), 185.

53. Ellen Willis, "The Velvet Underground," in Ellen Willis, *Out of the Vinyl Deeps* (University of Minnesota Press, 2011), 56; Ellen Willis, "The Big Ones," in Ellen Willis, *Out of the Vinyl Deeps* (University of Minnesota Press, 2011), 78.

54. Christgau, "The Rolling Stones," 184.

55. *Ibid.*, 216.

56. Stanley Booth, *The True Adventures of the Rolling Stones* (Acapella, 1984), 50.

57. Cohen, *The Sun*, 24.

58. Ellen Willis, *Out of the Vinyl Deeps* (University of Minnesota Press, 2011), 90.

59. Cohen, *The Sun*, 256.

60. *Ibid.*, 200.

61. Booth, *True Adventures*, 134.

62. *Ibid.*, 153.

63. Keith Richards with James Fox, *Life* (Little, Brown, 2010), 18.

64. Booth, *True Adventures*, 132, 179.

65. *Ibid.*, 82.

66. Ellen Willis, "Sympathy for the Stones," in Ellen Willis, *Out of the Vinyl Deep* (University of Minnesota Press, 2011), 121.

67. Booth, *True Adventures*, 177, 136.

68. *Ibid.*, 280.

69. *Ibid.*, 269.

70. *Ibid.*, 195–196.

71. Christgau, "The Rolling Stones," 187.

72. Norman, *Shout*, 380.

73. Booth, *True Adventures*, 245.

74. Cohen, *The Sun*, 240.

75. *Ibid.*, 242.

76. Booth, *True Adventures*, 354, 357.

77. *Ibid.*, 370–371.

78. *Ibid.*, 373.

79. *Ibid.*, 372.

80. Cohen, *The Sun*, 246.

81. *Ibid.*; George Trow, "Eclectic, Reminiscent, Amused, Fickle, Perverse," *New Yorker*, May 29 and June 5, 1978, 253.

82. Cohen, *The Sun*, 246; Ethan A. Russell, with Gerard Van der Leun, *Let It Bleed: The Rolling Stones, Altamont, and the End of the Sixties*, 295.

83. Cohen, *The Sun*, 290.

84. Richards, *Life*, 490.

85. Cohen, *The Sun*, 292, 9.

86. Richards, *Life*, 159.

87. Kirchherr, "Foreword," xvi.

88. Cohen, *The Sun*, 136.

Chapter 8

1. Ellen Willis, "Dylan," in Ellen Willis, *Out of the Vinyl Deeps* (University of Minnesota Press, 2011), 125.

2. Alexander Bloom and Wini Breines, eds., *Takin' It to the Streets* (Oxford University Press, 1995), 278.

3. *Ibid.*, 27.

4. Joe Boyd, *White Bicycles: Making Music in the 1960s* (Serpent's Tail, 2006), 270–271.

5. Greil Marcus, *The Doors: A Lifetime of Listening to Five Mean Years* (Public Affairs, 2011), 95.

6. Joan Didion, *The White Album* (Farrar, Straus and Giroux, 1979), 41–42.

7. Mikal Gilmore, *Stories Done* (Free Press, 2008), 266–267.

8. Elektra Records, *The House That Jac Built* (Apple, 2010).

9. Marcus, *The Doors*, 106–107.

10. Holly George-Warren, *Janis: Her Life and Music* (Simon & Schuster, 2019), xii.

11. Greg Tate, *Midnight Lightning: Jimi Hendrix and the Black Experience* (Lawrence Hill, 2003), 14.

12. Didion, *White Album*, 21.

13. Jim Miller, ed., *The Rolling Stone Illustrated History of Rock and Roll* (Rolling Stone Press, 1976), 262.

14. Gloria Lloreda quoted in George-Warren, *Janis*, 52.

15. Tate, *Midnight Lightning*, 19.

16. Eve Babitz, "Jim Morrison Is Dead and Living in Hollywood," in *Shake It Up: Great American Writing on Rock and Pop from Elvis to Jay Z*, ed. Jonathan Lethem and Kevin Dettmar (Literary Classics, 2017), 316.

17. John Densmore, *Riders on the Storm* (Delacorte, 1990), 68.

18. Tom Dicillo, *When You're Strange: A Film about the Doors* (Wolf Films/Strange Pictures, Rhino Entertainment, 2010).

19. Elektra Records, *The House That Jac Built*.

20. George-Warren, *Janis*, 73.

21. *Ibid.*, xiv.

22. Marcus, *The Doors*, 98.

23. Jacob Brackman, "Overdosing on Life," *New York Times*, October 27, 1970.

24. George-Warren, *Janis*, 56.

25. *Ibid.*, 187; Philip Elwood, "The Most Dynamic," *San Francisco Examiner*, March 22, 1967 (clipping pasted into Janis's scrapbook, with the title missing).

26. Willis, "Dylan," 130.

27. Tate, *Midnight Lightning*, 39.

28. Charles R. Cross, *Room Full of Mirrors: A Biography of Jimi Hendrix* (Hachette, 2005), 161.

29. Miller, *The Rolling Stone Illustrated History*.

30. Tate, *Midnight Lightning*, 25.

31. Paul Friedlander, *Rock and Roll: A Social History* (Westview, 2006), 218.

32. Babitz, "Jim Morrison Is Dead," 315.

33. Densmore, *Riders on the Storm*, 59.

34. Gilmore, *Stories Done*, 257.

35. Marcus, *The Doors*, 116.

36. Cross, *Room Full of Mirrors*, 156–157.

37. Steve Katz, Email to the author, May 18, 2020.

38. Miller, *The Rolling Stone Illustrated History*, 276.

39. Cross, *Room Full of Mirrors*, 168.

40. George-Warren, *Janis*, 53.

41. Steve Katz, Email to the author, May 18, 2020.

42. Ellen Willis, "Janis Joplin," in Ellen Willis, *Out of the Vinyl Deeps*, 126.

43. George-Warren, *Janis*, 140.

44. Densmore, *Riders on the Storm*, 130.

45. Babitz, "Jim Morrison Is Dead," 325.

46. Marcus, *The Doors*, 15.

47. George-Warren, *Janis*, 193.

48. Gilmore, *Stories Done*, 258.

49. Mick Houghton, *The True Story of Jac Holzman's Visionary Record Label* (Jawbone Press, 2010), 210.

50. Babitz, "Jim Morrison Is Dead," 318–319.

51. Cross, *Room Full of Mirrors*, 186.

52. George-Warren, *Janis*, 282.

53. *Ibid.*, 316.

54. *Ibid.*, 83.

55. Cross, *Room Full of Mirrors*, 102.

56. Tate, *Midnight Lightning*, 47.

57. *Ibid.*, 20.

58. Cross, *Room Full of Mirrors*, 145.

59. Arthur Allen quoted in Tate, *Midnight Lightning*, preface.

60. Friedlander, *Rock and Roll*, 222.

61. Tate, *Midnight Lightning*, 11.

62. George-Warren, *Janis*, 91.

63. Cross, *Room Full of Mirrors*, 248.

64. Densmore, *Riders on the Storm*, 89.

65. *Ibid.*, 316.

66. Babitz, "Jim Morrison Is Dead," 318.

67. Steve Katz, Email to the author, May 18, 2020.

68. Gilmore, *Stories Done*, 250.

69. George-Warren, *Janis*, 691.

70. *Ibid.*, xiv.

71. Elektra Records, *The House That Jac Built*.

72. Cross, *Room Full of Mirrors*, 237.

73. George-Warren, *Janis*, 216.

74. Babitz, "Jim Morrison Is Dead," 320.

75. Steve Katz, Email to the author, May 18, 2020.

76. Gilmore, *Stories Done*, 262.

77. Miller, *The Rolling Stone Illustrated History*, 262.

78. George-Warren, *Janis*, 261.

79. Densmore, *Riders on the Storm*, 237.

80. Marcus, *The Doors*, 45.

81. Densmore, *Riders on the Storm*, 310.

82. George-Warren, *Janis*, 245.

83. *Ibid.*, 262.

84. Cross, *Room Full of Mirrors*, 179.

85. *Ibid.*, 322.

86. Miller, *The Rolling Stone Illustrated History*.

87. Cross, *Room Full of Mirrors*, 179.

88. *Ibid.*, 163.

89. *Ibid.*, 227–228.

90. Boyd, *White Bicycles*, 271.

91. Houghton, *True Story of Jac Holzman*, 205.

92. *Ibid.*, 206.

93. *Ibid.*, 207.

94. Densmore, *Riders on the Storm*, 93.

95. Marcus, *The Doors*, 177.

96. Warren Odze, Email to the author, June 14, 2020.

97. Amy J. Berg, prod., *Little Girl Blue*, 2015.

98. George-Warren, *Janis*, 136.
99. Willis, "Janis Joplin," 129.
100. Miller, *The Rolling Stone Illustrated History*, 280.
101. Houghton, *True Story of Jac Holzman*, 214.
102. Marcus, *The Doors*.
103. Willis, "Janis Joplin," 133.
104. Boyd, *White Bicycles*, 271.
105. Steve Katz, Email to the author, May 18, 2020.
106. Babitz, "Jim Morrison Is Dead," 325–326.
107. Gilmore, *Stories Done*, 264.
108. *Ibid.*, 251.
109. Berg, *Little Girl Blue*.
110. George-Warren, *Janis*, xiii.
111. Tate, *Midnight Lightning*, 69.
112. Willis, "Janis Joplin," 126.

Chapter 9

1. John Szwed, *Billie Holiday: The Musician and the Myth* (Penguin Books, 2015), 159.
2. Gillian G. Gaar, *She's a Rebel* (Seal Press, 1992), 31.
3. *Ibid.*, 216.
4. *Ibid.*, xviii.
5. Barbara O'Dair, ed., *Trouble Girls: The Rolling Stone Book of Women in Rock* (Random House, 1997), 130.
6. Holly Gleason, ed., *Woman Walk the Line: How the Women in Country Music Changed Our Lives* (University of Texas Press, 2017), 70.
7. Chris Albertson, *Bessie* (Stein and Day, 1982), 88.
8. *Ibid.*, 132.
9. *Ibid.*, 12.
10. Elizabeth Hardwick, *Sleepless Nights* (New York Review Books, 1979), 34–35.
11. Szwed, *Billie Holiday*, 104.
12. Hardwick, *Sleepless Nights*, 34.
13. Gleason, *Woman Walk the Line*, 17.
14. *Ibid.*, 5.
15. Sheila Weller, *Girls like Us* (Washington Square Press, 2008), 128.
16. Gayle F. Wald, *Shout, Sister, Shout! The Untold Story of Rock-and-Roll Trailblazer Sister Rosetta Tharpe* (Beacon, 2007), 153.
17. *Ibid.*, 96.
18. O'Dair, *Trouble Girls*, 39.
19. *Ibid.*, 7.
20. *Ibid.*, 191.
21. Gleason, *Woman Walk the Line*, 207.
22. https://www.goalcast.com/2019/02/21/dolly-parton-quotes/
23. Weller, *Girls like Us*, 251.
24. Gaar, *She's a Rebel*, 484.
25. *Ibid.*, 212.
26. Weller, *Girls like Us*, 242.
27. Lindsay Zoladz, "Joni Mitchell: Fear of a Female Genius," *The Ringer*, October 16, 2017.
28. *Ibid.*
29. Weller, *Girls like Us*, 59.
30. Zoladz, "Joni Mitchell."
31. Weller, *Girls like Us*, 209.
32. Zoladz, "Joni Mitchell."
33. Weller, *Girls like Us*, 92.
34. *Ibid.*, 433.
35. *Ibid.*, 442.
36. *Ibid.*, 462.
37. *Ibid.*, 18.
38. *Ibid.*, 444.
39. *Ibid.*, 372–373.
40. Zoladz, "Joni Mitchell."
41. Weller, *Girls like Us*, 468.
42. *Ibid.*, 105.
43. *Ibid.*, 327.
44. *Ibid.*, 108.
45. O'Dair, *Trouble Girls*, 95.
46. *Ibid.*, 95.
47. Andy Cush, "Barack Obama Understood Aretha Franklin's Greatness as Well as Anyone," *Spin*, August 16, 2018.
48. O'Dair, *Trouble Girls*, 242.
49. Gaar, *She's a Rebel*, 96.
50. O'Dair, *Trouble Girls*, 150.
51. Gaar, *She's a Rebel*, 223.
52. *Ibid.*, 403.
53. O'Dair, *Trouble Girls*, 467.
54. Orin O'Brien, email to the author, June 12, 2020.
55. Gaar, *She's a Rebel*, 209.
56. O'Dair, *Trouble Girls*, 106.
57. *Ibid.*, xxi.
58. Patti Smith, *Just Kids* (HarperCollins, 2010), 244.
59. *Ibid.*, 294.
60. Ellen Willis, "Beginning to See the Light," in Ellen Willis, *Out of the Vinyl Deeps* (University of Minnesota Press, 2011), 148; Ellen Willis, "But Now I'm Gonna Move," in Willis, *Out of the Vinyl Deeps*, 137.

61. O'Dair, *Trouble Girls*, xxi.

62. Jon Caramanica, "Powerful Song-birds with Clipped Wings," *New York Times*, May 27, 2018, AR15.

63. O'Dair, *Trouble Girls*, 389.

64. Zoladz, "Joni Mitchell."

65. Weller, *Girls like Us*, 348.

66. Ted Gioia, "Music Criticism Has Degenerated into Lifestyle Reporting," *Daily Beast*, March 18, 2014.

67. *Ibid.*

68. Zoladz, "Joni Mitchell."

69. Gleason, *Woman Walk the Line.*

Chapter 10

1. Will Hermes, *Love Goes to Buildings on Fire: Five Years in New York That Changed Music Forever* (Faber & Faber, 2011), 32.

2. Jonathan Mahler, *Ladies and Gentlemen, the Bronx Is Burning* (Picador, 2005), 224.

3. Hermes, *Love Goes to Buildings on Fire*, 276.

4. Mahler, *Ladies and Gentlemen*, 166.

5. Kembrew McLeod, *The Downtown Pop Underground* (Abrams, 2018), 1.

6. Ho Hoangmy, Julie, "Anya Phillips 1955–1981," *New York Times*, November 16, 2020.

7. McLeod, *The Downtown Pop Underground*, 238.

8. *Ibid.*, 2.

9. Hermes, *Love Goes to Buildings on Fire*, 38.

10. Stephen Petrus, *From Gritty to Chic: The Transformation of New York City's SoHo, 1962–1976.* sohomemory.org.

11. Richard Kostelanetz, *Soho: The Rise and Fall of an Artists Colony* (Routledge, 2003), 140.

12. Petrus, *From Gritty to Chic.*

13. Edmund White, "Why We Can't Stop Talking about New York in the Late 1970s," *New York Times Style Magazine*, September 10, 2015.

14. Hermes, *Love Goes to Buildings on Fire*, xi.

15. White, "Why We Can't Stop Talking."

16. Hermes, *Love Goes to Buildings on Fire*, 101.

17. *Ibid.*, 228, 140.

18. *Ibid.*, 147.

19. Mahler, *Ladies and Gentlemen*, 257.

20. *Ibid.*, 160.

21. White, "Why We Can't Stop Talking."

22. David Lanois, with Keisha Kalfin, *Soul Mining* (Faber & Faber, 2010), 165.

23. White, "Why We Can't Stop Talking."

24. *Ibid.*

25. Hermes, *Love Goes to Buildings on Fire*, 193.

26. Mahler, *Ladies and Gentlemen*, 309.

27. *Ibid.*, 239.

28. McLeod, *The Downtown Pop Underground*, 6.

29. Hermes, *Love Goes to Buildings on Fire*, 140.

30. McLeod, *The Downtown Pop Underground*, 234–235.

31. *Ibid.*, 255.

32. *Ibid.*, 279.

33. *Ibid.*, 280.

34. Hermes, *Love Goes to Buildings on Fire*, 55.

35. *Ibid.*, 89.

36. *Ibid.*, 66–67.

37. *Ibid.*, 248.

38. McLeod, *The Downtown Pop Underground*, 285.

39. Hermes, *Love Goes to Buildings on Fire*, 27.

40. Mahler, *Ladies and Gentlemen*, 156.

41. Hermes, *Love Goes to Buildings on Fire*, 236.

42. McLeod, *The Downtown Pop Underground*, 275.

43. Mahler, *Ladies and Gentlemen*, 186.

44. Hermes, *Love Goes to Buildings on Fire*, 251.

45. Mahler, *Ladies and Gentlemen*, 191.

46. *Ibid.*, 205.

47. *Ibid.*, 225.

48. Whitney Balliet, *Night Creature: A Journal of Jazz 1975–1980* (Oxford University Press, 1981), 67.

49. *Ibid.*, 38.

50. Kostelanetz, *Soho*, 223.

51. White, "Why We Can't Stop Talking."

52. McLeod, *The Downtown Pop Underground*, 318.

53. Hermes, *Love Goes to Buildings on Fire*, 292.

54. Kostelanetz, *Soho*, 185.

55. Petrus, *From Gritty to Chic*.

56. Lisa Robinson, *Nobody Ever Asked Me about the Girls: Women, Music and Fame* (Holt, 2020), 220–221.

57. Kurt Vonnegut, with Suzanne McConnell, *Pity the Reader: On Writing and Style* (Seven Stories Press, 2020), 381.

58. Kostelanetz, *Soho*, 201.

Chapter 11

1. Mikal Gilmore, *Stories Done* (Free Press, 2008), 1.

2. Elektra Records, *The House That Jac Built* (Apple, 2010).

3. Steve Katz, *Blood, Sweat, and My Rock and Roll Years* (Lyons, 2015), 218.

4. Walter Kirn, "Signals from Nowhere," *New York Times*, June 22, 2003, SM11.

5. Carina Chocano, "How 'Rock Star' Became a Business Buzzword," *New York Times Magazine*, August 11, 2015.

6. *Ibid.*

7. *Ibid.*

Chapter 12

1. Robert Henri, *The Art Spirit* (Lippincott, 1951), 37, 9.

2. *Ibid.*, 164.

3. Pablo Picasso, philosiblog.com.

4. Robert Drew, dir., *On the Road with Duke Ellington* (Drew Associates, 1974).

5. Henri, *The Art Spirit*, 241.

6. *Ibid.*, 114.

7. Arnold Weinstein, "Don't Turn Away from the Art of Life," *New York Times*, February 23, 2016.

8. *Ibid.*

9. Greil Marcus, *Mystery Train* (Plume, 1975), 24.

10. Henri, *The Art Spirit*, 107.

Bibliography

Albertson, Chris. *Bessie.* Stein and Day, 1982.

Babitz, Eve. "Jim Morrison Is Dead and Living in Hollywood." In Letham and Dettmar, *Shake It Up.*

Balliet, Whitney. *Night Creature: A Journal of Jazz 1975–1980.* Oxford University Press, 1981.

Balliet, Whitney. "Out Here Again." *New Yorker,* May 2, 1964, 52.

Bangs, Lester. *Psychotic Reactions and Carburetor Dung.* Random House, 2003.

Bangs, Lester. "Where Were You When Elvis Died?" *Village Voice,* 29 August 1977. https://news.google.com/newspapers?nid=KEtq3P1Vf8oC&dat=19770829&printsec=frontpage&hl=en.

Bell, Ian. *Once Upon a Time: The Lives of Bob Dylan.* Pegasus, 2012.

Berg, Amy J., prod. *Janis: Little Girl Blue.* 2015.

Bertrand, Michael. *Race, Rock, and Elvis.* University of Illinois Press, 2000.

Bloom, Alexander, and Wini Breines, eds. *Takin' It to the Streets.* Oxford University Press, 1995.

Booth, Stanley. "The Memphis Soul Sound." In Lethem and Dettmar, *Shake It Up.*

Booth, Stanley. *The True Adventures of the Rolling Stones.* Acapella, 1984.

Boyd, Joe. *White Bicycles: Making Music in the 1960s.* Serpent's Tail, 2006.

Brackman, Jacob. "Overdosing on Life." *New York Times,* October 27, 1970, 45.

Callahan, John F., ed. *The Collected Essays of Ralph Ellison.* Random House, 1995.

Caramanica, Jon. "Powerful Songbirds with Clipped Wings." *New York Times,* May 27, 2018, AR15.

CBS New York. *Biggest New York Events of the 1970s.* January 15, 2015.

Chocano, Carina. "How 'Rock Star' Became a Business Buzzword." *New York Times Magazine,* August 11, 2015. https://www.nytimes.com/2015/08/16/magazine/how-rock-star-became-a-business-buzzword.html.

Christgau, Robert. "The Rolling Stones." In Miller, *The Rolling Stone Illustrated History.*

Cohen, Rich. *The Sun & the Moon & the Rolling Stones.* Spiegel and Grau, 2017.

Cole, Bill. *John Coltrane.* Da Capo, 1993.

Connolly, Ray. *Being Elvis: A Lonely Life.* Orion, 2016.

Cross, Charles R. *Room Full of Mirrors: A Biography of Jimi Hendrix.* Hachette, 2005.

Cush, Andy. "Barack Obama Understood Aretha Franklin's Greatness as Well as Anyone." *Spin,* August 16, 2018. https://www.spin.com/2018/08/aretha-franklin-barack-obama-new-yorker-quotes-death/.

Davidson, Sara. *Loose Change: Three Women of the Sixties.* University of California Press, 1977.

Davis, Angela. *Blues Legacies and Black Feminism.* Pantheon, 1998.

De Curtis, Anthony. "Crossing the Line: The Beatles in My Life." In Sawyers, *Read the Beatles.*

Densmore, John. *Riders on the Storm.* Delacorte, 1990.

Dicillo, Tom. *When You're Strange: A Film About the Doors.* Wolf Films/Strange Pictures, Rhino Entertainment, 2010.

Didion, Joan. *The White Album.* Farrar, Straus and Giroux, 1979.

Dixon, Willie, with Don Snowden. *I Am the Blues*. Da Capo, 1989.

Drew, Robert Ellington, dir. *On the Road with Duke Ellington*. Drew Associates, 1974.

Dylan, Bob. *Chronicles*. Simon & Schuster, 2004.

Early, Gerald. *Miles Davis and American Culture*. Missouri Historical Society Press, 2001.

Elektra Records: The House That Jac Built. Apple, 2010.

Ellison, Ralph. *Living with Music*. Edited by Robert G. O'Meally. Random House, 2002.

"Elvis Presley Quotes." https://www.brainyquote.com/authors/elvis-presley-quotes.

Etheridge, John. Email to the author. April 15, 2020.

"Famous Quotes: Bix Beiderbecke." https://www.musicwithease.com/bix-beiderbecke-quotes.html.

Fortune, Drew. "T Bone Burnett on *Inside Llewyn Davis*." *Salon*, December 2, 2013.

Friedlander, Paul. *Rock and Roll: A Social History*. Westview, 2006.

Frith, Simon. "Music for Pleasure: Essays in the Sociology of Pop." In Sawyers, *Read the Beatles*.

Gaar, Gillian G. *She's a Rebel*. Seal Press, 1992.

Garland, Phyl. *The Sound of Soul*. Regnery, 1969.

George, Nelson. *Where Did Our Love Go?* St. Martin's, 1985.

George-Warren, Holly. *Janis: Her Life and Music*. Simon & Schuster, 2019.

Giddins, Gary, and Scott Deveaux. *Jazz*. 2nd ed. Norton, 2015.

Gilmore, Mikal. *Night Beat: A Shadow History of Rock and Roll*. Doubleday, 1998.

Gilmore, Mikal. *Stories Done*. Free Press, 2008.

Gioia, Ted. "Music Criticism Has Degenerated into Lifestyle Reporting." *Daily Beast*, March 18, 2014. https://www.thedailybeast.

Gleason, Holly, ed. *Woman Walk the Line: How the Women in Country Music Changed Our Lives*. University of Texas Press, 2017.

Goldstein, Richard. "We Still Need the Beatles, But...." In Sawyers, *Read the Beatles*.

Gundersen, Edna. "Dylan on Dylan, 'Unplugged' and Birth of a Song." *USA Today*, February 5–7, 1995, 12D.

Guralnick, Peter. *Last Train to Memphis*. Back Bay Books, 1994.

Guralnick, Peter. *Looking to Get Lost*. Little, Brown, 2020.

Guralnick, Peter. *Sam Phillips: The Man Who Invented Rock and Roll*. Back Bay Books, 2015.

Guralnick, Peter. *Sweet Soul Music*. HarperCollins, 1986.

Hadju, David. *Positively 4th Street*. Picador, 2001.

Hannah-Jones, Nikole. "America Wasn't a Democracy, until Black Americans Made It One." *New York Times*, August 14, 2019. https://www.nytimes.com/interactive/2019/08/14/magazine/black-history-american-democracy.html.

Hardwick, Elizabeth. *Sleepless Nights*. New York Review Books, 1979.

Henri, Robert. *The Art Spirit*. Lippincott, 1951.

Hentoff, Nat. *Jazz Is*. Random House, 1976.

Hermes, Will. *Love Goes to Buildings on Fire: Five Years in New York That Changed Music Forever*. Faber & Faber, 2011.

Hertsgaard, Mark. "The Breakup Heard 'Round the World." In Sawyers, *Read the Beatles*.

"Hillbilly on a Pedestal." *Newsweek*, May 14, 1956, 82.

Ho Hoangmy, Julie. "Anya Phillips 1955–1981." *New York Times*, November 16, 2020.

Houghton, Mick. *The True Story of Jac Holzman's Visionary Record Label*. Jawbone Press, 2010.

Katz, Steve. *Blood, Sweat, and My Rock and Roll Years*. Lyons, 2015.

Katz, Steve. Email to the author. May 18, 2020.

Kaye, Elizabeth. "Sam Phillips: The *Rolling Stone* Interview." *Rolling Stone*, February 13, 1986. https://www.rollingstone.com/music/music-news/sam-phillips-the-rolling-stone-interview-122988/.

Kemp, Mark. *Dixie Lullaby*. Free Press, 2004.

Kempton, Arthur. *Boogaloo*. Pantheon, 2003.

King, Stephen. *On Writing: A Memoir of the Craft.* Simon & Schuster, 2000.

Kirchherr, Astrid. Foreword to *Read the Beatles.* Edited by June Skinner Sawyers. Penguin, 2006.

Kirn, Walter. "Signals from Nowhere." *New York Times,* June 22, 2003, SM11.

Kostelanetz, Richard. *Soho: The Rise and Fall of an Artists Colony.* Routledge, 2003.

Kozinn, Allan. "Astrid Kirchherr, 81, Friend Whose Photos Portrayed Beatles as Tough and Tender." *New York Times,* May 18, 2020.

Lanois, David, with Keisha Kalfin. *Soul Mining.* Faber & Faber, 2010.

Lawrence, D.H. *The Spirit of Place.* Viking, 1964.

Lethem, Jonathan, and Kevin Dettmar, eds. *Shake It Up: Great American Writing on Rock and Pop from Elvis to Jay Z.* Literary Classics, 2017.

Lomax, Alan. *The Land Where the Blues Began.* Knopf, 1993.

Mahler, Jonathan. *Ladies and Gentlemen, the Bronx Is Burning.* Picador, 2005.

Marcus, Greil. "Another Version of the Chair." In Sawyers, *Read the Beatles.*

Marcus, Greil. *The Doors: A Lifetime of Listening to Five Mean Years.* Public Affairs, 2011.

Marcus, Greil. *Mystery Train.* Plume, 1975.

McLeod, Kembrew. *The Downtown Pop Underground.* Abrams, 2018.

Miller, Jim, ed. *The Rolling Stone Illustrated History of Rock and Roll.* Rolling Stone Press, 1976.

Morrison, Toni. *The Nobel Lecture in Literature.* Knopf, 1993.

Norman, Phillip. *Shout: The Beatles in Their Generation.* Simon & Schuster, 1981.

O'Brien, Geoffrey. "Seven Fat Years." In Sawyers, *Read the Beatles.*

O'Dair, Barbara, ed. *Trouble Girls: The Rolling Stone Book of Women in Rock.* Random House, 1997.

Odze, Warren. Email to the author. June 14, 2020.

Oliver, Paul. *The Story of the Blues.* Random House, 1997.

O'Meally, Robert. *Lady Day: The Many Faces of Billie Holiday.* Arcade, 1991.

Petrus, Stephen. *From Gritty to Chic: The Transformation of New York City's SoHo, 1962–1976.* sohomemory.org.

Piazza, Tom. *Devil Sent the Rain.* HarperCollins, 2011.

Porterfield, Christopher. "Pop Music: The Messengers." In Sawyers, *Read the Beatles.*

Ratliff, Ben. *Coltrane: The Story of a Sound.* Farrar, Straus and Giroux, 2007.

Remnick, David. *King of the World.* Vintage, 1999.

Remnick, David. "Soul Survivor." *New Yorker,* April 4, 2016. https://www.newyorker.com/magazine/2016/04/04/aretha-franklins-american-soul.

Richards, Keith, with James Fox. *Life.* Little, Brown, 2010.

Robertson, Robbie. *Testimony.* Three Rivers Press, 2016.

Robinson, Lisa. *Nobody Ever Asked Me about the Girls: Women, Music and Fame.* Holt, 2020.

Samuels, David. "Neil Young's Lonely Quest to Save Music." *New York Times Magazine,* August 20, 2019. https://www.nytimes.com/2019/08/20/magazine/neil-young-streaming-music.html.

Sarris, Andrew. "A Hard Day's Night." *Village Voice,* August 27, 1964.

Sawyers, June Skinner, ed. *Read the Beatles.* Penguin, 2006.

Sisario, Ben. "At Grammys Event, Bob Dylan Speech Steals the Show." *New York Times,* February 7, 2015. https://artsbeat.blogs.nytimes.com/2015/02/07/at-grammys-event-bob-dylan-speech-steals-the-show/#:~:text=Updated%2C%206%3A23%20p.m.%20%7C,on%20his%20every%20word%2C%20Mr.

Smith, Patti. *Just Kids.* HarperCollins, 2010.

Springsteen, Bruce. "Keynote Speech." South by Southwest Conference, March 2012. https://www.rollingstone.com/music/music-news/exclusive-the-complete-text-of-bruce-springsteens-sxsw-keynote-address-86379/.

Szwed, John. *Billie Holiday: The Musician and the Myth.* Penguin, 2015.

Tate, Greg. *Midnight Lightning: Jimi Hendrix and the Black Experience.* Lawrence Hill, 2003.

Torff, Brian. *In Love with Voices.* iUniverse, 2009.

Velsey, Kim. "A Soho Settler Moves to

Queens." *New York Times*, September 20, 2020.

Vonnegut, Kurt, with Suzanne McConnell. *Pity the Reader: On Writing and Style*. Seven Stories Press, 2020.

Wald, Elijah. *Escaping the Delta*. HarperCollins, 2004.

Wald, Gayle F. *Shout, Sister, Shout! The Untold Story of Rock-and-Roll Trailblazer Sister Rosetta Tharpe*. Beacon, 2007.

Walser, Robert. *Keeping Time*. 2nd ed. Oxford University Press, 2015.

Weinstein, Arnold. "Don't Turn Away from the Art of Life." *New York Times*, February 24, 2016. https://www.nytimes.com/2016/02/24/opinion/dont-turn-away-from-the-art-of-life.html.

Weller, Sheila. *Girls like Us*. Washington Square Press, 2008.

White, Charles, Richard Wayne Peniman, and Robert Blackwell. *The Life and Times of Little Richard*. Random House, 1984.

White, Edmund. "Why We Can't Stop Talking about New York in the Late 1970s." *New York Times Style Magazine*, September 10, 2015.

Wild, Jon. "Uncut Magazine, July 2004." In Sawyers, *Read the Beatles*.

Williamson, Joel. *Elvis Presley: A Southern Life*. Oxford University Press, 2015.

Willis, Ellen. "Beginning to See the Light." In Willis, *Out of the Vinyl Deeps*, pp. 148–157.

Willis, Ellen. "The Big Ones." In Willis, *Out of the Vinyl Deeps*, pp. 77–83.

Willis, Ellen. "But Now I'm Gonna Move." In Willis, *Out of the Vinyl Deeps*, pp. 135–139.

Willis, Ellen. "Dylan." In Willis, *Out of the Vinyl Deeps*, pp. 1–20.

Willis, Ellen. "Janis Joplin." In Willis, *Out of the Vinyl Deeps*, pp. 125–133.

Willis, Ellen. *Out of the Vinyl Deeps*. Edited by Nona Willis Aronowitz. University of Minnesota Press, 2011.

Willis, Ellen. "Sympathy for the Stones." In Willis, *Out of the Vinyl Deeps*, pp. 119–121.

Willis, Ellen. "The Velvet Underground." In Willis, *Out of the Vinyl Deeps*, pp. 53–65.

Williams, Mary Lou. Interview with Martha Oneppo. Mary Lou Williams Archives, Institute of Jazz Studies, Rutgers University–Newark, 1980.

Yaffe, David. *Bob Dylan*. Yale University Press, 2011.

Zappa, Frank. "The Oracle Has It All Psyched Out." *Life*, June 28, 1968, 82–86, 88, 91.

Zoladz, Lindsay. "Joni Mitchell: Fear of a Female Genius." *The Ringer*, October 16, 2017. https://www.theringer.com/music/2017/10/16/16476254/joni-mitchell-pop-music-canon.

Index